In The End, You Kill Us Both
V. Ivan

Copyright © 2024 by V.Ivan

All rights reserved.

No part of this publication may be reproduced, distributed, or transmitted in any form or by any means, including photocopying, recording, or other electronic or mechanical methods, without the prior written permission of the publisher, except as permitted by U.S. copyright law. For permission requests, contact V.Ivan at victorivanwrites@gmail.com.

The story, all names, characters, and incidents portrayed in this production are fictitious or used fictitiously. Any resemblance to actual persons (living or deceased), places, buildings, and products is coincidental.

Book Cover by V. Ivan

For the furious girl I still cache deep inside—
I will protect you with sharpened nails and
carnivore teeth for the rest of our life.

BEFORE YOU READ

Many intense and frightening topics are explored in detail throughout this story. Despite the importance of these scenes, no reader is required to blindly revisit past trauma just to read this book. If you've done me the honour of sitting down with the intention of reading my work, which at times can be quite brutal, the least I can do is give you the ability to prepare.

MINOR CONTENT WARNINGS INCLUDE *casual drug use including prescription drugs and cannabis, underage drinking, vomit, arson, drunk driving/car accidents, discussions of massacres, language (swearing, cussing), verbal abuse* and *mild sexual content.*

MAJOR CONTENT WARNINGS INCLUDE *past-and-present scenes of murder, suicidal ideation/language, mental health crises, explicit descriptions and depictions of cannibalism, parental abuse and first-person descriptions of severe/life-threatening physical assault.*

To retain full comprehension, many scenes *cannot be skipped.* The climax of this book contains *all* major content warnings, and *may* be as upsetting to read as it was to write. *Have patience with yourself,* assess *your needs and proceed at your own discretion.* More information on content warnings can be found at <u>victorivan.weebly.com</u>.

Victor

in the
END,
you kill
us
BOTH

V. IVAN

THE GAP

Just over the slush-patterned hill beside the duplex on Allenview, through the venous streets of Olympia's western outskirts, a holy church of spirits and gasoline sat wedged between a Dollar General and a two-story apartment. Florid lights carved its windows from the dark, slashed by splatters of mutilated leaves and muck. By the time I arrived I'd gone purple from a chill I no longer felt, and in the numbness where I stood, I knew the Devil was coming for me.

Only three days outside the Echo and the holy convenience was a sugar-encrusted fairground. Fluttering neon smothered every ounce of shadow, illuminating my oily face in stark, sanitary white. Alongside the counter squatted a shopping cart heaped with baseball cards and magnetic matchbooks and flat cases of rings that turned your fingers green. The treasure trove was haloed by a bulletin board swarming with fluorescent business cards and flyers in various languages, curling stickers promising deals on sofa cleaners, pressure washing, ballet lessons, curving like a moss around the plexiglass-caged register where a cashier with freshly dyed red hair peered distrustingly at me. Rapid-fire radio chatter swole inside the lonely bubble behind the counter. The topic at hand must've been serious, because she looked at me as though I'd interrupted an emergency broadcast begging her to seek shelter.

"Please tell me you've got Winston Blues," I begged.

Nicely, despite the fact that I'd spent a year and a half cooped up in training, gearing myself for suicide at my next petty inconvenience. Drumming her nails over cased-in lotto tickets, the cashier ducked from view, rummaging through a wealth of hidden shelves to find a pack just

V. IVAN

for me. As I waited, my knapsack erupted with an obnoxious wail of scattered, robotic beeps that sent my soul through the ceiling tiles. At once, the world was ending—the sky falling, the clouds melting away like ink caps.

Drawn like a cougar by the noise, the cashier returned, gripping a fresh pack adorned with an unimpressionable golden eagle. *THE RUSH ISN'T WORTH IT*, the eagle promised. *SMOKING KILLS*.

"Turn that noise down."

"Orange soda?" I asked, red-faced.

She cast a finger towards the left flank of the store. When I went for the pack, she recoiled from my reach. "When you *pay*," she cut. "I mean it. Shut that shit off."

I skittered through the aisles until the counter was out of view and I was flanked only by pints of ice cream, making friends of the Neapolitan variety as I dripped anxiety across the clean, beige floor. I'd failed to shake the sweats since day one, and the intermittent bolts of lightning that pierced my brain crept out the door at their own pathetic pace. I was improving at the same rate a punctured lung might heal itself, or a shattered leg might reconnect its own pieces; poorly and with much error, suckling air in wheezing gasps, every lightbulb a warm, grubby pill just out of my reach.

Somehow he knew that, the *cunt*.

Somehow, even several states away, Satan crept up on me in the frozen aisle like an old high sneaking back in—parading through celebrity magazine spreads, warping technicolor photographs, logos and babies on diaper bundles into oily, oblong sprites with black horns and daggered claws, or snarling dogs with chimney spoke ears gushing smog, their teeth of plastic price tags chattering wickedly. He'd always found my paranoia to be one great, big joke; he'd buy tickets for my anxiety attacks if he knew he'd get front row seats.

Laugh, I thought. *At this point, somebody ought to.*

There, crouched inside the holy convenience, I stripped the knapsack from my shoulders. I'd been too scared to open it when the discharge nurse dumped it back into my hands days ago; two years had made its every crease and sutured tear a stranger to me, turned the lifeless fabric into an unclaimed corpse. The zipper laid cold and waxen in my hand, stroked only by dust for God knows how long.

Onto the tile I gutted the last of who I'd been; a black and white pamphlet for Hau's Cuisine in Ruth, an eyebrow ring and the emptied dime bag I'd awkwardly crammed it inside, a heavily scratched ID and a Ziploc of loose pocket change and three Lincolns. I counted out a filthy thirty bucks and forced that eyebrow ring back through the warped hole at my brow bone until I bled, then dipped my face crudely into the bag.

Every fibre held a medical *reek*. The same sterile, cruel smell that touched the furthest corners of the duplex. White vinegar and Pine-Sol and lemon pin-pricking the hairs in my nose. It soaked everything, dirtied all the fabric, stained the wood. My skin was slick with it; the powdery residue of those people, the mothy dust they left behind after all was made anew for me.

Zzzzzrp.

I hadn't missed cell phones when I was in the bin. I'd nearly trashed the thing just days before admittance, and *should've;* the only people that ever called me ought not to be spoken to. Like a thrashing bug it skittered into my knee, flashing puke-green numbers at me, chirping and whirring, possessed. No contact name, unsaved because I hadn't given a fuck at the time or because I'd been angry, or because I hadn't known how. One hand rose and jerked the cooler door open, flooding me with a sobering spray of cold, and I just—swayed.

Supposedly, the key to rehabilitation was accepting the sound of the past, no matter its intonation. The bubblegum-and-soda version was that we weren't yet bad people, but inaction could change that. There in the frozen section, the past was a mere static, chipping hungrily over the tinkling radio like it was coming from within me, somewhere lightless. I snatched it up, still thrashing, reminding myself of this like it mattered as I hit accept and rested my thumb over the end call button like a trigger: *I am not a bad person, but I could be. I am not a bad person, but I can be. I am not a bad person, but I should be. I am not a bad person. I am not a bad person. I cannot be made to feel like a bad person. Not here. Not now.*

V. IVAN

Please.

From the other end came the garbled barking of a PA system, spread into illegible chunks. A shifting noise like a barrage of coats toppling over, a quick, sharp whistle. Then came the peculiar and all-too-familiar clearing of a throat to some lifeless tune, a callous, cautious voice carving a chunk from me:

"Lenore?"

Heartburn saturated the dense flesh of my chest, soaking all the way into my lungs. I kept quiet, mirroring the waves of static, imagining her as a motion-triggered monster seeking its young, or myself as a buoy on a green-black sea. The silence offered her a chance to regain her composure and she returned even sharper, even more concise.

"Lenore, *say* something if you can hear me."

I sagged against the shelving behind me, creasing the smiles of celebrities too new for me to recognize. Two twitching fingers toyed with the nodules in my throat.

"Y—op. I hear you."

There was more to say. I hadn't the luck to live in a world where I'd ever get it all out, and not while she was actively on the line. *"God. It's so bizarre hearing your voice,"* came a well-rehearsed exhale. "I caught your voicemail a moment ago, but I didn't leave a message—you sound older than her now." There was a third, garbled piece of that sentence but I lost it in a crossfire of radio rambling and jingling doorbells. Someone entered the convenience store with a child, hidden by high steel shelves, and all I could hear was spoiled whining. "H—ear m—?"

"Well, *now* I can't."

Shattered speaking. I furthered myself from the parent and child and communed with shelved loaves of half-off bread and bagels, passing towards the soda cooler as I chased my fleeting patience, wondering if I'd had any at all. My smokes waited by the cash register like a frustrated lover.

"Try again."

"In—for the—Can't—me—?"

"Maybe you should hang up."

IN THE END, YOU KILL US BOTH

Myra continued, her voice lilting in broken curses, diving headfirst and unsupervised into an unintelligible rant like a symphony of violent groans. For a staggering moment I just read the highs and the lows, the vague, interspersed consonants, the echoing of lost words. I could've let her bleed forever. Pitifully, my mind fled to all the conversations I'd survived with her, and how many would've gone well if I hadn't listened to her words—just her tone.

"Mom," I said, "I'm moving to a better spot. Just hold on a second."

That word crunched like cartilage between my teeth. I pulled open one of the cooler doors to free myself from it, but it clung. The distant, echoing background noise bled away as the chill of a cold bottle against my fingers weighed me down.

"Say something."

Without skipping a beat, Myra's clear, unbroken voice swept into my ear. "It's just because I'm in transit," she explained, comically clear now, mimicking small talk like a sheepish alien. "Working my way back from the Yukon. Three months—oh, you remember how it is. Not much of a minute here for me to settle, but I thought—*well*. A nice male orderly over there in the office called me to remind me of the discharge."

Thank God for that.

"I didn't *need* reminding," she guaranteed, "but I'm glad they did. I found some time. I would've called sooner, but I didn't know if you'd have your phone on. I half expected *you* to call *me*. I guess if I want to know how my child's faring, I've got to go find her myself."

I licked the back of my teeth like a thinning animal, sliding past the huge, bulbous jugs of spring water, eyes skirting blindly over the labels. I could've grabbed a bottle of soda or a tallboy; I was hardly looking, only knowing the cold through the relief of my thumping brow bone. "Why would I call *you* first?"

"Oh—*alright*, Lenore," came my mother, my *mother* once again, "because I expected that you'd want to *talk* to me. That somewhere within the past year and a half, you'd experience things that you'd want to tell me. Is that such a *shock?*" I stood with inherited impatience, waiting for the curt sigh, for the snap of her teeth as she came for me. Instead,

V. IVAN

there was a deep drowsiness in the way she asked: *"Do you have things to tell me?"*

I held my tongue as long as I could manage. Long enough that I knew she was mutely comparing me to Dad; the voice that bounced back again was thin and tough.

"Lots to readjust to, I'd imagine. I hope they *fed* you. Well, really, I *hope* they gave you lots of good skills in there for dealing with things. Did they?" She prodded, clawing for me. *"Help you figure yourself out?"*

Things. Oh, the *things* that had to be figured out.

Silence told me she wanted me to elaborate. She could only wade in it for so long before she spoke just to stay comfortable, but I lived in silence for well over a year; silence wet the barren vestibules of my heart, as vital to me as breathing. I basked in quiet. I baked in a suffocating tension, golden brown and warm.

This was not a sore, cold shoulder. This was an entirely new degree of rejection; a complete lapse of it. A well-earned nothingness between us. It was dead air and the gory, pestilent things that lived in the gap. These were the things that stained the lids of my eyes, things I couldn't outlive for the life of me.

"We don't have to talk about it," Myra interjected. "I just wanted to call before I got back to Nevada. To make sure you're adjusting."

"I'm living with an older woman in Olympia."

Those words hurtled forward without warning, carved from that nothingness with my own stained fingers. When I glanced over the shelves and towards the counter, the cashier was eyeballing me. Paranoid, I let the cooler door flop closed with a sticky thump, my spattered reflection marbled by the condensation.

"Georgia," I announced, tasting each syllable the way I'd done on garbage day when I'd arrived—my worn knapsack on my shoulders, three days into a withdrawal that'd kneecapped me before her, a shock of beauty thinner than a broom handle in a ketchup-stained tank and dense eyeliner. "At a two-story duplex on the edge of the city. It's a nice place, too. She finished the program long before me; says that folks from inside do monthly wellness checks, but otherwise it's *independent.* She's got a

little boy and a little girl, and a baby, too. I have my own room upstairs across from hers. She's really great, and so are her kids. Y'know what? *Honestly?* I've never slept better."

I said all of it just to hurt her; the voided response told me I'd succeeded. I wanted so desperately to love her, but I despised myself enough that it doubled back to her. Maybe it was the other way around, too. Maybe still, in contrast to life as I knew it, there existed unseen universes where my mother and I arrived at love in unison. Some other Leo was standing barefoot in the dirt there, glimpsing Myra's affection like a meteor on the edge of an oily sky. At times I was jealous of her, the bitch. At times, in *every* universe, I wanted her dead.

Myra struck back in the nothingness, as kind as a killer: "Should I be sending her some cash?"

"I'm not being babysat," I forced. "I'm an adult."

"Last time I saw you, you weren't." Before something could procreate in the quiet, Myra clipped its wings. "I should head over to my gate. I already put my bags through. There isn't much time."

Envisioning her amidst the airport chaos like a lone seal on a shale slab of iceberg, I waited for the finishing touches—tongue-in-cheek questions about Georgia and her background, about her children, about the insides of a home that she hadn't lived in, let alone *seen* before. In our time apart, I'd clearly forgotten who she was; she didn't fucking care. Those things only mattered if she thought Georgia was doing better in life than she was, and how could she be envious of *more* children? I lifted the phone from my face.

As if instinctually, Myra mewled: "Lenore?"

I didn't dare expect an apology. If that's what she was building up to, I didn't want it. I'd chew it up and spit it out. Still, the speaker crept back to my ear.

"*Hm.*"

A sudden moment of quiet poked through. I could hear her breathing within it, tracking through the labyrinth of her own words.

V. IVAN

"You shouldn't be quick to come back. Not—not for a good while, at least. It's better for both of you that way. To keep things separate while we work this out."

I no longer bled from Myra's words, but something about that stuck me. I knew I couldn't go back. It wasn't illegal, and it wasn't impossible, but even the consideration was inhumane. Still, it was only in being denied the opportunity that I was angry about the lack of choice. I *never* wanted to go back to Ely. I'd never wanted to be there in the first place. Something about Myra voicing it—the wound festered, gummy with old, brown blood.

"Location and rehabilitation," I rattled. "Of *course.*"

"And with work, and the sudden demands between Ely and the Yukon, you know—"

"It's fine. I'm fine."

"I would if I had the time," Myra supposed, "but I can't be bouncing all over the place. The plane rides, they—well, they're so exhausting, and I've got commitments that I can't shoulder."

I knew that, too. It'd been quite some time, if ever, since I'd been one.

"They're calling for me," she said, and I absorbed the sound of her shuffling jacket, wondered if it was the thick green one with the fur around the wrists. She looked like an old rich matriarch when she wore it and told everyone the fur was real. I never understood why. "I'll leave you here, alright? It was—nice to hear your voice again. You sound so much clearer. You really, really do."

I jimmied the knife from my chest, flicked my cell closed and returned to the register, sliding what ended up being a praline milkshake across the counter. Whatever colour the weather had brought out in me was waning, and I felt like a staunch bulldog in a tar-black hoodie.

"Waste of electricity," the woman murmured regarding the cooler, ringing me up.

I forked over half of the money I had, shambling with my tall paper bag back to the duplex and halting under every streetlight to trace the day-old purple curls of Georgia's gel pen on my wrist. *Pass hill and take right on Abenaki, Walk 2 law place and left, right, right at Newman, pass lights.* The snow, something I'd never acclimated to, sucked at my sneakers like still-wet sheets of gum.

My first winter in Washington was long, sheltered and built without choices, fitted just over a year ago inside my soggy memory. All that remained were the moments I spent wastefully, mooching cheap menthols from girls with no taste, dreaming of Nevadan varieties, glazed in the light of a fibre optic tree the size of a toddler propped distractingly aside the communal television. Then, aside from the excitement of snowfall, Christmas was a week straight of candy-striped pill cups and watered down eggnog, pre-unwrapped gifts of cheap chocolates and ankle socks. Sole reprieve—the Dobson Newham Healing Garden, a cube of pale greenery and boardwalk pathways walled by windows—became a mountain of filthy, murky beige and stayed locked for months. Lawn walks were spent smoking, chased by courageous breaths of fresh, polar-cold air, a trek across the green and back like training puppies with our tails squared away. Otherwise we were bound to the insides of the Echo, half of us unmarked by cabin fever while the others basked in it, clinging to the windows and marvelling at the skinned trees wagging their spiny fingers tauntingly from the cemetery across the street.

It was stranger on the outside, willingly entering the frigid outdoors with no restraints. The damp dark of Abenaki Road was little company, but I sucked back the taste of menthol to keep me warm and I was no lonelier for it. The corner of Allenview where the duplex huddled shyly between its neighbours was salt-rimmed with vehicles when I returned; old and new micro-cars, a burnt-brown beater truck with a tail light kicked out, motorcycles of all shapes cloaked in protective slips. Shadows skated across the whiteout curtains indoors, glimpses of bodies I didn't recognize through fat grubs of falling snow. Before the door light could catch me, I crept along the edge of the lichen-heavy brick, setting my breath to the repetitious vibrations of the hellbilly music coming from inside.

I shook it off to the best of my ability, halfway through my second cigarette, sliding my hands inside my sleeves and mocking the desire to

V. IVAN

strip the pain off as simply as a pair of wet gloves. It shouldn't have been so hard to dust myself of the echoes and shake the deadweight from my skeleton. That's all it'd been; an echo of my mother, an uncanny image sculpted by wires and circuits. A conversation I'd never be able to control. In an instant I was back inside the Echo, marinating in pink and blue Christmas tree light, wondering why the garden gates were locked if the snow was too high to trek through anyway. Wondering who would even try.

In the Olympian dark, the lights in Ely, as far and few between as they were, seemed suddenly so bright.

BUG PROBLEM

THE INDOOR CROWD FLOWED in tandem to the music, clustered gatherers swaying like garden eels in a lukewarm current. I drifted through them as a ropeless diver hanging over the free ocean, never sure I'd make it to shore. Splayed hands and elbows and torsos throttled me into the surf. The ancient speaker system underneath the living room's boxy television gargled around Rob Zombie's *Superbeast*, vibrating all the way into the dining room where I found Georgia Gwen mid-pour into a line of red solos for a group of burly men in tarnished leather vests.

She looked like a western barmaid from some old Clint Eastwood joint, if cheetah-print belly tops existed back then. Standing there with one hip against the counter, her lipstick bleeding around the corners, I wanted to hide in her shadow for a while; to live through her wide, uneven smile and its catlike teeth, her bony wrists buried beneath stacks of copper bangles, the uproar of laughter over something I hadn't heard tossing her bleached curls back with a rough bounce. They all paid full attention, even when she spoke over them. I could never command men that way. Then again, I never *really* wanted to.

"I thought you were gonna sleep all night," she cooed when she noticed me hovering, her pink face bright underneath the kitchen light. "You feelin' okay? Need something to wear? I bet I've got somethin' you could borrow."

I took a long look at Georgia's frame, half that of mine. My sleep-bloated body, tucked inside yesterday's clothes, suddenly felt so spongy, so absorbent of the light she gave off, and as I remembered the

V. IVAN

bedroom window I'd left ajar in my late-night escape I feared the chill I'd face that night in bed.

"I'll be alright." I tried not to sound sour, tried not to smell like *smoke*. "Those melatonin—they knocked me the hell out."

"Prescription shit'll do that to ya. Surprised you're on your feet, actually." Georgia turned her back to me and, like a magician, returned with a half-full solo. When I glanced uneasily into it, something piss-yellow stared back at me.

"*Uh?*"

"Oh, don't look so squeamish. It's only apple juice." Georgia slotted the cup into my reluctant hand, unfazed by the shingle-rattling music. When I met her eyes, she waved a dismissive hand. "I don't mess around with that underage drinking stuff. I wouldn't let my own kids do it if they were your age. Juice'll have to do."

I didn't *want* a drink, alcoholic or not, and my body rejected her sentimentality like a thorn wedged beneath my fingernail, a well of infection nested neatly below the surface. I clutched the cup, my every thought pounded from my head by the welling sounds of life, the flooding of the living room, the spattered groups of people in the kitchen; squawking migrant birds. My eyes landed on an owlish sort of man with a tattooed face, drowning his solo in cheap vodka, suffering inside a leather jacket a few sizes too big. I gestured lowly with my cup.

"Why doesn't that guy have apple juice? He looks like he just finished his SATs."

Georgia followed my invisible cast all the way to the Owl. As if supernaturally aware of the eyes on him, his head swivelled towards us, a disconcerted twinkle in his eye. For a moment there was only that stand off, unnoticed by the rest of the party, Georgia's brow crinkling as she fumbled over her splintered memory. The Owl must've known her at least as little as I did, because something in that stare made him respond with a muffled name.

"You just had a birthday," Georgia stated, half-questioning.

IN THE END, YOU KILL US BOTH

The Owl glanced at me, seemingly expecting that I'd answer for him. His stare seared the hair clean off my face. "Next Wednesday, actually," he reeled his attention back to Georgia. "The thirtieth."

"How old are you gonna be?"

He flatlined, wetting his lips. And then he smiled at her, some cheap, blatant grin. "Old *enough*, Gee. C'mon."

Alcohol licked Georgia's bare wrist as she craned across the counter and snatched his cup. Through a daggered smile, she tilted the lip towards him as if she were pointing a meter stick over a white-topped desk, glaring into his open-mouthed, wide-eyed face.

"My flat ass," she scowled. "Old enough. How old do you think *I* am? Jesus. Give me a *break*." She looked one of her leathered lap dogs in his expectant face. "Tell me you smoke. I need a fucking cigarette."

She was out the patio door before I could manage another word and I was left standing like a shrew in a cornfield, avoiding the hard glare that'd befallen me as I shuffled awkwardly to the sink. I grabbed a fistful of ice from its half-filled basin and pretended I was back in the Echo and away from all the noise, but that was no better. The sink's hard edge caught the light, and I drifted to harsher places.

"Hey," the Owl's voice bounced across the counter.

I poured the handful into my cup, quieting the urge to dump it all out. A large, pinching breath held within my lungs as I stared into the cool steel, the ice buzzing from the stereo's bass. It gave an odd life to the sink that I didn't appreciate at all.

When I didn't respond, I heard him shuffle and snarl, "Nice job being a total goddamn buzzkill."

Mid-memory, I turned. *"Excuse me?"*

"Ratting me out like that." He leaned hard on the counter, a pair of beady, globe-like eyes ogling at me from behind the dated eyeglasses seated on his forked nose. Under his biking jacket, I bet he had feathers. "We're all here to have a good time. One little drink won't kill nobody. Ain't no point in acting like such a narc unless you *are* a narc."

I wiped my hands of condensation. "Can't legally drink, but *sure*, I'm a *cop*. Take it up with Chief Georgia."

V. IVAN

My guard was readied like porcupine quills, itching to shoot. Something about him was disgustingly familiar. Without a doubt I'd never met him before, only men like him, and if you've met one you've met them all. And how *awful* to have met them all.

He stared at me for a long time, that Owl, wordlessly watching. His fingers found his specs and shoved them up with a mildly-annoyed sniffle. I darted out of the way of a lady on her way to the sink, overstimulated at best, craving another magic white melatonin and debating finding Georgia. All I could make out from the kitchen window were bodies bobbing about on the back patio, an infestation of faceless heads wading in the swirling dark, puffing smoke.

"Not much of a chatter, are you?"

A deep, pitted annoyance swelled in my stomach. "Did I somehow make you think I wanted to chat?"

"You go to parties just to ignore everyone?"

"I didn't *choose* to go, I *live* here." I was itching such a ferocious itch that instead of closing doors on the Owl, I'd been unintentionally clawing them open. I couldn't remember the last time I'd enjoyed simple, meaningless chatter like that, and he wasn't breaking any records.

His gaze lifted and a finger shot up, flicking towards me. "Right. See, I *heard* about you. You're the newest guest that checked into Hotel Georgia," he grinned, thinking himself funny. Rob Zombie skipped back to track one and, as if on cue, a slouching older man slid around the corner from the living room and cranked open the spice cabinet, which I was astonished to find packed with CD cases. "I tried asking her when you were coming, but she couldn't even tell me your name. She turned blue before she gave up. *Y'know,*" he warned, *"she's got a thing with that. With people's names."*

It wasn't just names, and there was a *word* for it—scribbled in doctor's chicken scratch on a bleached post-it inside the cereal cupboard, smacked to the door with tape the way all other things in the kitchen were labeled—documents taped to the walls out of toddler reach, juice boxes with tacky yellow post-its and black sharpie, shipping labels on every surface scrawled in her belligerent handwriting. REFRIGERA-

IN THE END, YOU KILL US BOTH

TOR, NAPKINS, BABY WIPES, TOASTER, SPAGHETTI, TRASH BAGS. Things that were pre-labelled were bolded for effect, underlined for certainty. I'd seen her pretty blue-faced on Monday just trying to introduce herself by name.

"What is it, anyway? Since she couldn't tell me."

I glanced back at the Owl, and winced as he tipped his head in a sore attempt at being charming. Would there be pills upstairs in the cabinet? I bet I could find them.

"*Lenore.*"

"How old *are* you, Lenore?"

"Seventeen," I lied.

"So you *are* too young to drink." *And too young for you to be hazing*, I agreed, trying not to squirm as the Owl craned closer, his eyes rolling over my face like toppling dice, drawing tingles to the patchy stretch of port-wine mopped around my eye. "You like to smoke, Lenore? Not just cigarettes."

I hadn't smoked pot since eleventh grade. The Owl gazed expectantly at me, wired by my inattention like he might blink one eyeball at a time and spin his head around just to entice me. In imagining his bulbous skull rotating and popping off like a tired bobblehead, I didn't think hard before I caved.

"We can *smoke*," I said through throbbing teeth, sliding my apple juice to the countertop. "But I've gotta piss first."

I didn't wait for him to agree or disagree. I was gone like Georgia, snaking through the foyer and along the shoreline of bodies bumping to a freshly-spun copy of *Shout At The Devil*, up around the stairwell and into the stale solace of the upstairs foyer. I popped the first doorway on the left and hissed at the hellish, unflinching cold. The borrowed bedroom I lived in was a wobbling blanket of coy shadows—the foot of my unmade bed slashed with moonlight, casting odd, misshapen faces up and across the walls, over the wardrobe, over the scraped-down wooden floor. When their features warped too close to comfort, a recognizable fear leapt up into my throat, desperate to be quenched, and

V. IVAN

I was thankful for the music if only so nobody could hear me slam the window shut harder than ever necessary.

When I tried the handle on the hallway bathroom, somebody balked from behind the thick pine door. Suffocating, I waddled into Georgia's room, a glorified mess strewn about a carefully-made bed, and dipped into her private bath, flinging the door halfway shut behind me. I was glad for the master bathroom and its mess—children's toys peppering the floor, occupying the sink's edge, pinky-sized toothbrushes, a mustard-walled freeze-frame of their little life. I parked along the tub's edge and loosened the neck of my hoodie, Georgia's stained shower curtain embracing me as I scooted into it, filing itchy baby hairs away from my neck. I sat slumped into that curtain so long that my body began to set, my fingers barely curled in clawing desperation over my thighs, knees trembling with an unmoving ache.

I sank before my humiliation like it was my childhood bed, preserved and waiting for me as long as it took. I couldn't handle five minutes alone in a crowd of booze-fuelled strangers and I couldn't handle a single conversation, as insufferable as it'd been. I could, however, count on one hand how many people I'd spoken to in the last year. Was it more pathetic to assume my social skills *hadn't* completely rotted? Was it plain as day that I'd been ruined forever?

Standing, I left my humility on the flowery toilet lid and avoided the Fresh Meat in the mirror, but she was terribly disappointed in me. Round-faced and sick looking, the stretching birthmark on her right side a polished red, her uneven jaw set behind a dense scowl. I pulled open the cabinet so her grubby reflection was flung towards the wall, glaring at coffee-toned wallpaper until I found my bearings. Pearls and thin chains on the bottom ledge shone in my direction. Kids mouthwash, pills unnamed and wrapped in plastic cling film, a bottle of toothpaste with a rubber band securing the top, volumes of orange bottles with white toppers consuming half a shelf. I reached past a dull razor and began spinning their labels to face the back, squinting invasively at their contents.

Foolishly, I hadn't thought I'd miss the medication when I left. I'd taken it morning and night and I'd scraped along every day in therapy with my buttons done all the way up to my neck, sweating out the last dribbles of emotion that the pills didn't clot and ferment. I ate oatmeal and pre-buttered crackers and didn't complain about how I felt because I didn't feel anything at all, and feeling nothing was better in every single instance I could think of. I left under the assumption that it was permanent, that I'd absolved myself of emotions and was henceforth reformed, quiet and honest, communicable and peaceful, oblivious. Nowhere near the kind of person who snooped through other people's stashes just for a taste.

Well, I was *right*. I had to be. It couldn't be snooping if I wasn't looking for anything but melatonin. Still, an odd, conscious sourness crept up my throat; Georgia had been kind to me. The thought that I might be crossing her was unwelcome, and the guilt it drew forth was honest but distant like I was watching myself on television acting through scripted emotions.

My guilt had always been genuine, just far outside of reach, and what I felt with my hands in Georgia's cabinet was nothing more than a trembling poltergeist in the dusty corner of my brain—an echo. If I willed it away, maybe it would lose merit, but I was still the newest rat in that hole in the wall and I hadn't healed a bit. I was only *just* coming down from it all, and trying desperately to claw my way back up. The revelation sent me trembling.

Not because I was sad, but because I was *useless*.

In absentia, I smacked aside a bottle and, in doing so, knocked several others into the sink where they clattered against each other like crooked, plasticine teeth.

"Shit," dribbled sloppily from my mouth. One bottle struck the edge of the porcelain just right and its protective white lid snapped off, flinging brown and grey pills across the floor. "Shit, shit, shit," I aimed at the bottles this time, with an extra gratuitous, *"Motherfucker. Dickface."*

I would've been thankful that the comedown was drawing splotches of red back into my cheeks if only I wasn't hot and dirty and swollen

V. IVAN

all over. Scooping scattered pills from the basin, I stooped to retrieve the empty lid behind the sink's neck. My fingertips nudged something slick against the unaligned tiles and stomach acid shot bullet-like into my throat. Recoiling, I grated my hand against my pants and hurriedly plucked the rest of the pills off the floor before begrudgingly sliding forth the metal trash can to ensure none had fallen in or behind it.

My hands stuttered on its tin lip and froze.

An old friend writhed at the bottom of that bagless bin. Six bile-yellow limbs and two twitchy antennae sat below the matte black eyes affixed to its cherry, boneless head. The steel was a slippery death; wherever it came from, it was wearing itself to death at the bottom of Georgia's garbage trying to get back home. Those slanted, pinching mandibles curved and twitched over a stray pill that sat inside the can and I watched in dumb silence as it climbed over the little brown capsule and carried on, frantic.

I sat on my knees for longer than I even realized. The music's faint buzz radiated through the floor, changed over a few times and I remained paralyzed, each hair on my body drawn tight and straight like flagless poles, pointed at the ceiling. It might've been excruciating, but I wasn't present enough to know.

Instead, I circled what memory I had left of my childhood home in Ely, a hearth which the Devil I knew had never crossed upon. A pale green single-level buried deep on Lyons Avenue, right across from an Episcopal Church with muted brown brick and a patchy, sloping lawn. I couldn't walk that house quite as well as the last, but that was fair enough; the fresh hell of the last house on Carpenter Street loomed like a planet, powdering anything that dared challenge its burdensome weight on my memory. Beneath its shadow, the Lyons house faded over time as good things often did, accentuated like constellations puncturing a horrific, endless sky. I could beg for the memory but I was beyond retrieving it—I could sketch out a kitchen with grey cupboards and wine-red backsplash, a peony rug in the living room and a banker's lamp on a slug-yellow coffee table and none of it would mean anything. I had no way of knowing what was true to memory and what was merely the

IN THE END, YOU KILL US BOTH

last nibbles of that old, rotten fruit. The time and space between my collapsed body and the framework of the old house was a choiceless hazmat suit.

In its place, Carpenter hung off my back like a sack of dirt. It was formed from whatever oily shit covered the tiles behind Georgia's sink and old, cakey black blood, the sort that gets jammed under your fingernails. It stung like tripping in the kitchen and hitting your head on the counter, the stars and fractalized vision that follow. A tall glass of water hurled through an open entryway, bedroom to living room. Glass littering the linoleum like gravel, dredged in by old work boots.

The home on Lyons had one big, bad remaining memory, tumescent in the mental map which had long ago worn away. It was a glaring red nuclear leak stemming from the treeless backyard where only fountain grass survived and the weeds all burnt to an aching crisp, ribbed against the exposed dirt and the quartz-rimmed fire pit, ensnaring the legs of my childhood swing set with its rubber seat half-amputated and dangling in the windless, tyrannical heat—the last bones standing in the robbed grave of my mind. That horrific summer, the Nevadan heat had turned our elderly air conditioner into a useless box, and hiding behind blackout curtains transformed the home into an ever-churning kiln. I'd never been so desperate for school, in such withdrawal of the opulent bliss that came with walking into an icy building, the relief of cold water fountain sips and laying my head on a frozen desktop.

Myra's remedy was to leave the back door wide open each afternoon so the stuffiness behind those curtains wouldn't kill us. God knows if it really made all the difference, but my father hated it, warned her against it, and so she always made sure to close it by the time he got home—had gone as far as to glue me to the front windows from five to six as a self-described *lookout*, sweltering beneath a blanket of wiggling heat so she'd know the exact moment his car pulled in alongside her Buick Riviera.

Early one sticky Sunday morning, off duty from the front window, I found my father with his sleeves balled up to his elbows, digging beneath a loose kitchen tile with a pocketknife the size of my little fist. Upon seeing me he'd risen, his pink, unshaven face flooded with sweat, ushering me towards the counter and hoisting me into his arms, the burning scent of scalding tar still smoky on his clothes. He tilted me down towards an overturned glass on the countertop, and though at first I'd had no clue what I was looking at, I shrieked regardless.

Earwigs; two grubby redheads with pinchers like grabbing fingers, bumbling stupidly around the edges of the glass. I squirmed similarly until my father put me down, only to duck behind his trunk-like thigh, watching the glass as if I expected it to crack.

When Myra got home, he asked her about the door and she denied it, staring at the egg-carved tile he'd jimmied from the floor with green-faced disgust. He never got angry when she lied, even when he knew better. He was good that way—not as hypocritical as he could've been—but it was the *dark* and the *dampness* that they ached for, and he told her so, wide-eyed and careful as he hammered the words down. The door needed to close. It wouldn't work otherwise.

Myra didn't listen. Even in the presence of evidence, she didn't believe him. She kept the door open when my father was at work. He'd never know the difference.

In two weeks, they were everywhere.

Nested inside the pleats of the living room curtains, inside folded clothes, clinging to the ribbed necks of bottled jam and cupboard foods, underneath the handle on the toilet and inside the bathroom faucet—warm, narrow, damp. They were sneaky, and *worse*, they were tactical. Bedsheets were also preferable; in due time I slept less and less, and when I did I dreamt of the Episcopal church and their air conditioning. The people that mingled about on the lawn every Sunday looked bright and cool and happy all the same. I thought of asking my father if they would let us sit inside, just for a little while, or if the church had air conditioning because its people believed in God. But there were no answers for those sorts of things.

The day I came home readied with questions, I found him standing above the fire pit he'd dug out years before. His hair was sopping with sweat and his arms were red-brown, baked to a crisp in the summers he spent roofing and landscaping. Before him, the pit gushed with a hungry flame, devouring a mountain of mismatched fabric. Kitchen rugs, armfuls of clothing, a set of curtains. Old bedsheets of mine, bathroom towels, pillow cases. From beyond the patio door, the clashing fabrics squirmed against lashing blue tongues.

I froze in the doorway and asked aloud, speaking openly into the world, what he was doing.

Eventually, he turned. The right side of his face, overexposed, had started to blister by July and it wouldn't fully heal again until fall. Glancing into the fire, he debated it. Then he stared at me, smiling as if to tell me nothing was wrong. The lie hung heavy on his brow where sweat coalesced. Before him, the egg-infested fabric crackled and popped with machine gun fire.

'All those earwigs,' he explained. 'Once they root like that, you've gotta destroy the nests. Otherwise they'll keep coming back.' His eyes fell upon the debris once more. 'You've got to burn them.'

Briefly, I lost him to the flame. Something crude and adult haunted his burnished gaze, pointed into the coals or somewhere deeper, far beyond it. The roofs were so hot in July, and twice that in August. I'd often worried as a girl that the sun would bake the soft tissue of his brain. Even more often, I'd begun to wonder if the same might eventually happen to me.

'You've got to burn them. Kill them,' he had commanded. 'Otherwise they'll never go away. Not fully.'

THERE WAS A TIME when I liked to think about my father. Kneeling on Georgia's bathroom floor with dust-painted knees, watching that monster struggle for freedom—that wasn't it.

I rose from that terrible daydream, the fire whittling away my bones like a dull knife as I nudged open the cabinet once more, incessant. Costume jewelry, medication, toothpaste—all inflammable. I looked to the ceiling, thick curls sticking to the sweating sides of my neck, and

V. IVAN

made quick work of popping free the smoke detector from its ancient casing above the toilet.

My father's face lingered against my eyelids, muddled and off like an old memory left out in the sun, burdened by green and purple water spots that made his proportions disjointed. He occupied my body as I parked myself on the edge of the bathtub, lighting a cigarette to keep myself warm. A bright, dopey-eyed bath toy eyeballed me from behind the toilet. I debated towels, facecloths and old blister packs but settled on toilet paper, fashioning kindling in the palms of my hands, rolling until there was nothing but a shell of cardboard swaying on the holder. I dragged the basket across the floor with the tip of my shoe, observing the beast as I shredded the tissue with my nails, dropped flakes into the basin, watching it scrabble across newfound surfaces.

It couldn't know what hopelessness really felt like, but I could almost put a method to its scrambling. I dumped more into the bin, balancing my cigarette like a scale on my fingers. It hovered over the steel lip, barely smoked, a waste if I'd ever seen one outside of a mirror. Indifferent, the beast kept crawling. Blissfully unaware, even as I let go.

With the cherry pointed downwards like a diving missile, the mound winked and caught and in the mere moment it took for the flames to soar, the body of that pinching creature jolted, fluttered an inch across the grimy steel and cracking clean in two. I was awoken by the lapping yellows, blues and reds coalescing, rising in the pot. White ribboned into black, ashen and powdered before my eyes. It wasn't kind to sit in a memory so painful yet I was at momentary peace in that pool of blood, displaced from my body. It wasn't the first terrible memory I'd guarded, seeking comfort in the fact that it belonged to me. It wouldn't be the last, either. Defocused, my hands sitting at the edge of that heating steel looked mineral, quartz-like.

The fire nipped promptly at my nose, the tips of my bangs twisting from the clarifying heat. The Carpenter house passed overhead, a meteor gaining traction as it spun directly for me.

Without a thought, I dumped the weakening fire into the tub, the flames whining and shrinking against leftover water droplets collected in the basin. Flames sought the shower curtain but failed to reach, my hands spinning the tap, flooding the embers with a gush of freezing water. With a snap and a hiss, it was gone, little else left but a pile of damp, muddy ash clumped around the drain, the earwig indivisible from the remains.

I'd lost my breath. Cranking the tap off, my fingers smoothed across the chest of my hoodie, over my throat. I hunted down the pack of cigarettes in my pocket with twitching hands, regressing to the porcelain as I hoisted the garbage can back onto the floor. It was all too much—humiliating, of course, but *pitiful*. It would never *not* be too much. Things would always be that way—overpowering, suffocating. Wading in blood. I lifted my head to light a new smoke and caught, through the trembling flame, the silhouette of a body, a *corpse*, lounging there.

From the footlong gash in the bathroom door, a Wolf was watching.

THE WOLF

Straight from the forest and into the tungsten glow of Georgia's bathroom, the Wolf had crept—feral behind a mute stare, dressed casually to mask the claws and the robust canines.

I wasn't *clueless*. I could *see* the uneven, broken nails beneath the wrists of their coat—could smell the blood, too, despite knowing I always smelt it coming back from the fire at Lyons. They were just so *still*, like someone had swept silently into Georgia's room and left a standee in the unlatched doorway. Inhuman at first, as their mere presence wracked my body with a blatant, uncontrollable shiver.

With a tilt of their head, the shadows withdrew around the Wolf's scar-warped face, diving beneath their uneven, narrow nose, forming two beetle eyes with sparse lashes, lips wrapped in fishline scars that drew a permanent wince. The fur was no longer fur, not *ever* fur, but a mop of scissor-cut chunks of dyed sable hair. An inch of coppery roots painted their scalp bloody. It was the sort of face that pries its way into your dreams, suctioning you awake, not feminine nor masculine but indistinguishably *other;* blunt, as was the rest of them. I'd left the door open—had invited the Wolf in, if you really thought about it. As their head stooped just below the top of the doorway, I thought *hard*.

Sniffling, the Wolf lifted a bony hand, flashing a palm dotted with half-missing tattoo, and a ragged slush of lazy Southern poured from their mouth.

"Good choice. That detector's got a sister in the hallway and a cousin downstairs that's prone to waterworks. Wouldn't want everyone gettin' pissed on."

IN THE END, YOU KILL US BOTH

I was a rat in the field, motionless but for a heartbeat which steadily climbed into my throat, holding my cigarette like a blade of razor grass. "Happy to grab it," they offered. "The damn sister."

"*Occupied,*" I finally managed.

Their unbothered gaze rotated around the room, up and over the shower curtain, into the basin half-drenched in ashen bathwater. The eyes that caught mine were a cavernous black; light quivered before their clueless stare. Innocence, feigned or real, I couldn't be sure.

"Been' lookin' for the smoker's corner," the Wolf admitted. A scuff of their muddied sneakers, not daring a step beyond the doorway, jutting a toe towards the ashen bin. "Must've found it, then, eh?"

Heat rose blotchily to my cheeks. "Flicked the cherry off by accident. My own dumbass mistake."

God, they weren't *blinking*. Eyeballing the trash can, their raw pink mouth a taut line, assessing the crime scene.

"I can wait 'til you're done. Don't wanna smoke you out." They took a wavering step back. "Or I can go outdoors, but it's cold as a witch's tit out there."

From somewhere deep in my tensing ribs, possessed by the embarrassment, I grumbled. Hospitality—as little to none as I'd offered—was nothing but a ruse to keep that humiliation from crushing me. "You're fine. It's whatever. Power to you."

The Wolf idled, perplexed.

"Sit," I pushed. "If you really want. Shut the door, since I didn't. Or don't—I don't *care*."

They did as they were told, a perfectly obedient stranger, sliding inside the bathroom like a cornered shadow and gently shrinking to the floor beneath a shelf of mismatched towels. From the wrist of their jacket came a set of crooked fingers, tapping something hand-rolled from their pack and shaking the lid closed, the snapping spark of their chrome lighter scorching the end of a pencil-thin joint. We sat in the muffled leftovers of music for some time, puffing into the open room, cloaking the place in a fog. Beneath the Wolf's unrelenting stare I draped my eyes

V. IVAN

over the toilet again, skirting over the lid's embroidery. I was still basking in the afterglow of that havoc when their pleasant voice rose.

"Ain't fond of company?"

The bathroom reeked like soot, pot and canned air freshener; the most human symphony of smells I'd known in years. I withheld a cough, peering over the tile. "How'd you guess?"

"Hidin' upstairs, startin' fires," they suggested, not as a joke but a flat-ironed fact. "Can't get much more antisocial 'round here. Still—I'd grab the hallway detector, if you're super set."

"On?"

"Burnin' the hair clean off your head."

I balked, leaning onto my knees. *"How long were you watching me?"*

The Wolf's button eyes flickered away in consideration, diving into the cracks of the air vent with a lolling head. "Long enough to get the picture."

"There's no *picture*. It was an accident."

Amusement caught the corner of their waxen lips. *"Sure,"* they said lowly. *"No, I get it."*

The earwig was gone, the pest temporarily banished. Still I sat, suffering through the end of my cigarette, trying to glare their urge to speak into nothingness, into grime on the floor.

"Tough mask, but there ain't no shame in it," they added, proving me unsuccessful. "Plenty of folk on the inside would rather be doin' whatever the hell you're doin' instead of inhaling percs and Ritz. So if that's what speaks to you, have at it. *Live that dream.*"

I squinted. *"Inside?"*

The Wolf flexed their fingers around one bony kneecap. *"Eden Valley.* You got the full lease of the place, right?"

The way those words flowed from their cracked lips was entirely surreal, words so private to me and so known all at once. For a moment I felt I was speaking to someone I knew, someone I'd known for some time, a glimmer of casual trust stretched between us like fine, fragile silk. I stared at the middle ground where a white flag would sit if I had one to surrender, and took such a deep drag that my lungs clenched alongside a singular heartbeat.

"Never heard of it," I said through the smoke.

The exit wounds of their eyes held me still. *"You haven't."*

A resounding knock rattled the bathroom door, and I nearly dropped my smoking cigarette into my lap. The Wolf never even twitched. Between us bloomed a silent debate as to who would answer until a clueless, low voice slid through the crack beneath the door.

"Lenore?" the bird-eyed freak called out, like a lost boy in a grocery store. "Hey, Lenore? Takin' your sweet time?"

I'm going to stab myself in the face, I thought. *Right now.*

Another knock rattled the frame.

"Lenore," the Owl cooed. "Smoke break. You coming or what?"

The Wolf stayed hunched in the corner without a hitch, puffing lazily. Under their tired stare I sluggishly rose to my feet, cracking the door a few inches. The Owl craned towards the light, sloped against the trim, eyeing me with a smugness I despised.

"Seriously?"

His hands rose, fingers long like wing bones. "Just came to check on you." Pinched between them was a sloppily rolled joint, half-bent in his grip. He waggled it like a dog bone. "It's good stuff. Promise you that. Shit, this stuff fucks me up for *hours.*"

The Owl, though I didn't care to know, looked like a Todd or a Lucas, or a Damian if he was so lucky. He barely fit into the clothes that he wore—I imagined he thought himself rather cool for drowning in that old leather riding jacket. The peeking tattoo on his collarbone had bled so much that even upon closest inspections, it hardly looked like anything more than a smudge of chain grease, and when he sparked up that shitty joint right there in Georgia's bedroom, the cutting scent of rubber on an open gas burner filled my sinuses.

Todds and Lucases always left nasty little wet spots on your cigarettes, didn't they? Out-of-town college types, the ones that wanted back-home character without suffering for it. Sure, I wasn't the kind of person to dictate character; I hadn't much of a personality but the shredded mess that remained when the drugs were gone, when the flowers in the hospital garden were wilted and petal-free and the winter chained me inside with nobody to play with—but at least I *knew* that.

Under the Wolf's watchful eye, a lump inflated in my throat. The Owl turned his unshaven face, sliding the joint my way, and I couldn't help but grimace.

"Actually," I tensed. "I'm good. You enjoy that."

In moving to shut the door, the Owl jammed his foot in between the crack. I could've sworn, though I'd done my best not to look, that the Wolf twitched—not much at all, a mere jolt of the shoulders as if they thought briefly to stand. They hadn't—they only hovered in my peripheral, a cataclysm of brown, grey and black. A lunging dog behind chain link, barely expelling a breath to let me know they were still alive.

The Owl's eyes hardened. "C'mon, be serious for a little bit. You were into it downstairs and now suddenly, post-piss, you're—what?" Whatever expression crossed my face, he felt it necessary to scoff at. "It's just a little smoke. You can't handle that? How long's it been since a guy's been nice to you?"

Never crossed my mind, but little did boys in general. My eyes hit the floor, scrutinizing my dull green socks, one loose thread hovering over the floor in moot escape. My skin ached beneath every inch of my shirt, dizzied by the haze in the air. Was the smoke hovering just above my head? I felt like running for a wet cloth to cover my mouth. *Fire, fire,* I could scream. *Fire, fire, fire,* and nobody would hear me. No one but the cunt on the opposite side of the door and the Wolf on the inside.

"I don't have any money, and I've got nothing else to give you, man."

"You're cute enough. *C'mon.* We can work the details *later*. Let's take a load off."

"*Move your foot.*"

"You're not really gonna make me beg."

"I'm not making you do *anything*. Just move your *foot*."

His cool-guy tone dropped. "You don't have to be such a tease. It's just a little weed."

I didn't think before I kicked him. Didn't need to—I nailed the toe of his foot with my booted heel, earning a sharp yelp as he recoiled from the door. Through the slit I stared unwavering at him, pressing closer, forcing through that shying space a hard, mean sneer built on months of zero privacy.

"I don't fucking know you, dude. How many different ways should I tell you to fuck off?"

The Owl's wide, optical eyes burrowed into me, the lackadaisical boyishness dispelled. There as he'd always been, he was just a man, glaring into my face the way I knew all too well. I wondered what he was thinking about doing to me. I wondered if he would try to kick in the door. I bid him to try.

Instead he snickered, his lips peeling back.

"Whatever," he spat, turning a cheek, begging me to bury my fist in it. "All you whackos act the goddamn same. Fresh off the fuckin' funny farm, you'd think at least *one* of you could realize how lucky you are that people are even *talking* to you."

Retreating, The Owl turned from the door and hurled something over his shoulder, a volleyball he'd been too cowardly to lob at my face: *Ugly bitch.*

In that brief moment, while the slash of wine across my face was all of me and I was nothing more or less, I wondered what his teeth would feel like uprooted from their gummy sanctuaries by my knuckles, pulpy tissue caked against their pointed little feet. I dreamt of the snap of his glasses and the crunch of his nose against hardwood, spiralling in on himself, weeping like a degenerate on the floor. I didn't hit him despite that cold, displeasing wave of desire. Instead, I glared into the back of his stupid jacket as he stormed childishly from Georgia's room, waiting for the nuclear fallout of my rage to subside. Once it began to lax around my lungs, returning to coil around my calloused heart, only then did I finally look down.

There we were—the Wolf, the truth and me—my lie waving like a bloody tie caught in a sharp breeze. That faraway guilt crept closer until

V. IVAN

I was on the floor again by the bathtub, face-to-face with it, my knees halfway driven into my chest.

"Sorry," I feigned, though I'd long forgotten how to be. No explanation required, I sought my cigarette but had laid it down somewhere, my eyes rolling over the sinks edge hungrily. "There's just not much of a point to this."

The Wolf's knowing gaze punctured me. *"This."*

"Small talk. Chit chat. I don't really enjoy talking, especially with people I don't know—y'know, *clearly*, so—we can just skip it altogether. I'm almost done with my smoke."

I found it moments later, lining the grit between the tiles, crushed and torn and made mostly of compound ash. I turned my face up, heated. From where I sat, the Wolf's outstretched arm was frightfully angular, growing from their coat like a warped branch. Their joint hung before me, dangling between their fingers, eyeing me with one glowing, red pupil.

I wasn't an idiot; I took it, stole its smoke, their homemade filter as dry as old bone, no rougher than smoking tobacco. Their emptied hand lifted in questioning, but fell just as quickly.

"Say it," I beckoned, losing steam. *"Go on."*

A scar-warped smile drew across their lips—*tempted*, if I'd read them right. "I was gonna hold off, but I don't actually think you recognize me."

Their expression was indistinguishable—dancing a razor-fine line between baiting and genuine. I had to wonder if they were just trying to keep me talking, then subsequently had to humbly remind myself that not a single person in that house gave enough of a fuck to waste the energy. Still, they were watching me with a peculiar stare like they were winning at some unspoken game. If they were, I wanted to play. I'd been desperate to—so I sank forward.

"You don't ring any bells."

"Didn't think I would. We only overlapped a couple weeks. You got in just before I got out, and we never spoke or nothin'. But I *remember* you. Remember your face, really." They flattened themselves against the wall. "Knew you had an L name. Didn't think it was Lenore, though."

I stared at them until my eyes began to ache. Until the worm and the hook tempted me. "Leo," I bit. "Lenore's—a dumb joke."

"Y'don't got a last name? Just Leo?"

A poorly-withheld frown worked over my face.

The Wolf waved their spiny hands in defeat, retrieving the joint once I'd mooched enough to settle my shoulders. "We don't have to talk about nothin'. You said so yourself. I'll zip it."

That lasted all of a minute. Something glimmered in the dark, cranial pool of my thoughts. I broke first.

"Two weeks?"

"Mhm, but my stint was a good while longer than that. Did the whole thing hopin' nobody would remember me, so don't feel bad or nothin'. I thought about talkin' to you, but you didn't seem the type to answer."

"You're talking to me now."

"Hm. Happy to be proved wrong."

I held onto the peculiar image of that scar-faced little Wolf, hiding amongst a sea of white scrubs like blood on fresh cotton. "Just funny you remember me. That's all."

"Is it? Like I said, memorable face."

"Yeah. *Of course* it is."

"Sure. Birthmarks are memorable, whether you like 'em or not."

I wasn't embarrassed of my own face. Some had *tried* to make me, tried to find a way through the slats, but I built the walls without one goddamn crack and beyond that, I'd never found a good enough reason to feel shame; I spent so little time with the mirror that I hardly knew the shape of my own eyes. Still, I waited for the Wolf to do what everyone else did—to ask me what I'd done to God to earn it, to ask me why I *looked* like that, if there was some way to *fix* it. Instead, they lifted two fingers and gestured to my cheek fearlessly, their sunken eyes falling calm and cool on my skin.

V. IVAN

"Especially yours. Never seen another like it. And I've been around, Leo, so I'd remember."

I sought out maliciousness or disgust and came up empty handed. Nothing in their whistling comment prodded me to fight back. Only my name, oddly comfortable in their lacerated mouth, and the aching skin where they'd nearly touched me.

"Been out for almost two years an' I don't miss it even a little. Them grimy white walls, always goddamn freezing. And the *smell.*" The Wolf cocked their head, finding me across the floor. "What *was* that? It was cleaner, but it was fuckin' gruesome. Like they mopped the floor with peppermint oil and shit water."

"It used to keep me up sometimes," I admitted, staggered by a flush of adrenaline.

"In the summer." The Wolf nodded. "Think somethin' was rotting in the vents above 2-C. Raccoon or somethin'."

"Rats," I whispered. *"Stole my fuckin' earplugs every now and then."*

"Christ," the Wolf cackled, their thrilled laugh like the bouncing clack of hooves on cobblestone. "An' I did a whole *year* of that stink. Wouldn't do it again if you paid me in gold."

"A year. Try eighteen months."

The Wolf peeled themselves from the wall.

The truth fell on pale, pointy ears. Later I'd be humiliated, but in that moment I could only retreat deeper and deeper into myself, scrabbling for freedom while the Wolf unearthed their half-crumpled package of cigarettes and wordlessly slated their lighter inside.

"Must've done somethin' awful to land yourself in there *that* long."

I didn't like the place those words carried me to. A place of ruin, a vault long welded shut inside of me bursting open, spilling gunk into even the lightest thoughts that passed by. Acidic and warm, tickling the back of my tongue, pouring from my mouth into words that came out much too hard:

"Maybe I just liked being *alone.*"

I waited for them to stick up their thin, uneven nose and scoff, to tell me to relax. I waited for anything to burnish the image of them, to seal what could've been a drive-by conversation in its tomb. But there they were, marble-eyed and curious, my spite barely powdering their nose. I thought to tell the truth, just that one time—that I could've gotten out sooner if I'd wanted to get better. But that was no one's business but mine.

"What'd you do, then?" I asked instead. "Since you want to talk about it."

The Wolf's fingers rolled over their cheek, itching sluggishly. Finished smoking, they could get up and toddle off at any moment and I would've been completely okay. Yet they sat, debating it, formulating some great, elaborate tale.

"Don't lie," I warned. "I don't give a shit about fake stories."

Their eyes flicked towards the sink, staring right through. "It's an interestin' situation, y'know. But since we're not gettin' to know each other, maybe I don't need to answer. Right?"

"You don't have to."

"Not sure I *want* to."

"So don't."

The Wolf sought something from my face, but found nothing in the mask I'd spent so long chiseling. Out came their smokes again, as if the mere thought of what they'd done warranted another.

"Me an' this old fella got into it real bad back in Boise when I was a teenager," they gave. "Things ended ugly."

I tried to conjure that. The Wolf, tall and fragile with a thin neck and twiggy wrists, hurting someone badly enough that they'd been sent away. They didn't seem to have the temperament. Suddenly the odd, murky swing in their voice made sense.

"Idaho," slid from my mouth, not entirely uninterested. "You're far from home."

"Ain't home. Not really." They sparked up evenly, taking their time. "Ol' friend of a friend had a little too much to drink and pounced on me. Landed a few good ones, too. Broke my damn nose. Not to sound like I'm givin' myself a pass, but it *was* self defence. Guess sometimes it's not so easy to look at it that way."

V. IVAN

Acutely aware of that shattered bridge, I followed it down as it melded into the scars at their lips. They looked as though they'd kissed the mouth of a shattered beer bottle, but when they spoke they seemed no more in pain than I was.

"The Echo's all about rehabilitation," I poked. "Big and heavy into the first-time perp concept, inpatient with reparative conditions for most of the kids I toured with. Sounds more like he should've done the time instead of you."

The Wolf eyed me through the smoke. "There's excess damage on my end. Makes it hard to come across as *victimized*."

"Someone took a swing at you, and you swung back. What part of that's so complicated?"

"The part where I bit him."

I waited for the joke to land, for the punchline to bounce into view. It didn't. Instead, a clearing vision came to me—plastic canine teeth, ketchup blood and wailing terror. A daydream more akin to a frightening children's cartoon. The reality of it stumped me, so much so that an irreversible, awkward laugh spilled freely forward.

"How—I mean—that's kind of weird, right?"

The Wolf didn't say a word.

"I mean, biting someone. That's worth a whole entire year of your life?"

Their head twitched. "Y'don't believe me?"

"I never—said that. It just seems far-fetched."

Another lapping silence slicked us both, and the Wold scraped teeth-first along their cigarette.

"When the medics were finished with him, the surgeons had to remove most of his right cheek and jaw—'cause the tissue was too torn up to be repaired. Someone told me that... y'know, workin' with somethin' so mutilated... it's like tryin' to stitch up suet. I'm not up to date on the details—they recommend y'don't look at that stuff, so I don't—but I know it was bad *then*." A sour smile of sorts winked at me, and was gone again. "I'd imagine it's *still* bad."

The movie in my mind no longer replicated some lost, banned Disney short. I vied for something more—the grit of unshaven skin, the pop of relief as it gave way to sharp, uneven canines. Gushing blood, fatty tissue. Could the human jaw lock the same way an alligator's could? I didn't puke. Instead, I traced the Wolf's unchanging expression, the lost, searching look in their eyes. They sought out the memories, unhappy with whatever crossed their mind.

"I don't remember doin' it," they slowed, ashing into the floor vent. "I'm not an—angry person. There've been times, alright, *sure*, but I don't remember makin' that choice. I remember coming to, an'—not movin', just watchin' him squirm and scream like a leech in salt. And me, just—standin' there in a pool of his blood, *our* blood. It's different when you're in it. If you give yourself time to think, you're dead. I guess at that point, I wasn't sure if I was *okay* with that."

The words stuck in their throat, grated out by force. I knew the lives that a single expenditure of thought could cost. By proxy I felt I knew them in some way, but I didn't; we only knew similar Hells. It was as strict as that.

"Jesus," I thought aloud. "Mine isn't worth telling."

The Wolf's head shot upwards, snapped free of their old torment. "Don't say y'don't talk about it. I've heard that before."

In the middle I met them, my outstretched leg inches from theirs. Briefing it would be easy: slot the details into place like dominos. Arson, battery, self-annihilation. If I arranged the memories inside of my skull like pictures on a zoetrope, animated and chalky, I could avoid the true dangers and keep it bare—a spinning, sputtering image of an old blue mobile home under a venomous sun. A ranch-yellow beater truck with the plate stuck in the back window. What else was there to see when you strayed no closer than the curb?

"No," I agreed. "I don't talk about it. You really did beat me."

The Wolf didn't push. They stuck their nose right where it belonged, against the butt of their dwindling smoke, before crushing it on the tile and swiping away the ash with their finger.

V. IVAN

"But that says it," I spoke suddenly, and could've sworn their ear twitched my way. "Self defence. Acting without thinking. That's what happens, right?"

Something unreadable tugged on their lips. "Sure. Maybe."

"When you're fearing for your life, things are different."

The Wolf debated that. Lashes fluttering over wide, lightless eyes. For a moment, they seemed to understand where I was coming from. At least, they seemed to *try*.

"I imagine things would be different," they agreed, "but I wasn't afraid; I was pissed. An' that big bastard wasn't the worst thing in the room."

For the first time that evening, I *saw* them. Someone's child, someone's baby, a Wolf in the bathroom of Georgia's party, puffing like a chimney to drown that bloody memory. Where were their parents? All the way in Idaho, perhaps, buried somewhere deep within those mountains, or alive and well on a lakefront property. Regardless, away from the Wolf. Away from their terrible, biting child. I saw them. *I did.*

The debilitating throb of that pill-free evening came sliding down over me, ripping me from thought. I shut my eyes, cushioned my head between my knees and didn't come up until I heard the Wolf rise and depart, shoes like gravel-torn claws on tile, shutting the door behind them wordlessly.

Me and the zoetrope of my life, left alone.

GRAVE ROBBERS

Early that next morning, it hit me hard; I was *out*, free and alone in a city I'd never even dreamt of visiting. I could do anything I wanted, at any given moment, without a written and signed permission slip. The headaches had finally subsided and the house was ice-cold and silent when I awoke. By the time I crawled out of bed and the gears of my brain began to grind forward, I was thinking about ending it all again.

When I first got to the Echo, I was desperate for results. Looking for quick and *accurate* ways to end things, despite the fact that I could barely swallow the pills I needed let alone the ones I didn't. I didn't have the power to speak to *anyone*, never mind about how to kill myself under constant surveillance, and by the time I felt well enough to speak I'd begun to preoccupy myself with other tasks. In the last stretch, I'd been so doped up I hadn't cared if I lived or died. Some people would consider *that* progress. Death's booming voice had dulled into a medicated whisper, which made it easier to distance myself from it.

The sacrifice of medication in order to feel something ran the risk of those feelings returning. They'd only be placated until I left the windows of my mind unlocked once more. At Georgia's, *sober*, I was once again plagued by that deeply-clawing *want*. Instantaneously, it came to me—the desperation to seal off the Allenview bedroom and light it ablaze. Anything I did could be done in the company of that unavoidable want if I could only remember how I'd lived on the outside—that morning it was the simple act of dressing myself, hauling on my second and last clean pair of sweats. Though I wasn't sure there was any merit to those thoughts, I feared the simple fact that they were back, knowing they wouldn't settle for anything other than divulgence. Once you've made the mistake of considering it—taking your life—only a complete reinvention of who you are might give you a shot at shedding the desire for more than a moment. In no place to reinvent myself by desire *or* assets, I stayed stuck with death in the waiting room of my life. Even my clothes sat on my skin like silk draped over a coat rack.

Scrubbing scum from my eyes, I left the bedroom and was greeted by the tip of a baseball bat inches from my jaw.

I staggered, still drenched in sleep, pinned to the doorway. Hunched before me, Georgia was wild-haired and wrapped in a scant purple robe, clad in neon Hello Kitty pyjamas and manically clutching a steel-capped bat by its taped handle. We stood frozen like two territorial cats, hairs on end. Lowering my hand from my rubbed-raw eyes and meeting hers, their silken grey melted from fear to comprehension, and the bat's head smacked the hardwood with a *thwack* and a long exhale.

"Fuckin'—*Jeezus*," Georgia said, wiping her mouth. "I forgot you were *here*."

I hadn't the time to be scared of the bat. I'd nearly forgotten as well, standing partly present in the hallway, listing the details with a bobbling head. Georgia, two kids, the television running downstairs on some fragrant action film. Sunlight on the runner. Labeled house. Olympia, unaccompanied. Housewarming party. Hungover? No, I didn't drink. No, Georgia hadn't *let* me drink.

"I'm working on getting a name tag."

"Nice, jackass. I'm gonna start up breakfast. You lookin' for some?"

My stomach lurched. "Not hungry."

"Then you can help," Georgia rolled the bat's handle against her palm. "You'll be by yourself this afternoon. Got a custody proceeding to attend, kids and all." She cast me a peculiar glance. "I can trust you here alone, hey?"

Stepping out onto the cool hardwood, I wrapped my arms around myself, the compulsory way one hugs distant relatives at family gatherings. "I won't touch your stuff."

"Ain't what I mean."

"What, then?"

Georgia studied me mutely, trying to worm her way inside my brain. Something about her attention was ungodly and penetrative, shovelling deep into my mind where dark particles swirled in a suffocating mist, seeking the right way to say what she needed to say. Before I could swat her away, she dragged herself on with a shrug.

"Nothing," she cut, setting my teeth on edge. "You'll be fine. It's just nerves."

With that long, gutting stare she'd almost found me out; I would've preferred the bat. I watched her descent downstairs, envisioning an inaccessible steel gate between us, barring her from the frostbitten thing that pumped my blood. Then came the mumbling, the switching from gunfire to chatter on the living room television, childish mewling. When I sensed she'd reached the kitchen I returned to my sunlit bedroom, staggering to the dormer window and sticking my nose to the glass. Across the rooftop of the laundromat next door, two wind-burnt men stood puffing on cigarettes like huddling penguins, their faces ember-red from the cold. I'd stopped sweating overnight, the last dribbles of medication petering out of me. Only one smoker remained, so I kept him company at the windowsill until the wind beat his wits from him and I was left alone.

I still fought the urge to call over the bannister to tell Georgia that I understood—that if her children were afraid of the howling demon I'd made of myself the week before, writhing and sweating through fractured dreams and migraines like interspersed lobotomies in a bed that had once belonged to someone else, then I couldn't blame them. If she was afraid, and if she'd had guilt about forgetting me because I'd been so strangely quiet without the withdrawals, well, she could let go of *that*, too.

I was always either howling in pain or hardly there at all.

V. IVAN

IT WAS DESPERATION THAT carried me through the house. Desperation that poked into the hall closet and huffed the waxy scent of Seafoam Sparkle dryer sheets stuffed into each jacket pocket, rolling the fake fur of their wrists between my fingertips, rubbing them raw on silky sleeve lining. Desperation tiptoed through the foyer, a caramel-coloured hub with a left-leaning, ancient staircase, into the living room now absent of gunfire and children, burying me in the television channel guide, every available station bound to ancient reruns of COPS and Springer.

It'd been so long since I'd been alone that part of me had forgotten how to survive it. An overabundance of wildly-grinning ladybug figures, salt and pepper shakers and Blue Mountain statuettes of shadowy terriers and glossy horses infected the unit's dated shelving—I stole them away, lined them up upon the countertop and made them an audience. I tried asking if Georgia had given them any long forgotten names when she'd bought them, but none answered. *Bet she didn't buy them herself*, I thought, taking a slow, swinging scan of the room. Perhaps she hadn't bought anything in this place. Perhaps it was all pre-decorated by some wide-eyed landlord so infatuated with chubby figurines that they had to store the tail-end of their hoard at Allenview in the name of *beauty* and *preservation*.

Once I'd walked my laps, I could no longer deny how easy it would be just to get it over with. Instead of scrounging up the effort, I draped myself across the grape sofa, a fast food kids toy jammed against my tenderest rib, and tried to distract myself from it all by allowing the blood to rush to my head, dreaming of what the weather was like further South.

It was only ever hot or fucking hotter, but in what formation were the clouds above the old house, above the Episcopal Church across the street? Cotton trails like shredded pillows, spirals, toads with plush swells of cumulonimbus for eye sockets? Somebody new must've moved in by then—maybe they'd finally painted over the water stain on the living room ceiling, or maybe the ceiling was nothing but whipped polystyrene now and my childhood bedroom was painted a screaming blue, the kind I'd been denied as a kid.

The speculation fed that deeper ache inside of me until I started to plan it, so I pried myself from the couch and went to gather my leftover change, counting it in the bedroom and then creeping upon Georgia's bathroom to glare into the trash can. In death, the earwig was nothing but powder; I'd wiped the bin clean with paper towel last night before retiring to my bedroom with nothing but the dripping mental image of an excavated cheek to keep me company. Paranoid, I carried myself downstairs. If I still wanted to die after the stomach ache subsided, after I went to the holy convenience for ginger ale—my last line of defence—then kill myself I would. I hauled yesterday's hoodie on at the door and stepped out, swiping dollops of ash from its stretched front pocket, narrowly halting before I ran head-on into the body on the steps.

Shrouded in a gaudy, pink-checkered button up, the Wolf was surreal in the unforgiving daylight. Each old slash of scar tissue a pearlescent paint stroke on their tight cheeks, the purple wells of their eye sockets threatening to suck their eyes into their skull. It wasn't just the dimness of the entryway—even the sun couldn't colour their wide, stunned stare anything but polished black.

Their fist, mid-knock, recoiled against their chest. One flash of jagged teeth and I almost called them that foolish nickname aloud.

"Leo," the Wolf recalled eagerly. "You look well-rested."

I felt suddenly half dressed before them, clumsily sliding a veil over my bewilderment. "It's a touch early for jokes."

"Did I catch you at a bad time?"

I stared long and hard at them, willing my memory. The cramps wringing my guts guided my body into the doorframe. "Did I tell you to come back around or something? Not—to be rude, just—"

Around a peculiar, painful sort of smile, the Wolf shifted their weight, glancing through the doorway. "You didn't. I was actually wonderin' if I could take a look inside for a second."

I cocked a brow. "For fun?"

"I left somethin' here last night. Listen, I can see you're tryin' to leave. Only need *two minutes*. You got a job already or somethin'?"

V. IVAN

My stomach shrank. "Two minutes." I stepped out of their way and they moved into the foyer with the effortless balance of a tree in the wind, maintaining its composure. "I don't have anything but fucking cramps."

They caught the wall with a tendon-white hand. "Two minutes. Then I'll get outta your hair."

"One. One minute now."

The Wolf disappeared into the den and I shrank to the floor below the coat rack, drawing my knees pitifully against my chest. I sat just so, bordering comatose, until the Wolf came silently padding back across the runner. Stepping easily over a pair of abandoned toddler sneakers, they fitted a thin silver chain between their teeth and used their freed hands to dig into their pockets. From one came a square of folded saran wrap housing two fat, red pills.

"Ibuprofen," they said through gritted teeth. "Can't keep a bottle on me 'cause I take 'em like candy if I do. God made me wrong, an' I don't do surgery. *Here.*"

Unsurely, I accepted. The Wolf disappeared into the kitchen without question, returning moments later with a half-empty carton of juice hooked around their knuckles. The necklace was freed of their canines, sitting pretty on their slender throat, a penny-sized seashell. I swallowed the pills like small, salty pebbles.

"You like the ocean?"

"*Whassat?*"

After a mouthful of juice, I nodded to their throat. "The ocean," I said, drained of patience with my own body more than them. "Dolphins. Fish. *Seashells.*"

"Never actually seen it myself," they admitted. Halfway through screwing the cap back on, the Wolf wandered towards the fridge. "Saw a documentary about the Sulu Sea when I was locked up, but that's the best I can offer. *Oh*—do y'know how cigarette snails got to bein' called *cigarette* snails? If y'get stung by one, y'ain't got the time to finish a smoke 'fore you're dead." Returning empty handed, the Wolf took the coil of saran wrap from my fingers like I was a toddler with a wrapper and shoved it into their jean pocket. "Should start workin' on that job thing by the way, if you plan on stayin' out of the Echo. Even somethin' shitty would please those monthly visit suits."

I buried a snort at the lip of the carton, setting it between my knees. "Everything's shitty. I don't want a job. Don't think anybody would want me, either. I don't like to work."

"Who does?"

"Right. But I'd rather blow sand." I stared at them hovering there before me, ghostlike. "People in Idaho must not like introductions, huh?"

Unblinking, they asked naively, "How so?"

"We've had two whole conversations now and you haven't told me your name."

"Y'didn't ask for it."

I waited them out until their silence fell beyond awkwardness and towards uselessness. Until the tension of their shoulders shifted and they couldn't look at me any longer.

"Elowen."

It seemed an oddly tender name, but I couldn't comment; my own was a sudden slap on the fingers, one I avoided at all costs. "Where's that from?"

"It's Cornish, but I've never been. Y'know, there's more pills in my truck, too, if you need 'em for later." Elowen staggered to my wall, leaning as if they intended to stay. "I don't like workin' either. It's all bull crap. I only do it to run my truck and my habits and that's it, but I hardly do anything 'sides stand around like a sittin' duck. A job where you hardly do anythin'," Elowen reiterated. "That'd work for ya?"

"I don't do illegal shit. Immoral, maybe. Illegal, no."

A petrifying laugh spilled from them, rousing me from my pain like a wheeze of dead, dark wind. "It ain't illegal, just damn boring. Y'ever heard of the Anchor? The bowling alley on Loregan Drive?"

"I don't know Washington."

"Right," they nodded. "Sure, neither do I. But *look*—I'll even take you to get stomach pills, if y'don't trust mine. But I think I've got a good money opportunity here for ya, if you're not busy."

V. IVAN

I *was* busy—trying to kill myself. Or trying not to; I wasn't really sure anymore. They'd pulled me away from my deliberation and as the pills painted my stomach in numbed relief, I took pity on them, hanging around in Georgia's foyer like they were desperate for company. I walked myself up the wall with my hands and stretched, the cusp of my belly sore as if I'd been punched.

"I don't like working. I meant that."

"I heard you." Elowen approached the door. "Keep your casuals on. It'll prove my point." A canine grin nudged me out from under the blackened cloud I'd parked myself beneath. "Give it your worst, if you gotta. You'll see what I mean. How else're you gonna afford smokes?"

"I won't have to afford them if you keep bugging me. I'll take yours as financial compensation."

Elowen eyeballed me, dragging their keys from their pocket with one bony finger. In their stare hid something hellish, something warped by curiosity. Before I could comment, they turned to the door and caught the sunlight like a white-hot dinner plate.

"I like you," they said, flattening my disagreements. "I'm helpin' you out here. Hey, tell me more jokes on the way. Maybe you'll change your mind about gettin' to know people if you just let all that snark out."

Doubting it, I followed them to the rust-kissed truck at the curb as if I'd known them for years.

T HE DRIVE FROM GEORGIA'S to the Black Anchor was a miniature road trip through crumbs of late fall construction, businessmen swarming like gnats outside a newly-renovated conference centre, the fenced-in arboretum on the edge of the city stripped down to its whiskers, reaching for the truck as we traced Olympia's lower shelf.

Elowen's truck gushed with an earthy perfume like a lawn of old, wet leaves, layered over Golden Earring on the fuzzed-out radio. I allowed myself to be nosy—if they noticed, they never said so. Nature magazines and coffee cups with gnawed rims carpeted the floor, my shoes pinned against the dash to avoid crushing them. Only a miniature plastic skeleton hung where the dome light would've been, and knotted around the rearview mirror's stiff neck was a string of clear, pearlescent beads lumped around a worn silver cross. That surprised me; I chose not to think too hard on why.

The rattling of their chewed nails against the steering wheel kept me lucid for the entire trip. Hooking right, we followed a sluggish moving van down 4th Ave, sneaking past a cafe doused in a neighbouring bar's lime neon, an old theatre screening twenty-year-old movies, a watch repair shop with a spinning clock sign representing the hours as seconds. I'd just begun to worry about the repercussions of getting into a stranger's truck when we turned into a starving business park and crawled to a stop before a beacon of soul-illuminating pinks and yellows.

"Behold." Elowen stretched forward, slotting the gear shift into park. "The beast."

On the city's limits, the Black Anchor stretched like a greedy abscess, scabbed by pawnshops and dives dipped in dashed sunlight, stolen away by the high stalks of the downtown high rises. Stepping through the Anchor's patterned sliding doors gave way to the fierce buzz of overhead lights and a hexad of bowling lanes, centre-striped with red paint to promote accuracy, the walls suffocated with neon signage. Before I could try running, Elowen jutted their head towards another set of double sliding doors to our left, beyond which the mouth of an awkward, narrow hallway laid in waiting.

"I've gotta clock in," they said, flicking a hand towards a faded blue door pasted with a half-peeled 'No Smoking' sticker. "Just knock and wait. The Captain'll holler."

T HE OFFICE IN WHICH the Captain of the Black Anchor sat was a room lost not only to time, but sense. No bigger than a walk-in freezer, its walls were crowded with old fishing trophies, a wire-reinforced jaguar's skull on a plaque with a date kissed by dust, old and

V. IVAN

current health and safety certificates for Pinhead's Pizza. Somebody had let him string up a pressed geometric suit like a bewildering souvenir. Somehow, all of this was made *more* peculiar by the Captain himself.

Against the sickly aster wallpaper, the tiny, elderly man bent behind the desk was unlike a captain. Maybe in another life, perhaps, unless he'd been beaten into retirement by callous waves and sea monsters and found his next calling among children's birthday parties and drunk businessmen. A netting of thin, overgrown hair spun behind his pocked ears, his face set behind a grey, incomplete beard that did little to buff him up. He'd hollered me in, pampered me with softball questions then dove into a lengthy stretch of thoughtful silence, palming his wired desk mouse, sinking inside an oversized dress shirt covered in miniature eight balls.

"All those kids out there," the Captain whispered, leaning forth on weak elbows. "They're all *gems*. Do you know what I mean when I say that?"

I blinked, long and sluggish. The meds were kicking in and I was in pure ecstatic silence, left only to shrug as the pain shrank.

"Ripe for the picking." His trembling fingers went itching at the remnants of a spiny floral tattoo winding around his neck, its thinning lines more like a dotted *'cut me'* than a proper stem. "It's nice to get you in the door and teach you how to do a job *right* out of the gate. None of this half-assed, new-age ethic. Not all of you have the gumption. You said your last name—what was it? Welch?"

"Uh—I—legally, yes."

A coy glance slid from behind his drooping eyelids. "You seem young to be married."

I tried hard to quench my horror. "My mother remarried. Had it changed."

"You know much about bowling, Leo?"

"Should I?"

That made him laugh. A sore, dusty laugh in which he reached for his throat, to comfort the ragged chords that worked his vocal box. "Oh, God, no. Pardon me. You're just setting up pins. General maintenance, keeping the bathrooms *clean,* you know. I went over it. We went over it, didn't we?"

"We did."

A malnourished glimmer passed over the Captain's face like a fugue. He reeked of a man doing his damndest to cling onto the little life left inside of him. Some odd part of me felt bad for him.

"I used to be a real big shot out there," he quieted, as if divulging a secret. "Working that job, keeping things in line, doing all the hosting. Back when we used to advertise at the cinema down the way, it was *my* mug on the posters. But the frontline work doesn't suit me now; not much of a people person anymore. You lot, though—much younger. More spry. More social, if you can believe it."

"Hardly."

Something in the dryness of my voice mistranslated. The Captain sparked, a lively militia in his eyes. "Do you work out often, Lenore?"

"N—No?"

"No," he repeated, flattening it as meaningless chatter. "That's alright. It's not overly physical. Not much pay at the start, but you don't strike me as an expensive girl. You *smoke,* though. I can smell it on you. No judgment," he said, spotting my mortified face. "I used to be a pack-a-day sort of guy. So the money's minimum, but there's *always* room for improvement. Stepping stones, weekend work. *Specialty* weekend work. *Late* shifts."

Elowen promised the job wasn't illegal, but something about the way he spoke made me question what stepping stones the Captain had laid. Setting up the pins first, then being the pins second? I wouldn't mind getting beaten up by bowling balls.

"You don't seem convinced."

I recoiled from the image of myself in a god-awful checkered button up. Protruding from it, sized too small, filling drink machines and cleaning toilets and setting up pins for lonely old perverts and baked teenagers. But it was money, and it was an offer, one which Elowen had eagerly brought me.

For whatever reason.

V. IVAN

I chewed around my thumbnail, unthinking. "I've never worked a job before," I assured the Captain. "I don't even have a resume to give you. I don't know anything about bowling, and I don't have a car."

He sat mutely eyeballing me. Flatlining like a streetside corpse. In the silence, I squirmed.

"It was nice of Elowen to bring me in. Trying to help us both out. I just don't know if I'm what you're looking for."

In that quiet, I glanced at the mounted jaguar skull, its marbled, devilish eyes boring down on me. Beside it, above the Captain's head, hung an empty gold hook—only a cigarette-stained rectangle on the wallpaper as proof that anything had been there.

"El's a new one," the Captain finally said. "New, but a solid worker. Friends helping friends. That's nice, isn't it?"

The casual dropping of Elowen's vowels made me quiver. They were suddenly delicate in my mind, working until their hands throbbed, feigning odd, unfriendly smiles at guests, having earned the affectionate sleight from someone like the Captain. I wouldn't wager anything on a friendship I'd made: it'd tear as soon as it was tested. I cracked a wincing smile.

"Friends are fine," I guessed.

The Captain lowered his voice again, his intentions a mystery.

"I like your honesty, Lenore. It's not common in kids these days. But some of you are special ones—my, *you're special, aren't you?* You've got good, clean foundations." The Captain placed his interlocked fists on the desk and gave me a smile that cleared my confusion. The same smile that orderlies gave when you needed more water to swallow your handful of horse pills. "I'm looking for *trainable* people. Are you trainable?"

"I... think so."

"If a customer comes in here, cash willing for tips, *heavy tips—*" The Captain's eyes steeled with something younger. "Are you willing to kiss ass?"

How nice it would be to have spare cash for cigarettes. Snacks, clothes, stomach medication when I needed it. It would be nice to go somewhere else eventually—tuck away a dense stack and just hit the asphalt running, flee to Pismo Beach and live where I could spend my mornings watching the elephant seals.

"I—maybe I could, yeah. Yes."

Without an ounce of warning, the Captain opened his hands to me.

That was something the Echo hadn't prepared me for—contact. Some folks liked to touch you for seemingly no reason at all, as if to make sure the prescription pills and tap water hadn't turned you as mushy as wet clay. Like a slapped child, I lifted my hands and presented them inches from his, where he craned closer and took them. His skin was icy and wrinkled, yet somehow still soft from sitting behind a desk. He felt around the tips of my fingers and clutched onto my palms, trying to devour them with his. It took everything left in me not to scream in his face.

"You tell me if you need *anything*. Any accommodation, any assistance or extra time around work. I'm always, *always* willing to negotiate. The point's to keep you, not to shuffle through folks day by day. I want to get to know *Lenore*. M'kay?"

The cracked smile he gave me was transparent. An unmissable pity, at peach-pit depth inside his brain. Utter disbelief that someone like me might need help just being alive, just breathing. A pity that catered to his sense of self, a feel-good button being pushed.

"I like you kids. Fresh out of it and into the right place, you're impressionable. Your friend steered you right. You could really have a good shot at this, not just the job. Not many people get that second chance, but you're lucky. Lucky, lucky, lucky."

My fingertips boiled inside his grasp, but I didn't yank free. Instead, I tried to find the luck in leaving the circus and being thrust back into a cage. Like some oddity, a terrible chain of events pivoted towards the light, towards a job, towards communal acceptance that what I'd done didn't define me. Except it never mattered *what* I did, only that I'd done *something*, which made me helpless and desperate through the lens of the Captain's imagination. People like him always felt better about themselves every time they thought of people like me. Each time they

V. IVAN

remembered the wild animal in its cage, they'd congratulate themselves and each other for being more civilized. For having domestication. For being a *dog*.

The Captain gave my hands an affirmative squeeze.

"You're lucky," he purred. "Some people don't get to turn their life around. They just live life in the shadows, wondering when things are going to brighten up again, clinging to what they know. But it never does brighten up again. Not for some."

I FOUND ELOWEN AMONG a maze of purple and green chairs to the right of the entrance, bathing in the candied light of a checker-bottomed counter that glowed in swirling bands of red and blue, reeking of pre-spiced meats and thawing, eggy dough. *Pinheads*. With their dark head buried in an inventory sheet, gaze moored on some distant plane, they paid no mind to me or the flimsy, depressing assortment of nibbled food on a nearby paper plate. The closer I got, the better I could make out George Michael's voice leaking from the thin pair of headphones looped around their scrawny throat.

"I survived," I announced tenderly. Elowen lifted their head, a murky fog of deep thoughtfulness lifting from their stare. "Where were you just now?"

"Here." Arachnid fingers muffled one side of their headphones as they nodded towards an untouched slice of pizza cooling off before them. "Help yourself, seriously. I brought my own."

My hands hovered over the adjacent seat. "You didn't need to—"

"Sure, I'm well aware." Elowen placed a thinly-cubed segment of carrot into their mouth and bit down distrustingly. Once they'd swallowed most of it, they shrugged. "Can't eat it anyways. This is, uh—what'd they call it—a—*healing* relationship with food. I'm in progress."

I sucked in hard. "Right."

"Your body is your temple and all that shit."

"Okay, gross."

I glanced past Elowen's shoulder, pink checkers searing the edges of my vision. Behind the Pinhead's counter, a pimply, half asleep teenager hung out beside an emptied pizza display case, sneaking glances at both of us from behind the glass. I gestured in his direction and Elowen craned their head to the side, slouched shoulders acting as cover for me.

"Is he gonna make me buy something?"

Elowen scooped a hand under the pizza plate and raised it in the air wordlessly. The kid whipped his head in the opposite direction, sneakily drawing his cell from his pocket and muttering to himself. Elowen returned to me, dropping the rubbery slice back onto the table with a dissatisfying *plop*. "Sure y'don't want it?"

"Very."

"Then what's the deal? When do you start?"

Recalling the Captain's scraggly beard and the hard wrinkles beneath his ball cap, the way he'd cupped my hand and spoken to me like one of those Episcopal pastors at the stone building in Ely, I winced.

"I don't know. I'm not sold."

Elowen raised a wild brow. *"Oh?"* A passing glimmer of intrigue laced their words. "Strange. Never seen him send away an applicant since I started. No offence. I'm sure you did a whole tap dance routine or somethin' to seal the deal."

Words bubbled from my throat.

"Your boss is a creep," I said first and foremost, "and somebody should teach him how to talk to women so he stops acting like an old, stupid *dog*. It's dehumanizing. And *disgusting*. And it's probably not just me, either. He probably talks to you like that, right?"

Elowen stared hard at me, their mind left blank to process the few simple words I'd said, expression mopped over by a remarkable show of attention. After a long, motionless silence, they *finally* blinked.

"Did he say somethin' *crude* to you?"

"Not—crude," I corrected. "It was just—bizarre." As if I could critique. I came to a job interview in my suicide clothes, like I could somehow stay alive to take the job if it were offered to me. I was just a

V. IVAN

banshee in wool sweats. "Couldn't even get a proper read, except that we're both *gems* and the rest of the world is *fucked.*"

Elowen dug a thumbnail into the edge of the pizza plate, busying themselves with rips and tears. "He *does* talk to everyone like that," they quieted, "to answer your question. Probably finds you pretty. Probably held your hands, right? *You look like the kind of angel who needs a shitty part-time gig slinging pins.* He's like that. He might ask if you have any sensitivities he should be worried about. He doesn't mean allergies, so state those separately."

I paled. "Puke."

"Right," Elowen agreed, "and it's disgusting, but talk's the extent of it. Y'told him you weren't into it? That you don't want the job?"

I'd laid my hands out and allowed them to be taken. Was I there for that? No—I'd been somewhere else, pretending I'd knocked him flat on his back in that tarnished leather desk chair. I felt like shrinking into my shell and staying there, still dizzy from that scattered morning.

Elowen slid off their headphones. "If y'don't want it," they said, "then don't take it. But it's brainless work. All the drunk fools that come in here through the week give real good tips. They come to this joint for beer and pizza and to hit somethin', 'cause this corner of Olympia's nothin' to look at and bowling's all they got when the bars stop servin' 'em. Cap's a gross old fuck just like 'em, but you'll hardly see him. He's an ant in a colony of worse people, y'know, and worse people won't bother you as long as you're willing to scare 'em a little. It's nothin'. Not really."

I almost laughed at that. Almost.

"Scare them? You think I'm capable of that?"

Elowen frowned, swallowing an apple segment with the ease of a boa constrictor inhaling a lamb. Two glassy eyes found their way to my face.

"Y'just have to let 'em know why they shouldn't fuck with you. And if y'can't scare 'em, well." Elowen shrugged, and my nerves drained like I was bloodletting into a styrofoam cup. "You'll be workin' with me. Folks don't usually talk to me, not even poor Avan over there. Workin' with a friend has its perks."

I froze. "A friend."

Elowen ran a tongue over their teeth in mute amusement. A vague smile breached the hard line of their mouth. "We're friends. Y'don't think?"

"*Explain.*"

They gestured to the glowing Hell we sat in. "I handed you a job on a—fools gold platter, I s'pose, for starters. And I'm not sure about you, but last night felt pretty chummy to me. Saved you there, too."

"Oh, my *hero,*" I said, a touch meaner than I'd intended. "I saved *you.*"

Elowen didn't even flinch. They reached into the neck of their shirt and dug up the seashell, thumbing it in front of me. "Then it's mutual. Plus, you were kind enough to let me have my things back." Before I could take a good look at it, they shielded it once more against their throat. "During your busy mornin', too. I don't keep friends usually, so help me out. Does that sound right to you?"

They weren't telling me; rather, they waited to see what I might do with such a bewildering suggestion. To see if I'd be disgusted by the mere thought of it, as if they didn't think themselves deserving. All the same, I wondered if I was even capable of such a commitment. It'd been easy to abstain from friendships in Nevada. I never initiated and ducked when I was spoken to, kept far away from group activities, walked home much later than others. For a while I was phobic to any human interaction; even Myra kept me on a questionably long leash.

Yet of all the impossible situations where I'd been forced to engage, to *adapt,* Elowen instilled none of that familiar hatred. Somewhere deep within that antisocial nonsense, there was a well-ignored part of me that knew I'd never be able to nurture a friendship, that it would blow up in my face or spiral into abysmal nothingness as all other pitied attempts had. A still water like theirs had never put me at ease.

I understood very well my insufferable nature. Eventually Elowen would too, if they weren't such a way themselves. Even if I'd had bountiful company back in Ely, none of it would've prepared me for them. Not an ounce of former experience could help me imagine what our friend-

V. IVAN

ship might look like; I drew it much like a beast in my mind—horned, snarling teeth, unable to frighten myself away.

"I guess it is," I caved. "I guess it is."

I watched my first friend work around their food like a poison-testing rat, afraid of the unknown bite which held the most painful end.

I LEFT FOR ALLENVIEW just after six, cloaked beneath a reluctantly-accepted jacket from Elowen's own shoulders, the daylight curtained by the skyline's uneven teeth. Along the city's jawline, street vendors offered me handmade purses and shawls with beautiful beaded fastenings on the throats, wicker gift baskets, hand-hammered jewelry and vintage broaches. Without currency but my smokes and my cell phone, I shrank along the sidewalk and crept past the undulating fencing of a century-old graveyard, traipsing home like a collarless cat with a belly full of feral rodent.

Georgia's car was long gone and the house was lifeless when I arrived. In that comforting dark, I felt my way up the staircase, peering blindly down into a milky well of shadowed hallway. I left the bedroom light untouched, shutting the door tightly behind me, minding the whispering of the wooden bones that held everything up. I peeled my clothes off with the window cracked, puke green curtains ribboned by the musky, frozen Olympian breeze. Trembling and half naked, I draped Elowen's jacket across the lap of an old pine dining chair sandwiched in the corner across from my bed. Then I switched on the nightstand lamp and studied it, just to see how it looked sitting in my space.

With the window slammed shut, I wound myself in blankets, retrieving my cell from the limp pair of sweats I'd been wearing. One text message waited for me. Though I hadn't saved the number when it'd been given, I knew damn well who it was.

```
UNKNOWN — 8:43 PM, 10/08/2002
Come on Wednesday. Clothes here 4 you. Size??
```

IN THE END, YOU KILL US BOTH

My fingers hovered over the keys, skirting around the letter *I* for what felt like an eternity. Another text swept in.

```
UNKNOWN — 9:12 PM, 10/08/2002
Don't b afraid. I will show u the ropes
```

I clumsily typed in a single word and pressed save. Elowen's name appeared in all caps at the top of the string of text messages, the letters melting before my bleeding vision.

```
                      DRAFT to ELOWEN — 9:13 PM, 10/08/2002
                                              large is fine
```

I danced over the send button, every dark corner of my room like a pair of scrutinizing eyes. There, the silence devoured me, starved by the day.

Someone must've died, came a whispered thought. A death could've soaked up all the sound, leaving behind that foul stench and a sullen quiet. Once you've lived in a wretched place for long enough the rot sticks, carried by you like a pollinator into each new home, gushing anxiety onto the floors, afraid to turn your back on insensate walls. I'd lived with live grenades prior to Georgia's; the weight that came with this meaningless quiet was excruciating.

With my back to the mattress and my eyes wired shut, I charted the floor map of Carpenter blind, starfished on a bed hundreds of miles away, mouth breathing to block that godforsaken smell. I carved out the water dispenser shoved up against the fridge and the poodle-black blankets as curtains in my bedroom, rolled and tied at the ends with loose brown elastics when the weather was too humid. A skin-stained shower curtain, askew floral tile in the bathroom. My mother's suitcases a fixture in the dining room corner because she was an after-dinner flier, a 'dine-and-dash' woman. The relentless Nevadan sun roasted that house.

V. IVAN

Sometimes when its skinny bones creaked, I used to pray it would catch flame right in front of me.

I rolled over and plugged the prepaid lazily into the wall, squinting at its scornful glow. My head began to thrum once more with a sleepless ache and I caved, the imagined remnants of Ely scattered around me like dried petals. I wasn't there; I was nowhere at all, drifting on a bleak ruby sea alone, no faces, no punches to be thrown, no catches to be made. I willed it over, and over, and over. I willed it until the words began to grow meaningless. I fell asleep to the off-key lullaby of ten dollar wine and cigarettes calling my name all the way from Ely. It was a good dream for the first time in a long time. When I awoke to the sound of sirens sometime during the night, I clumsily patted the mattress until I triggered my cell, the faceless wall flooded with sour light.

> **To ELOWEN — 9:13 PM, 10/08/2002**
> **large is fine. will i see you wednesday?**

> *From ELOWEN — 1:02 AM, 10/09/2002*
> **Sooner than later. Promise**

I turned onto my sweating stomach, the words seared into my eyelids as I shrank back towards a dissatisfying sleep.

LIFE, OR HOW IT SHOULD BE

THE FIRST PAYCHEQUE CAME two weeks in, hand-addressed in a clean white envelope. I'd stood there at the Pinhead's counter for the first half hour of my shift, cloaked in the Anchor's gaudy pink checkers, eyeballing it until the numbers began to blur.

Never known for my wise decisions, I sank most of it into cigarettes, orange soda, a sensible amount of thrifted black tees and a cellphone with a slide out keyboard, which made me unreasonably happy. When all was said and done, I asked Elowen to drive me to the corner store in the middle of an evening snow to buy Ibuprofen, though my stomach aches had disappeared almost entirely. Back at Georgia's, where the last of my money earned us a midnight screening of Eyes Wide Shut, I got to watch the side of Elowen's face turn mottled red every time Alice Hartford appeared on screen.

Despite deeming this whole job to be *bull crap*, they worked twice as much as I did; until nights like those began, that didn't phase me. I watched them come and go like a roadside car crash, all spinning tires and going nowhere. They were prone to taking doubles, early morning opens and late evening closes with a scrawny half hour in between, yet were rarely ever scheduled to. So long as my shifts hinged on the afternoons and never the opens, I took my breaks just before they clocked in or just after they clocked out. For that fraction of time before they were off again, I had them to myself.

I couldn't pinpoint when that began; it cropped up naturally. On the nights after closing when they couldn't make it as far as Sixth, they camped out at Allenview, staggering in and collapsing drunk with ex-

V. IVAN

haustion across a makeshift bed on the couch. I'd think about it then while allowing the television to roll, tracing their spindly form with my eyes as they laid motionless in a tangle of blankets. They had their own place to stay, their own apartment to go to—roommates, a television, a couch. Yet like a stray, they ended up under my exhausted watch more often than not.

Was that what it meant to be their friend? Some days, that question plagued me more than my scant memories of home. Each time I wound up staring at the back of their neck while we were pin-setting, I thought to ask them about it—or if they'd even noticed. But each time I started to speak, I found myself losing courage.

I'd observed friendship from afar. I'd studied the girls I went to school with, etching in my mind the emphatic way they touched and fussed with each other's sleeves and hands, the sacred way they conversed; mouth-to-ear, a cock of the head, sometimes simply *eye-to-eye*. I'd seen the other end, too; deliberate silence, girls that stood in pools of each other's anger and self doubt and fed each other breath minds and hand sanitizer, the girls whose dark lipstick and shadowed stares I felt tiny yet complete under. It was nothing like that. I was *relieved* when they were around. When the Ibuprofen stopped working and my teeth seemed cemented together for good, I kept close to Elowen until I could eat again. I stayed up staggeringly late just to catch the jingle of my cell phone, left charging behind the mattress, telling me they'd gotten home to their apartment. Piece by piece, they replaced the urge for rest with an impenetrable jitter; whatever it was, it held me to the earth, kept me conscious, kept me frantic.

Christ, the thought of them made me nauseous.

It was on one of those gaps between Elowen's shifts that I sat beside the Pinheads register where the sun couldn't touch me, filled to the brim with piss and vinegar, my mail and cellphone both laying open on the countertop where I'd left them after punching in Myra's number. My thumb hovered over the call button. Inside my stomach, fury sloshed about with a gaseous sizzling.

It arrived that morning, her return address stamped on the outside as though I might lose the job before it could arrive. Inside, she'd left her handwriting in areas where it to be personal, my full name spiralling across the deliveree line, her signature splashed over the corner. On the memo line, she'd written 'FOR CARE', knowing exactly what that would do.

I was taunted by anger's rearing head. There it was, half-buried by the Echo, no longer withheld by a pill-fuelled haze. I had little idea what I'd manage to say to her but I called anyway, surrounded by dial tone as Avan stripped stale pizza from the heating case. When he caught my eye and gestured to the old slices, I shook my head.

Staring at the cheque before me, the dial tone cut out and acidic bile rose in my throat. Myra's voicemail broke through like a beacon in the night, a whistle skidding across a cold, black sea. My fingers twitched above the end button, tensing in the brief moments I'd thought her there. Just a glimpse of her had me reeling, her voicemail like a dated Christmas commercial. I sought the anger but it cowered from me, tangled within my organs. I was her daughter again when she was not near, when she could not see me. I was her daughter, unobserved, the way she hated me most.

At the beep, words slithered from my mouth. Pitiful, infantile words.

"I must've just missed you," I said, sounding just like a gramophone—all hiss, struggling substance. "Things are fine here. I've been working a lot. Georgia's perfect—she's great. You've got nothing to worry about."

It needed to come out spiteful, but it sounded like I was tracing a shaky finger down a grocery list. Like there weren't so many more things to *say*. Like a successful scream into the microphone wouldn't suffice. I'd sat at this bus stop before, waiting for her to meet me. I'd told myself to seal it up. Before I left Ely, I thought I'd never find myself waiting for her again. And she wasn't even *there*—just a ghost of her old self, whispering through her voicemail.

So where had *I* gone?

V. IVAN

"You don't need to come to Washington," I whispered. *"Just do what you normally do. I'm okay. Alright. Okay. Bye, Mom."*

I slid the phone shut and traced the light fading against its glass cover. Pushed by a wave of hatred, I stashed my knapsack in my locker and walked three streets over to a bank with snow hiked up the windows and a doorway that blasted you with warmth upon entry. I cashed and withdrew that cheque, walked myself down the block where I'd seen the sidewalk vendors, found the woman selling hand-stitched, glimmering coats and I picked the brightest one.

I'd never been so happy to see money go. I split the rest, shoved half into the pocket of that goddamn coat, and walked frozen-stiff back to the Anchor. I knew where my chunk wanted to be. When I arrived, Elowen was skulking about and I'd missed two of their phone calls. I met them in the break room among debris from a children's birthday party hours before; that *and* their uniform made their bare arms look frostbitten, and in the wake of a double shift the day before, they hung from a fraying thread.

"C'mon," they beckoned, setting a can of lukewarm orange soda on the table before me. "I pushed my start time for twenty but Marian's only got fifteen. If I've gotta do another week a' this shit without a top up, God forbid, Leo, let the right folks know that I wanna be cremated."

On Mondays and Thursdays, if Elowen minded their promise to come to work early and I hung around a little longer than scheduled, we'd manage to catch the Pinhead's delivery truck just as it backed in between two titanium goal posts at the loading dock.

It was the second truck of the day that intrigued us—one with a large, red-lettered shipping company logo on the side, chock full of bulk tomato sauce, dried and bagged herbs and freeze-dried mushrooms for rehydration, the smell of which made me gag when I pressed my face to my uniform after a long shift.

IN THE END, YOU KILL US BOTH

The stench was rotten, but worth it—the Romanian that drove that truck held the real gold. Marian Barbaneagra was nowhere near a high school graduate; he was a soft-spoken loner with a pleasant voice and a strange youth about him, but he was just young enough to talk to Elowen and I without seeming like a desperate old man. Really, his age was as much my business as the reason he'd gotten into selling bowling alley workers weed as secondary income. That afternoon he'd already checked off his deliveries and parked himself post-drop at the back of the lot, as far from the security cameras as he could manage. By the time Elowen and I made it outside, trickles of smoke were already unspooling from the open back doors of his truck like coils of incense.

A creature of habit, Marian positioned himself like a hawk across from Elowen, his feet up on the levelled shelf so he could study his truck cab and whatever took place through its large sheet window. He seldom smoked when we did—he had the good sense not to drive impaired—but he hauled off cigarettes like a vacuum, impartial to any particular brand. Marinating in a perfume of fungus and pot inside the cab, I followed Elowen's swinging ankles like a metronome, pinning my own legs silently out of reach. After a sufficient bake and a money exchange, Elowen hauled themselves out of the truck, myself in tow. From above, Marian handed them a sealed black baggie and warned, his voice thick but ever-gentle despite its seriousness, "Don't handle the leaf too much. You'll wipe away the good crystal."

"I'm a professional," Elowen promised. They didn't bother looking in the bag: a marker of their trust or simply not giving a shit, I couldn't be sure. "I wouldn't dare. Ask Leo."

"*Eh,*" Marian muttered, seating himself near the front of the cab as habitually as a domestic cat. "It's only *your* loss if you do." He hadn't shaved in days and as he sat itching the unruly beard he'd begun to tender, he caught my wandering eyes and the apples of his cheeks rose around a sparse, coarse moustache. Before he could speak, another van entered the pothole-kissed lot and Marian's gaze darted out the front window. He watched it pass completely before he turned and gestured with two wiggling fingers for the lighter. I passed it off to him, eyeing the beaded straw bracelets that dangled from his thick wrist. "I won't be working this coming Monday," he said, trapping his smoke between bruise-coloured lips. "Family obligations, but you can still reach me as usual. Thursday—same time, yes?"

"Sure thing," Elowen hummed lazily. It took much less to smoke me up than it did for them, and while I was mesmerized by the smoggy weather, they were only halfway in the bag, sloped against the truck's side. "Suppose I'll probably survive. I won't go through it all before then unless Leo gets into the stash."

"Which won't happen," I purred, eyes pointed elsewhere.

Elowen cast a cunning glance in my direction. "Y'think I haven't noticed? If you're gonna nip a few buds, don't leave me breadcrumbs."

"You know," Marian spoke suddenly, as if sensing my hesitation, "if you want to buy, I can give you a text. Or you can give me one. Your friend has my cell phone number, and I have more to sell. *Anytime.*"

Something in the tenderness of that offer frightened me. Rain tickled my hands and wrists, so I tucked them beneath my armpits. The money in my pocket, Myra's money, sung.

"I'll let you know," I nodded. "Really, though. Elowen's tugging your leg; they're happy to give me a taste of theirs, and I don't smoke alone."

Another car wobbled through the parking lot and when Marian's eyes fell from me, my shoulders sagged beneath the uniform I'd yet to change out of. With his attention briefly elsewhere, I was all too aware that Elowen was watching me. Instead of giving in, I stared just as hard into the back of Marian's head as it twitched towards the loading bay.

"You shouldn't smoke with people you do not trust. *Or* alone," he murmured. "It's much better to enjoy these things with friends, isn't it?"

It made him feel good to be needed. So I nodded, and pretended I couldn't taste the loneliness beneath his kindness like a bitter, juiceless fruit.

IN THE END, YOU KILL US BOTH

THE WEATHER DROOPED WITHOUT fail—the clouds splitting, slinging flat slashes of icy rain across the parking lot. I hid still underneath the truck's overhang, dragging my feet in finishing a cigarette I'd started before Elowen scurried off to work. Inside my pockets, one dry hand thumbed Myra's money like a worry stone, wearing Andrew Jackson's face to a smooth finish.

"No need to be ashamed."

My hands stuttered over the bills as I whipped around. *"Sorry?"*

From above, Marian busied himself, slamming the truck's shelves into their upright positions with his sleeves drawn back over his thick forearms, the muscles flinching as he worked. "You don't need to be shy," he grunted, hoisting his weight into the last shelf with a heavy *thwok*. "If you are looking to buy. I don't think that Elowen is the—judging type."

My heart floored it into my stomach. Relief, accompanied by sudden panic, swept over me. "Don't think so?"

He made an odd face, waving a dismissive hand. *"Phft.* How much? You can show me."

I folded the bills, bound them in a hair tie from around my wrist and tossed them into the truck. Marian caught them easily, made a sharp tutting noise and disappeared into the front cab, returning momentarily with a stiff, double-wrapped baggie twice the size of my curled fist.

"Remember; do not smoke it all alone," he commanded, tilting the package into my fingers. "Bad for the lungs and bad for the brain." As I jammed the small boulder into my knapsack, he dropped down from inside the van. "I meant to ask you something."

I couldn't be rude, but I wanted to go home desperately. Wanted to go home and strip off my work clothes and hide under the covers, one headphone-clad ear crushed against the pillow.

"Go for it," I said regardless.

Marian hesitated, seeking the right words. He patted for his truck keys and, upon finding them, peeled the ball cap off his head, a spray of granite hair kissing his temples.

V. IVAN

"I have two entry tickets to Green Nomad this evening. It's a Romanian bar—they're doing some live entertainment downtown around eight. You like music?"

"Depends what kind."

"Rock music," he explained slowly, gathering his thoughts. The longer he stood, the straighter he got and the quicker he found his footing. "A few friends of mine play together as a band. They're *very* talented—we could go," he caught my eye, "you and me. Could meet you near the information centre, just down the street from the new library they constructed last year."

Like a broken record, I said, "I'm not from Olympia. I don't know it."

His hands went airborne as if he'd just passed a major revelation. "Then we *must* go," he assured me. With fallen fingers, he toyed with the brim of his hat. "It's small, but respectable. Could have a few drinks, enjoy some beautiful music. What do you say?"

Elowen was, at best, reclusive in terms of friends; for all I knew I might've been their *only*, but if they vouched for Marian then he couldn't be too bad, and if it was harmless fun he was after then there was little to be afraid of at all.

Still, though I agreed, unsureness crept over me as I watched Marian jog promptly back to his truck with a fire underfoot.

That evening, Georgia looked right into my reddening face and said, without a doubt, "It's *obviously* a date." She'd been mashing slices of pot pie into individual bowls for the kids when I got back and though I'd been sheepish in showing her the coat I'd brought home to her, she'd chosen—albeit dramatically—to wear it immediately, leaving its pockets thankfully untouched. Glinting and jingling under stove light, she scraped down the pie plate and stuck a flaky scab of crust in her mouth, casting a curious eye at me. "You're gonna walk to that centre all by yourself at—what? When're you leaving?"

"Half—an hour?"

Swiping at a swath of sauce on her lip, Georgia made a disagreeing noise. "If you care about impressions, you should've left ten minutes ago.

IN THE END, YOU KILL US BOTH

I mean, if *he* cared about impressions, he should've picked you up. He can drive, right? He's not some bummy forty-year-old, is he?"

I shook my head, growing sticky and gross in my uniform. I'd yet to change or even brush my hair, let alone put some effort into an outfit that might make me look the slightest bit appropriate. I had no fancy clothes whatsoever and Georgia sensed it. After watering down a bottle of juice for Andy, her grabby but sweet toddler, she took my arm the way mothers do when they're leading you through a store. "Come upstairs," she whispered, tight-lipped and brisk. "I'll spiff you up and give you a lift over there, but you owe me cigarettes, 'cause I know you've been mooching off my pack."

"Even after the coat?"

What crossed Georgia's lips was a goofiest grin I'd ever seen, and it disappeared just as quickly in the staircase's shadows. "Smoking on that coat won't stop me from punching people, kid, but you're still sweet. Just let me dress you nice. We'll swing by the 7-Eleven, split a pack of smokes and nobody has to punch anybody."

I HATED PINK ALMOST as much as I hated *zebra print*. Yet there I stood, idling on the sidewalk a few businesses down from the information centre with a mini-skirt hiked halfway up my thighs, in *both*. If I didn't look impressive, and I was *damn* sure I didn't, then the entire evening was about to get a whole lot rougher.

Georgia had fun with it; that's the only reason I left the house looking like a bird of paradise. Bouncing light like a disco ball, Marian found me easily, working his way down the opposite end of the sidewalk with a tired black wallet in one hand and a pair of sunglasses tucked into the pocket of his patterned, silky button up. Rounding the jagged, misshapen lineup sliding down the street, he came upon me like a giddy fan, only five minutes later in arrival and thus five minutes warmer than me.

V. IVAN

"Wow-ow-ow," he exclaimed, casting his arms out as if he was coming in for a hug. My heart flattened, and only swole again when he dropped them without an attempt. "Look at you. *Zebra.*"

"*Mm.*" The bitter Olympian winter lapped at the backs of my legs, my sole sense of security laid in the fabric of Elowen's jacket around my shoulders. "Look at *you*. Much nicer than a work uniform."

"It's Persian," he spouted proudly, thumbing his silken shirt gilded with exotic florals. His thick cheeks rose in an appreciative smile and he coaxed me down the sidewalk like a sheep towards a navy blue bar front, only to pass by it completely. "Come. You've never tried Romanian brandy, have you?"

"Never heard of it. They serve that?"

Marian yielded to a darting couple in matching coats and drew me to the curb, his hand careful but scalding on my clothed elbow. When he leaned in close, the spicy cologne on his throat wet my eyes and I watched in anxious intrigue as he reached into his shirt pocket and withdrew a ruby-glass bottle with a golden label. Looking just as young as me under the streetlights, Marian's face flooded with a bright, mischievous grin.

"*They do when I am here,*" he whispered, uncapping it and tossing back his share.

Mine went down like a warm, relaxing sip of paint thinner, enough to cool my nerves and get me moving. The Green Nomad wasn't a large space, nor was it even all that close to the information centre. Instead, The Green Nomad was a shy little dive one street over with a chainsaw-carved crane on a stump outside its doors and a clueless bouncer who glossed over my ID as if he was asleep. Marian bought me a drink without question, a topper after that emptied brandy bottle, and didn't introduce me to anyone in particular. Relief collapsed over me like a windblown sheet.

The venue's interior was ripe with liquor-sticky counters and deep prune stage lights. We moved through a turret of suffocating perfumes and loud voices and I did everything but cling to him, riding close behind until we squeezed through to the small searing area opposing the stage where half a dozen tables and steel chairs were staggered in uneven clumps across the floor. By the time we found seats without beer bottles already glued to the tabletop, I was mutely exhausted.

He blasted me with questions the entire way—I tried hard not to mind. He was just excited that I was there, and I was happy enough to be doing anything at all rather than staring at my bedroom ceiling at Georgia's. I only hoped he wouldn't notice that my mind was elsewhere; even when the lights dipped and a chubby boy my age stepped onto the stage in dark plaid and brown eyeliner, trailed by monochrome bandmates, I wasn't present. Ripe guitar riffs bounced off my ears, the lead singer's voice muffled and sore, sanded down to an elegant whisper. Warm, fluid drum beats crashed over my head. Synchronous whoops and hollers sat me at the edge of a Roman pit, watching bodies tumble into the dark.

Apart from the crowd, I imagined that Elowen would've liked this little spot—a deep purple hole in the wall where the music took every howling patron by the collar and slapped them silly, where the drinks were strong and sour and the air gushed with the scent of pumping blood and sweet-smelling lotion. Admittedly, I wondered what they liked quite often, but trying to wrangle answers from them was like setting broken bones; messy yet brief. I wondered if they'd even *been* to a bar before or if they'd ever had a drink, if they had a *favourite*, and when I started wondering too much I nursed on brandy until my eyebrows grew hot and my jaw loosened, my head nodding like a dashboard bobblehead.

What would they think of me going on a date with the older man who sold them weed? In a blink I was struck by their face, painted with a strict kind of disagreement that I'd never actually seen them wear, and as if I was possessed, one hand flew to my lap and drug the edge of my skirt down to my knees. Something about that thought roused me like a child caught sneaking peeks at a gory movie from a shadowed hallway. Nowhere to be seen and *still* they were on my mind, the speculation of their disapproval a silent and venomous poison. By the time the band rounded out their third song I'd drained the last drops of my drink, rising shakily from my seat.

"Bathroom," I answered Marian's fretful face, crouching to make myself smaller as the band rattled on.

V. IVAN

"Don't be long," Marian urged. "They always do a wicked *Distrus* cover at the end of their set. You will enjoy it."

I bore a smile that matched my clothes, fake and unbecoming, and disappeared through a cloud of vapour into the ladies room, plunking myself down in one of two graffiti-eaten stalls. The bassline hummed through the plaster and hugged me from every angle, palm-sized tags of unreadable names, slurs and swears etched in sharpie and scratchy pen across all four suffocating walls. I hauled out my phone and scrolled through the last texts I'd sent, biting my tongue to contain a hateful grimace at the childish way I spoke. Underneath a midnight conversation about their roommate's late night eating habits, I tapped out a few words and read them over until my eyes burned and my cheeks began to ache.

```
To ELOWEN - 9:29 PM, 10/28/2002
you still working?
```

Somebody came in, blew their nose over the sink, swore and left. I leveraged my feet against the stall door and slid the toe of Georgia's shoe over a graffiti face until only the eyes were peaking out. When my phone double buzzed, I turned it over much too quickly.

```
From ELOWEN - 9:32 PM, 10/28/2002
Like usual
```

```
From ELOWEN - 9:32 PM, 10/28/2002
Everything ok?
```

I thought to joke, or *funnier*, to tell the truth—but something pulled at the very base of my throat, a swollen, viscous lump.

```
To ELOWEN - 9:33 PM, 10/28/2002
i'm out for a bit. don't want to walk home
```

IN THE END, YOU KILL US BOTH

From ELOWEN — 9:34 PM, 10/28/2002
Where?

To ELOWEN — 9:36 PM, 10/28/2002
meet @ anchor. just wait for me?

It didn't sit right, but neither did the thought of Marian finding me in the women's bathroom, texting Elowen to rescue me so that he wouldn't have to take me home. They'd see right through me—I'd come to realize that wasn't something they found very difficult—and the truth would taste shitty on my unwilling tongue.

My phone vibrated one last time.

From ELOWEN — 9:39 PM, 10/28/2002
You know where to find me

After a flash of frigid sink water to the face, I left the bathroom and traversed the ultraviolet tunnel back into the main bar. Down three brassy yellow steps, I sank into my seat next to Marian.

Though I wanted to apologize for my prolonged absence, I couldn't quite find the right moment. Opaline blue and yellow glazed the audience and coated Marian's thoughtful face in hues of holy light. For the first time since I'd met him, I found him oddly beautiful. The music deified him, washed his mortality away within a melancholic riff, turned the water in his very being to wine. I sat in silence with my elbow against his until the stage lights bled into darkness, until the band disappeared behind a fluttering curtain and the whistles began. An eruption of applause and the clinking of glasses gave way and, half blind beneath the sweat-heavy air, Marian wiped his misty eyes with the back of one dewy hand and slammed the last of his drink.

V. IVAN

Marian's SUV puttered across town towards the bowling alley, the horseshoe-shaped air freshener dangling lazily around the neck of the rearview mirror like a simple charm of luck in the dead backstreets.

He offered more than once to drive me home but each time I considered it, rejection poured willingly from my lips. He didn't take it to heart—too busy waving one freed hand while the other gripped the steering wheel, telling me all about the meaning of the music, the importance of it, the merit that it held. We passed walls of sardined businesses, brick shopfronts spliced into one another like Cronenberg abominations, gaudy glowing signs that doused the sidewalks in angelic light. I wound the window down and draped my arm out, subtly afraid that the posts might take my hand wrist-down and leave me with a gouged stump. We struck a patch of late night construction, orange and highlighter yellow suits and blinding stage lights casting ominous shadows over scraped-down potholes, thick workings of tar and splattered machines whirring and snarling their way through the evening. At a sign holder, Marian slowed to a halt and gave me a meaningless moment of quiet before he finally turned to seek my attention.

"I'd take you for a coffee or a tea," he said rather apologetically, "but I need to be home with my daughter. My mother watches her during the evenings, and she's quite old herself."

I blanked. Somehow, I'd forgotten how much older Marian really was in the smog of that bar.

"Your—daughter?"

"Andrea." Light caught his rounded, prideful face. "She's very little. She'd like you very much, I think."

"Why's that?" I asked, still swallowing that jarring fact like a python inhaling a football.

Marian fell sheepishly silent, red even in the highlighter glow. The sign holder spun his pipe handle and waved us forward. Nauseous from the pungent stench of tar, I rolled my window up.

"Fine by me," I promised him. "I told Elowen I'd meet them, so I can't stay out."

Marian's fingers slid over the leather wheel cover, eyes on the reflective suits before us. He turned an ear towards me. "You and Elowen. You've been friends for some time now?"

"A month—little more, I guess." Adjusting the seat belt at my throat, I rubbed at the cologne stink from my nose, itching at the sore sinuses blooming beneath the flesh of my cheeks. The earwig in Georgia's trash spattered the backs of my eyelids and sent a jolt through my shoulders. "It's no—wild story, honestly. Just a party. Just a coincidence."

He gave a small grunt under his breath. "You two—you—*uh*—" A knitting motion with his hands, threading his fingers together against the leather. "You *mesh* together very nicely. A month is—surprising. I didn't know that Elowen kept friends until we met, you and I."

Glancing unsurely upon Marian's silhouette, I sought some kind of mockery in his words but retracted into my seat when I found none. "It's—unorthodox, but yeah. We're friends."

"*Unorthodox?*"

"Unusual."

His head bobbed. "Ah, yes," he purred. "So you noticed that as well."

"What's that?"

Snagging my attention with a glance, Marian's eyes rolled across the street, pearly and knowing in the dark. "They *are* unusual." He spoke quietly, as if they might hear. "I noticed when I met them. Unorthodox? It's a good word to describe it."

I didn't care much for gossip. I liked it less than leaving voicemails for my mother, like proof of my own vulnerability might make its way around the world in the wrong hands. I leaned into the turn as we crossed a small bridge towards the edge of downtown. Chicken wire fencing licked all the way up the bridge's rungs in a macabre, wordless warning.

"How long have *you* known them?"

"A year or so," Marian guessed. "They looked very different. Not like they do now, but this isn't surprising. They eat very little, and sometimes I find it hard to understand the things they say. All the morning shifts they take—no breaks, I've heard. I am not complaining, of course. I'm

V. IVAN

only saying. They come from a family of hippies; if this is the normal attitude amongst those people, I am not familiar with it."

I ate every single word, cramming each syllable inside of my mouth like powdered glass, chewing until my tongue turned numb and irony.

Unfortunately, my silence made him feel comfortable enough to add, "I'm glad I am not the only one who noticed something wrong."

That string of words threaded through my skin like a dull needle, shredding the uneven terrain of my heart. I bristled.

"There's nothing *wrong* with Elowen."

It came out hard enough—Marian's eyes flickered across the dash to me and back upon the road, paling as the seconds passed. *"No,"* he hurried. "No, no. The words came out wrong. *Different* would be a better choice."

He looked to me for approval but I gave none. The city forked off into lower-income housing, accounting offices with gaudy white and red signs, billboards with half-torn faces plastered on them, then finally the Anchor's candied glow. As we rolled to a stop at the curb, I resisted the urge to jump out and run. Elowen was likely changed already, or perhaps they were still waiting aimlessly in the corridors behind the bowling lanes, resetting pins with their headphones on.

"I had a nice time with you tonight, Leo." When I turned, Marian was wringing his tough hands, his gaze flicking between the sidewalk and me. "I hope you had as nice an evening as I did."

"Of course," I assured him, though I'd hardly been there. "Your friends are talented, and they put on a good show. What's not nice about that?"

Marian pressed a palm against the wheel, distant in thought. He struggled around the ledges of foreign, unsure words before his fingertips dug into the leather and he found me again, sheepish this time.

"I wanted to tell you earlier that you look very beautiful tonight. But I was—too nervous."

Skin-and-bones compliments always made me feverish, a bit disgusted. It wasn't Marian—I'd come to find him almost sweet. It was *me*, stuck there in the passenger's seat, squirming to be free. I slid one ankle under the other. "I don't know about *that*."

He shied like a shy teenage boy. "I mean to ask something of you, but I don't want you to think of me as some old creep. You understand?"

I didn't at first—really, at all. At some point I must've uttered a stationary *no*, and Marian faced the passenger's side and planted an elbow on the armrest.

"I'd like to kiss you goodnight," he said. "If that is okay."

I was camouflaged against the seat by my own stillness.

Not since the bumbling days of prepubescent junior high had I kissed anyone, and never *seriously*. Instead of dreadful, mind-rotting nerves I was struck with an unsure curiosity. If it'd been as much of a date as Georgia had suggested, then this was warranted, right? He'd been kind, courteous, had bought me drinks and fed me stories and politeness all evening. I had no complaints. Was I not indebted to him by then?

Was this even something that could be owed?

I searched his softened, nervous face and found within that man a boy as young as me, bloody-nailed from picking away. He'd been *kind*. Was there more to it than that? There didn't *have* to be.

Marian leaned across the armrest so suddenly that my acceptance felt pointless.

A sudden, suffocating guilt stripped the air from my chest. I'd lay in bed later that night and think about how afraid I'd been among a full range of worse thoughts. I'd recall how I'd frozen like a block of solid, frostbitten meat, how I'd let him kiss me on the mouth without another word. Marian's tough hands captured my face with ease, his lips dry and cool and firm on mine. When he withdrew, I wet my trembling mouth for the taste of him to make sure the kiss counted, like that might stop it from happening again. All he'd left was the unappetizing cocktail of winter mint cough drops and tap beer.

I stood on the curb, my soul dangling inches from my body, pulling Georgia's tight rings from my frozen fingers as Marian hauled out of the parking lot. The multicoloured sign above me sent the snow aglitter. Once I was sufficiently alone, I untucked the silky blouse Georgia rented

V. IVAN

to me, readjusted the front of my skirt and let my posture collapse. I dropped onto the curb next to a group of concrete-bolted trash cans and tested my pulse. It was slow and thrumming, my veins irate from the disruption, squirming feebly against my finger.

Debilitating loneliness rushed in. There was no sparkling, incandescent feeling that came with being kissed by Marian for the first time. I liked his sweet face and I liked the way his breath had hiccuped when he met my lips, but it stopped there on the sidewalk and forked away from me, pooling in my lower intestine the same pounding ache that accompanied me in bed at night when my full bladder woke me and the quiet became conversational. I hadn't expected much at all and yet somehow I'd wanted more. Something, *anything* at all.

I pulled out my cell, squinted at its nauseating brightness and followed my directions to the one thing that had remained in Marian's absence, sliding by the faded, poster-plastered brick siding of the Black Anchor towards the lip of the basement stairwell. Seven steps below beneath a bug-encrusted bulb, Elowen leaned slackly upon the wall with their knapsack strapped to their shoulders, a dark brown hoodie thrown over their work uniform, their lightly-greased hair pinned back by the band of their headphones. I lowered my defences against the guilt that struck me as I stood, dressed in their jacket with my midsection baked warm by fur-lined denim, while they seemed unfazed by the reddening of their bare arms, milking a half-drained cigarette.

They studied me like a golden lion platformed at the zoo. I couldn't ask for anything less. Hell, if it were me and I hadn't any clue where they'd been, I'd have *laughed*.

"*Goddamn,*" is all they could manage. "Who're you supposed t'be?"

I grasped the memory of the bathroom at The Green Nomad, bracing my legs on the stall door and wondering when I'd find the right moment to tell them about Marian. As the opportunity presented itself, I willed myself to say something but I hadn't even a shred of excitement or desire. Marian's kiss *spoiled* it all. I couldn't tell Elowen about anything. I was suddenly, truly cursed.

"It's Georgia," I tried, shrinking inside the zebra print nonsense I was cloaked in. No wonder Elowen looked at me so sternly from that bottom step—they were trying to recognize me. "We played dress up. I didn't want to change back into my work clothes to go out, and nothing else was clean."

A deep, foreboding rot bubbled around that lie, a feeling that never graced my skin before then.

Elowen shrugged, rising from their slouch, their pointy face almost strife in the dark. "You look great. It's not *you*, though. This is my first time seein' you voluntarily wear a skirt."

An embarrassing noise crept from my throat like a frightened kitten. "I don't waste money on expensive clothes," I said defiantly, "and it's the middle of *winter*. I'm hardly acclimated as is. Besides, I'm itchy and I really fuckin' hate this pink shit. Just *look* at me."

I regretted it the moment the syllables left my mouth.

Not because they were already looking, but because asking turned them *thorough*. Rolling their eyes down the sleeves of their own coat, tracing the scar-tacky skin of my knees and the peculiar lace of the tights I was suctioned into, Elowen seemed to count each individual slash of zebra striping before they stamped out their cigarette on the asphalt. Their fingertips inched uncomfortably close to the edge of the cherry—even from the top step, it was clear they'd been furiously picking their nails. One finger kissed the ground, grazing the cement with blood.

"*Was it dead?*"

"As hell." They stuffed their hands, and the butt, deep into their pockets. "Couple a' bozos came in an hour ago wanting to play slots. Told 'em we didn't have any and they got real colourful about it. Drunk bastards have amazin' vocabularies." They marched up the steps towards me until I had to step back to keep from bumping them. Their boney fingers fluttered inside their pants pockets for truck keys. "I'm just ready to get the fuck outta here."

They crossed the pavement in front of me and spun. I didn't move an inch, landlocked by the cloying smell of them, holding my arms to my stomach in a lopsided display of comfort.

V. IVAN

"C'mon, Lee," they coaxed. "Let me take you home."

Guilt kept me glued to the sidewalk, studying the lumps of Elowen's pocketed hands. I wanted to tell them about the Romanian Rock music, about my first time drinking brandy, about Marian crying to lyrics I wished I understood. I wanted to tell them about the way he'd asked so politely at the end, the way he hadn't waited for my permission, the way that he tasted. I wanted to ask them if it was normal that I didn't feel a damn thing. Instead I knew only the remnants of that inescapable disappointment, and how the sight of Elowen at the bottom of the stairwell had stolen it away.

"Somethin's goin' on in that head of yours," they cut through my thoughts. "I see the cogs turnin'. Maybe you can think about it in the truck."

Elowen and I weren't friends. If it was that simple, I wouldn't have hid it. I thought to ask if we'd ever make it there or if we'd always remain in limbo between nothing and something, neither defined by such a *stupid* word as *friendship*. But courage—that slimy, slippery bitch. I lost it.

There weren't answers for these sorts of things, anyhow.

"I think I want to keep your jacket," I said aloud instead. "Just for a little longer."

Elowen took a step back to observe me, assessing their belief in that. Suddenly shy, they turned to the parking lot and wrestled free their truck keys, the tips of their angular ears purple-red.

"Sure," they muttered. "Looks better on you anyways."

Maintaining the gap and putting it past me, I began walking and Elowen followed. I knew exactly the footpath back to their truck, parked in the same place they always were—as far away from the rest of the world as they could get.

UNORTHODOX

After arriving at Georgia's and watching Elowen cruise from our narrow one-way street, I sucked back a cigarette and a few gulps of laundromat fumes before creeping into the warm, dim duplex. The kids were well in bed and I'd barely scraped off my shoes before I was dogpiled with questions about every aspect of the evening by a wiry shadow staggering from the couch.

She didn't *chastise* me, not in the nauseating way I was familiar with. If anything she was leeching off my crumbs, bloodsucking and whining when my answers were undoubtedly dry. Owing her the basics at the very least, I met her protestingly in the living room where Maury Povich was playing on the television lower than a gravelly whisper.

"Fine is not a good word to use when you're talking about a date," she told me right off the bat.

"I'll take 'nice' for 200, then."

"Fine and nice are practically the same thing, you bird. What I'm sayin' is, if it was just *fine*, then how *good* could it really be?"

I had no reason *not* to like Marian, and certainly no reason not to want to go out again. No logic held up my own frustrating hesitance. It was impossible to explain—I nixed most of those details from our conversation, cutting the story just before Elowen drove me home while I neglected to tell them anything. Their jacket groped my shoulders as I sank into the couch; the same denim that once warmed their pink arms now held my bones together.

V. IVAN

"It *was* good." I yearned to take a razor blade to my polished nails, to bathe away the animal print that was melding to my skin. "He's polite. And the music was good. Drinks were—" Good. *Good, good, good.*

"He didn't try to get frisky with you, did he?" I balked and as Georgia's eyes rolled, her head followed, exposing her sinewy throat. *"C'mon.* You teenagers have hormones shootin' out every pore. Y'think I wasn't your age not too long ago? It's not a stupid question."

Raising a clumsy hand, I swiped foolishly at the sudden flush painting my cheeks. "I don't do that stuff."

Not before or after Washington. Not because I didn't *want* to. Lots of people *wanted* to, at least a little bit. I just hadn't wanted to do it with anyone in Ely. Now that Georgia had me thinking about it, I had no clue if I wanted to do it with Marian, either.

"Well, yeah, 'cause the Echo has some legal voyeuristic thing going with all those cameras. But before—"

"He didn't do anything weird," I reeled her back in. "He kissed me goodnight. That's it."

Georgia savoured that, shrugging away a dusting of surprise. "Well, *good.*" Then, to incite panic, she rose from the edge of the couch and collected two child-sized sippy cups from the coffee table, trekking to the kitchen and hurling back at me a casual, "Invite him to dinner. *Here* this time. Maybe he'd like that."

I stared frozen at the space where she'd been moments before, overcome by a large, looming dread. Whatever was wrong with me, I was already spent by it. I held a hand to my chest, willing it to give me some reprieve, to haul itself onto some other unsuspecting victim, someone still alive enough to benefit its devouring appetite. I had little left of my soul as is. I'd be empty before the spring came.

Still, it was the most I'd felt since I left Nevada.

MARIAN AGREED TO COME over for dinner that Sunday, only after I'd given him a fully baked, thirty-second pity invitation that left me clawing at my eyes on the way back inside the Anchor. The weekend came and went, hitched to a bizarre silence; I hadn't seen Elowen outside of work since they'd driven me home. A month ago, that wouldn't have earned a blink from me.

By Sunday afternoon, I was a glittering, flighty mess, this time without zebra print. All morning I willed myself to cancel, but without his phone number nor the will to ask Elowen for it, I paced uselessly in desperation. I inhaled black coffee straight from the pot and smoked myself raw, delving into the light rain only to buy a fresh pack of Winstons and a frilly-sleeved shirt from a thrift shop opposite the public library—which, through my window at Allenview, became a distant, copper-tipped beacon since I'd gone out of my way on Saturday to find it. I tacked posters to my bedroom wall, flimsy magazine cutouts of sperm whale skeletons, Sex Pistols album covers, blow dried show sheep with decorations in their fur, and studied them criss-crossed on the floor until the wooly black eyes of those sheep wore holes into my skull. At one point, Elowen tried calling me; I couldn't even find the courage to answer.

Only Georgia's promise of culinary help kept me afloat. Her face was warm and exhausted in the kitchen that evening, explaining step-by-step instructions, half-certain I wouldn't remember. She chased me away from her cigarettes more than once and promised she'd give me one without strings if I remained in the kitchen with her, but I idled and trembled and stared at my cell phone screen by the kitchen island, vibrating and distressed until she grew bored and kited me in front of the stove to fry onions in a dizzying melange of heavy, fruity spices.

"One of these days," Georgia warned coyly from over my stiffened shoulder, "you're gonna have to learn how to do this shit yourself. And *trust*—I'll be expectin' a whole chicken cooked just like this, *just* for me."

Her voice rattled me from the chambers of my stuffy mind. I wet my lips, knee-deep in a daydream, the kitchen damp with yellow steaming light pluming towards the range fan. "I know how," I lied. "I'm just not good at it."

"That's what practicing's for."

V. IVAN

"Yeah. Lots of Little Tikes stoves in the Echo."

A raw, butter-glossed chicken in a black roasting pan winked at me from the countertop. I scraped a few slivers of onion free from the pan, bullying myself with that heat to keep me centred as Georgia peered over my work. Satisfied, she hooked a skirted hip against the silverware drawer.

"Find it awfully hard to believe you've never cooked chicken before. Your mom never taught you how to cook?" The sudden prickling in my neck earned her silent, shouldered twitch. "You got a mom?" she rephrased. "Sorry, didn't ask. Serves me right."

My soul waned, slipping into the pan to fry. "She doesn't cook."

Georgia stared hard at the onions, translucent under my careful watch. Then she slipped away, returning to sweep a cutting board of ribboned peppers and a teaspoon of sugar into the pan, her hand cupped beneath with odd, unbearable care.

"Well, it's not for everyone," she purred. "Yeah, just stir it in. It'll start to caramelize. Oh, careful. *Careful*. Aw, Christ. Here."

Georgia's hands, dusty from the sugar, slid over mine, spittles of oil hissing like begrudging snakes. A veil of panic curtained my senses—a projector fluttered to life, pulling me in a dozen directions. The warming light, Georgia's perfume, dates and honey and something almost *powdery*. Her cigarette stained fingers protected my hands, the onions taking on a tacky stench the harder I seared them. Myra's perfume had always seemed so citrusy, sour and bleak; God must've thought himself fucking hilarious, because it rose to the ledge of my upper lip right there in the kitchen, erupting from the warmth over the oven.

"Agitate that shit," Georgia goaded. "Y'see what I mean? Agitate the fuckers." Her arms skidded away, disappearing from the corner of my eyes. "It's easy. Just let it cook, an' keep stirring. Add a little oil if things get rough. We'll top the chicken, throw it in the oven for a while and Bob's your uncle. You'll be a professional by the night's end."

"Think so?"

Her lips curled. "Well, it's sort of hopeful. But we'll see."

"You're just loaded with faith in me."

"Of course I am," she said sincerely. "Ain't anythin' in the world that *someone's* Ma can't teach you if your own can't. Besides, you're a smart girl. If you're anythin' like me, you'll figure that shit out on your own whether someone helps you or not. You didn't *need* my help, but—I'm glad to do it."

Georgia hovered faithfully by my side. She was a mother, had been a mother, which imbued her with an immunity to bullshit that few others had such ease in handling; she could sense I'd gone elsewhere, that my attention had shifted. Regardless, she leaned over and huffed the smell with a gargantuan sigh.

"Still can't believe this dude's got a car and he let you find a way to Legion Street all by yourself. That constitutes a red fucking flag to me." She turned to see if she'd made me laugh.

Her expression morphed like thumbed clay, splaying hurtfully along the lines of her widening eyes.

"Oh—oh, *kid. Hey.*"

I didn't clock the sting at first, not until Georgia purred at just the right volume to make me rest that wooden spatula against the pan and touch the rotten cheeks she was ogling at. I found dampened skin beneath my fingertips, thick as blood and clear as spit.

Oh, I agreed. Like we'd just discovered mouse shit in the cupboards.

Georgia straightened, suddenly so firm before me that fear caught me and thrust me back.

"*Honey. Hey. Did I say something?*"

The tears were free flowing. I clutched my face like I was bleeding out, frantic for a towel, near-begging for stitches right there in front of the stove. The floor, growing uneven like a hillside, swayed beneath me.

I'm sorry, I was saying. *I'm really sorry. Sorry.*

"*It's alright. You're alright.*"

Georgia's kind hands sought me out. I fled them like Death's cold, skinless fingers. *Can you—*

She was already on the move. I danced out of her way with ease and she lowered the burners without a second glance as my body swung towards the kitchen entry. I hadn't remembered the scent of Myra's perfume until just then. It was in the air, fragrant, odd and disenchanting. I hated that old perfume. Not once in the years I'd been gone had I wished I could smell it again.

Why was I fucking *crying?*

I gestured towards the stairs, wordless.

"It won't burn," Georgia promised, her eyes poised on me. "I've got it. It's okay."

I climbed the stairwell without a sound. All the clothes on my body, the thickened skin beneath, my bones, my blood, all of it soiled and black with gunk. I'd bought a lacy shirt just for that evening and still I peeled it off and abandoned it, stationing myself in the middle of my bedroom floor in the dark where nobody could see me. When I reached for my phone, the castoff light erupted across the unrecognizable mass of my body. I sank to the floor, my back flinching from its frigid surface. Myra's name was still unsaved in my phone, but there sat a message with her stink all over it, puncturing the screen like a blade.

From UNKNOWN — 8:13 PM, 11/01/2002
Lenore. You sound exhausted in the voicemail you left. Did you get my mail? Let me know. Mom.

I laid in the quiet until the tears stopped, until the lights dimmed downstairs and the front door snapped closed, sending a wild cold dancing through the unit. When I came down once more, clothed and dry-eyed, the chicken was rendered a dark, glistening brown on the stovetop and Georgia was gone.

"I T WAS NINE YOU wanted me, right?" Marian asked, a step down off the front porch. I'd opened the door by chance—not to *run*, I swear—and found him climbing the steps quietly like a stray breeze, his SUV parked awkwardly in front of the laundromat.

I hovered in the caramel porch light, bound inside a clean, olive green tee I'd thrown on last minute. With a frail breath, I shifted my weight and laid off the hefty anxiety that was trying to break me. "Quarter after," I assured him, "but no worries."

"Early is better than late?"

"Always."

He cleaned up well; his beard had been trimmed short and his hair pooled in dense, spiralling waves around his jaw, his stiff frame bundled inside of a well-fitting polo. It wasn't often that men were much to look at, but he was handsome and almost feminine in ruby red, a thick glass baking dish with foil wrapping tucked under his arm. "Plum dumplings," he explained at the kitchen counter, peeling back the aluminum from that still-steaming bounty. They were golden and fragrant, glazed in rich, raw honey. He gave another name to it, something sleek and Romanian, but I turned such a deep purple at my own butchering repetition that I couldn't stand to breathe.

I'd never eaten dinner so fast in my entire life. The longer he stayed, the worse my budding stomach ache became. The more idle chatter, the further I wanted to be from him. I preoccupied myself with collecting our dishes afterwards just to avoid his eyes, but even that didn't dissuade him. Instead, he parked himself along the countertop next to me and, after exhausting nearly all of his pre-rehearsed chitchat about the day's events and weather, he simmered down and got to washing . I only took up drying duty because he'd gone quiet, and because he didn't fill up the sink the way Myra had always done. No painful pleasantries, no murky water for my unhitched mind to spook from. *Really*—I thought I was in the clear.

Well, I've *always* been a dumbass. The moment my shoulders slackened, he sawed through my peace and quiet without a second glance.

"I haven't seen you in Olympia before now. You haven't been here long, have you?"

I glared at a shrivelled piece of onion cemented to the pan I was drying, digging painfully at it with my fingernail. "Olympia's pretty big," I murmured. "Even if I was, you might've never seen me anyways."

V. IVAN

"*True.*" He shrugged, idling until I was free for another glistening plate. "But you *are* from another state. Somewhere hot; I remember that much."

"Nevada."

"Ah, yes! Las Vegas." I fought a tall, looming wave of irritation brought on by foolish pride. "Why move here from warm and sunny Nevada?"

I dried silently, masking my thinking face with a grimace. "Change of pace. Why'd *you* move here?"

"Better housing than in Baia Mare. More bang for your buck. I always wanted to see the Americas, and my second choice was Medellín but the heat would've been too much for Andrea. She loved Washington the moment we set foot in the streets, so we decided to stay." Corkscrewing the sponge into a mug, Marian turned from the sink. "You and Elowen—you've been friends since you moved?"

Something deep inside of my stomach fissured, and I itched my face with a slick hand. "You ask me lots of questions about Elowen."

Marian's hands stammered on the edge of that glass, wiping the lip of it clean. A faint noise slid from him—it took me a moment to clock it as a laugh. Burning up, I cast a life raft his way.

"It's not—inherently bad. Just something I noticed."

"I apologize. I guarantee it's not intentional."

"Right. It just *happens* a lot."

Marian slotted each polished glass into the dry sink one at a time, his ringless hands scrubbing down the lid of the baking dish like the success of this night depended on it. "You are friends, but your interests seem quite different. I couldn't imagine what it would be like to attend a dinner hosted by someone who doesn't like to eat—drink—party, even." He leaned to find my eyes, caught them then bowed out with a cautious smile. "It is not—my interest in *her*, of course, but in *you*. That is why I ask. I'm just surprised that you don't wish to talk about her as she wishes to talk about you."

My towelled hand slackened inside the soapy throat of a juice pitcher. *"They* talk about me," I corrected, not sharpened by the miscalculation of my interests but by the repeat offence.

"About *you*," Marian repeated, blissfully unaware. "Often—affectionately, and in good spirits. At times, out of the blue. It is part of the reason I became interested in you in the first place. *This is what I meant,"* he whispered, *"when I said they are unorthodox."*

For a long while, I didn't move. Marian took the pitcher from my hands and stole away my towel, but didn't dry and slot it into the cupboard with the rest of the glassware. He just stood, wiggling me from my stupor by ducking to find my face. The kitchen was suddenly so stuffy that I wondered if Georgia had left the oven on.

Without an ounce of warning, Marian reached out and brushed a speck of soapy debris from my cheek.

"It doesn't matter," he assured me. "Strange friends are friends just the same, and it's good to keep friends about in a new city. Isn't it?"

That fingerprint left a dusty, cauterizing feeling in my jaw, criss-crossing down into my lymph nodes. Adrenaline—of a positive or negative kind, I couldn't be sure. Marian was cocked like a gun, waiting dutifully for the sound of my voice. Sure, it could've been anyone standing there, but he was listening to me, hearing me, all eyes and ears. It was nice to be noticed. It was nice to be paid attention to.

I caved, resting my towel on the sink's edge and meeting him in the middle, travelling through the solitary vein tethering us together; them, them, *them.*

"You're wrong," I told him quietly. *"It matters very much."*

T HERE WAS NO NEED to sit down for dessert. He tasted just like it—plum, tart and warming, like he'd eaten some on the way over before dinner and somehow, he was still starving.

We made it to the couch—*how,* I couldn't be sure. What felt like an eternity only really boiled down to a few minutes of tense, fumbling

V. IVAN

nonsense. We collided at the kitchen sink, my hands flecked with dish soap, him dusting kisses at the side of my neck like polite offerings. Before we even breached the dark of the den, his arms went snuggly around me. It was all I could do not to bite his tongue clean in two; to be kissed was *one* thing. To be held was another *entirely*.

At first, it was—fine.

Thick, rough hands worked their way over my cheeks, my throat, my shoulders, the muscles belted around my hips rubbed sore by digging thumbs. His hands descended to the tender flesh of my legs and I parted them without thought, allowing him to rest in the crook of me. The sigh he gave was understandably grateful—that was the sweetest part of all. He was *grateful*. How lonely he must've been with nobody to kiss him. How much he must've hoped, on his way over, that this could happen. That he could make this happen.

My mouth stiffened at the thought. He never even noticed.

I sort of hated him for that, but I didn't stop him. Instead, we went on like that for a while: plush kisses and sharing breath, my arms knotted against the back of his neck, tensing and loosening, repeat. His wide, sandpaper tongue slid into my mouth and I permitted it, not knowing any other option. I swatted away all attempts to undo my shirt, redirecting his hands into mine. The intimacy made me frigid. I had to relax. I had to.

But I'd hit a wall.

I tried to imagine what we looked like from where the television sat. I played it in reverse, that black screen voyeuristically capturing our entanglement in the raw dark, stumbling into the living room and climbing onto the couch as one, his frame swallowing mine whole, our mouths molten and indistinguishable, asking me how much I liked it. All of me *wanted* to. Maybe deep down, I did: the kissing, the frantic touching, the awkward writhing, the denial of more and the equal yearning for it. The scalding, squirming sensation it gave, though that passed through me like a wicked period, deliberate pain in my abdomen superseding every touch. There were *things* to like.

Just not enough to measure.

Halfway through getting my bottoms awkwardly pulled on, an uneven rapping at the front door sent me scrambling like a rat. Marian chased my mouth and I wedged an arm between our chests, a notion that came more naturally to me than the awkward mouth-to-mouth. He begged weakly for me to ignore it, but the opportunity was just too delicious to refuse. I wormed out from beneath him, leaving him on the couch and staggering to the door with fixing hands tidying my blouse, my bottoms, my face. I hadn't worn lipstick because I didn't care for makeup, but what a mess I could've been. I wouldn't have been able to face myself in the mirror afterwards to wash it off; the embarrassment would have annihilated me.

I half expected to see Georgia, keyless and frozen on the steps. Instead, I swung open the door and looked upon Elowen's narrow, rosy face.

I'd watched their fiery roots burn down the sides of their face in the weeks past. The stark black dye held little ground now, casting them as a bludgeoning victim in the bleak porch light. Flecks of snow powdered the useless skim of a windbreaker they'd thrown over their work uniform. The smallest sniffle, the *slightest* cock of their head and I was dust on the doormat.

"How's it that every time I see ya now, you've got somethin' fancy on?"

Time and space skittered to a halt, decaying behind me. Something spasmed inside of my ribcage—whether it was relief or desperation, neither came kindly.

"*Hi,*" plumed from my lips.

"*Hi, yourself.*" They ducked towards the shadows to get a better look at me, their hollow cheeks a lively red in the cold. Much like a vampire, not an inch of their body passed into the foyer uninvited. A non-committal smile toyed around their lips. "I've been ringin' you, but you've been some hard t'get ahold of."

One arm went across the doorway, pinning me inside its narrow frame. I prayed they couldn't see how goddamn *hard* I was shaking. "We're cool. I was learning the art of brazing from Chef Georgia."

V. IVAN

Darkness traced the curious shells of their eyes, an unsure glance bouncing from my wrist to my shoulder. My lips opened and closed soundlessly, and every nerve that'd failed to tense under Marian's groping palms went firing like a jammed rifle—*bang, bang, bang, bang, bang.*

Elowen crouched, speaking lowly and just to me.

"If you're busy, I'll fuck off. I just happened to have some spare change rattlin' around and a couple decent grams. And I thought, knowin' *you*—"

Heavy footsteps crossed behind me, accompanied by the wounded whimpering of floorboards, and I bore witness to the horrible, slackening way that Elowen's smile spoiled.

Marian craned over my shoulder to look out the door. The mile-deep pool where my heart once lived stung with a corrosive, chemical sickness. It was that visceral emptiness I'd felt outside the Anchor, post-date. It was the nothingness, clarified. It was shame like an old dog, one I'd never had the courage to put down.

"Ms. Reeves!" Marian boasted, his voice ragged from my own spit. "Nice to see you. *Fantastic* to see you." He turned, inches from my ear, and I paled all over. *"Did the two of you have plans?"*

The weak light held in Elowen's eyes bled, leaving behind a gaping abscess, unwavering from my face. "Nothin' concrete," slid from their parted lips, each syllable a jagged tooth tucked within their tense, unsure mouth. "Didn't realize I was interruptin'."

"Of course not!" Marian's hands, excessive in their enthusiasm, waved Elowen closer to no avail. "Of course not; we were just finishing up. It's freezing outdoors. Step in, step in. Do you like dessert? Plum pastries? I made them myself."

"Impressive."

"You will love them. I will set them out." He stooped his head again. This time, I flinched. "Leo, you don't mind?"

I numbly shook my head, drowning in the retreating sound of his footsteps. Alone on the porch with Elowen, I met their straining stare. Anger, confusion—neither graced their face. They were blank, the same wretched look I'd learned to identify when they were processing information that, for the most part, they didn't like.

"I left you a message," they finally whispered, quieted by the snow.

"I know. I saw."

Their eyes fluttered across my face, reading me like a book, its last page torn mid-sentence. "Got nervous when you didn't answer. Figured—*don't know*. You weren't on the schedule, but *usually*—" Before I could prod, they shrugged and wiped slush from their laces onto the calf of their jeans. "You just go on an' delete it next chance you get. Ain't worth listenin' to, now that I'm lookin' at you."

Dizzy, I placed myself right in front of them, even as that wounded dog of shame nipped at my ankles. Something about the way they said it lit me up—forced words that might've never voluntarily come out into the light like a pale vomit.

"It's only dinner."

Shaking their head disagreeably, Elowen slid a fingernail between their nipping teeth. Once it popped free, they stuffed their hands back into their pockets and stepped to me. Air suctioned from my lungs in a silent burst.

"Y'know," they lowered, briefly shedding that blank expression for something raw and red, *"you can tell me the truth."*

How could I formulate the truth into words with my mouth sewn shut? With a brain full of muck? Marian could've been back, hovering over my shoulder like a mayfly, and I wouldn't have known.

"I know," I offered. *"I do."*

They didn't accept. *"Do you?"*

Elowen's wolfish stare wandered past my face and into the entry—through the kitchen archway, through the living room. Much too late, the state of things clicked inside my skull; the pillows and blankets hurled corpse-like onto the floor, their borrowed jacket draped against the coffee table, the cushions sloping where my body had been wriggling. Their face morphed again. This time, the glimmer of canines and the flinching wrinkle above of their eye were all for me.

V. IVAN

"*Right,*" they purred, finding the step behind them. One hand gripped the railing for balance. "I'll let you get back to *eating.*"

The warmth indoors wasn't enough to pin me there as they left. Out onto the porch I went in my bare feet, bouncing down the stairs after them. I followed the zigzagging patch of roots at the back of their head like a northern star as they fumbled for their keys, unresponsive, my toes wailing in agony from the frigid earth. I hardly knew I was talking, only certain that in doing so I was further embarrassing myself. As they climbed into the cab I ducked into their cracked passenger window, glaring at the stubborn fumbling of their keys into the ignition, the truck retching around them before chugging to life.

"We're just having dessert," I was saying as I slid back into my body, the door of their truck sandwiched between us. I tugged on the locked handle, tilting up on burning toes. "He's already setting it out. There's no point in rushing home now."

"Pass. Thanks for the offer."

"They're homemade. Just stay for *one.* I'd be *glad* if you did."

The *hmm* that rolled from their throat crawled down my back. "Don't think I can do that."

Frustration rose in the back of my throat, a second pair of snarling jaws. "Y'know," I burned, bracing my hands on the window, "*you* can tell me anything."

Cranking the radio up, Elowen's face was cast in a mottled costume of shadow. "Then I'll call when I've got somethin' to say."

"Don't be such a *dick.*"

One spidery hand froze above the volume knob, their twitching fingers coiling into a fist around the steering wheel. Stooping, their shadowed face was ignited by the laundromat's outstretched fluorescence, a stare of complete unease pinned on my bloodless face. I felt like I'd caught a possum in a trash can.

"Don't be standin' out here talkin' to me when he gets done with that," they urged, dry and rusty. "It ain't me that needs your immediate attention."

IN THE END, YOU KILL US BOTH

Bewildered, I stood there in my stupid little outfit, the ghostly remnants of his hands on me, and I couldn't lie. I hadn't the power anymore, not when I knew they could see the truth and smell it on me like a sickness. Lying to them outright would do something irreparable to me. To us.

Whatever the fuck that meant, I felt it in my skin, my bones and everything in between.

"Go back inside, Leo," they demanded. Though it was soft, I felt scolded. "You'll freeze to death. I'll call you."

I flinched from the passenger's side window as it zipped upwards and the truck cut away from the sidewalk, powering past the laundromat and around Allenview's bend. I waited like that dying hound of guilt with the front door wide open behind me, bare feet pin-cushioned by sidewalk gravel, until Elowen's truck was no longer audible. Then I wiped my lips on my blouse, spat where the truck had been parked and forced my feet across the sharp stones all the way back to the steps.

THE DEVIL, YOU & I

Over the next week, I successfully drove myself insane.

I really had tried talking to Elowen about it, more than once. Despite the quiet, unsure air that loomed overhead I never once waved them *away*—hell, if they were truly upset, *they* should've been the one to keep their distance. *Tough luck;* Georgia's tacky purple couch was their midnight sanctuary, a flood of quilts and a glass of lukewarm apple juice with Ibuprofen, *lots* of Ibuprofen, and absolutely nothing to be said about Marian and his plum dumplings nor the goddamn mess of the living room couch seared into their memory.

Thursday night, I swore I'd find a way to expel the shitty little worm that took residence in my stomach and fed from my discomfort; no games. They were right in front of me, glossy under the TV castoff, their ankles resting across my knee as infomercials whispered them to sleep. I had prime real estate, sure, if I could've *woken* them—if I'd found it in me to reel them out of a sleep I knew they rarely endured. No matter how badly I wanted to slide out from beneath them and force them to talk, I didn't dare move; if they sensed my intentions, they'd clam up and withhold every damn word like they'd done all week.

No matter what bait I cast into their waters, they refused to bite. They refused to even *entertain it,* especially at work. Garbage duty, phone calls, order sheets to be filled out. I let them go each time with a pinched nerve in my side, aching for a word, aching to understand why beyond my own irrationality, *my* business felt so much like *theirs.* I finally caught that pin-chaser late Tuesday afternoon in the hallway behind all the reset machines, slatted by castoff light from the customer floor like sunlight drifting through blinds. They were alone, narrated by the electronic buzz of late-seventies funk whining from the headphones hanging loosely around their throat. From my perch in the doorway, I could see the tension puppeteering them—they knew I was there. They were just being *stubborn*.

"*Okay, I'm sorry,*" I finally burst. "Just *speak.*"

This was the first time I'd seen that expression on their face—one awash with blatant confusion that I wasn't sure was real. Dulling the volume on their walkman, Elowen spun away from their work, both of us cloaked in the backwards reflections of the bowling lane light strips.

"What're you sayin' sorry for?"

"The Sunday before last," I said, no courage to elaborate. "When you showed up at Georgia's."

"O-kay. Sunday."

"With Marian," I added, hitting the nail into splintering wood. Finally, as their face flashed with something other than complete obsoletion, I jabbed a finger at them. "*There.* You do remember."

Elowen cocked their head—*God*, they could be incredulous. "I remember, Leo. Just ain't really sure why you're apologizin'."

Neither was I. The need had fermented inside of me over the weekend, reactive to their absence, slithering out of my throat like a tough, chronic mucus. Without my answer weighing them down, Elowen drifted back to the machines with a sniffing sound that came uncomfortably close to a laugh. Something was hiding deep behind their sunken eyes, peeking at me, *dissecting* me. I couldn't grab hold of it.

All of me wished they'd just unveil their anger towards my secrecy in a way I found familiar. I'd gladly freeze if they'd just commit to a cold shoulder. I'd cower from a hurled cup or a raised voice, a bark, a deceptively soft spoken interrogation—something I couldn't possibly *owe* them. But if secrecy was the standard by which I was measuring things, there was plenty between Elowen and I that warranted dead silence. Why was I so ashamed of this? Why wouldn't the pit in my chest go away? Why couldn't I *rest?*

Was I broken?

V. IVAN

I lifted my head, finding Elowen's expectant face in the hard slaps of light.

"*Time,*" they repeated, their distracted gaze darting across the floor. "When're you off?"

I faltered. Usually they just *knew*. "In—thirty."

Elowen finished setting up and moved onto the next lane. I followed like a puppy. "I'll take my break when you get off."

"For—what?"

They turned to me and calmly lifted two pinching fingers to their lips, a crude display that any fourteen-year-old boy would recognize. "Like we always do. Right?"

I didn't answer—had no clue how—and they went back to inspecting the duckpins like I wasn't there at all.

B EYOND THE STENCH OF freeze-dried mushrooms, spiced cologne and Elowen's indecipherable, close-proximity sweetness, there wasn't enough pot in our collective possessions to strip me of my nerves.

I couldn't even sit between them; I dragged my feet to ensure Elowen climbed in first, because the mere thought of the two of them flanking me seasoned our entire session with a brutal nausea I tried desperately to toke away. Devouring half of Elowen's joint, I watched in swirling silence as both of them fought for the right to comfort like dogs trying to share a cushion. Ladling each other's laps full of surface-level conversation, baseball recaps, discussing the goddamn weather like I'd imagined Tuesday night, like I was the *only* one who found the awkwardness unliveable. Elowen set their legs up on the shelf that I was seated on, slicing the group in two. They passed the joint my way and I stifled a flinch when their fingertips got too close to mine, bathing in a low, distracting grumble of nu-metal that ground my eardrums to a pulp.

"You've been treatin' me lately, Marian."

I glanced up and caught the sharp curve of Elowen's throat in the cloudy daylight, the hard line of their stare darting across the cab from beneath the grey Rangers ball cap they'd begun wearing to hide their roots. Entrenched in both our damper moods, Marian shuffled in his seat at the head of the cab, shielding his discomfort with the fog of his foul-smelling cigarette.

"More than usual, you think?"

"Oh, *sure*. You've been gettin' high quality buds, right? 'Cause this—" Elowen draped their newly-purchased baggie over their palm as if to study the molecular composition of the dope inside. "It's real dense. Good stuff. My man."

A small, honest smile cut through Marian's nervous, watchful eyes. Coyly, he glanced at me—despite my eyes remaining glued to the coil of smoke fluting from the joint as it slowly went out—and chuckled. "Anything to please."

"Well, sure. I can *see* that." Suddenly the joint was gone from my fingers, and as Elowen hauled a fat dose of potent courage into their lungs, their voice rose through the smoke with the feigned innocence of a church boy. "It's just 'cause you an' Leo are fuckin' now, ain't it? 'Cause I never heard you say *nothin'* like that when you were givin' me crumbs."

I dropped the lighter in the midst of handing it to them. It didn't draw a single eye when it clattered to the floor of the truck.

Fucking. I could barely kiss him without getting ill. How difficult it was, just for a moment, to determine whether or not I'd started hearing things. That wouldn't have surprised me one bit; only Marian's chalk white face sold me on my sanity, his astonished stare drooling past the end of his cigarette and onto Elowen, who reached down and calmly scooped the lighter from the floor before my feet.

"*Sorry?*"

"S'alright," Elowen assured him. In fact, it was almost grossly sweet the way they smiled then, like a wild cat with sharp, finger-length teeth. "Not askin' for sorries. Just figured that was the reason. *So?*"

"*So?*" whistled from my throat.

"Is that it? The reason why you're givin' me your good stuff all of a sudden? If that's the case, then you oughta be giving *her* your good stuff. That's the whole point of that sorta thing, right? Hell, if you're doin' it

V. IVAN

for *me*," Elowen flicked their pointed gaze my way, inquisitive, "trust me, I *don't* want it."

What split down the middle of us then was something unspeakable. Some grotesque, hidden wound they'd sheltered away since last week, allowing it to grow pestilent and swollen. Had they thought of doing this after leaving me on the curb? Had they been driven home, tight-handed on the wheel, boiling?

I didn't find that in them. No hatred, no anger. Instead, honest concern accumulated on their scarred face, the debris of their care splintering in my hands, segmented by a hairline fracture of *hurt* that could've been fixed before now, before this, if they'd only opened their mouth.

That's what infuriated me.

Marian bristled, his back pin straight. The wrinkles at his eyes and lips collected shadow. Even if he'd been stretched tall and thin through medieval torture, he didn't begin to broach Elowen's size, but hate rolled off his tongue as if he were ten feet tall.

"*What a disgusting way to be,*" he whispered tensely, like he was scolding a pissing house pet. "Apologize. *Now.*"

Cold wrapped a thin arm around my shoulder. I wondered if he spoke to his daughter like that; like an animal. Suddenly, even through everything, I felt less comfortable sitting across from him. Elowen must've had the very same thought; before I could find enough anger to bite, they'd already sat forward.

"*Disgusting?*" poured eagerly from their smoking mouth.

"*It's fine,*" I tried breathlessly. I'd express the opposite to Elowen in private later, but I was buried almost instantly by Marian's smothering voice.

"*Apologize to her.*" He pointed his smoke at me and I flinched. "You do not get to speak this way in front of her. It's none of your business what we do, whether you are there or you are not. You don't get to *choose.*"

"Hell, were that the case, we'd already be *past* this."

Marian's eyes went white with disbelief. For a long, baffling moment, *neither* of us had enough words to string together a response.

"Leo's my friend," Elowen levelled in his contemptuous quiet. "Her best interests are *my* best interests."

"And yet, she is only your friend. Nothing more. Correct?"

The truck fell into a deafening silence. The breeze picked up and the light snowfall outside nipped at my exposed ankles, my numbed hands sandwiched weakly between my thighs like frozen, dead things. Every part of me wanted to reach over, take Elowen by their exposed upper arms and *shake them*. Shake the gentle calm right off their face and wipe away at it until I unveiled all the harsh words underneath like skin scrubbed raw. If they were doing this to spite me, even just for the plain crime of being left out of the loop, I couldn't *entirely* blame them. If it'd been the other way around—*well*.

See, I just didn't like to think about it if I didn't have to.

When I landed back on Earth, Marian had ceased smoking and had risen from his seat, dabbing his cigarette on the inside wall of the truck with thick, rough fingers. He'd gone almost blue in the seconds I was away.

"Out," he waved his hands. "Out. Back to work."

Elowen's joyless expression broke into a snort. *"Pardon?"*

"Get out of my van. You're wasting our time being here. Embarrassing your friend. Embarrassing yourself."

"Emba—" Elowen turned to me, blunt and deeply focused. Their eyes caught mine and I was jolted back into my body, pressed into the truck's cool shell. *"Am I embarrassing you right now? 'Cause y'know I'd never—"*

"Get the hell out of my sight."

Though I froze before Elowen's devastatingly chilly stare, I wasn't its intended recipient; merely collateral. When they found me through the gun smoke, they softened as I knew they would. "All 'cause of an apology? Sure—I *am* sorry, Leo. Really am. If I knew you were gonna get yourself involved in somethin' so unrewarding, I would've steered you clear *long* ago."

Marian surged forward and caught a hold of their shirt.

V. IVAN

In the brief seconds I was given to react, stripped of the motor function to intervene, murder flashed grotesquely upon Elowen's startled face. Murder in all honesty, two flattened black coins for eyes, their cinched lips drawing tight like the furious snarl of a startled dog, reactive enough to snap and sever an earlobe or the tip of a nose. Before they could grope for his hands, the moment keeled and died and Elowen was out and over the step, stomach first in the damp gravel, one knee bouncing off the metal overhang on the back of the delivery van.

I hardly knew I'd made the choice to stand until my body was wedged between them, swaying like a spinning drunk. *Enough,* I was spitting. *Enough. Fucking quit it, the both of you. Take a pill.* It came out mangled, and amidst my fear I'd likely made no sense. Marian was eyeballing me like I'd gone criminally insane, the clay mask of his face posing a million and one questions, why I was doing it, what I was doing, why I was on *their* side. If I'd had the time, the sense, the grip on reality, I'd have explained that only fights had sides.

This wasn't that.

Elowen wasn't swinging, or screaming, or threatening. They'd never had a hold on Marian the way he'd seized them by the collar. There were no clawed hands raking my back to get through me, trying to kill him. Instead, they were small and painted in dirt, silent as a slapped child as they wobbled to their feet and patting their blood-streaked palms on their work pants. Wordlessly, they stumbled into the cement-lined culvert a few feet away to grab their soaked ball cap, flicking debris from the brim, so red they looked sunburnt in the smog.

The end took place far from me, with Marian's shouting like a distant television playing through a thickly-insulated wall. Before I could determine who I wanted to strangle first, I lowered myself from the van, avoiding eye contact with Elowen as they limped across the parking lot in sopping wet sneakers, blood dripping eagerly from their fingertips. I stayed leagues behind, wrapped in a rained-on sweater, gluing myself to the bathroom wall as they washed their hands under hard, cold tap water. Marian didn't dare follow us any further than his tailgate.

Not a damn word all the way back into the bowling alley, and not a damn word when I disjointedly asked if they wanted help, so I wandered off alone to pry the first aid kit from the break room wall. They were sitting on the bathroom's flat-lidded trash can with their palms pressed tight to their pants and their cap tossed into an adjacent sink when I returned.

"*Go on,*" they begged, their voice whittled away. "*It's your turn now. Have at it.*"

I knew anger. Knew its presence and its nature, always close, always tucked against the back of my neck, fangs bared. It didn't strike despite its attendance, despite knowing it would later when the image of them sweating and filthy against the bathroom counter *might've* dulled.

No—when I looked at Elowen, anger took a step back from us both.

"Alright," I said still. "I will." Then I unpackaged a wad of silken gauze and began winding it around their gravel-shredded palms.

We stood like that for some time as I tidied them up, tracing my eyes over their muddy fingernails, the split seams on their shoulder, the dampened back of their shirt as they swayed beneath the bathroom lights. They stayed still as I secured the gauze with steel viper pins but bolted to the bathroom door the moment I was finished, stopping in its arch just to stare at me through the piss-stained yellow light, pawing at their wrapped palms like they didn't quite understand what I'd done.

"He doesn't suit you. I've gotta *say* that." A wild, jerking shrug. "Give a shit or don't. Do whatever the hell you want. It ain't my business."

I was at the sink still, rinsing my hands of their browning blood. A clouded lump of something sinister weighed on my throat.

"I know," I agreed. "You're right. It's really *not*."

Wide eyes, dark as sin, held me there. They slid past the bathroom doormat.

"It's not. I'll get over myself."

I worked the rest of that awful shift hoping to understand what they meant. What hill they had to climb, what hill I'd sent them upon. I walked home without answer, and when I came in the following morn-

V. IVAN

ing to hide and smoke out of the cold, the customer bathroom still reeked like old, rabid blood.

I STOPPED SMOKING ON Mondays and Thursdays.

It was my own idea; cut the cancer out before it spreads, score the remaining skin. My lungs ached, or I'd convinced myself as such, and I needed the break from pot more than anything else. I'd grown up around cancer, hung out around cancer, all my life. I told myself that I didn't want to get *sick*. I didn't want to riddle myself with it before I ever had the chance to form a life. All vague truths to keep me company.

Only somehow, in the days that followed my decision, the cancer started calling me—having swiped my number from some incredible source, a contact list or a discarded sign-up sheet, because Hell would've frosted over before Elowen voluntarily dished it out. I'd have been more pissed at the time if I hadn't felt so guilty; surely I owed him an explanation. Instead, I left him alone with the ability to leave long, question-addled voicemails morning and afternoon, to call me even if the morose way he spoke made me ill, even if I never intended to pick up, even if I had no answers to give.

Then the morning calls stopped and the evening calls began, pushing deeper and deeper until I was rousing between the dead hours of two and four to voicemails with no more questions, because he'd answered them all himself and was desperate to share his findings. All that was left was the switching of my shifts from afternoons to opens, something I'd previously bitched against doing, which made *asking* for them so difficult. Then it was *Marian* rousing me in the morning like an alarm clock, beep-beep-beeps of expletives, demanding communion, demanding I *listen*.

I knew I was being cold; I came by it honestly. I just cared about other things.

Those red-eye mornings kept the afternoon delivery truck away from me. Yet in their haze of green-blue morning light, I never found the courage to tell Elowen about his pursuits; beyond everything else, I was still angry—with myself, *and* with them.

It was natural to be mad at myself, so I had no need to search—the reasons were bountiful and I'd been made sure to know that my entire life. But being angry with Elowen came with its own unique collection of challenges. The truth was that it didn't matter how frustrated I became; I couldn't withhold *all* of me. I buttered my toast at the counter each morning, texting them haplessly, reeling when they answered. I accompanied them on smoke breaks, took my lunches in the passenger seat of their truck, bathed in the uncommon silence like a duckling in oil. My organs curdled at the mere thought that I'd wounded them in some irreparable way. I fell asleep writhing and still woke up with them on my mind. I took them everywhere with me, allowing the new quiet to salt my wounds until they were drooling, bound in red infection, my patience descending until I was inarguably *pissed*.

It was a gloomy, grouchy Friday before Elowen came around Allenview again, and I was quite sure they'd mostly agreed for Georgia, who had only one child old enough to behave in court alongside her.

For that reason alone, Elowen sat like a sloping hill on the living room carpet with Georgia's youngest in their lap, drowning in a shirt three times theirs size and painted like a macabre mural in splatters of yellow and swollen pinks along the cheekbone that struck the parking lot asphalt. Andy must've seen something in them that fine morning; though he'd never spoken to me, he had plenty of jabbering to do when Elowen started toying with his blocks. They'd just pushed the L into place at the front of the word LAKE.

"*You're gonna wait forever,*" I whispered, cradled by the deepest valley in the couch. "Just like me."

With their attention pinned on the little boy against their knee, Elowen never flinched. "What're we waiting for?"

"An apology. A late one."

"For which crime?"

"The crime of being a total asshole."

V. IVAN

Silence. Their eyes fluttered sideways and up, gliding along my face with flattened intrigue.

"For making comments like that out of nowhere," I continued. "For talking out of your ass right to Marian's *face*. You weren't even subtle about it, but y'know what? I don't think you even *tried* to be. *That* calls for an apology."

At the mention of his name, Elowen turned towards the TV with a grimace. "I didn't plan on apologizin' to him. But if that makes you feel better—"

"To me." My voice shrank, incapable of rising above a whisper, so I craned closer. "I thought you respected me more than that. Where did all of it come from, Elowen? Everything was fine. You didn't even *have* to pay him for that shit, he would've given it to you for free. And don't look at me like that. You *know* I'm right."

Elowen was staring at me, firm and bladed. Something haunted them, something so steady they'd surely take it home with them.

"You think I don't respect you?"

"Not as much as I thought you did."

My face had begun to burn an irate, stressful pink. When Andy noticed Elowen's attention had shifted, he began scrambling his blocks gleefully. Elowen's long gaze darted over my face, drawing thoughts together like string-connected pins staggered across a wall of newspaper cuttings.

"I *am* sorry," they said aloud, toying with a few ousted blocks. In the gruesome silence, they spelt FLOAT with slow and tidy precision. "Really, I—I know I sounded like I was talkin' out of my ass in the truck, but I meant it then, too. I'd never say anythin' to hurt you, but I did anyway. I see that."

Spit stewed in my mouth. "Oh, *bullshit.*"

Elowen's fingers froze over an A. "Bullshit," they repeated slowly, dragging in new letters. The fucking nerve. "Bullshit. B—U—"

"See, I don't think you're sorry at all."

I'd noticed it before, but I was struck again by the sheer lack of blinking that Elowen did. "I've apologized."

"I heard you. I just don't believe it."

Halt. *"So now I'm a liar?"*

Elowen wasn't afraid of being sharp, even if it cut me. No, something *had* changed over the weeks since that cursed dinner, something that sizzled whenever I thought too long and hard about it. Of one thing I was sure: wedged deep in the crevices of their mind laid something Elowen wasn't letting on about. We were both that way—jammed closed by insecurity, sealed by secrets.

You can tell me anything.

My Elowen hid things, and coveted themselves as I did, but they weren't a liar. And perhaps if I stopped trying to get them to speak, I'd have figured out a lot more, a lot sooner.

"*No*," I assured them. "But you're *lying*, and I'm not stupid, Elowen. You're *angry*."

Behind their still head, a cartoon duck rattled on about manners and alphabetical jingles. Wide, hardening eyes traced the lines in my own face, seeking the soft spots of my bluffing like a tiger leech.

"What am I *angry* about, Leo?"

It was more a jab than anything, and some darker part of it held weight. "You don't like him," I guessed. "Not even a little bit. You don't like that I was hanging out with him, even in my own free time, because I had to split it and spend less of it with you. You've been *bullshitting* me about being fine with it and I'm—*tired, Elowen*. I'm only—I saw him *twice*. If you don't like that, fuckin' *say* so! You have a right to say it. Why can't you just *say it?*"

They sure looked like they wanted to say *something*—something drawn-out and crude, something mean, something they'd been strangling with rubbed-raw hands just to keep down. Wide-eyed, pale-faced, a scarecrow on the living room carpet fighting back a grim sort of smile. The dimpled kind, the mid-argument tie-breaker—*if I was going to say anything, I would've said it by tearing a chunk out of him.*

I hated planting words between us like branching thorns, cutting my fingers as I tried to reach for them. I wanted to throttle them. I wanted to grab them and shake them and scream at them that I'd never

V. IVAN

wanted him to touch me at all. I didn't owe them, no, I was *beyond* that excuse—now, I just wanted them to *know*. I wanted to see their face transform with relief, as selfish as that was of the both of us. I wanted to see their shoulders lax, their jaw loosen. I wanted to know that I was *right*.

But they sat, the accusation undenied, their expression a reminder of why I'd given it up. Words slid through their beaten lips, nothing but an exhale.

"I want you to be happy." Before I could demand more, they asked, resolutely: "Does *he* make you happy?"

My mouth snapped shut like a bear trap. Elowen waited dutifully, as I knew the answer and still chose to say nothing like a goddamn *hypocrite*. After a while they returned their attention to Andy, reorganizing his blocks, allowing me the silence. Our conversation and the opportunity to continue it disappeared eagerly on the horizon. I didn't dare stop it.

Elowen left before dinner as usual, scared off by the prospect of food, or maybe the prospect of spending further time with me. I laid like a bloated corpse on the couch as the city grew dark. I rose once to slip outside and smoke, to feed Andy a few lukewarm spoons of mushy banana and carrot, then I returned and curled up even tighter with him like an iron weight on my ribcage.

When the girls arrived home, I hardly noticed. Georgia had been quiet for days at that point, her mood sullied by a smog of courtroom conversation surrounding the rights and responsibilities of a baby I'd never met. She'd spent all that afternoon guzzling legalities, and by the time she returned to the duplex she was deathly silent—I only recognized her through the scuff of her socks and the jingle of her coat as she walked through the den, as she nudged a few toys into the corner with her toes, as she peeled Andy's sleeping body off of my chest and spread an itchy throw over me. I burned the entire time she was in the room, and continued to char as her footsteps grew muted, separated by the kitchen wall.

It wasn't Elowen that ruined things. I made my own choices. I could've kept seeing Marian if I'd really wanted to. We could've spent more time, done more things, but I'd ended it as I always did before anything remotely decent could come of it. I needn't ask myself for the hundredth time *how* to make myself happy, or *who* I should be happy with. I wasn't as stupid as that. My best guess was this, had always been this, and always would be; there wasn't a single person in the world that could be happy with me, not for any meaningful period of time. That was the truth I knew. I'd been molded by the devil long ago: happiness would never fit inside of me. I no longer held the space for it to grow.

As I laid encased by the scents and sounds of Georgia's presence in the kitchen, I wondered when our time would be up, too. And that shook me so terribly that I didn't sleep a wink.

GHOST TOWNS

Something died in the Anchor's party room.
 Something nobody wanted to deal with. Something left for the morning zombies to tackle. All that remained were slashes of oily rainbow gore smattered on the polkadot tablecloth, shrapnel of sullied red foam noses and tattered balloons, lukewarm poundcake on the counter. That was my morning, bright and early against the salmon pink dawn, scrubbing down tables and stacking chairs, scooping frosting from the floor with gloved hands. In the days prior, I hadn't been sleeping; waking up held little difficulty if I never even made it to bed.
 Starving, the gloves came off around nine. Using the last clean solo cup as a plate, I stole a sagging slab of untouched cake and dug around at it, pulling apart the dense icing, letting the bowling ball of my head loll towards the floor—dialling into conservation mode, licking away crystallized sugar with my tongue. I stood just like that for some time, even in the face of passing chatterboxes and the grinding struggle of the AC unit adjusting the temperature above freezing. Some part of me hoped that someone would see me there and remove my malfunctioning battery as a courtesy. Hell—a slap of frosting across the cheek might've successfully set me straight.
 A slash of colour fluttered past the doorway—tan and red like a flailing robin, a ghost of the abandoned party. None of my business, and under none of my authority—the exhaustion of six successive openers had worn my brain to silt. Mashing the cake into an indistinguishable paste, I stared longingly at the clock above the water cooler, my joints non-lubricated and my teeth chattering. Elowen wasn't due for another

half an hour; by then I'd be nothing but clear mush on the retro carpeting.

I turned, staggering towards the door in pursuit of another task, and halted at the displaced sight of Marian, snowed-on and bewildered, bound in a cherry-red racing jacket that made him seem tougher than he was.

A mirage, I guessed, trying and failing to fight off a typhoon of panic. Just an image from my tormented brain, seeking things to fear in a place where I should be *safe*. I didn't cave. I wiped my mouth of slippery icing, dropped my plate in the emptied garbage can and moved for the opposing door, the one that led out into the back parking lot, to prove to myself that his truck was nowhere to be seen. It wasn't *anywhere* near the afternoon, let alone three. I wasn't about to be fooled by some shadow in the woodwork—not after all this time.

Marian dove to block my way, and the smell of him shot like a bullet through my sinuses.

His exasperated voice sawed through me, splitting the mirage in two. When I went for the door handle and his arm darted over it like a slash of blood, I spun for the exit on the other side of my room. He jammed himself pathetically before that one, too, his two open hands vying for me. My throat sealed like a tomb.

"Leo. *Stop, now.* You know I just want to *talk.*"

"Like fuck," I wheezed. "Get out of my way."

I tried to duck under his arm. That must've been a mistake, see—must've made him feel small when I did that, because he rapidly cornered me, grabbed the sleeve of the thin longsleeve I'd thrown under my uniform and thrusted me back into the events room to keep me where he wanted me. If Myra had witnessed it, she would've been *relieved*, because it didn't cost her a thing compared to a plane ticket and yet it sent me right the fuck back home.

Ely was crisp that day in my eager mind. Soft wrinkles of wiggling heat reaching like fingers from the dashboards of cars, wild sagebrush in jaundice yellows burying the legs of street signs, sunbaked dogs howling in the low humidity. My lungs cauterized with scummy dish water and

V. IVAN

soot. The over-encompassing stench of fire-split wood, ash in the passages of my nose, water in my eyes, soap in my fucking *eyes*.

Marian jerked my arm hard and I sucked back a lone breath.

"*—what she told you, but we could have a good thing together,*" he spat. Slammed back into my body, I wrenched my arm from his grip, bumping into the table. Even if anyone was in earshot, I was too afraid of what might happen if I called out. "*You listen to your friends too much. And when they do not want to see you happy—*"

The Carpenter house had walls shorter than those in the break room, with tears in the wallpaper and messy white-pink stucco. They reeked of hot dirt and Tropical Breeze air freshener, but smell of burning Pall Mall always rose above it. You could taste it when you sat down on the furniture, the cushions gushing tobacco spores into the air. Dad *never* smoked. Myra found it *disgusting*. The Lyons house only smelt like detergent and carpet cleaner and burning wood from the stove. That was it. That's all there was.

My voice wobbled as I fought for air. "This isn't about my friends, this is about me. If I don't want to talk to you—"

"*I'm talking to you now!*" Marian's hands cut maddening shapes through the air. I couldn't keep track of them; too busy trying not to pass out. "I'm talking *now*. Because I take you out, I buy you *drinks*, I am *kind* to you, and now—"

"I don't owe you anything." Humiliation clogged my throat. "You asked me to go out. You were *nice* to me."

"And now you think I am not nice because I am interested in you? Because I am showing initiative? Do you enjoy playing games like this with people like me?"

There were, of course, other differences between Lyons and Carpenter. See, the windows at Lyons used to open on both sides and swing outwards into the backyard, but Carpenter's windows jammed and leaked and shattered at the worst times. Carpenter hadn't the few well placed trees that Lyons did. It was so hot all summer in the clay-coloured desert, and in winter nothing kept out the chill. The locks on its windows didn't work, but we never used them. No one ever came to visit, and we weren't scared of anyone that might break in. It was nothing, comparatively. Nothing at all.

"*Not even a conversation?*" Marian stared into my face. "*You hate me this much? For what—defending you from your bitch friend?*"

When I looked at him, I croaked.

Through Marian's eyes, Kev poured over me. Marbled and warm like an oil spill, a familiarity behind those hateful lenses which taunted me from hundreds of miles away. I carved from Marian's pupils the image of his sloping figure on the sofa, a mess of greying black hair and a still-shitty beard, smoke gushing from his rotten mouth. There was a death pit in that look—I was well acquainted with the monsters that lived at its deepest depths.

I shrank so small that everything *ached*.

I'd seen a print of his mugshot once, years ago. His wallet left out on the countertop, hazardous material exposed to the air. The novelty surrounding such an artifact was the only reason I'd dared to peel it apart; he never left his valuables out of his reach, despite forever blaming me for anything he misplaced. It felt cursed to even know its existence, let alone *see* it; dirt-bordering his acne-scarred face, his wide, inhuman eyes, his mouth like an old scar snapped and split by the dry Nevadan air. His own name was etched on the bottom in ballpoint pen so he'd never forget where he came crawling from. *Welch, Kevin J.*

He was still there with me, the Devil. He'd always be with me. Even if I'd skipped town before everything had gone wrong, I'd have still found him miles away in someone else. How deserving of a lifetime in Hell, I was.

With all my strength, as cold as a curse, I whispered, "*I don't want to see you ever again.*"

That silenced him for all of ten petulant seconds. Listening closely, I caught the hum of Carpenter's ancient radiators on Marian's furious exhale.

"*I don't like you,*" I whispered, crushing my wet eyes painfully against my arm. "And Elowen—you hardly know them. So don't call them a fucking *bitch*. Don't *ever* say that shit to me."

V. IVAN

Marian regarded me like he was seeing me for the first time. Then, coming to a conclusion within the boiled material of his brain—cooked from a summer spent baking in a big steel box—he sneered.

"*She* is interested in you, too. Like I am."

Nothing came from my open mouth.

"She is," he cut again, the words numbing my ears. "Both of you. You're both *sick*. *That's* why you cannot see a good man when he's right in front of you. You're *blinded* by your own filth."

Rage's familiar moon eclipsed me, shattering over my head and piercing me with its shrapnel.

"I see *you*, Marian, and what I see is a grown *man* who can't talk to women his own age so he spends his time engaging with *girls*, teenage *fucking* girls, who want nothing to do with him! And y'know what I think? I think the reason I changed my mind—which I can do as I *please*—has *nothing* to do with Elowen and *everything* to do with you."

Much like Kev, I flinched when Marian lifted a finger and pointed at me, his wide eyes two bleached saucers.

"*You should find it in yourselves to repent for your ways,*" he swore. "*You are a selfish, heartless person. If I see you again, I'll make sure it happens.*"

Marian pulled from me and stalked towards the back door, finger wagging promisingly as he went. With one hand on the push bar he halted, sweeping his eyes around the room to survey the damage he'd done. Satisfied, he disappeared into the back lot, the November air nipping me as he went.

I hovered on that breeze long after it departed, just a child on a playground too scared to touch the sun-boiled pebbles. The worms in my skull began to whisper, all the potential outcomes of this conversation wetting the soil of my mind. My pulse delivered wild punches against my ribs, echoing the promise that at some unforeseeable moment, I would pay for what I'd done to him. For not wanting him. For whatever he deemed fit, at whatever time he deemed fit. Who was I to know? Who was I to say what he'd do?

"You slackin' off?"

I hadn't even heard Elowen come in, but there they stood at the furthest edge of the party table, their ragged hair flat-ironed by a light greasing of snow, sliding their knapsack onto the table's wiped-down surface. Parting with an odd frown as their icy-red hands buttoned up their uniform, forever coatless despite how shredded they were by goosebumps, they shuffled across the events room towards me, ducking in an attempt to meet my drifting eyes.

"That's one sorry face you're makin'." Fruitless, they shook away the cold. "Y'know, I'm pretty sure if the wind changes, you'll stick that way."

I was grimy and filthy and I couldn't get that mugshot out of my head. *Repent*. Repent for what? Kneading my fingers into my jaw with closing eyes, I lowered my throbbing head from the wall clock—for twenty minutes I'd idled there like a dead crow on the side of the road—until I could see nothing but Elowen's winter boots.

"*Marian was just here.*"

Saying his name aloud pressed on the fear like he might come back, and when I glanced riskily at the door I was all but subtle about it. Elowen, the *observant*—all they had to do was recoil and I knew they'd caught me. In a heartbeat their shoes slid from view, padding across the carpet towards the other side of the room, the back door popping open as if punched by a gauntlet, bouncing into the brick wall outdoors. The sound snapped like a gunshot and my attention flew to them.

A clear, brutal shiver broke over me.

Elowen was straight as a pole, hunting the backlot with a darting head and a jaw screwed too tight. Their pallid face weakened me—from it came the bubbling, inky murder I'd seen in their eyes weeks before, accompanied by something else altogether, something I'd never seen on *anyone*. It washed them white like a leopard in the barren snow, their wide, pinheaded stare growing frantic and ready to devour. I tried to prepare myself for what they might do if his van was still parked in the lot, but all I could think about was the Idaho drunkard with half a face. Corn-syrup blood and Wilhelm screams; I rubbed until black blobs dotted my vision.

"*Elowen?*"

V. IVAN

No response. Wind fought the ledges of their clothing, pinching feverishly at their wrists.

"*El?*"

Only once they found me did a flush of human emotion rub their hollowed cheeks with colour. Something other than the murderous nature of an indoor cat hunting birds behind plates of glass passed over them like a fog.

"I want to go home," I breathed. Snuffling, quiet, dissolving. "I want to go home." Then, as if I wasn't mortified enough, I started to cry.

Immediately Elowen palmed for their keys, and I wagged my head back and forth, pinching my lips shut tight. "Then you're goin' home," they said, "and *I'm* takin' you there. It's alright."

"*I'll walk.*" Then, to myself, "*I can walk home.*" Ely or Georgia's, I imagined Marian following me either way. My chest clenched and I winced, lips morphing into a wobbling line as fat tears drooled down my cheeks.

God, how *humiliating*.

"You're not walkin' anywhere," Elowen swore. They came to stoop before me and offered their hands, which I placed mine inside as trembling fists. They didn't squeeze. "*Hey. Look at me.* I'm not lettin' you leave by yourself. Not right now, not in your state. Got it?"

"*Okay.*"

"I've got my keys *right* here. I'll pull up out front and you can jump in."

"*Oh, God—*"

"Leo."

I met their eyes, recalling the daggers he'd swung at them when they weren't around to defend themselves. However angry I'd been at them before now eagerly melted away. I could've *killed* Marian for that single word alone. A blooming, aggressive migraine painted the walls of my skull; yes, I wanted to *kill him*. I wanted to maim him. I wanted to punch his head into the wall and hear it bounce off the cracked wallpaper, watch it pour free its contents in horrible shades. I wanted to let anger wet my mouth. More than anything, I wished he'd had the guts to say it again; I could get so fucking ugly when I was pushed.

When I wasn't *afraid*.

"Leo?"

"Mm."

I met Elowen's eyes. Something hidden swam through their stare, something that roared for murder through steel bars, a passing adrenaline in the eyes of a wild thing fresh off the kill. Whatever it was, it clicked together inside both of us like stolen puzzle pieces, sealing us in the events room together. As soon as I saw it, it was gone like a burnt out bulb.

"Nothing," Elowen whispered. "C'mon. You can sit out front and watch folks hit potshots until I pull up outside; I'm only parked a shot away. If he comes back in that time, he's gonna fuckin' regret it."

THE DEVIL HIMSELF COULDN'T have pulled Elowen from my side.

And not once did they demand any kind of explanation. We laid together all afternoon without question or concern, the sky puckering from pink to orange beyond my frost-hemmed bedroom window before diving into a deep, rolling navy. I passed in and out of sleep gracelessly for hours, awoken more than once to a rhythmic banging on my the inside of my skull, both imagined and all-too-real. Twice Elowen left my bed—both times at my unwilling expense—to retrieve extra strength acetaminophen and lukewarm water, though I'd made it clear that I could get things myself.

In reality, I'd stopped being sure. I'd gone and melted into a seamless nothingness on the mattress, beyond reach. My body was in Olympia but my mind was on leave in Ely's blackened Hell, just after the chaos cleared, all my goodness scorched to nothing but an ashen mattress hauled to the side, the surrounding carpet cratered like a dirt-rimmed blister, popped and peeled away to expose an uneven subfloor. There was little left of me to entertain; my existence boiled down to few old

V. IVAN

posters and photographs now splintered from existence, some powdered and others removed, ash-rimmed squares spattered on the walls where they'd once been hung up.

If I'd stood against the wall that day, would I too have left an impressionable outline in the soot?

Elowen's voice rose in the dark and I turned from that memory. Night had long filled the space and they'd moved in the time I was gone, parked now before the entry to my bedroom like a bodyguard. A towel laid against the gap beneath the floor and the door, the glowing cherry of a cigarette barely visible, hovering above a silken pile of ash dripping onto a folded napkin atop their knee.

"Where were you just now?"

I slid into a sit, my back to the wall where the exploded television sat in my mental mappings. *"Nowhere,"* I lied. *"Thinking."*

"Anything interesting?"

I wanted to be done lying, but the truth came out like a damaged record, bumbling over the beginning over and over. *"About—about—"*

"Don't make something up."

Their shadowed silhouette stretched its gangly legs. Like the rustling of a beast in the dark, I clang to their image in desperation for reality.

"It's alright if you don't want to talk," they whispered. *"As long as y'tell the truth when you do."*

I laced my hands over my face and peered through my fingers. "Just trying to figure out where I'm at."

"Georgia's," Elowen said without hesitation. I wondered why they'd sat themselves so far away, and why that even bothered me. "Round ten o'clock, last I checked. She's downstairs. I helped get the kids to bed. Was it about today? That thought?"

My frail heart stuttered. *"I guess,"* I whispered. "Starting to feel like I'm in a therapist's chaise, though. Just saying."

"Is that bad?"

"They didn't even *have* chaises in group, remember? So I guess I wouldn't know." In the static dark I caught their stare, hooked somewhere deep inside of me, tugging. When silence found us again, I fought away the invasive image of Marian's gritted teeth. "Sort of; to answer your question. Today made me think about it."

"It?"

"Home. Nevada. An armpit called Ely, north of Vegas."

"Somethin' special caught your mind?"

The stomach aches from months before crept close. I rubbed a hand over my churning gut with a quiet hum, a wordless disagreement I needn't explain.

Elowen's voice waned dangerously close to a beg.

"It's nice and quiet here. Lots of space to think, and you're thinkin' about it. So what's in Ely?"

"Nothing," I said after eons. "Old ground. Hotels. Schools. A movie theatre. Copper mines that opened long before I was born. Are you sharing that thing?" They offered me a fresh smoke from their pack and I shook my head. "Just blow it my way."

"There's somethin' else. Otherwise you wouldn't be thinkin' so hard."

"I don't know." I fussed with the blanket's lumpy spread, but realized quickly that my own body was the source of my discomfort. *"I don't know,"* I parroted to cover the terror. "I lived there my whole life. There's things to do, but not much to *be*. Shops and museums, parks and doctors. Dad lived there. Mom still lives there—whatever I had to think about, I destroyed, or tried to. So if you're looking to make sense of it, join the club."

Elowen said nothing. I shrugged the rest away, turning my face to the open window.

"Isn't that enough for one session?"

"This ain't therapy," they caved. *"It's just two friends talkin'."*

"So much for not getting to know each other, huh?"

Elowen's silhouette bent and shrank as they folded their napkin ashtray. *"Well, shit.* I never agreed with you in the first place."

"About?"

"Not gettin' to know each other. All *that*—" Their fingers fluttered up and down, gesturing to the crumbling brick wall I'd built between

V. IVAN

us. "That's all you. I've never *not* wanted to know more. And I've never found myself wantin' *less*, either, for the record."

I'd played the ruse well, but my desire to know them wasn't new. It was my own life from which I fought off interest. I didn't want anyone, even Elowen, to see me. Of course I'd always been *curious*. Even listening to them talk made me unfurl with questions; their odd, mushy twang, peculiar enough that I knew I only held a fraction of their truth. Though I prayed otherwise, I felt in my soul that Elowen could see me through the shadows as clear as daylight.

I feared how deep their probing could reach.

"S'alright, Lee. What took you home today?"

The image in my head was hardly Marian anymore. His puckered jaw took on a prickly, matted beard. Hot metal shavings flecked scars on the cheeks of that mottled, fused face of theirs. There was no more separating them. In went a winded breath as I crept across the words.

"Marian sounded just like this—*vile* bastard Myra and I lived with. When he put his hands on me—when—he grabbed me as hard as he did, it just—threw me right back there." My vision began to wobble again, and I seethed. "*Elowen*—you didn't see the way he *looked* at me. It was—God, I just *know* that fucking guy. I've seen that face everywhere. The things he was saying, all that bullshit, it didn't even *matter* anymore; I wanted to claw his eyes out just for *looking* at me."

Silence befell the room. After a moment I lifted my head, seeking Elowen's blurry frame against the door.

"I'm still here," they promised.

"It sounds fucked up. It—*is* fucked up. But this look; it's like nothing else. It's like they want to *eat* you. Not in a hungry way but in an *angry* way, like they want to scream at you until they hear what they want to hear, otherwise you're not worth much at all. All *I* wanted was for him to shut up. *Repenting,* he was talking about. For what? I earned the shitty way I am. I earned it 'cause of people like him."

I was well beyond catching my breath, exhausted by the memory. Only the soft creak of Elowen's chair kept the room alive.

"And that feels like home to you?"

"Bold of you to think I've got a choice in what *home* feels like."

With that exhaustion came a low, taxing nothingness from the painkillers. All my thoughts dribbled out of my ears, peppered black fractals of light danced across the ceiling. I *loved* that feeling. God, there wouldn't come a day when I didn't *ache* for that feeling. In the Echo, when I tucked in for the night and their top-grade prescriptions fell over me like a collapsing parachute, I used to map out those stars and try to find words in their glare. Nothing kind ever bounced back to me. I laid my head against the pillow and forced my eyes upon the wall, trained on their breathing, smoker lungs whistling in the dark.

"You're not *there* now," Elowen said slowly. "You're not even in *Nevada*. Far from it. If y'don't wanna think of it as home, then it's not. You can pick somethin' else. Got that?"

"I got it."

"And me," they tacked on at the last minute.

My heavy eyelids slid open just a crack. *"You."*

I listened to them stretch in that chair, but they moved no closer. "I'm around, s'what I mean to say. That makes a difference, too."

The cold, dead thing that pumped exhaustively inside of me stilled. Though Elowen might've spoken after that, sleep crept in and took me away from them, lulling me into a fragrant abscess until the darkness began to take shape again, starved this time.

FEED

MARIAN RETURNED THAT NIGHT. In a dream, no less.

If it wasn't for the clumping of time and the washing machine spin of my surroundings, I could've been awake. Each line in the unearthly emptiness before me was a painterly stroke, each vague sensation cast through a fractal lens. I'd been dreaming of something else before I was transferred back into that bone-cold bedroom. Something lighter, something further from reality—my childhood retriever, Tiger, playing tug of war with the forearm-thick bullring of a Black Angus. A melting cathedral of severed fingers and glue and spit and wire, coming apart in my clumsy toddler hands. A nine-armed mandrill chasing me through a decrepit alleyway that never narrowed to an end, walls of brick sizzling like sun-hot beach glass in every direction.

Still, the bedroom I'd come to know was more disorienting than any of it. Surrounded in a swath of cool, milky sheets, I reached across the mattress for Elowen—to make sense of the empty chair at the door—but they weren't anywhere and the room was frigid without them. Coils of colour danced across the ceiling, veiling my eyes.

Surely they'd just gone adrift in the muddy black sea lapping at the bed frame; out in the bathroom perhaps, or snagging a lung-full of cold, murky air on the porch. That's where the *real* Elowen would've been. I left in a frame-by-frame haze with the blanket around my shoulders and crept into the hall to find them. An overwhelming and brittle cold encompassed me, as if all the doors in the house had been propped open overnight. Maybe in whatever world I'd been suctioned into, the chair in my bedroom had been empty all night and Elowen simply didn't exist. That was leagues more frightening than the apartment, emptied of life.

The hallway towards Georgia's room stretched infinitely past me, draped in a liquorice blackness that made even my sleeping body shudder. Her door was ajar but no light crept through its razor-fine opening, not even the sharp, snotty slash of yellow from their bathroom bulb. I crept on, trekking around the corner past baby photos on the wall of Kennedy and Andy, quite like the ones that were in the real upstairs foyer. A thought passed over me the way they do only in sleep; a small explosion, gone as soon as it detonated.

Even the house isn't breathing.
Even the bones are still.

Silence bore down on me, suddenly sentient. It knew I was listening, seeking anything that could prove to my unsure mind that I wasn't wandering the halls in a fugue. All that greeted me were hair-fine sounds—the minute clicking of the freezer downstairs adjusting its temperature, the magnified hum of commercial washing machines purring next door. The whistle of white noise that filled all empty houses wasn't present.

Instead, something else lingered.

Something urgent and unrecognizable. A repetitive gouge, rip, gouge then a gushing sound like water inside suctioned cheeks. From over the banister that symphony echoed, amber light pierced the knowing dark and spilled upwards from the kitchen onto the bannister and along the ledge of each stair. I tiptoed across silent floorboards and rested my hands on the icy railing, stretching to peer down at the foyer below, hunting through my consciousness for a shape I could make sense of.

Each otherworldly stroke of line and light turned to hard, crisp steel.

Marian was reclining in the middle of the hallway. Lax and dribbling coils of heat like a spent candle, his pearl-glazed irises were devoid of warmth and pointed upwards in an oddly expectant stare, looking not at me but *through* me, towards God. Tangles of crystallized blood framed his open mouth, his throat, his cheeks, coagulating in the corners of his eyes unbeknownst to him—it was as if he'd been picked up by a

V. IVAN

gargantuan vulture and dropped from a hundred feet, left to spoil on the carpet of black vinyl garbage bags that blanketed the floor. The stove light trickling into the hallway snagged on chunks of gelatinous blood, shredded flesh, split fingertips—everything but the gaping hole in his chest, lined by shredded Persian silk. Whatever pooled beneath the puckered edges of that ribless pit, light wouldn't dare touch it.

Something was making a sandbox of him.

Something was digging for collectables, devouring what could be salvaged and toying with the rest. It was little more than an entanglement of crouching limbs at first, starving and desolate. Its needle fingers dove into that cavity—something stretched, something suctioned and popped, and there was no complaint from Marian as his eater stooped its head and began tearing at whatever it found with its teeth.

What viscera painted its hands was then lapped up by a meticulous tongue. Beneath a blue-black slick its palms were white and human, brittle nails rimmed with gore. It reared its head, peering directly up the stairs at me, and suddenly the waxing of blood across its craning skull was not blood but a zigzag of filthy roots. My sleeping body rocked with a debilitating shudder.

The dark found its edges and Elowen was terribly human beneath it all. No extra limbs, no pulsating fangs, just their moon-white face angled upwards, a predator caught feasting on a snake split from throat to rattler. Their eyes were hollow and focused, off in a distant dream on their own. Blood drooled down their jaw and forearms like rainwater, spilling eagerly onto the plastic beneath their knees.

There was no more chewing, no tearing. Hell, no *breathing*, both of us marble statues in wait. A sledgehammer of dizziness struck me across the face, slackening the strength in my ankles. I was the first to move and it was only to stagger away from the banister, my eyes sinking back into my head, bare whites exposed.

I left the nightmare forcefully, thrown into sleep with the strength of a shotgun blast, carried from the voracious scene at the stairwell by the sudden bounce of my head against the floorboards. A spike of light shattered across my dwindling vision like a burst of blinding sunlight, sending fractals every which way, spit swelling in my open mouth.

I entered the void, the picture of Marian's emotionless corpse burned into my eyelids, and in that silken emptiness the chewing began again.

T HERE WAS NO BODY on the runner when I awoke. No blood, no bones, no hollow carcass with a plastic-white face. I awoke in bed, wound in the sheets like a thrashing child, bent to the throes of a stabbing headache before my eyes even opened. When I did, Elowen's chair was empty—fear was the only thing that forced me off that mattress. I flew downstairs in a full-fledged panic, my cornered vision painted with bleach spots, only to find them glued to a chair at the kitchen island, playing Cheerio soccer across the countertop with Kennedy while Georgia fussed at something unseen over the sink. No more stark yellow light cutting through the darkness. The curtains were wide open, the radio was whispering, and my heart was *hammering*.

"Sleep alright?" asked Elowen, catching me idling in the doorway. They were already dressed in checkered pink, overseeing a barely-nibbled boiled egg, their fingers and wrists and exhaustive little smile perfectly bloodless. "You should eat."

"In a minute."

"Cereal?" Georgia turned from the sink, mid-refilling a zippo over its basin, fluffy hair in a mop at the nape of her neck. "Could have some toast. I've still got the toaster out."

"*In a minute.*" I followed the Cheerio flying across the tabletop like it was a detached eyeball, dragging silky connective tissue behind it. "Yeah—maybe."

I caught Elowen's stare and held it. The light burn of that dream framed them in a grotesque, blood-sticky cavity; an old photo in a brand new frame. I shovelled through the passive glaze over their eyes and dug for something deeper, some glint of awareness, and found only a still,

V. IVAN

black river unbeknownst to my dreams. I painted viscera over their lips and watched it drip away with nothing of substance to cling onto.

Without another word I waddled back upstairs and unplugged my phone from its fallen position behind my headboard, dialing the Anchor's office number. Nobody answered. I called twice and was bounced right through to a grating electronic beeping like Cap had forgotten to check his voicemails after a long day of doing shit-all. The next call and the next and the next wouldn't go through. Crouching at the edge of my bed and leaning into my heels, I prayed to a God I didn't believe in, but if there was a God cruel enough to build a life like mine, then a fleck of graciousness such as giving me a goddamn day off would be totally uncharacteristic.

I should start praying more, I thought. Then I rose and undressed, pasting my uniform onto my body and trying not to hurl.

Elowen was no closer to finishing that single egg by the time I returned. They'd long abandoned it, and their skeletal back was pressed to the wall beside the stairs when I returned. We were matching then, polos buttoned to our throats like Santa's two fuckiest elves. One long, bewildered look upon me and they went whipping their head back and forth.

"No. Nope."

I stared at the carpet, waiting for blood to bead around my sneakers. "It's four hours. I won't burst into flames."

"Just call in. It ain't worth the pocket change."

"Tried that. Cap's voicemail is full or something. I wonder if he even knows how to check it."

Elowen shuddered. "Then *I'll* tell him when I go in. I'll work the double. Wednesdays are dead, anyway."

"I've gotta do *something*, otherwise I'll go nuts. Besides, I need the money. *No*," I sharpened when Elowen reached for the thin slice of wallet they kept in their back pocket. "I'm already dressed. Just take me in with you. I'm not asking, 'cause if you don't, I'll just walk. I don't *care* how cold it is."

I wanted to be stronger than Marian's words, his looks, his threats, yet I couldn't get past that staggering vision, that magnetic late-night feast I observed from the stands. Elowen looked nowhere near as animal as they had in the dream, but I still couldn't shake the feeling that they'd *seen* me. That even alive and awake in the foyer, they could sense I'd dreamt of them, and was painting them red as we spoke.

They observed me the same way Georgia did when she had something caught in her throat that she knew I wouldn't like to hear, only Elowen didn't say a word. They plucked their jacket from the railing and unsurprisingly sacrificed it, swinging it over my shoulders, allowing me to stuff my arms inside the waves of denim.

Then, with fingers that tore Marian's ribs free like sun-bleached splinters, Elowen fixed their collar and opened the door, suckling at their shredding teeth as they guided me into the morning's fresh snowfall.

ELOWEN KNEW MY FEAR well, and kept the air conditioning cranked low and the radio at a high hum just so I couldn't think without being derailed.

An unfamiliar urge bloomed on that very drive. Not the adrenaline, which had drawn me like a puppet into their truck—that sense of ungodly fear had dissipated, and even my puniest muscles had begun to throb cantankerously. My body wanted a punch in the ribs or nothing at all, certainly not a truck ride through the damp mid-morning blue that crept over our heads. All the terror, my body's limits pushed beyond capacity—I was possessed, desperate to reach across the console and demand Elowen's arm for comfort, for something to squeeze and break, but the mere thought of touching them made my empty hands numb. No abnormal comfort would settle me. Marian scared me so deeply I'd begun to feel like we were on our way to Nevada. A worse, more indignant nausea flushed my body in a sickly heat and I curled up in the passenger's seat, burying that thought deeply away.

Elowen hooked a corner, dead air freshener swinging.

V. IVAN

"Don't worry about seein' him," they said. "If he comes around, I'll be with you. You've got nothin' to worry about."

"*Okay.*" Nothing seemed a stretch.

"He's full of horseshit. Can't take rejection, so he throws a hissy fit." We pulled up to a red light and I fixed my gaze past the business strip and across the scattered buildings edging the city as they turned to look at me. *"Hey. Y'know I'm right, don't you? There ain't any merit to it."*

Tucking myself behind their jacket collar, I found an odd, trustable seriousness in Elowen's presence. It was all in their voice: a low, surprising hum of emotion from their typically mild mouth.

"Nothin's gonna to happen to you," they steeled. "Not a *thing.*"

Only when I nodded did Elowen face the road again, steering us into the business park at the first glimpse of a green light. As we encroached upon the Black Anchor, I talked myself into taking long, deep breaths, counting them out in my head. By the time we turned onto our street and the red and blue strobe slid over the truck, painting us in mottled purple, I'd made it to *eleven.*

"Fuck," was all Elowen could manage, cranking us into a spot along the sidewalk.

All the Anchor's morning staff were out in the cold, mingling like seed-desperate sparrows on the grass ledges of the parking lot. Looking over them were half a dozen police vehicles, sirens muted, flashing lights casting rave signals across the asphalt. The *open* sign next to the sliding entrance was powered down and caution tape choked the doorway. Officers darted back and forth beneath it like ants, entering empty-handed and exiting with bagged paperwork, walled decorations, personal belongings. One swung by with a baseball figurine from Cap's desk, the next with the trophy jaguar from the wall, handled by baby-blue gloved hands.

My throat dried of spit.

Where the Anchor's restricted side doors dribbled off into a stretch of sidewalk that met the street, Avan stood like a decoy goose on a manicured lawn. The closer we got to the crew, the more their muddled, overlapping whispers grew. I didn't have a hold of Elowen but my elbow stayed pressed tight to theirs as I wandered mindlessly along, pinching distractingly at my exposed wrists.

"Isn't this fucked?" Avan asked upon seeing me, pointing with a lit smoke towards a cruiser stuffed to the brim with evidence bags. "They're piling everything in *there*. There's gotta be a neater way to deal with this."

"*This?*" Elowen muttered glibly.

Avan startled as if he'd just noticed them. As expected, he glanced unsurely around them to find me, his cheeks rosy in the cold. "You don't start for a bit, right? 'Cause the whole morning's been like this, and none of us are allowed back at it until we're spoken to."

"About?"

His wired gaze cut across the cruisers, displeased at how behind we were. "Ship's sailing. The Captain's a *super* sick fuck," he said eagerly. "Sadistic stuff. Who'd have guessed? Well—I guess it's not *that* surprising."

A deep, rotting chill rolled down my back.

"I thought he was just a *perv* or something." Avan glanced cautiously at Elowen, a spectre in the corner of his vision. "Uh—*you* probably remember when he wanted to hire a bunch of teenagers as wait staff over the summer for Pinheads, right? Remember how set he was on those skimpy uniforms?"

Elowen's displeased face said enough. When I unconsciously leaned away, drifting further from their conversation towards a distant, pitch-black thought that made every logical muscle inside me tense, Elowen caught my sleeve and held me with a peculiar carefulness.

Magnetized to the darkness, my body detached from my soul. That wicked dream licked at the corners of my mind, and a white-dotted dizziness slid over me.

"*And—so—how do they know that he—?*"

Avan sucked eagerly at the pink filter of his cigarette. His voice lowered, as did my head to meet him in secret.

"This isn't like some cleaning crew at a hoarder house, hauling out everything in sight. There's proof. Like, *everywhere*. *Cum* and shit.

V. IVAN

Sorry—not, like, *human* shit. I mean blood and fingernails and—*hair*. In his car. In the office. Hell, all *over* the place, for all we know."

The parking lot fell into an abrupt, echoing whisper.

My wandering eyes crept past the caution tape along the Anchor's neon edges, searching the cruisers for a sign of the old man. I didn't make it to him—instead, my attention snagged on the police cruiser backed against the Captain's office entrance. Zipped tightly in a plastic baggie and marked in dark, thick pen, a tangled lump of straw and beads sat atop the cruiser's hood. Baked in purple-black blood, left out under the daunting sunlight, the straw glimmered with fragments of bone and hair, glazed in a gluey residue.

Avan palmed for his lighter. *Fuck, I hate this thing,* he was saying, somewhere eons from me. *Never lights right. Fuckin' wind.* Elowen handed him theirs wordlessly and my sleeve slid from their grasp. *After all this shit's over, maybe we'll get the day off. Or if they've got enough proof, maybe they'll let us stay open. I've got half-cooked pies in the oven.*

I mouthed an answer, but nothing came out. Wheezing, I tried again, ending up with a dull noise of unsureness.

The mass, barely distinguishable as a bracelet, was amateur and colourful even beneath all the cracked gore. Marian's daughter must've done it up for him with the help of her grandmother. I bet he wore it with a stinging sort of pride. I bet when it'd been pulled off, it felt worse than shedding all that blood.

Slipping away from Elowen's light grasp, I drug myself down the sidewalk aside the Black Anchor, angling myself just beyond the caution tape so I could see the steps where Elowen and I took our smoke breaks, waiting to make sure neither of them followed. When I peered across the asphalt and found the dock empty, the afternoon truck nowhere to be seen, I clumsily pulled my hair behind my ears, curled up on the concrete and vomited, wiped my mouth on my sleeve, and vomited again.

And again.

And again.

DISTANT RELATIONS

Thomas Fowler—*the Captain*—was finally TV famous. He'd been putting up the schtick for years, only now it was true and he seemed rather glum about it. For the first while, he showed up diligently in mid-transportation questioning, tapped phone calls with tabloids, deep-dish interviews where he was dressed in blinding orange. He was ever-emotional and spitting everywhere, stripped of his coy personality, his head a mop of wiry, plasticine hair that drifted into his warped face. Demanding innocence, weeping for justice. It was hard watching someone old cry so much. It felt like I was peering in on someone's private breakdown, but then again, so was the rest of the state.

Within two weeks of the arrest, the deeper grime came forth, clawed from the mud by an ever-dredging siphon of journalistic curiosity. At first I'd heard it was around half a dozen cases, but the numbers swerved into double digits—workplace harassment, past and not-so-past. Sexual misconduct, indecent exposure; buried, dropped, paid-off. In two weeks, the colour left the Captain's television presence. Aged by a century, his skin hung from the sagging, brittle skull it sat upon. He stopped answering questions. He glared into cameras. He sat in the stands in the courtroom like a dead body, haunting every juror. During the last trial, which went swiftly and without mercy, he'd dribbled fat, thick tears onto the stand without blinking once, a wounded animal seeing death climb through the floorboards to take him away.

His expression never changed, not even as he claimed guilt.

V. IVAN

During those empty days with the Anchor shut down, when the kids were gone and there was little else to do but sleep or watch television, I listened to the updates over Georgia's couch-cradled shoulder. Once he got cold and unapproachable, once his mind began to decay from the prison food, I stopped watching altogether.

Marian did his best, wherever he was discarded, to haunt me. Each time I slept I was greeted by his gnawed-off face, pursued by his armless torso thudding around in the dark, stalking me from behind corners even in my waking hours. I started sleeping with the lamp on, casting hard blades of light into my throbbing eyes just to placate the memory of him. I'd hardly say that even *worked*, but it certainly pissed me off enough to redirect my attention for a few moments at a time.

I'd been questioned, as had everyone else, by two balding men with dark, crime-worn faces in a white walled interrogation room that reeked of disinfectant and old carpet. I was the last person to see him alive and that *alone* was worth hours of discussion, yet with those hours came a horrible, *knowing* comfort; I could tell them whatever I wanted, because the only man to challenge me was dead.

So Marian sold pot. That *was* the truth. He'd come to Elowen and I because we took smoke breaks together, but I'd never seen him otherwise. He'd thought that we'd be interested. Not something *I'd* ever heard of. *Elowen* wasn't into drugs. Elowen was clean, straight, recovering.

Just like me.

For days I awaited a call. A knock at the door, a pair of blood-scented handcuffs and the end of everything. Alongside Marian's corpse, I dreamt of how Elowen's face might've looked when my name was brought up in that white walled room. The familiar, distant guilt that came with that pulled the blood from my extremities.

Those men found nothing of substance, not an inkling of the dream I so desperately buried away. The last of Marian was painted on the documents and furniture in the Captain's office. A bracelet, tacky with blood, a debit card, two bills stuffed beneath a bookshelf with fingerprints and cocaine trace elements. Only after the dust had settled could

IN THE END, YOU KILL US BOTH

I understand the circumstances in which we'd been together, and find a shitty sense of relief in the radio silence.

Marian never said a word about me to anyone. To him, I'd never really been anything at all.

I WAS SITTING BENEATH a ribboned white table cloth, rubbing my thumb over water-splotched silverware, the first time I saw Marian's wife.

On a dying restaurant's boxy corner television, at that: stretched over the heads of elderly patrons, milky from years of steam exposure. She was dark-haired and apple-cheeked, an artificial blush keeping her alive in front of the bulbous microphone she spoke into. No matter its size, I couldn't hear a word over the restaurant chatter. She sucked up every drop of light that touched her, basking in the attention regardless of its reason. Ivory cotton spun around her throat, a heavy golden dragonfly pinning the hair back from her weeping face, which she swept with a ringed hand. The name YLENIA BARBANEAGRA hovered underneath her petite frame.

It was almost as abnormal as Myra seated across from me in her brilliant grey pantsuit, poking at her salmon entree and ogling at the television.

I cursed myself for ever mentioning the trials. In my desperation to give her something to pacify her prodding, I'd made Olympia interesting enough to visit. She arrived that morning before the sun came up. Hadn't dared ask, electing instead to let me know she was coming just days before. I wouldn't tell her Georgia's address until I'd been certain she had somewhere else to stay, somewhere she could crawl back to when she was done with me.

Three days was plentiful. Three days would last the rest of our lives. I didn't care where she was staying, as long as she wasn't around longer than that. Somewhere in the very pupil of downtown Olympia, in a hotel room that she'd booked by star rating, her briefcase and suitcase

V. IVAN

and business outfits and business *casual* outfits laid stretched across an unfamiliar bed. Why had the grey one been suitable? Surely she hadn't picked it for *me*.

Against the consistent chatter, Myra was a silent wraith. Her crow-black hair had grown down past her shoulder blades. Lengthy fingers draped calmly over her silverware, wind bitten from the Arctic circle, a permanent bloody pink dyeing her thick knuckles and crawling upwards past the wedding band that Kev had nearly pawned four years ago. It still sat habitually on her finger like an omen. With Marian's wife on the television above me like the voice of God, that gaudy diamond was all I could focus on.

"That *poor* woman." Myra adjusted herself snakily, splaying her fish in one paranoid slice. "To go on-air like that and expose yourself to the world. After such a loss, too."

"She's making decent TV," I muttered, dribbling oily dressing over the rainbow vegetables on my plate. Neither the sauce, nor the guilt of being cruel, did anything to spark my appetite. "I bet the networks are pleased."

Myra's head twitched disapprovingly. "That's hardly appropriate," she insisted, swiping a napkin from between us. My gritting teeth ached as she dabbed at the corner of her plate, cleaning up what the expeditor missed. "You wouldn't like someone saying things like that about you. It must be quite an unimaginable sort of pressure."

In truth, I might've appreciated some commandments for *my* performance. Sure, I was shabbily held together by tape and string and pot, but I was still *there,* wasn't I? Sitting at the table, passing through the motions. My *mind,* however, lost its tension—I'd left the present a few weeks ago, descending into a bleak nothingness, spiralling like a balloon with no tension anchoring me to the earth. It wasn't just Myra, though she would've been enough on her own to send me packing.

It was everything.

The fevered, haunting dreams. Being housebound for weeks, watching the Captain decay on live television, never working, hardly scraping enough money for cigarettes, mooching like a dog. It was my

IN THE END, YOU KILL US BOTH

last kiss being a dead married man who'd threatened me with biblical hearsay. It was Georgia and her kindness, the way I didn't deserve it. It was the Black Anchor in limbo, bought out by an up-and-comer from Southern California, according to Elowen.

And it was Elowen. Oh, it *was*.

The last threads of me were knotted around their fingers. In the gloom of those fragile weeks, something between us had taken on a terrifying, rocky edge. Against the shadow of death I clung to their presence, to be as close as I could get without souring things. In gaps of silence I eyed their uneven back, spinal knots spilling from the neck of their bargain t-shirts. I knew the hiss of their exhales in the depths of uneven sleep. I knew the whimper of their nightmares, the smell of their unclean skin. I knew so much, and so *little*.

I never told them about the dream. I didn't need any more difficulty when it came to Elowen. In that regard, I was *bountiful*.

But it was torment, the way I'd begun to wonder. I could've been fine with a few secrets because I *had* to be, because I knew nearly nothing of where or who they'd been before Olympia, before me. Now it scared the *shit* out of me and that curiosity sought to ruin everything, Elowen included, casting them in an increasingly monstrous light as the days went—a great hairy thing with sharp teeth and a moon-like face, blood hungry, eager, *solid*. I'd given myself plenty of made-up reasons to run.

And yet, there I was. Thinking of them before the larger threat of my own mother. When I roused, Myra was rattling her fork quietly against her plate, watching me with low, accusatory eyes.

I speared a chunk of steamed beet. "I'm listening. I hear you."

Her jaw rolled with a sarcastic click.

"Once you start making friends, you'll feel better about things," she said. "You need someone to talk to about everything that's gone on. Anyone would."

I had someone, but we chose to talk about other things, and from Myra I hoarded their existence like a dragon coalesced in gold. "I have Georgia," I offered instead. "I'm perfectly alright."

V. IVAN

Myra's hand waved as a wand might. "Someone your age, not a superior or a roommate. *Oh*—I *will* see that place you're staying in before I leave, by the way. Don't think you're getting away from that."

My jaw screwed so tightly it popped. I fixed my eyes on the television, only a bluish light burn left in Ylenia's place. "I *live* there."

"That's what I said." The prongs of Myra's fork snagged on the edge of her plate, her voice wrapped in a venom of fake kindness. "I just *have* to meet this lady that you like so much. You don't usually take to people like that, so she must be *awfully* special."

"Well, she's working a new job. So that's unlikely."

It was a convenient truth. Some bakery on the edge of town, early mornings and overnights—that's where Georgia had started to donate most of her free time. Something happened at the custody hearings, something that dried her bones to powder. I couldn't bring myself to ask anymore than I could bring myself to bite off my own fingers, and I'd seen so little of her in the past weeks that our early dinners became sacred. Some evenings, all I could do was sneak glances at her and hope to God she knew I was there. That I was available. That I was bad company sometimes, but I could hold the weight of her mind for just a while. It was the *least* I could do.

Myra beady eyes were affixed to the plate I'd hardly touched. A pitying smile framed her lips.

"Maybe you can *try* to arrange something. And while you're at it," she followed up after a puny bite of fish, "do *me* a tiny favour and think more about a future visit. I'm not—asking for a decision. Just think."

Haunted by the image of Myra at Allenview and the staunch, sweaty perfume of elderly folks and businessmen brining in their dark suits, I could barely see, let alone *think*—but I knew. Just from the way her words slowed coming out, I *knew*. Still I fell into her web, time and time again.

"*Visit?*"

Myra found me through my nausea, gun drawn. "Home," she levelled. "Ely."

I only blinked at her.

"I know we discussed that it's not a good plan, not for a while. But in the long run, I think you'd be better off at home. Closer to things you recognize, people you *know*. You need that sort of stability, especially right now. Don't you think?"

What stability could come of brushing shoulders with the dead things I'd left in Ely? I wouldn't last one trip to the corner store without falling into complete psychosis. I wouldn't sleep. I wouldn't eat. I'd die in a bed that wasn't mine anymore, nothing but a skim of bones on a splintered duvet.

"I'd like to know," Myra continued when I didn't answer. "We can't do anything about it now. But is that something you think could happen?"

Was that a glint of hope in her polished voice? Was that a tiny sliver of vulnerability in her unflinching eyes, or maybe impatience? I'd mistaken the two before, more than once.

"No." I rested my fork on my plate. "It's not."

Myra stopped chewing, and the AC perfuming our table went lukewarm.

"*No?*"

"If you want the truth."

"Well, I asked for it." Her tanned hands folded against the tablecloth. "Not now," she repeated, "eventually. You could behave for a shorter visit, couldn't you?"

I knew the homesick weight of my mother's hatred, the weight of her words, how she'd chosen them. My mouth ran irony as I realized I'd been gnawing on the gummy inside of my cheek.

"*Could I behave?*"

An unsurprised sigh spilled from her. "You know it's a valid question at this point, Lenore."

"No, that's alright," I strained. "Let's talk about—*literally* anything else." When nothing from the restaurant registered in my brain but television whimpers, I improvised. "See lots of polar bears in the Yukon? Do folks really have to do safety training so they don't get themselves mauled? Have you ever *seen* anyone get mauled? Is that a higher risk for your patients than the earaches you're treating?"

The eyes I'd inherited bore down on me. Ogling like I was brainless—like I was the only one not grasping the joke.

"There's a certain degree of forgiveness you must have in order to make life work for you, Lenore." I bet she thought she sounded so smart, climbing the saddle of her goddamn high horse. "Please tell me you grasped that much during your stay, at least."

"Oh, *forgiveness?* So *that's* what I'm missing."

The truth laid like a flattened house cat on the side of the road, slinking tensely from Myra's pinched mouth. "He wants to make amends. And I think you should take some time to consider that."

Everything blistered. Suddenly, the threads of my own sweater were hair-fine and biting. The shard of carrot stuck at the back of my molars splitting my gums. A warm, sick throbbing filled my belly full of warm pebbles, and I lifted my gaze from the depressing pile on my plate.

"*Make—fucking amends?*"

Myra couldn't even restrain a conscious glance at passersby. "*Lower your voice, please.*"

"And how could you possibly *know* that?"

"It's my opinion that he is. We've talked about it extensively. It's really—a big part of the reason I made this trip."

There was the kicker; she was clear from the start, but it didn't strike me until that moment and when it did, it punctured an artery. Losing blood rapidly, I tipped closer to my plate, spinning, circling that word. That *specific* word.

"*Extensively—so—so you're still—*"

Myra pointed the heft of her disappointment upon me, speechless. When I laughed it was in fury and not humour, bubbling at the first glint of worry in my mother's eyes.

"What in the ever-loving *fuck.*"

"Lenore."

I lifted a hand to speak but dropped it onto the table's edge when the words spun out of my control. All that time in the polar caps could've been worth something, the very birthplace of a fresh start. Myra never wanted a fresh start, though. If she did, I wasn't certain a half-assed apology could absolve the broken bones in my throat.

"*You.* Oh—oh, *God. Wow.*"

Myra raised a mirroring hand; I nearly vomited on the spot. "Lenore, if you'd just give me a *chance* to explain before you go rushing into things—"

I rose with a familiar, knotting dizziness that budded behind my eyelids and palmed my pockets for my keys. "Amends. That's—that's—*what?* An *apology?* Just *his?*"

Myra's eyes cut around the room, ensuring the few elderly folks in the breakfast nook nearby weren't staring. People she didn't even *know.*

"Look at me," I demanded, winding skywards. "You're both still living there, aren't you? In the same *house?* You didn't even *move,* did you? You're—And he's—"

Myra retrieved her fork and brushed a thick tendril of hair calmly behind her ear. "Sit. You've got a lot to say."

I gazed at her until each similarity we shared began to mar. Until our faces were complete opposites, absent of the features we'd both inherited. Until that filthy *fucking* rhinestone on her finger was all I could see. Once I'd taken my entire life's fill in those fragile seconds, I folded the napkin I'd soiled and dropped a twenty atop my plate.

"Enjoy your fish." I salted my words. "Try not to choke on any fucking bones."

Metal and porcelain clattered together; from the corner of my eye, Myra shielded her face with splayed hands. Like I was a dog, and she was the tormented owner who couldn't touch me without fear of being bit.

"Oh, Christ. Lenore, *sit. I didn't raise you to fly off the handle like this.*"

She committed to her role by not moving an inch as I fled through the restaurant's double doors in an airless stumble. I dodged the cab drop off as a group of college-age kids spilled onto the sidewalk, shrouding me in cabbage rose and nicotine perfume, marching myself down the street and rubbing away the vinaigrette aftertaste with the neck of my

V. IVAN

sweater. Once I was far enough I lit a cigarette, sucking in tarry puff after puff as I scoured my phone for voicemails, retrieving one from Elowen a month back containing half-drunk documentary recommendations relayed from their eldest roommate. I forced my pocketed headphones into my ears and listened, parking my ass on the edge of a wooden planter until my breathing deepened and my anger cooled into hard, unflinching steel. Only then did I walk myself home.

There was a hapless, frightened child inside of me somewhere that could've forgiven Myra if only for the nostalgia. It was often that I had to remind that girl that she was motherless, that she walked the streets in a body much larger than she felt she needed, one she'd spend the very remainder of her life swallowed by. I'd scoured that body over and over in search of its sick points. Still, I'd yet to discover a part that could do such a gracious thing in Kev's name, save for a deep, creeping rage that defined forgiveness as swallowing him whole. *That* was amends.

That was peace.

UNSURPRISINGLY, ELOWEN WAS ALREADY at Allenview upon my arrival.

With the kids in bed and Georgia parked at the kitchen table with her headphones jammed in her ears, I crept into the hallway just as Elowen emerged from the den, dripping with dim lamplight. They asked if they could touch me before greeting me—I agreed, only because I'd caught their shadowed hands mid-rising to push wet, stray curls away from my face and behind my frozen ears.

"She doesn't mind you being here?"

"She's payin' me to babysit tomorrow." Upon seeing my expression, "You pay your rent in smokes. No cut for you." They unhooked my bag from my shoulder without touching me and ushered us upstairs into my bedroom's chilly arms. Across the alley, an evening ensemble of roofers lined up their beer cans on the cement overhang, the warming stench of day-old tar wafting through my split window.

IN THE END, YOU KILL US BOTH

Aching, I fled to the dresser and grabbed the first soft bundle my hands could find. The window slid shut with a grunt, followed by the shuffle of bedclothes. I peeled off my sweater in response, my slick back beet-red in the awkward quiet, and redressed in a weighty silence. When I turned, Elowen was already draped across the bed, their purple-rimmed, sleepless eyes pinned on the ceiling.

Eagerly, I dragged the curtains closed and climbed in next to them.

There would be a goodnight, a tug of the comforter, a ritualistic arm-to-arm brush as Elowen rolled to face me. I'd gotten used to having them in my bed, though I woke them up most nights mid-flight, dry heaving and spitting nonsense about dreams and nightmares and the foolish Ely heat, sweat tracing my sleeping calves like cottonmouth snakelets. They never complained. Not aloud, anyway.

It was ghostlike the way Marian came to me, the dimpled thumbprints he'd left on my subconscious. The dreams rarely featured him yet he appeared punctually, even in the odd and surreal expanses with puffy mushroom trees and oblique cities of multicoloured melting buildings. There he'd be, bleeding in the background, shackled around the ankles by his own glittering guts, his long-deflated eyeballs resting inside the hollow cradle of his skull. Taunting me, asking why I didn't save him, asking why we couldn't try again, asking if I wanted to go out to dinner one more time, a great Thai place on Graigola, the very best. Always punctuating each sentence with the last thing he'd said to me. Elowen and I—broken, bathing in sin, helpless. In need of repentance.

It made me wish I was *capable* of holiness. I knew plenty of folks that needed to repent, folks more capable than me. I was guilty for things—had been born guilty, you could ask *anyone*—and for the things I was not guilty I often felt the crippling weight of responsibility. I had nothing to say to God that wouldn't get me in trouble. Despite that, none of what *we* did was *wrong*. If I was born guilty, then I was born to be this close to them, too; if anyone else but Elowen dared to lay with me in such sobering silence, I wouldn't have lived through it. It was how things began, and how they remained—raw instinct, the way some elephants walk hundreds of miles in the killing summer heat only to march back

V. IVAN

home empty-handed. Necessary but misunderstood, only knowing that their reasoning was far beyond their own comprehension.

"You're gone again."

I found their expectant stare, glinting in the dark like forgotten marbles, inches from my face. *"Did you say something?"*

Hesitation stalled them. After a brief pause, they asked, "Is this it for tonight?"

"Is *what* it?"

"Sleep? Nothin' else?"

I traced the haloed curl next to their ear with my eyes, the crude scar beneath their pierced earlobe. The urge to squirm took hold of me, itching against the butterfly bedspread, a staggered pattern like globs of soot in the dim light. *"What else is there?"*

Elowen swallowed tenderly, a wordless response. Their knuckles brushed against my stomach and I flinched, settling once I realized they were only adjusting.

"Just thought you'd wanna talk about lunch." They worked slowly, tasting each word with care. "You were stressin' before, and you're stressin' now, too. Did y'think you were doin' a good job of hidin' it?"

I ran a hand up my neck, worried they might hear my pulse spiking. *"No,"* was my answer, whistling at the back of my throat. *"I left that back there. I'm with you now. It's past me."*

Sucking at their tongue, the silent flex of Elowen's jaw prepared me for their whispered sigh. *"Leo."*

I draped a wrist between our chins. *"Okay, alright. So it was fucked. But I knew it was going to be. I think—I definitely made it a little more fucked, too. Don't get me wrong."*

"That's—"

"I did," I whispered, turning my nose to the pillow. "I set expectations. It'd been so long since I'd seen her that I sort of—punished myself by finding her in my own reflection. Now that she's here, it's wild just how different we look. I hardly resemble her at all now. When I walked in, y'know—I looked past her twice before I realized who she was." My

eyes cut to Elowen, searching deeply for their disapproval. *"What kind of asshole forgets their own mother's face so quickly?"*

Elowen's eyes traced along the hill of my cheek, avoiding my stare. Words coiled on their tongue, fighting to get free, ground to a paste by their teeth instead.

"It's past me," I assured them. "It's past me. We talked about bullshit, and she's—so fluent in it. I forgot how bad her *taste* is. Lunch was just a steaming plate of hot garbage. Plain greens with a dish soap glaze; it was fucking pukey."

A humorous exhale shot from Elowen's nose. "Couldn't've been *that* bad."

"It was," I assured them. "Never heard of the joint, and now I've gotta wipe it from my memory. If their ancient clientele don't want the sugar-free Jell-o they get back at their nursing homes, I'll take it over those mildewy vegetables *any* day. No, don't laugh. I'm being *so* serious."

But they did—that uneven, wild giggling you might hear from miles away across a night-blanketed safari. It unnerved me when I hadn't known them—now, my stomach bottomed out from another inexplicable feeling. Something more uncomfortable than that. Something stinging.

For weeks, I tried desperately to pinpoint it—some crossbreed of shot nerves, stomach pains, a skin-tingling fever, the horrendous byproduct of them all. I blamed it on Marian, but quickly realized it wasn't him that triggered it. Whatever it was, I'd become so overwhelmed by it that I hardly remembered life without its ache—and at the oddly sanctimonious shift of Elowen's body towards mine, my mouth permeated with spit.

When they asked if they could touch me again I nodded, and as their fingers curled into the fine hairs beneath my jaw, I did my best not to beg: *"Don't pull. It knots when it's wet."*

"I wouldn't," Elowen said. Then their breath fish-hooked my bottom lip, moody with cinnamon gum and nicotine, and they pressed their open mouth against mine.

V. IVAN

Whatever proboscis creature had been growing in my unsettled stomach hurtled forward and took a chunk out of me. Sank its teeth into my plush throat and ripped, dribbling air into Elowen's eager mouth. Their kisses came languid and curious, peppering two on my trembling lips before something wet and tender grazed my teeth.

With my rolling eyes squeezed shut, I laid bare to the chill that slid over me.

I'd thought about this before. In passing, in the brisk infantile morning as the world slept and the streets were quiet. Just once before *everything*, and then once again on a recent lonely night, but it'd been just a harmless thought, a passing glimpse of desire that slid down their wall-facing shoulder one evening, their rising and falling ribs a hill I'd wondered about climbing. I never found the courage to think about it again, only the cowardice to hide it away like a bloodied sheet. My fingertips flirted beneath the edge of their sleeve as a sudden, staggering urge to hold them burrowed parasitically inside of me. I wanted to mimic them, cocoon them in my bare skin, tie a noose of my fingers and feel their throat rest upon it. But by the time I'd built the courage to give back they'd already retracted, wiping a dot of spit from my cheek.

Inside my skull, a swell of bees buzzed to and from, doused in flushes of pollen, the remainder of my compromised thoughts parting for a hive miles away. Atom-sized flashes of electric white peppered the corners of my vision. Elowen's thumb scrolled over my ear.

"*Leo?*" they whispered. *"Are you gonna puke right now?"*

I wheezed: *"I'm dreaming."*

That murky afternoon faded into a whisper, pilling on the bed sheets beneath my head, dripping from my ears like spinal fluid. Horribly, Elowen's hands left me.

"*Stay asleep, then,*" they whispered, undefeated. *"I'll come with you."*

My mind would swirl until the first hours of the morning when I'd exhausted every facet of my brain, spinning sorely into a deathlike sleep. I'd been muted by Elowen's mouth—maybe I'd remain that way, with the ghostly impression of their lips on mine, unless they kissed me again. I could've asked and they might've done it, but they would've laughed at me for being so worked up. My silence was well spent, yet torturous all the same. Greater and more agonizing than *anything* I'd ever felt.

That night I dreamt of Marian in the same way I'd dreamt of him in the weeks since his death, only his body was in the bedroom this time, not the hallway or the stairwell as I went for a midnight glass of water. Idling by the bed, guts unspooled like a great wind of thread, grinning like a split-cheeked lamb. The *feature*.

There is an end, he said, but he didn't sound like himself. His voice was nasally and high and dead. *There is an end, and you'll be lucky to see it.*

Who keeps the Shepherd safe from the wolves once he's been seduced by their bleeding fur?

Marian folded himself into the cushion atop the corner chair, a symphony of crunching bone and popping cartilage, a tight papier-mâché square in waiting. When I awoke the next morning, Elowen was tip-toeing down the stairs and the chair was waiting, unencumbered by broken limbs.

Where the line between that dream and the others blurred into reality, I hadn't any clue.

BRAVE LITTLE SURVIVOR

I'D GROWN TIRED OF dreams. Tired of that which plagued me even when I was no longer asleep. So I waited in bed with the rotten fragments of that nightmare until the sky swelled with early morning blue-black, until the front door dipped shut and the mangled sound of Elowen's truck engine dribbled down the street. I bundled up until I was twice my size, crushing the painful tingles in my stomach and heart. I'd put an end to the dreams. At the very least, I'd dissect them until they meant nothing anymore.

That was the plan. Only when I dragged myself down the upstairs hallway and to the stairs, a cherry pit of fear sprouted in the lining of my stomach, rooted in the hazy, dreamscape glow of yellow grinning at me from the edges of the railing. That deathly light—lemon-curd and glassy, brutal against the morning blues, pilled on the walls atop the landing. I was shell shocked for a few debilitating seconds before I could walk again, my fingernails scraping the railing as I glanced feverishly below.

A breathing body clad in a nutmeg apron and work pants tiptoed back and forth across the living room carpet. Georgia's arms, tan in that golden light, threaded through the boughs of a plastic pine tree, its feathered branches stretched in uneven sprays. I shrank down the stairs, arrested at the bottom with my side melted into the wall. Only the crinkle of unfurling instructions burst the den's web of silence—it was entirely premonitory the way she spun around and caught me, wrinkled booklet in hand, masked from the light.

"*Fuck. Did I wake you?*"

I wiped the murderous dream from my mind, rising and creeping towards the glistening martyr set before the living room windows. "Couldn't sleep. Not your fault." I glossed over pre-lit bulbs, scattered upwards to the tip of the tree, inches from the ceiling. "I thought you nixed the idea of a Christmas tree this year."

Georgia's shoulders drooped, her ponytailed hair chaotic from a night spent with yeasty, heat-gushing confection ovens. She fell upon the tree again with worn hands, her back pointed at me, tightening a loose bulb until it sprung to life.

"Yeah. I said that, didn't I?"

Something stalled her, prompting a glance back across the carpet at me with an expression I could've clocked even in the dark. The same look that told me there was something lingering inside the confines of her mind, then on the edge of her parted lips, tracing my figure in the tree light. I didn't need to ask about the coat I'd brought home to her; she'd worn it thoroughly.

"Tips around Christmas are hefty," she said, unconvincingly. "You leavin' right now?"

An instantaneous shrug. "Don't have to."

Georgia held onto a single blue bulb, warming her cool fingertips. "Help me dress it, then," she asked carefully. "So it's all pretty when they wake up. I'm dyin' for a little joy."

Without question I abandoned Elowen's jacket on the couch, taking to the ornaments like a bored kitten. With the two of us staggering candied reds and greens across the branches, the work was miniscule. We powdered the boughs with cheap silver tinsel that snapped with light each time we nudged the branches. Only the shuffle of our muted footsteps waltzing around one another in the brutal silence, no Christmas music jingling on the radio, no whispered conversation.

Hinging on the last few ornaments, dull light crept through the curtains, casting grueling shadows across the branches. The sun's sleepy rise pushed me to focus away from the dream. I tried my damnedest to pay attention.

V. IVAN

But Georgia was so much to take in, and that was grand because this was something I loved to do so very much; finding peace in the baby hairs along her hardened jaw, the sugary scent of her conditioner when she reached past me, the scrappy, illegible name tattooed on her wrist in flailing cursive. Shuffling cards like a Vegas professional, Baby Phat pants in varying shades of denim, the baseball bat in her bedroom corner peppered in Kennedy's Powerpuff Girls stickers. In the creeping daylight, I saw for the first time what'd always been there—the exhaustion of wearing two lives, the fatigue of running at full-tilt into oblivion, auto-piloting the bulbs onto the tree with a rubber mask of pleasantry slipped over her reddened skin.

It ached. It ached to know I couldn't reach inside and drain it like an abscess, as many times as needed. Horror and desperation, the culmination rotting my heart—she'd die one day and I'd never be remotely ready. A gauntlet of fear struck me so forcefully I lost track of the empty boughs I'd been dressing.

"I want to say something," I whispered, *"but I don't want you to take it the wrong way."*

A spectral flinch split across Georgia's face. "Well, we'll both live if I do."

How far from the truth; I could crush her if I wasn't cautious. So I went tenderly into that dance, tucking the necessary words neatly among the pine needles.

"Are they letting you see Bela for Christmas?"

Georgia fell brutally silent, as expected. I waited as long as she needed, only certain she was still alive by the sudden clearing of her throat after a long, arduous silence. All I could think of was the rotten taste I'd just put in her mouth.

"No." A great heaviness sank her shoulders and burrowed deep into her throat. "Not for Christmas. We'll visit a few days after. Maybe Boxing Day, with supervision."

I dredged for the last silver baubles at the bottom of the tote, her words a noose looped keenly around my throat.

"I see what you do for the kids, y'know," I told her, hating the way I sounded when I said it, always dancing on the brutal edge between constipated kindness and condescension. "I could *help*. If that's something you need. I could talk about it to someone who matters. I could vouch for you."

From Georgia came a wounded sort of laugh, if you could even call it that. *"I don't need a voucher."*

"But if it would help—"

"It's not about *character*, Leo," Georgia shot, her voice lilting above a whisper. "It's not about not knowin' who to talk to, it's not about what I *do*, and it's not about a lack of vouchers. So don't even bother."

The house gave a great, fussy shiver. As I anxiously searched the boughs for an empty branch to hang myself on, neither of us said a word. Then Georgia's hands fell from that golden light, tucking into the pocket of her apron.

"Look—I'm sorry," she mumbled genuinely. "That wasn't about you. I know—where you're *comin'* from, but—you didn't *know* me before I was in the Echo. I wasn't the person I am now. And on the inside, the person I was becomin'—it was goddamn ugly. I was so much better at handlin' all this shit before my stint. I'd ask people's names and I'd remember 'em. I had all my babies with me, I had a little house over in Poulsbo. I *had*. But I shacked up with some nasty folks, got into some—ass-backwards situations. I went batshit. Hurt myself real, *real* bad."

My curiosity writhed like a caged, wailing animal. I'd never dared ask Georgia what she'd done. She'd never had the courage to ask me either. Either way, there was relief in never knowing each other's worst parts.

Something akin to anger curved Georgia's brows. She went back at the tree, her voice hushed like God was listening.

"See—when I look at my little girl, I *know* I named her after someone important. Someone I really fuckin' treasured. But for the life of me, I can't remember who. Y'don't know what that's like. I'm *glad* you don't. I wasn't a good mom when Bela came into this world, and I'm not the only person who knows that. Second chances—they're nice if you can get 'em. But getting 'em's the hard part, and once you've got 'em, if you're anything like me, you'll waste all your time trying to figure out whether you deserved it in the first place. I've had vouchers. *Lots*. But it doesn't matter, 'cause—because—"

"I know," I said, foolishly. "I'm sorry. I'm sorry." For a million things.

Georgia took a step back from the tree and gave a great sweeping look over our work, past the work, through it and beyond. She wasn't *really* checking. Even paralyzed at her side, I knew that much.

"It won't be enough for me, just to see her once in a while," she said, "but that's what I get now. All I can do is try to be better for what comes after, once all the bad shit takes a backseat and the healing can have some room to start."

Her distant stare landed on me, snagging the light, absorbing it before the sun crept past the blinds and stole its thunder.

"Sometimes second chances just feel a little too close to punishment. That's all."

A LL THE WAY ACROSS town, I debated taking a detour to avoid The Green Nomad.

I was too much of a pussy to walk on that side of the street, even bundled up beyond recognition. Under a fog-laden mist, the bar's entry glowed in an ultra-maroon whisper and the sidewalk reeked of piss and beer and mint-scented cleaner, muffled music chattering through the cracked front doors. It was nowhere near as inviting in the daytime, and I knew damn well there'd be no tables or chairs inside; just an empty, liquor-sticky floor and Marian's body, carved out like a marble statue, bloodless and angry and wobbling around, looking for his bracelets and his credit cards and his innards.

I was a fleck of dirt against the greying cityscape, hidden beneath the looming ebony pillars that made up the public library, a well-packed joint overrun by college students and dull-eyed baristas that sniffled at me as

IN THE END, YOU KILL US BOTH

I shoved past the coffee bar. Working my way up two flights of marbled stairs, I cornered the scrawny volunteer at the second floor help desk and before I could figure out what I was doing, I'd signed myself up for a basic library card just to use a boxy computer that sat blue and stoic on a shared desk in front of me.

I had no fucking clue where to begin.

There were backseat options, the sort I had little faith in but needed to cover; *dream meanings*. I started on a deep purple website with yellow embellishments, pixelated moons and glutinous stars humping the text. Issues with that search arose immediately. The meanings were overabundant. Trouble with interpersonal relationships. Perpetually stuck in dramatic situations. Inability to intervene in stressful moments. I clicked through side searches, barely legible sentences at times, until I'd landed on a dead forum dishing information on fertility herbs and their benefits.

The browsers at the library found my baseline search for cannibalism appalling and gave me medical hearsay. I sat forward and peeled Elowen's damp denim off my back. *Cannibalism science*, then. Historical cannibalism was irrelevant—I didn't need to know *how*, but *if*, and I'd settle for a brisk *why* if that's what it came down to. As the dusting of snow at the nape of my neck began to melt, I feigned for clarity. I tapped, backspaced, scrolled rapidly away from the images that rolled like film stock, scrubbed clean by censor bars, taphonomy research and criminal sciences, body fields, corpses with their pecked-away faces skewed towards the sky, left to the elements.

The dream grew sillier with each lap it took. The more credit I gave it, the angrier I became, the harder my fingertips came down on the mouse, clicking irately over pictures and willing each censor to crack, to flash the despair and pulpy entrails they coveted. It could've been the surreality of the entire situation that was to blame for my lack of fear, sitting desk-side, nails bitten down to their blood-laced quicks. I preferred not to consider why else I might be so eager for clarity and yet lacking in fear of the answer. It was a dream; that was all it could be. A paranoid nightmare. A lapse of my triggered mind.

V. IVAN

I'd wanted him dead, just so it was all over. Terror was enough to seed a dream as ripe as that. I sat back with a dull creak and webbed my frigid fingers over my face, prodding my imagination, baiting the fear to come out.

Elowen killed Marian, I told myself as convincingly as I could. Though I'd always had trouble picturing much of anything, I willed a mirrored image of myself to the forefront, taking hold of my shoulders and violently shaking. *Elowen murdered him in the downstairs hallway. They split him open like a roast and devoured him. They ate his body, his organs, his hands and feet and eyes, and left the rest where it won't ever fall back on either of you. Doesn't that sound like something they would do for you?*

My pulse didn't even flinch. I rose from my tacky orange seat, slammed the browser shut and walked to the holy convenience to buy a new pack of smokes.

Anything but menthol smelled the same to me after Nevada, so it never mattered what regulars I bought when the money was shabby—in that way, I'd never left home. I walked back to the library, puffing like a smokestack outside until I felt hateful eyes on me. Then I reentered with a handful of change, knowing where to go, how to shut my hapless brain up.

I typed slow, so nobody would notice my trembling fingers and their misspellings. *Cannibalism Idaho. Idaho murder,* I tried next. Then, *Idaho missing man. Idaho murder cannibalism.*

A page full of results rolled forth, a communal muttering of the same sentence, variegated. The fourth result caught my eye and refused to let go.

COP-KILLING VAMPIRES OF THE PANHANDLE: IDAHO'S CANNIBAL DEATH CULT

A gaudy website patterned by slashes of pixelated gore flooded the screen. Loud, murderous text rolled in staggered chunks across the page, littered with black and white scanned photos between walls of sensationalized headers. Polaroid images stuttered by as the browser loaded in, flickering like a slideshow across my eyes—a group of cops in dated uniforms standing before a decrepit shack in an overgrown forest of red firs, a spread out collection of filthy, bug-eaten knapsacks, sacks of rice and root vegetables smeared in a nondescript black paste, littering the soil outside a sloping cabin of hand cut planks. The first few lines spoke of a cold-blooded commune of flesh-eating settlers in the untrodden wilderness near Coeur d'Alene, wedded to the underside of a protected mountain, and the two lost hikers from Chesapeake that stumbled upon a litter of human remains amongst a bed of wildflowers three miles from the beaten path. The commune itself, so the website claimed, was discovered in the days following. Glowing from the screen like a portal to another realm, I was stupefied by the images of an S-curved pathway snaking through small and wide shacks of natural wood, a nearby bending stream, desire paths from the shoreline to each shack, clothes on a fishing line, the oily slash of a bonfire in the background.

 The bones of all twelve residents laid in those wildflowers, not counting the half-devoured corpses of two missing police officers that were found in a doorless shack north of the camp. Aside from two deeply-buried dogs and a single arm belonging to a young child, the remains were unearthed with a quick sluicing, and many of them bounced back as reformed criminals or parole-jumpers fleeing everything from petty theft all the way to aggravated assault. I scrolled. Below a sparkling divider of beaded blood sat another photo, a patchwork of filthy clothing strewn across a bank of moss growing between two cabins. Shack doors ripped away from their hinges, abandoned like Christmas sleds in the nearby dirt. A riverbed of damp, grey soil, skinned and sparse trees patterned and rooting beside—

 The soil was so saturated, I'd first thought it was clay.

 I scrolled hard just to get away from the blood, and swung across a pasted scan of an autopsy report for an Officer Daugherty. I only eclipsed half of the graphite drawing of his devoured body before I realized the second half simply didn't exist. Nausea conked me on the head like Georgia's bat, and I closed the tab with held breath.

V. IVAN

If Elowen had bitten off a man's face, and I had more trouble picturing them outright lying to me than doing such a thing, it ended there. That memory and its mental stimuli—irregular teeth sawing through tissue and fat, lapping blood from a carefully excavated jawline—paired with the stress of horrible afternoon was more than enough to spark that dream. I could *force it* to end there. I wasn't hashing out the reality of vampires or monsters, especially those of the Panhandle; I had them. I had them in my hands.

I spelled their name out like a curse and hit enter.

There was only one story, reiterated in different voices through different publishers. Otherwise, they didn't exist—the most damning proof of their existence written in stark navy print across a scan of The Boise Reporter from three years ago. There, I found every ounce of information that they'd given me, only *altered*—not a fight but an *attack*, not a mention of their broken nose but the staggering, half-blurred images of a torn apart face, stretching up and towards a pixelated eye splashed in soil red, a ribboned set of thin lips coiled in pain.

My hand flew to the screen and my stomach bottomed out. Only when I knew nobody was watching did I keep going.

They were sitting right at the bottom of the page, waiting for me. The eyes of their seventeen-year-old face were obscured but I'd know them by the shade of their blood alone, and they *were* bleeding—profusely from each nostril, the hard shelf of bone split in two and lacerated at its middle. It soured their mouth, swole around fresh scars that bordered old ones, dribbling down their chin and speckling their exposed ears framed by jagged slashes of natural ruby hair. Beneath the torn collar of their damp shirt, one line gave a snark to the image that I couldn't stand:

Reeves (fig. 2) to be sent out of state for reparative care as per request from their designated legal team.

I fought with my cold sweats, forking the desk chair out of my way as I shuffled to the front desk. That poor volunteer jumped like a kicked dog when I dropped my change on his countertop.

"I need print tokens."

He surveyed me closely, something dense and annoyed in his disrupted stare. "*Okay.* So print and pay here after."

"I'm in a rush."

"Waste of time to walk all the way here, then, wasn't it?"

I scowled all the way back to the desk. It took the last of my change but I didn't give a damn, avoiding eye contact as the teenager stapled and scrutinized my printout. *"School project,"* I soured, wrenching it out of his hand before he could finish. Suckling at my staple-punctured thumb, I took the elevator down and out of the library, folding the pages over and filing them into my knapsack as the rain began to trickle.

Where the urge came from was a complete mystery. It was interesting, depressing, *a mild violation,* but didn't tell me anything that my conscious mind hadn't already known. As foolish as it was, I was no closer to determining whether the dream meant something or not. It wasn't plausible to think so much of it.

Still, I printed the article like it meant something. Like my daylight, half-awake sleuthing was adding up. My brave little survivor didn't speak to me like some archival tablet behind museum glass, or a prophet, or a God. They were silent, imposing, a morbid Rockwell in some cheap family doctor's office. I had a lot to learn from this other version of Elowen, whether I liked it or not; how to stand still despite your anger was *one.* How to move past the blood and the guts and look on was *another.*

When I'd placed *weight* on the dream and demanded a simple answer for its convenient timing, the troubling and entirely foolhardy implication that the dream hadn't been a dream at all, my pulse hadn't flickered. My fingers didn't run numb, my mouth no more dry than it usually was. I paused under a pawn shop awning to light a half-spent joint buried in my knapsack pocket, smoking until I felt the owner might come and beat me away from her door like a rain-drenched cat. *That* made my fingers numb. I prayed the joint wouldn't go out as I took the shallower, quieter sidewalks to Allenview.

At a crosswalk I found the article once more, peeking eerily from the mouth of my bag. Pages and photo proof of wretched details I had no

V. IVAN

need for. I'd end up shredding most of it when I got the chance, just so I couldn't reread it. Still, I felt better taking Elowen home with me, not only to keep them company but to lighten my own loneliness. I wrapped my bag beneath their jacket to keep the both of us a little bit extra warm and continued against the elements.

It was cold in Olympia that December. Sure, it must've been even colder in Idaho, up in those mountains amongst the doorless sheds and the bodies zapped of their heat.

ROUNDING THE BLOCK WHERE our building sagged and the air reeked of commercial laundry detergent, I skidded to a halt like a frightened dog.

I wasn't quick enough to stoop and put out the joint on wet pavement. A pinched face rose from behind the steel rails of Georgia's porch, bitten red by the cold and molded against the throat of a dusky winter jacket, waving by a tense hand in curt beckoning. I was a teenager again, sweating after my first cigarette, watching the crescendo of lights from hallway to kitchen to back porch.

"Lenore," Myra barked, shamelessly loud. "Lenore. Come *here*."

Oh, Jesus. I collected globs of slush on my boots as I went, abandoning the joint hatefully in the snow at my back, taking in the salt-kissed rental at the curb.

Myra futzed with her coat zipper. Her eyes, sharp like tacks, rolled towards the doorway with an irate snarl.

"That stupid *cow* wouldn't let me in," she balked, wet froths of snow painting the throat of her jacket. "What a *ridiculous* woman you live with. *Ridiculous.* Where *were* you? How often do you wander like that?"

I stood at the edge of the steps, blue in the face from holding my breath. Paranoia scraped at the walls of my throat, wailing and yowling and *nipping.*

"You sound pretty strung out, considering you could've just sat in the car and *waited.*"

Before I could finish, Myra took a long, studious assessment of me. Then she leaned forward without warning, scowling.

"You *stink*. Why do you *stink*?"

"I try really hard to smell like shit, actually."

"You stink like pot." Myra's face swam with disgust. "*Jesus,* Lenore, are you smoking *pot? Who in their right mind is selling you pot?*"

The curtain in the living room window stirred, struck by a phantom breeze. Vibrating, I climbed the steps and hoisted the screen door between us, the same way Georgia must've when she'd seen Myra coming at her full-force. "Not in the mood for this conversation right now. Let's try tomorrow."

"Oh, so—so you think that's the best thing for you to do when you're in recovery? *Really? Smoking?* What, you're probably drinking as well, then? That woman, does she—"

"*Oh, God, please.*" I released the knob, bumping between the doors. "Georgia's not my babysitter. I don't know why you're blaming her for not letting some random woman she's never met into her *home.*"

"*Because you're my child!*" Myra's hands flew skyward, catching flakes midair as they coiled to fists and fell. "Because you're *my* child, Lenore. And if you're in the custody of a woman that I'm supposed to trust, then I expect her to be reliable. I expect her to be communicative or, *Christ,* at the very least *willing.*"

She approached and my hands skidded instinctually to my bag, a gurgling heat blooming across my chest. Inside, the printout could feel no second hand embarrassment for me, but I supplied enough for us both.

"You're *barely* nineteen," Myra added, "but that's *besides* the point. I only came to take you out, seeing as I spent all this money to come and visit *you,* but you've clearly done your wandering for the day. Let's go inside and catch up, since we've got plenty to talk about."

I'd felt her voice on me for years, unwavering in its magnitude, looming like a distant, dormant volcano. I used to wonder if every daughter was born wounded, and that might've been true all along, but deep down I knew it really only hurt *this* much because I was hers. On the best days,

V. IVAN

I ached like old bones in deep winter. When Myra looked at me, I knew she felt it, too—it angered her to witness a misprint of herself, lacking in humanity, lacking in capability, desire, honour, femininity. A brutal, unthinkable mistake. I should've stared her down and told her my closest friend would eat her alive if she spoke badly to me. Salvation was merely a phone call away.

But I was tired and ready to cry, so God forbid if my resolve wasn't strong.

"Whatever." I shook the keys from my pocket and cradled my knapsack against my chest. "But fair warning: I'm in no mood."

An infuriating snort hit my back like a bullet.

"Good," said Myra. "For once, we're on the same page."

Inside, the stiff heat from the registers fell sour on my nose. Georgia's shadow lingered in the kitchen entry, a banshee in a cable knit sweater, a terribly tight look scrawled across her face as we trekked snow around the foyer. No words were exchanged—they'd clearly done enough of that through the wooden door—so I walked Myra upstairs wordlessly, flinching at the sound of her short-heeled shoes on the steps. I wanted to block her out of my room instinctively, my only solution being to pretend she wasn't even there as I stashed my knapsack at the foot of bed, that it was just me among the magazines and shreds of unlaundered clothes on the floor.

Framed in the doorway, Myra's pestilent stare rolled across the room like marbles in a ceramic dish, over furniture, the taped up posters, Elowen's jacket freshly draped over that corner chair. There was a perpetual stiffness to her that I'd expected and still resented deep down in my guts. Her attention snapped to me at the subtle creak of the nightstand under my ass.

"What then?" I asked. "Get it out."

She looked as though I'd slapped her. At first I thought she might try feigning a tear or two, but nothing came from her dry, withered ducts.

"I expected you to be *better* than this. I don't quite understand what's stopping you. I thought you being here and having a distinct change of scenery would give you the opportunity to grow up. You wanted that, didn't you? That was why we agreed on this course of action, because whether you like it or not, Lenore, you *agreed* to this. That was part of the exchange. You had to be *willing* to get better."

My jaw clenched like a pulled muscle. "You wanted me here."

"*Here? Here?*" The way she glared around the room made me want to drive my fist through the dormer window. "Here is *nothing*, Lenore. Here is a dead end. You need to turn around and walk the other way."

Right then, the No Exit sign at the head of Carpenter waggled behind my slanted vision. It seemed almost orange filtered through all that red. My mother was the most impactful person in my life, despite everyone and everything; I learned all about my nature by watching her chase dead ends for years. She made my brain go terribly fuzzy. Always had.

"*Is that it?*"

Myra smoothed her hands over her coat and shook her head at the floor. "Oh, God, you're so painfully stubborn. You *promised* that they gave you better assets in there. That was the entire point of you being committed, so you could get better and move on. You've got nothing to say about that?"

"I didn't promise *shit*."

"And this is what came of it." Her hands flopped against her sides and in her exasperation she'd resorted to pacing, criss-crossing the old bedroom like the ghostly remnants of a previous occupant. "Silly me, because I expected more. I really, *really* did, because if *I* were you, I'd have put the effort in. I thought things were getting better. You had a job, you were on your way to some sort of normalcy. And you've fallen back again. *As you do.*"

I was vibrating. A slippery, hateful thing crawled over my back, dousing my vision with grey. "*That's why I'm here, Myra? Self improvement? Not—not because—*"

"It's *part* of it." Myra gathered her courage, eyes pinning me like a sticky note to the wall. "It's part of it, and you *know* it. And the studies map it out for you; oh, Lenore, the attitude problems these drugs cause, and the *health* problems. You're making yourself *worse*. And how—how

V. IVAN

long have you been doing this? If you think you're friends with the sort of people who sell this stuff, I've got sorry news for you."

I watched her pace like a dog until I felt she was going to catch the floor aflame.

"Stop," I finally cracked. "Stop moving. You're driving me fucking *nuts."*

She halted so hard I swear she left drag marks. *"Pardon me?"*

"Stop pacing. Stop preaching. Stop fucking *poking*. Stop talking from all the way up on that pedestal like you've never done any of this shit before. Even if you *did,* you'd never tell me. What's it matter where I got it? What're you possibly going to do? What does any of this really matter? Self improvement. Oh, God, both of you can *shove it."*

Myra took a long step further into the room I'd hoped she'd never set foot in. Then, as kindly as ripping a tooth from the sober mouth of a child, she whispered, *"Do you need me to make a call to your counsellors?"*

Pitiful. The exact way she must've sounded in the groups she visited, the ones for troubled parents, the ones for grief counselling. Like I'd killed myself and gone to hell. Like she was wiping her eyes with a hanky and telling everyone how much she *adored me.*

The veil fell briskly.

"If you need to make that call, then make it. Or let me do it for you before you don't have a choice anymore, because I don't recognize this person I'm seeing. I don't recognize this place you're living in, the people you're surrounding yourself with. I don't recognize you at *all.* What *happened?"*

The rubber of my heart pulled to its limits. *"Go home and take a look around. Then ask."*

Myra placed her forehead in her palms and shook. Then her hands clenched in prayer. *"Lenore,"* she whispered. *"Sweetheart.* You can't blame him forever."

"Fuck you, I can't!"

Snap. Like the cracking of a cattle whip, the searing of burnt skin and throbbing, puking grief. If there was an anger inside of me strong enough to kill someone, it was split at the core there like an apple, bare to me. I ran my hands up the sides of my skull, trying to contain the spillage.

"*I can't*—I can't *believe* you can stand there, right there, and *look* at me and tell me you hate this place I'm in, the things I do, the person I live with, when *you* put me here. *You* did. I never *asked* you to come watch it happen, I never asked you to *look*. You think smoking is the worst thing that's happened to me? After everything? After every *fucking* thing you both *did?*"

Myra's lips opened and closed like a carp. "I didn't—"

"You did! But you *did!*" I stalked around the nightstand until I could see her face without my own shadow cast across it. "You told me this was the *only way*. *Y'know how much of a crock of shit that was?* You flew me across the country for some dumpy inpatient program that I could've gotten at William Bee so *he* wouldn't have to see my face again across from his fucking Cheerios. So I wouldn't make a scene for the two of you. So you wouldn't be a conversation piece for the Petersons, or the Doucettes. Well, you are *anyway*. But I should be *thanking* you. Christ, who *am* I? You covered the plane ticket and the hospital fees and the cost of fucking melatonin and everything. You're so great, Mom, really. Do I owe you the money back on top of my *eternal* gratitude? Or would you just give it right back to him to spend on the fucking *slots?*"

"*Stop it.*"

Downstairs, a floorboard creaked knowingly. Oh, surely Georgia was listening by now. I didn't care—I was right. Myra knew that, too; she couldn't even look at me.

"At some point," she spoke to the walls in peculiar prayer, "you'll have to take responsibility for your own actions. It'll hurt when you do. But it's an important part of being an adult. You're *almost* there."

Without caring that Georgia might scold me for smoking with the door open, I tore into my knapsack for my pack and crammed a cigarette between my lips, turning to the unopened window to tease the brutal cold that I refused to invite indoors.

"Go home," I hurled across my shoulder. "Go back to the Yukon or Ely, I don't care. Just get the *fuck* out of my face."

V. IVAN

I braced a trembling hand against the sill and stooped my head, forcing my eyes on a gushing chimney several buildings away. When I heard no movement, no attempt to yield, I spun and glared at Myra, standing statuesque in the afternoon light.

"*Haven't I made you uncomfortable enough yet?*"

She debated that—shifted her handbag up onto her shoulder and looked at the bed I'd made that morning. "Every single day." Seeing the knife was not yet deep enough, she pushed further, slower. "Sometimes I think it's not even the state we're in. It's just *you*. In every situation, you've never excelled. Even when you were little. Even when you were pushed."

She let me get a good look. I was glad for it—I absorbed every inch of her so if I ever got a chance to compare her to my mother, I would. The byproduct of those wicked years set between both our shoulders, shared unequally—I hated Myra. I hated her as a person, as a concept, and all the same I missed my mother and wished for her still, when the sky was clear and those bleak universes laid just beyond my grasp. I had no hate for the woman that fed me and loved me and baited my jokes as a child, the same woman who'd once thumbed my doughy toddler cheeks where the birthmark had been painted and sang of red, red wine because it was funny, because she loved the pieces of me that looked nothing like her.

The Devil hadn't killed me though he'd tried hard, but he'd killed her and she'd let him. *Continued* to let him. The woman in my doorway was but a fragment of something worse. A stranger, entirely. An echo.

And still, though I begged, the world did not tear apart.

Myra walked herself to the door. Ten minutes later I followed, towing a clean set of clothes tightly packed next to my printouts and what little savings I'd kept for Somewhere Better. At the base of the stairs I avoided Georgia's maternal questioning with a cold shrug and left on a goose chase through the first floor cupboards for antacids to dissolve my swelling nausea. By the time Georgia found me and plunked a capful of oily pink goop in my hand, I'd already mindlessly stolen one of the ladybug figurines sitting on the cabinet and stuffed it up my sleeve. I swallowed every drop. I didn't even throw up.

Instead, I repackaged myself in stolen denim and stepped outside into the venous alleyway that laid between Georgia's and the laundromat. Lemon soap punched me in the nose and I wiped a thick swath of snot onto my sleeve. Briskly checking that no one could see me, I pulled the ladybug from my sleeve and gave it a final once over before tucking it into the snow-trimmed asphalt beneath the duplex's brick siding.

Then I brought my shoe down so hard on the paint-caked ceramic that I nearly broke a toe.

It *could've* broken; that wouldn't have stopped me. I stomped on the cute little fucker until its beet-red cheeks and wide, oblong eyes were nothing but glitter. I stomped until the muscles in my leg twanged with pain, branching into the crook of my hip. Then I kicked its splintered corpse into the wall, for good measure.

I stood heaving in the dirty snow with my hands on my knees. When I looked up, those two penguin men were huddled atop the rooftop for their smoke break, peering at me. Without any greeting, I kicked loose ice over the ladybug's massacred body and crouched to pick fragments of porcelain from my sneaker.

Then I began to walk. If I didn't, I would've burned everything to the dirt.

EVERYWHERE; EVERYWHERE

EXCEPT FOR THE GHOSTS of people more fortunate than us, nobody was home at the apartment on Sixth.

Sixth itself was an older neighbourhood, and relatively well-tempered from what Elowen had told me. Dated structures with snow-suffocated lawns, a small sitting park with steel benches, a quietly abandoned community garden topped with flaps of mud and unbroken ice. The street sat beneath a woollen blanket of night that evening with no porch-sitters, no cars painting the sidewalk in fluttering yellows and greys before skidding downtown. Even the streetlights were asleep, the only sign of human life coming from the very end of the street—two bouncy teenagers beaning each other with snowballs.

The violent chill did for me what that lonesome, peaceful walk only dreamed of achieving; it forced me to slow down, to focus on something other than touring downtown Olympia to find that puss-white rental and beat its headlights out with a brick. I'd formulated an entire daydream about it, right down to the holes I'd kick in the casings themselves to ensure the bulbs couldn't be salvaged. I debated how difficult it would be to find the money for a plane ticket back home, just to meet the both of them there and set us all ablaze. By the time I'd arrived at Sixth I'd gone and scared myself shitless, but I was too numb in the fingers to do much damage to anything.

After rage-puking ungracefully a few blocks back behind a dumpster, I gummed at a mint from one of my tins and stumbled up the curb in the wicked dark, approaching the hollow skull of the grainy blue apartment. Even standing atop the edge of the flowerless bed beneath the front windows, the place was lightless—more of an abandoned house in the middle of a ghost town than a place where people lived and healed. Shadows warped into boney and splintered leftover furniture, moldy food and animals, dust and debris and bird shit. I dropped down, extinguished my cigarette on the railing and stuffed it back into my pack. When I knocked, the door trembled under my fingers.

Silence bounced back at me. Tired of waiting, I tried the knob and it turned with an eager click. A swinging look around told me no one was watching but even if someone had been, I looked like I belonged there. I stepped inside like any bad natured person might do, but instead of looking through the flattened dark for money or valuables, my groping fingers sought a lamp. When I found one, I nearly knocked its glass shade onto the floor, fumbling for the switch which did—nothing.

Cussing, I felt my way through the shadows and into the room with the wide casement window that overlooked the road. Now adjusted, the apartment's melting pot of darkness took shape as a dusky blue couch pasted with woven blankets, a scatter of clothes and a peachy suitcase, a stack of encyclopedias near a reading chair and a pair of eyeglasses sandwiched around its corduroy arm. Of the posters on the wall, all I could make out were gleaming, open-mouthed faces, howling with laughter.

As the hairs on the back of my neck straightened to attention, a muddled coughing rose from just outside the sliding patio doors. Through the inky kitchen towards the cracked slat in the patio door I crept, welcomed back into the night, sticking my head through its breezy opening.

I could've picked out their back from a seamless crowd. Poor posture framed inside a swampy green tank-top, shoulder blades sharing wells of darkness with their exposed tailbone. Their wiry hair and the latticed scars zippering along their hairline, overgrown and curving gracelessly behind their ear. No coat. Never a goddamn coat. When I reached for the door and slid it open, they surely heard but didn't say a thing. I gestured unseen to the beer bottle at their hip.

"Need another one?"

V. IVAN

Elowen found me sluggishly, their pitted eyes carving across my face. Squared away by ribs of chain link, the glow of a sheltered fire pit in the yard opposite the fence traced ghostly shapes across their startled face.

"Where'd you come from?"

"I ask myself the same question all the time." When I gestured again, they shrugged.

"They'll go warm if we don't. Get one for yourself, too, if y'want."

I returned with two, cracked and handed one to Elowen, then plunked down clumsily next to them. They were barefoot on the snow-kissed grass, their red, freezing toes painted an untidy black. Even in the wake of that hateful afternoon, I took in the peripheral blur of their cheek and wondered if they still felt the ghostly tickle of my mouth on theirs.

Elowen tossed back a solid mouthful. "Did you break in through the front door?"

"It was unlocked. Doesn't quite count as breaking in."

"Everyone's at Golden Dragon. Power's out, so we can't cook." They pointed the mouth of their bottle across the lawn, towards the fire. "They're settin' off fireworks in a few minutes. You got here just in time."

I forced down half of bottle and laid appreciatively in the sudden flush of warmth it gave, toasting the roots of my anger which, as usual, had begun to give way to a horrendous ache. What would it be like to douse myself in beer and stick my head over the flames through the fence slots? I came back and Elowen was looking at me, hard and curious.

"No comment? You don't like fireworks?"

I studied the ledge of their reddened cheekbone, the hollow of their jaw like a ladle I could drink from. It was good to see them, even after everything. I didn't care for fireworks, never had, but for them I could deal with quite a lot. I decided, stupidly as I was already shivering, to peel off my sneakers and socks and join the party. When I wrangled my second sneaker off and dropped it into the step, I was greeted by a bloody, sticky sock glued to my foot. Peeling it away revealed an uneven chunk of ceramic ladybug embedded in the corner of my big toe.

"It's fine," I spat before Elowen could dare ask, though they didn't seem inclined. They just watched, hunched and silent, as I pinched at the adrenaline-numb wound, dislodging the shrapnel from my pulsing skin. When I stuck my foot in the skiff of snowy grass, I nearly moaned.

"J'eat? I can ask Xianne to bring something home."

As I inhaled the last of my bottle and sat it next to theirs, creating the smallest of glass walls between us, I shelved the pang of hunger deep inside my gut, my very last meal both unfulfilling and now more than a day old. "I don't need anything," I whispered. "Just want to sit with you. That's it."

Elowen took my words into them, and chewed well before swallowing. They rose stiffly and crept inside, my eyes trailing after the wet footprints they left in their wake. Upon returning they switched our empties for fresh bottles, sliding an open pack of waterproof bandaids into my frigid hands. "Feel like talkin' at all? Or do you want me to be quiet?" When I did nothing but stare at the box, Elowen popped it open and did it for me, and didn't dare ask for permission. "I can't *make* you. Just wanted to offer, since y'don't usually come over bleedin' and all."

"I don't have anything nice to say."

"Mm. I ain't easily bummed."

Their eyes fell upon me and I smiled like a dog, euthanized and waiting, fighting off the rage tears as my voice sank to a furious whisper. *"I don't want to ruin your fireworks."*

Elowen leaned into their knees, stooping close to me. I dissolved beneath a cloud of their shampoo, dense and spicy, smothering the ripe, *real* smell of them.

"Ruin 'em." They nudged the glass mouth of their bottle to mine. "Go right ahead. Everythin' else but this is—y'know. It's background noise."

I looked at them long and hard, the way I looked at magazine photos of celebrities until my own face felt gummy and unreal. Wet spatters hit my knees. I licked at the tears pilling on my lips, trembling hard in the cold. They didn't turn away, even as that nasty, ugly smile pulled taut. I wanted to bite something and bite it *hard*.

V. IVAN

"I think I've had it," I admitted, not for the first time in my life. *"I'm tired of this shit now. Oh, I just want to sleep."*

Elowen twisted off the cap of my bottle with their bare hands. I cringed just watching them. "Take a breath. I know you're holdin' it."

I shuddered one out. *"Fuck,"* I said. *"Fuck this.* God, I don't even want to *think* about it anymore. Or *talk* about it. I talked for months and months about it inside and it never changed a thing. And—and here's the worst part, El, here's the worst part—*I'm* the fucking idiot. Don't look at me like I'm wrong; I *am* an idiot. I don't know why, but I felt like—for some reason, I just thought things would be different. Some childish fuckin' part of me expected something else. Anything else. Just not *this* shit again. It's *her* blood in me, y'know, so how come I can't put it to rest? She's got all the strength to do this to me. *Why can't I end it?"*

Elowen offered me a cigarette. I recoiled, waggling my head.

"It's *normal* to hope for somethin' else," they quieted. "Just like it's normal to be disappointed when things ain't different. It'll happen again, too. Don't matter if y'think you know better now. Hope's a cancerous thing. Doesn't even need your permission to kill you."

I wet my sleeve with the snot that painted my top lip, slugging it off onto the knee of my jeans. *"I'm sorry,"* I said, despite Elowen's shaking head. *"I know. But I am."*

"Said you could talk to me, didn't I?"

"Yeah, but I *hate* talking." I heaved an embarrassing sigh. Possessiveness lifted my voice, entangled with the pearls of hatred strung against my throat. "Not to you, but to *anyone*, about *any* of this shit. It's mine. *Mine. I* think about it every day. Why would I tell it to someone else, someone who's just gonna *forget it* later on while I'm still *living* with it?"

An assaulting pop and scatter of golden tendrils shot off in the swollen sky above the campfire. Pouring voices of encouragement rose, drifting through the leafless maples edging the backyard. Despite the exhaustion, despite my feverish mind collapsing, I considered telling Elowen everything from the very start. The kitchen sink, the fire pit, the Episcopal church. The matchsticks failing three times, sitting among petunias with soapy hair. A broken neck, my first week in the Echo, unable to speak. The crawl space where I smoked cigarettes, the holiday road trips to Reno to eat shitty rest stop food and visit relatives I hardly knew. Every puzzle piece of me, draped unevenly in their hands, *might* be solvable. But I'd have to risk it.

When the words tried to leave my lips, I bailed.

"Back at the Anchor," I whispered. "That afternoon. *Before—*"

Elowen made an affirmative hum.

"It brought everything back. I was right there in Nevada, when everything went to shit. I wanted to punch his head into the wall and he *wasn't* Kev, I knew that much, but he looked just *like* him. I felt that angry today, too, just talking to my own mother. I always feel that way when I talk to her. Like she can spy a hundred things wrong with me, like it's so *obvious,* and for some godforsaken reason I'm *blind to it.*" I rocked forth, clamping onto my knees. "Sometimes I think about that day and I wonder what would've happened if I'd swung on that motherfucker just once more, hard enough to jam his nose into his brain. I wish I'd blinded him. I wish I'd killed him. I wish I could kill him now. If he was here, I *would. I'd kill him and burn his fucking body until I couldn't recognize him any other way.*"

The relief of saying it aloud outweighed my embarrassment. The beers were almost warm, so I leaned down and set mine in the snow drift aside my foot, just beyond the pinkened snow. Elowen didn't say a word; I joined them in knowing silence as gold and ruby fractals of light painted the grass in lapping rays like a great, rolling sea before us.

Something called me forth, then, something I'd never quite understood. A brutal, unforgiving beast of an urge settled across my aching shoulders. When I was a kid, I'd been convinced that if I didn't suddenly grip my fingers as hard as I could or if I didn't hit the curb a certain way when I stepped over it, the entire world would simply cease to exist. That goading feeling was back; if I didn't give in, all of life would starburst around me, flame and debris and retribution. By the time I grew the courage to fulfill that urge, there'd be nothing but bones left for me to cling to.

V. IVAN

So I went without courage into the cotton of Elowen's shirt, crushed against my forehead as I sank into their bony shoulder, and the world didn't cease. Instead the sky flooded with colour, whistling bangs shotgunning into the dark, spatters of firework gunfire igniting the dead evening.

Their shoulder muscles twitched beneath my cheek. I remained still as a corpse, fighting the urge to run. I never enjoyed being held, and always wondered if someone had done it the wrong way and my mind had blotted it out or if I'd never quite understood the necessity. All I knew was that I didn't like it, couldn't *bear* it, and yet right then I was certain I needed it, and through all the urgency of that peculiar desire I was exactly where I preferred to be. Of all the places, of all the people.

Elowen was just as still, the two of us suddenly so nervous of each other's shadows. I wondered if anyone had ever held them before, or if we were both strangers to it. When the fireworks took a brief intermission to reload, I buried my wounded heart deep away.

"D'you remember that orderly at the beginning of my tour and the end of yours?" I whispered. "Bozzelli. He was from Pocatello, but you two sound nothing alike."

As startling as a needle prick, Elowen's frozen fingers slid through mine and took hold stiffly like I might jerk away. "No," they quieted. "S'pose we wouldn't. I've got Texan and English pig slop. Boz sounds like every other city boy I knew, though."

"*Texas?*"

"Nn-hn. Dad was from Laredo. We grew up out in the sticks, away from the city. We only moved to Idaho when I was nine—same deal. Minded our own damn business. 'Fore that, we were—*hell.*" Their voice knitted several notches too tight. "Well, I don't really *remember.*"

"Sounds lonely."

Elowen startled as the fireworks coughed above the maples. "Not so much. We were a tight family, and I wasn't in school. Ma was a youth teacher in Cornwall around her twenties, so she taught me all the good stuff. Dad's fault it got all fucked up—spent more time talkin' to him and shootin' the shit than I did with Ma, so things got scrambled."

"She doesn't teach anymore?"

Elowen fell quiet. Head pinned upwards on the sky, not a twitch of their lips to suggest an answer they felt like sharing. A low, creeping feeling nipped my ankles.

"Too far?"

"Mm." They stooped their head as another firework whistled. "They passed ten years back. Both of 'em."

Stupefied, I could only swallow and shake my head.

"I know," said Elowen. "Yeah, I know."

"I hope they went peacefully."

Elowen paused, perhaps hoping their mother might chime in from beneath the frozen earth. *"Sure,"* they said, when nobody came. "Me, too."

The lone, biting child left behind in the world by their star-crossed parents. Were they buried in Idaho's wicked cold, somewhere near the Panhandle where the blood of that rampage could leech into their graves and pull them, zombified, back through the dirt? I could've stopped there, but the sooner we ceased talking, the sooner Elowen might've pulled away.

So I told them, "I like your slop," which roused them from deeper thought. "Keep talking."

"About?"

"Anything." Then, with courage drawn seemingly from nowhere, "About *you*. Tell me about *you*."

There came a sheepish silence in which I wasn't sure if Elowen didn't know where to begin, or if they weren't actually sure what to say for themselves.

"Tell me about your Dad. Or your Mom. Tell me about Texas. *Anything.* Just don't make me ask again."

Faintly, Elowen exhaled—a stiff, unsure *huh.*

"Ma was always a teacher, I think. Even before she was trained; she was born one. In and out of work, it's what she did—pickin' up languages just to teach others a hundred different ways to say sorry and I love you and thank you. She enjoyed roughin' it the way Dad an' I did

V. IVAN

for the most part—liked to catch an' release, but killin' made her sad, so she rarely ate any wild game. She was—*well.*"

Elowen's hands flexed and relaxed midair, seeking words that never came. I'd never understood them better than I did right then—what, really, could we say about our mothers when all was said and done? Nothing *just*. Nothing that could even come *close*.

"Dad," they said instead, when their mother turned them fragile. "He was—a fisherman near Wallace when I was old enough to remember what he did. Catfish and cutthroat, mostly, but he'd been a little bit of a farmer, too. Wasn't very good at it, 'cause by the end he was only dealin' in fish. Fish and God. Tried preachin' after I turned ten and stuck to it—wanted to make himself whole again after all the shit he got up to. He was—a *good* man. I knew folk who'd disagree, but they'd be *wrong*."

Something held on Elowen's lips. *"Leo—"*

"I'm listening."

Elowen leaned into the railing, slackening my resting head. Their empty bottle dangled between their fingers like an oblong jewel, eyes cold and marbled in the dark, deep in distracted thought.

"Just keep going," I begged. *"It's too quiet without one of us talking."*

Sharply, they said, "I'll do it."

I lifted my head, catching the rise of goosebumps along their collarbone. "It?"

"Like you said." Their face rippled with colour. "You'd feel better if he was dead. So I'll do it for you."

The air laid thick with a feverish humidity laced about by the beer, yet I could've sworn that through the haze, they were certain of themselves. Like they knew they could manage it. Unable to do much else, a peculiar cackle bubbled from me.

"You're really goddamn drunk."

"Takes more than that," they said. "We don't have near enough. Sorta wish we did."

"You wouldn't kill anyone," I retorted, my voice unclear—my last words enunciated by the memory of that dream. For a brief, frightening moment, the glimmer in Elowen's eyes had me wondering if they could read my thoughts.

"Sure. Why not?" They licked spilt beer from the mouth of their bottle. "Used to skin pigs and cattle when I was a kid. Fenced-in sort, so it's a little different. You wouldn't let me do it?"

Sure. Setting down my bottle, I leaned into my knees. Our fingers were still knotted together, and I thumbed a weird, bolt-like scar between their thumb and index as I tried to process it. "It's not—I—so, I think *food's* a little different."

The way they shrugged made me run cold.

"It's different," I squinted. "It *is* different."

"Would it make you happy?"

I hesitated. "That's easily not the *point.*"

"But it would," guessed Elowen, their attention wired upon me. "It'd make you happy to see him dead. Hell, the way you talk about it, Lee, it'd make *me* happy. I don't *blame* you if that's the case."

In the open night, a great weight slid from my shoulders. There were no faces through the trees staring at me, no one to peg my answer as good or bad, evil or kind. If there was a ploy to be had, I could at least entertain it as I'd done so many times alone and without sleep. When the scattered pops above seemed loud enough to shake the city, I dove in with open, willing hands and bled a touch of truth:

"Sometimes I don't think anything else could do the job."

I drained my second beer and relished in the sweaty calm. I wasn't drunk, still present enough to know what we'd instilled by speaking aloud. If my fear of them were to come, perhaps it ought to arrive sooner than later, but there was no glimmer of it on the horizon, no mirage of shadow and terror.

A cut-free voice ran rampant across my thoughts in fear's place: *Sure, I'll kill the Devil for you, Leo. It's no big deal. Neither was Marian.*

I said, "How do you suppose we do it?" just to shut it the fuck up.

Elowen gestured aimlessly with their bottle. "We'd pack and leave Olympia in the truck. Stop and get gas when we need, sleep when we need. Parking lot or motel, if y'want a bed real bad. It'd only be a few

V. IVAN

days to Nevada, even if we took our time. We'd drive over for a visit, and when it's night and the bastard's sleepin', you'd spell out the directions to his room and I'd slit his throat. So you don't get your hands dirty."

Sitting there on the porch, our hands welded together by the cold, I was slowly thawing. Nobody had ever offered such a thing to me. When Elowen digested my expression, which must've been one of faint disbelief, they dropped their head fatefully close to mine.

"If you wanna get your hands dirty," they whispered, *"I won't take that away from you."*

With a spinning mind, I rested my upper arm against theirs. Flashes of red rolled over my eyelids and I turned to the sky, envisioning it as I'd done so many times before, embarrassed that they could see me until I realized they weren't only observing but participating.

"I could get my hands dirty," I thought aloud.

"Sure," they enthused quietly. "Yeah, 'course."

"But then what would *you* do?"

Elowen didn't miss a beat—had, perhaps, thought of this before and engraved it upon the gummy inside of their skull. "I'd show you how—and watch your back. Keep you safe. I'd make sure he bled out right, that it ended right. And if he tried anything, then—"

"Then?"

A firework shattered overhead and squealed in the darkness. "Then I'd make it worse," Elowen guaranteed in a low, knowing whistle. "I'd tear his fuckin' heart out before I'd let him take you away."

We sat for what could've been another hour as a brutal cold whistled through the chain links. Georgia was back at home, possibly cooking dinner, *likely* worrying about me. The thought alone made me jolt, made me rise and sever the inexplicable grip between us. Elowen's hand retracted into their lap like an eel between two rock faces. Something deep in my stomach sang formidably, and I crouched to grab the necks of the four beers we'd demolished.

"I'll take 'em in," I whispered, to no response. "More?"

Elowen was much too busy to look at me—their fingertips trapped in their mouth, gnawing through a sudden swell of anxiety. I suspected their mind had wandered back to Idaho, into the slop and shit with the pigs and cattle or reviewing alphabets with a dead woman. I climbed the deck in my bare feet, gingerly moving through the half-open sliding door with one last look. I couldn't help it—they sat abandoned in the snow like someone's house pet, searching the stars for a set of headlights that wouldn't come. My stomach swelled with something greasy and demanding. Something unavoidable.

"Elowen."

They suckled a jewel of blood from their finger and pressed it against their knee, swivelling towards me.

"Come inside." I leaned on the door and raised the bottles. "C'mon. It's too cold. You'll freeze."

They didn't fuss; that could've been what made up my mind. My hand, the one which held theirs moments before, trembled as they rose and padded indoors. When I took a clumsy step back and let them by, they shut the door behind us, the frigid shell of the apartment greeting us crudely.

We were inches apart then, a melody of clinking glass trapped between my knuckles. In the deeper dark, their skin was white as styrofoam and somehow still alive, still thrumming with blood beneath its surface. Mindlessly, I mouthed the bottle they'd been drinking, the last of their beer slithering down my throat which cinched tight from the faint wetness where their tongue had met the glass ridges.

In the shadows we were safer, but from *what* I couldn't be sure. *Everything,* I guessed—whatever lingered beyond, God or his angels or an absolute, impenetrable nothing; it couldn't see us, couldn't pass onto me the insurmountable self hatred I always feared I'd feel. A stomach full of rocks was enough of a hold. I set the bottles down by the back door and when I came back up, Elowen's frozen hands were on my back, curling like spiders into the fabric of their own coat.

Without warning, I sucked in the last of the air from their open mouth and kissed them like I wanted to hurt them.

They were a fever on me. My hands grappled across their valleys, latching onto their throat, their elbows, their hips. The bottles teetered

V. IVAN

over with a faint clatter but neither of us flinched. Their ribs against my clothed belly struck a match to my bones. My hands worked over the back of their head and brushed across their body's patchwork, and *oh*, how I wished I could peel them apart and curl up inside of their skull, smothered by the warm flesh there, their lips mine, their eyes *mine*. The sparks I'd been missing with Marian were found in the rough sanding of their skin against mine, catching like gunpowder, sprouting flame and sparking when touched.

Like two dancers, we staggered through the entry of a void-like bedroom, into the edge of a bedpost, my calves nipped by a metal box spring. I'd idled in the entryway foyer of this apartment once as Elowen had flown upstairs to snatch their uniform from their bedroom; with a jolt of adrenaline, I realized we hadn't made it there. Without the light, there was nothing to do but feel, awash in the fingertip strokes on my throat, over and under clothing, across the rounded edges of my thighs, lips bruising from a force I'd die before pushing off.

Then air. A jerking away which left me loathing the need for oxygen. On top of me, Elowen weighed nothing, a net of thin, fragile limbs wheezing in the dark.

Tell me where you want me.

I understood then for the first time what it meant to be rabid as I pulled Elowen's hair into fistfuls and went crashing in again, teeth and nails and scratched-raw skin.

Everywhere, I bit. *Everywhere.*

Their vulnerability overcame me. What wretched things plagued me all day and all week and all year were made swiftly meaningless. My thoughts quieted to a polite exhale, tears blooming around the mouth I was feeding into mine, spilling without comment or care. I let them go.

Elowen's teeth skated across the exposed flesh of my stomach, denim stripped down to my knees, scattered nips and tongued apologies along the flesh of my inner thighs. The beer bottles were broken in the kitchen and I didn't give a shit. I writhed over the mattress, that twinkling silver seashell dragging past the notch of my bellybutton—how I ached to suckle it into my mouth, to run my tongue over its faint indents, its polished curves. Then came a rolling wave of sensation, kneaded free like hands over plush dough, and a nothingness so powerful it wrenched a sob out of me. At one point, that alone could've been enough.

But I wanted them *whole*. To devour them, every inch of their skin, to know what they tasted of. To feel them slip through my fingers, soft and fresh and flayed apart—just for me. To be in their mouth, sandwiched between their teeth, no better than the remains of a satisfying breakfast.

Suddenly, that month-old dream was the only thing I could relate to.

THE POWER RETURNED LATE in the night with a choir-like buzz from every appliance in the apartment.

I awoke to a swell of light, artificial and crude, on the edge of the early morning. Elowen was asleep at my side, their sutured back pointed at me, hunched tightly in hiding as the morning sky took lapping glances over them. I laid there easily for an hour, guiding their form into my memory, absorbing their printer-paper posters and assessing how and when we'd climbed the stairs, the dull thrum of my pulse luring me from the mattress.

I didn't dare wake them. Instead I hauled on a wrinkled costume of them, a gaudy yellow Rottweiler tee and a pair of star-spangled boxers, and trudged downstairs. The first sign of life I found was Xianne, Elowen's youngest roommate, traipsing about the backyard in her balloon animal-patterned scrubs, collecting scattered casings and shreds of flamboyant plastic advertising, chip bags, labels ripped crudely from bottles blown past the ripped chainlink.

"I fucking hate this dump," Xianne said when she spotted me.

"I hear you." I rubbed sleep from my eyes and left to grab my sneakers. Returning, I padded down the back porch through biting shards of icy snow, piling debris into my hands as I went, my toe humming with a light pain. "Sometimes feels like being an elephant in an enclosure."

V. IVAN

"And people throw garbage at you to get you to move," Xianne lamented dryly. Her thick, dark hair hung limp along her round face. When she rose, she gave me a desperate look. "This is *typical*, isn't it? Just being watched and poked through the bars all the time? No privacy, no space—that's what regular people deal with, right?"

I offered out my hands and Xianne gave me her plastic bits. "Maybe," I supposed. "But someone's always gonna be the elephant."

"Well, if I ever escape this enclosure, I'm crunching one of these asshole's heads between my jaws like a grape." She worked a moment longer then pawned the rest into my hands. "There's leftover breakfast on the island. Elowen won't usually eat, so don't feel like you've gotta save any."

I couldn't scurry inside fast enough. By the time I'd emptied my hands and reached the countertop, I was salivating. Bread and butter in a small dish, digestive biscuits, a box of cereal I didn't dare touch. Hot coffee. Tea. Sugar. I bumbled about like a clueless housefly to make toast, two cups of coffee and collect the largest orange in the kitchen. All the while I painted them in my mind, unclothed in bed, their resting back forever stiff and spattered with freckles and ancient scars, sap-swollen rivulets in old, patinated wood.

When I returned to Elowen's bedroom with plated breakfast, I was stunned to find them awake and dressed from the waist down, shoulder deep in their closet. Just the sight of them buzzing about roused a soreness I'd yet to acquaint myself with, and without fail I turned red before I could even greet them.

"Your neighbours are fun, but they're scummy," I opened, sliding the tray past the edge of the mattress.

Elowen acknowledged me with a lingering glance and a still-sleepy smile, coiling charger cables around their bony fingers, stuffing them into the open knapsack at their feet. *"Mm.* The duality."

"Xianne's out there picking up trash in her uniform."

"Happened before. Y'know what their excuse was? Ain't nothin' they can do to control the wind."

"Bastards."

"*Hyup.* If she's late again for it, she'll come home swinging."

The politeness was a curt, frustrating swell. Surely we were both thinking about fucking again—at least Elowen made themselves seem occupied, scurrying about the room, collecting objects: a baseball cap, a thin velcro pouch, truck keys directly into their pockets. When I plunked myself down on the bed and drug their knapsack open with a hooked finger, there sat a layering of poorly folded clothes, headphones and a tired red wallet much older than theirs.

"Sit," I begged. "Just for a sec. Share an orange with me."

Elowen freed themselves from whatever purpose had awoken them from sleep, dragging the first half-clean shirt they could find from the floor over their head. They came to me like scrabbling creature, only just discovering the bliss of free will and the ability to sit down. Next to me, they swallowed throat-fulls of hot coffee like nectar, picking at the fruit I'd split for us, whispering to me about a dream of flooded tunnels and algae-encrusted monsters before devolving into chewing silence. I couldn't trace the curves of their face without my own heartbeat goring my eardrums.

"In a rush to get away from me?" I half-joked.

Tearing meekly into a slice, Elowen stopped as if ripped from a trance. I gestured to the bag and they bit, juice dribbling down their chin. "I'm packing."

"Sensed that. Where are we going?"

Was that a difficult question? I didn't think so, but the look on Elowen's face rode the fine vein between confusion and wonder. Just as carefully as they licked the last dribbles of coffee from their mug, the realization crept into the room, knife-wielding and desperate for blood, draining my face of colour.

"*No,*" I said. Then, "No. Oh, *that—*"

Elowen kidnapped the remains of their orange half, rising from the bed to return to their relentless task. "You wanted to go."

Words fell away from me.

V. IVAN

"If y'don't, just say that," they tacked on, jamming the last slice into their disinterested mouth and hauling a pair of socks on with sticky fingers. "But it sure sounded like we were fixin' a pretty solid plan."

For as long as it took Elowen to finish chewing, I did nothing but stare at their open knapsack, working over the cords, the restless sight of them rattling me like a jar of nails.

"This isn't like a trip to Disneyland."

"That's good. I ain't packin' sunscreen."

"Elowen." I inched closer, minding their carefully balanced mug on the tray. "When I said that, y'know—I *did* mean it. But I wasn't *asking* you—"

"I'm offerin'."

The thought of driving back to Ely had me suddenly, ferociously sick. Weighed down by it, my fingers throated the t-shirt I was wearing. If I stepped back into the state, acclimated to Washington, maybe I'd just melt and burst into crackling flames. Then all of this could be painfully, *painfully* easy. Only it never *was*.

"It's not worth the risk just to vent *my* grudges."

Elowen spun from the closet. Their stare sawed clean through me before darting discontentedly away. "That's what this is? Just some *grudge?*"

No. It was divine hatred in a neighbourhood where grudges lined the soles of my shoes. "I don't think it matters," I whispered anyway, "because rebuilding's the choice that I have. *That*—I don't need to involve you with that. It's more trouble than I'm worth in a million years. Seriously. Okay?"

I hadn't *really* meant it as a question. They took it as one however, and stood framed against dark shelves for some time before they could chew and swallow it. They grimaced all the way down.

Resolutely, they said, *"No."*

A car whizzed by outside; the first sign of life outside the apartment's dense bubble in the last twelve hours. *"No,"* I parroted when the rumbling tires ceased to reach my ears.

They fought against whatever waited behind their lips. Bit at their mouth, glaring holes into the bedspread, fisting one of the hung garments tickling their arm. "No," echoed from them once they stopped resisting. "I don't actually believe that, Leo, 'cause none of this'll be worth shit if you're dyin' here."

A scoff shot unwillingly from my mouth. *"Dying—?"*

"What about this place is all that much better?" Elowen's angular shoulders rose in defence. "I mean, *really*—is any of this better if he's still all you think about? If you're gonna live here, and—and *rebuild*—are you gonna settle for always wonderin' about what you could've done, an' what you *wished* you did, 'cause you only ever did what you were *supposed* to do? What's anythin' worth if you're still killin' yourself over somebody else?"

You, I wanted to say, *are worth a great deal.* But I knew better.

"Say what you want about everyone else hearin' you out and goin' about their day," they cut, "but *I'm* right next to you, *I'm* not movin' and *I'm* not askin' what you think is right. What do you *want?*"

Funny—I couldn't remember the last time anyone had asked me that. Couldn't even remember the last time I'd had a choice in it. Rebuilding was all formula: I rode the ramps of what people told me I should want, followed the patterns that were recommended to me, and in trying to piece together my own version of life and living as I sat on the edge of Elowen's bed, I fell ill and couldn't collect my own thoughts half as well as I did last night. Still they were there, hiding in the corners, baiting me towards darkness. What could I reap from their scattered shadows?

I sat in Elowen's shirt and thought about killing the Devil, my desire an open, sugar-rotted wound.

To see him not removed, but *gone*. Utterly unreachable. Away from me, from Myra, from humanity entirely. What kind of world would that be? The kind where I could take a shower with my eyes open, where I could light matches without the shakes pouring through my hands and into my shoulder blades. The kind of world where dead men no longer

V. IVAN

visited me in the evening hours, painting macabre faces across stucco, mocking me.

From my throat came a needy exhale. A ribbon of want, now too familiar to me. Suffocating me until I was reaching for them, until they came to my groping arms as if we'd done this exact thing a hundred times, in a hundred different spaces. My hands on the ledge of their boxers, clinging to sheets of shale sliding from a mountainside.

"I want to go," I said aloud, through the ringing of my eardrums. *"I want to go."*

I DIDN'T WANT GEORGIA to be afraid. More than that, I didn't want her to narc. So I didn't call, even when I knew I should've.

I would in a day or two. I'd make up an excuse, something to pacify her mind which I knew would be racing if she thought I'd disappeared off the face of the earth. But as I climbed into Elowen's truck, I didn't need her worry. I needed the money I'd tucked away, what little I'd saved to escape Washington, which sat squarely at the bottom of my knapsack. I needed Elowen, cloaked in a fibrous crewneck and a horseshoe-stamped tee, their rough hand fluttering against mine as I anchored my seatbelt into place. I needed a glimpse of awkwardness, the bumbling skid past it, the lack of worry about whether things could ever be normal again because things hadn't been normal in the first place.

The truck flew through town all the way to a gas bar several neighbourhoods beyond Allenview, where I kept my face cool against the fingerprinted window and studied the city's unfamiliar, leafless wings. We were off again as quickly as we'd stopped. Olympia began to slide away and I sat weaning off my second coffee, sweltering under the truck's heat and staring out the fog-rimmed windows. A violent pearl of doubt curdled inside me, made of regret, bidding me to be more cautious with what I was doing.

The Elowen I knew would stop the truck if I asked. *Only* if I asked.

IN THE END, YOU KILL US BOTH

I was held in silence by an idea. The single lane road ahead was damp and uneven, paved by bloodshed. There might be nothing to return to if things went wrong *or* right. That alone parted the curtains of my mind further, cementing the thoughts I'd begun to wipe away. It was odd, knowing the destination and pledging to get there. It only made sense as a joke, but the Elowen I'd dreamt of was more than capable.

And they were so willing.

If all went as we intended, then every little girl in Ely would be safer than she was on his last living morning. If all went well, the heat would be a little less excruciating, the truck he cherished would be buried in a cavernous lake a hundred miles from that humid little trailer, and I'd take a long, hot shower with my eyes crammed shut the entire time. I'd stick my head under the kitchen faucet and plunge myself into a basin of warm water, and I'd rinse myself clean of him, every inch of him, every breath and word and worn-down slur at the arm of the couch. And if all went as planned, then the ground where Kev laid would serve as foundation for me to accept that as much as I'd tried to convince myself otherwise, there had been no nightmare, no hazy midnight sleepwalking fugue. There had only been the waking dream, the hazy weight of being alive and aware. Of seeing it, and choosing not to believe it.

Elowen had *seen* me on the stairs in that piss-yellow evening, sleepwalking and stupid, and in a fit of hunger and rage that I only ever grazed the corners of, they killed Marian and devoured him. Had held the chance to consume me, to quench a nightmarish thirst emboldened by something deep, deep inside of them that I might never know, and had left me living. Had carried me back to the bed we'd shared, leaving not a crumb of skin, or blood, or viscera. Had kissed me with the mouth that left nothing but bones behind, that trimmed the meat of him with their uneven teeth. Had wanted stronger to consume me in other ways. Had killed for me. Had eaten for me.

As I imagined they would again in Ely, if I dared to ask.

There was something putridly beautiful about that, something so gutting that I couldn't shake it from my mind, even as Olympia melted

V. IVAN

in the dead-morning sunlight and the lull of snow-paved highway reeled us closer to sin.

DEADWEIGHT

When I slogged forward out of the dream, groping the dashboard of the truck for balance, I was stunned to find there weren't a pair of necrotic hands crushing my throat.

I *swear* he'd been there, the Romanian fucker—devouring my sleeping body, ripping me into strips like old, wet newspaper. Now half-awake, there were no more sticky thumbs working into my splitting lymph nodes, no gnawing, toothless mouth gumming around my jawline. No floral bedsheets, no burnt sugar stench, no earwig mothers sliding into the narrow tunnels of my ears.

No bedroom at all. Instead, I tossed and turned on tan leather upholstery, soothed by murmuring Blondie on the radio. Beyond the truck's rain-slick windshield lounged a coiled steel serpent of a building, beached on yellow-striped asphalt, pulley steel doors and windows scaling its flanks. Some sort of garage attached to a pocket-sized convenience store, not surrounded by Washington's familiar skyscrapers but by sloping birch trees and tangled telephone wires. Somewhere within reach, a grating ringtone wailed.

I cracked the window and let rain paint the sill, suckling fresh air as I fumbled through the cab and found my cell, popping it open with vibrating hands.

"Oh my God," came Georgia's voice through the speaker, laden with rock-hard annoyance. "You're not *dead*. It's a Christmas miracle."

Pestilent-yellow panel lights inside the store blasted an absolved sense of Heaven onto the pavement. How long had it been night? *Was it night?* I squinted through the windows and found God, stocky and

V. IVAN

pug-faced, manning the counter and picking away at a peeled label on a new hubcap.

Georgia said, "Hey, *Christmas Miracle*. I almost called the cops on you."

Almost was the keyword; she'd never do it. The news broadcast on the corner television inside, skewed by a tall, plastic pothos, was not one I recognized. Salem, KSLM. Salem, Oregon I prayed, though nothing seemed impossible anymore—of all the things I surrounded myself with, witchcraft was the last I needed.

"I fuckin' *should've*." The rain started to rally, beaten by wind, and I cranked the window closed. "You just disappeared after your little meltdown. If you didn't pick up just now—well, there wouldn't be any choice. It's not like you *have* to be home, it's just—I mean—*God*, Leo, y'know girls go missing in the city all the time, don't you? And don't give me none of that bullshit about you not knowing 'cause you aren't *from* here. Girls go missing *everywhere*."

Through the mesh of water gliding across the windshield, I picked out a garish form against a blurry shelf stuffed with breads and potato chips. With a flick of the truck's headlights, Elowen squinted across the aisles and out the window, tossing into the air a pointed wave, begging my patience.

"Hey. Are you listening to me?"

"I'm listening." Shaken, but not looking away. "I know."

"I'm not gettin' in trouble for you. I waited as long as I could. I didn't *call* them, Leo, not the cops or the damn *staff*, but y'know what would've happened if you didn't pick up? After all that business with your mom being over here, and you—"

I barked: *"Alright! Shit!"*

Nothing came for a moment but muted guilt, weaponized and pointed at my heaving chest. With all the delirious strength I had, I barred the truth behind my gritting teeth, skimming all I needed from it.

"I'm *sorry*, Georgia. You deserve an explanation, I know, and I'd give you one but it's—really—nothing interesting. I'm with El. We're being total hermits, but everything's cool, I just—after all of that, I needed to breathe. Y'know?"

The dead air shifted. Beyond the crackling of our sucky connection, Georgia scraped around at something, a distant noise that guaranteed she was trying to keep her hands busy as she determined whether I was being honest or not. The subtle jingle of her bangles twisted my lungs into irreparable knots.

Her voice came back, shelled of its former irritation. "At least shoot me a message next time you're gonna fuck off. It's fine—*it's fine*. I'm just *saying*. Motherhood requires me to shame you a little bit."

"I know." If Myra's tart perfume came back to me now, I was going to punch a hole through the windshield. "It's okay. We're fine here. *I'm* fine here."

"Happy to swing by if you need anything."

Cold crept across my shoulders. "Just space. That's all I ever need."

"Leo?" After a held breath, Georgia cleared her throat. "She didn't come looking for you again. I'd say that's a good thing, but—*well*—I don't want you thinkin' I support it. If she's around, you should *try* to mend something. If you don't, you'll get eaten up about it."

She'd earned the right to step on a few of my toes; that didn't numb my nerves to the agonizing weight of her worry. I hung up and rucked my seat back, glaring up at the cold, painted eyes of the dome light skeleton until Elowen returned, knapsack crinkling when they stuffed it aside my legs. Their smell, tinny from the rain, roused me from the last dredges of sleepiness.

"D'you remember?" they whispered.

How could I forget? I also remembered calcifying the dream. Sitting in that ravaged gravel lot, sprayed by mellow light, not a single person on earth knew where we were save for each other.

"We're just outside McMinnville," Elowen said. "Oregon."

"Did I say something?"

"I could see you wondering. *McMinnville*—just a midpoint. Here." Elowen leaned over me, flipping their knapsack onto the floor. "Keep

V. IVAN

your eyes in the cab. The only thing I paid for was a bed next door. And we've got a roommate."

The omniscience of their words forged a still-dreaming paranoia deep inside of me. As they backed the truck out and curved around the corner into the parking lot of a dumpy, espresso coloured inn, I did as they asked and kept my eyes far from the knapsack and on Oregon's last remnants of fall, clinging like bloody lace to the boughs of its spindly, night-covered trees.

T HERE HE WAS, THE little demon. Stout-nosed and copper-furred, snarling in the corner of the bathroom like a wet rat.

I didn't notice him at first—too shrouded in the scent of baby powder and cigarette scum climbing the walls, perfuming from the starry, ash-pocked comforter of the double bed and the nightstand's laundry tablet-stuffed drawers. When the light above the bathroom vanity shuddered to life, I dropped my knapsack on the tile and tossed Elowen's coat crudely over the curtain road where it could drain off. From the basin came a grossly human wail as a tomcat-shaped blur hurled spastically from the tub, butterflying the shower curtain and sailing into the far wall, scrambling behind the toilet like a fumbled bar of soap.

When Elowen reached the bathroom, I was white and flat against the doorframe.

"Should only be one, he said. Don't think this place sees many folks. I told him we didn't give a shit, long as there's a decent bed."

With adjusted eyes, I took in the bathroom—cat food dishes and old coffee cans, cookie tins filled with semi-fresh water. Tufts of fur and dust, tasselled pillows like mangled children's toys. *"Decent."*

Elowen nudged my arm. "Do we give a shit?"

"I'm fine with cats."

Disbelieving, they leaned closer to examine my face.

"Mr. Tubs over there can hang," I huffed, not unaffectionately. "Don't be dumb. He just—startled me."

Satisfied, Elowen peeled off their soaked layers, hanging them above the tub alongside mine and moving to the sink. Even as they clutched a dusty hand towel to their freckled ribs, I couldn't bring myself to look. I was no better than a teenage boy with a locker room chest ache.

"There's a couple hair dye boxes in my bag," they said, draping the cotton against the counter. "Can you grab 'em? And razors in the front. Shaving ones."

I returned with both and sat along the edge of the tub, supervising as their blunt fingers scraped into the package of razors. Their thumbnail punched through the skin of plastic, grazing the blade guard on one of the cheap blue sticks, and my stomach wretched. After surgically laying out their tools, including an unworn pair of powdered disposable gloves from one of the boxes, Elowen rose as if guided by a holy spirit. They scoured the drawers underneath the vanity, grew stiff at the presence of a lone bible and left the room, returning momentarily with a palm-sized leather sheath, urging me towards the counter. As I lifted myself from my sit, Mr. Tubs took to murmuring furiously until he realized I wasn't coming for him.

Unsheathed from its flimsy scabbard, the knife Elowen offered up was of flaked, blackened steel, sporting an oily sheen of colour within the deep rivets of its sharpened edge. Engraved in the rich wooden hilt, a woman with fat, golden curls and silver rings reared, laughing at nothing but the two letters etched beneath her broad shoulders—*T.D.*

"*You got a boyfriend I need to worry about?*"

I couldn't even look at them when it poured out of me—slicing without warning, burning right beneath my eyes with embarrassment. That was alright; I wasn't the only one smiling, just the only one doing it with humility. Elowen's odd smirk turned their voice to a soft purr, the handle of the knife cocked towards me with the blade pinched between their fingers.

"Ain't nobody *you* need to worry about. Swiped it years ago. *Cut careful,*" they warned. "It's real sharp. It'll blind you, easy."

I plucked it carefully from their hands like a loaded gun. Letting the weight loll against my wrist, my thumb a pad of heat upon its worn

V. IVAN

surface, Elowen's demand wore into my mind and an acute, whipping selfishness came over me.

"*All of it?*"

"It'll grow back," Elowen promised, guiding my bewildered hands, nudging the tip of the knife flat against their skull among easily scalloped skin. "Leave a couple inches. Don't care how uneven it is. I'll take a razor to the edges."

I peered over the crown of their head where that lovely red expanse wiggled amongst the blackened rest. Elowen's expectant eyes were already on me and so I set the knife to their hair, twisted several scattered strands around my fingers, and began to saw.

They were good the way treat-expectant puppies are good; sitting still and straight amidst their clear but unvoiced contempt. I'd never known them to be nervous, yet it spilled from them in waves—fearful of the knife or the hand wielding it, their fingers wound into fists upon their lap regardless. Where their knuckles rutted against the raw skin peeking through the torn slashes of their jeans, I spotted scabs reopened, their kneecap scuffed sparsely as if they'd fallen. I paused and stared at it forever.

"Am I hurting you?" I asked.

"Not even close."

Still, I laid my weight off the knife.

Elowen uncurled their crushed fingers and waved dismissively. I waited for that fist to reform before I took to their scalp again, cutting as close to that pocked, pink skin as I could bear. I pretended I was sawing away at their dense exterior, flaying each translucent wound on their sun-cooked shoulders. *Snip, snip, snip.* Goodbye to the memories of their mother and father, dead in unison. Goodbye to the bastard with the torn apart face. Goodbye to the Echo, its pulsating white tile lights and alcohol-drenched hallways that never darkened.

What else would I find if I shelled them like a pomegranate, sucked away at their seeds until I'd torn the exhaustion from their bones? What other names were wedded to the belongings that kept them safe? If I peeled back the neck of their borrowed jacket, would I find their father's bleeding penmanship? Could I somehow earn theirs on the faded tag of my favourite shoes?

Their fists wrapped around the fabric of the tee I'd stolen, eyes swollen shut by sleepiness. I pressed their ear down carefully with my thumb, their rough pulse twitching hungrily beneath.

If I dug the corner of that blackened blade into the river of scar tissue running alongside their hairline, I could dispel Marian from their mind, too, and remove each and every bit to privately examine. Then I'd be left with a gory, tumescent mess of things I was certain I already knew. I hadn't *forgotten*. Moreso, that slow realization had metastasized in the lining of my brain, consuming my very soul. It wore me like a skin, the knowing feeling of it, the desperation for something other than curiosity or relief. Fear, anger, repulsion—I ached for each.

I tapped the hilt of the knife resolutely against Elowen's unflinching ear. *Take it away from me,* I willed them. *Take it away before I try to dig my own brain out.*

It was a shame to see it go; even the ratty pieces looked sweet, snatched strips of marmalade orange in varying lengths, shaggy and ruined. I'd done a horrific job, yet they'd taken a long look over my work and snuffled a pleased response before tenderly twisting a razor around each unkempt edge. I'd never seen anyone's hands so careful, even in sliding on those skin-fine gloves and alchemically mixing up their dye.

I lowered my head from Elowen's busy frame, staring at their ankles in desperate prayer, curtained by sawed flecks of hair. "Me, instead."

They peered around their own reflection, rattling the bottled dye in their hands. "Huh?"

"I need a trim, too. You can use it up on me—*I don't care*. Just—do me this *one* solid and leave it be. Just for a little while."

Elowen's body sank against the countertop, wedged beneath a boulder-heavy silence. On went the sink full-force and after a quick skim of water to wipe down their neck of biting hairs, they shuffled from the bathroom onto the faded carpet, beyond my puffy gaze. When they returned, the air between us had replenished and with a timid scoop of

V. IVAN

their arachnid fingers parting hair away from my neck, I was roused back to life.

"Keep your head straight," they instructed.

Those hands could've been wielding a knife as striking as the one I clutched, but I couldn't bring myself to look. Fixed on the sink, I waited for the seizing of my hair and the demand for their blade, but it never came. Instead, nesting their hands in my scalp, the paper-thin snip of scissors whispered to me. Out of my sore chest came a stagnant chuckle.

"Somethin' funny?"

Falling hair licked at my neck. "You said it didn't hurt."

Elowen pulled a few strands from behind my ear and lined them up. "Said *you* didn't hurt me. It fuckin' kills, though. An' it'd probably hurt you more than it hurt me."

"I could handle it."

They went quiet, focused on trimming.

Elowen was as capable of hurting me as anyone. I didn't live on another plane of reality. If anyone could do it *right*, it was them. They were as close as needed to inflict something meaningful, something that drew no blood yet left me lifeless. They knew I'd lived on the knife, too, that I'd been cut by worse things than a stolen blade.

If I placed myself in their hands, could they take that ornate knife and part my throat into sections, skinning the fattened tissue of my vocal chords, splitting me open at the sternum? If such things were based on urges or impulses, they surely would've done it already. There'd been no better time than when I was wrapped around their fingers the night before, but the bathroom with its film of grime worked in a pinch. I was water in their torn hands, held innately by their cushioned palms, ready to be drank from. I was surely the most fragile thing they'd ever touched. When the scissors stopped snipping, I nearly wept.

A fat glob of alien black hit my sock, sucking a weak noise from me.

"It's gonna be cold," Elowen warned.

"*That* cold?"

"They were shelved next to the freezer. We're sorta lucky they ain't frozen." Another frigid dab of dye smeared across the back of my neck and behind my ear. I clammed up, squeezing tight like a statue until the chills grew intimate. When the sensation of their careful hands glazing my scalp fell through and I was struck by another wave of bloody delusions, I trapped my hands between my knees.

I could be relieved if logic gave me an answer that I didn't need to ask for. I could go ahead and speculate about the body and where it had gone and who had put it there, who made it a carcass absolved of its rich, fibrous organs. I could speculate, so long as it remained just that—a guess. The truth, harboured in my gut, was that I was afraid of not being afraid. That was the horror of it; the fear of acceptance, so long as it never fell back on either of us.

Elowen's fingers snagged in my hair, and I jerked so violently I thought they'd taken a chunk of me with them.

Standing before I could even register I'd done so, I swayed and shook like a smacked wall hanging, watching them watch me. Their mitts raised passively, purple-black like they'd been crushing wine grapes with their plastic fists. For a long while, they said nothing. Neither of us did. If I spoke, I couldn't even be sure I'd be addressing them instead of someone or something else—the sink, my howling scalp, the muffled screaming through waterlogged ears. Only once I realized I'd been gripping their blade in my pointed fist, prepared for a swift up-strike into a belly or groin, did I come around—sending it rattling into the sink and pretending with all I had in me that I didn't see their shoulders sag.

Quietly horrified, Elowen tenderly placed their scissors against the counter. *"Did I hurt you?"*

I was still on the wall, just a dress threaded through a hanger. *"I'm alright."*

I prayed for them to know that my lack of explanation wasn't synonymous for *yes*, but they held their hands out, low and slow, to the wounded animal I was. Right then, nothing could've felt worse.

"You wanna finish? It's—nearly done."

"*Nn—*"

"Gloves?"

"*In the—sink.*"

V. IVAN

They crept to the counter without question and peeled their second skin off tactfully, the chemical muck contained on the outsides, running them under the water like squid-ink balloons before dropping them dead in the basin. They departed the room with their knife in tow like a shunned child and I stripped clumsily, dumping our clothes on the floor and sliding the shower curtain closed around me, its pallid floral plastic like a sheer cocoon of light as I marinated in that pungent goop for as long as I could bear it.

Gloveless, I slid my fingers into the cushion of dye at the nape of my neck. There were no ribbons of blood, no tears, no breaks. It wasn't the pain at all, but the tugging—the ripping, the pulling. The memory of when it *had* hurt, when the skin there had been gummy and white and bloodless beneath the hem of a brace. I thumbed at the nodules of scar tissue beneath my hairline, reparative marks I could never wash off, and sucked gulps of air as if I'd been underwater all these years.

I was never important enough to be held carefully. Never so important for there to be repercussions from hurting me, never so important that others worried what might happen if they broke me. The last time I'd been worth anything, I wasn't old enough to understand the magnitude of my fragility. Now that I was no longer so fragile, I couldn't dream up a world where that kind of concern existed for me. I had it for *others*. I had it for Georgia, for Elowen, for Kennedy and Andy, and at a distant point in time there had been more. But what had I ever done to deserve it back? What had I ever done for anyone at all?

I'd never been worth a patient voice, two surrendering hands. Maybe I still wasn't. Before I could think anything worse than that, I cranked on the tap and shed my skin.

Lacy black water curtained my calves, like every negative thought I'd ever had was rinsed clean from between my ears, all the gunk and rot and hatred spiralling down the drain. It was ironic at first when the dye took forever to run its course, but after a while it stopped being funny at all, so I scrubbed hard until the water went as close to clear as the rusted taps would allow it and climbed out of the shower, ducking from the mirror while scraping myself dry with an old towel.

On the floor next to the toilet sat a smiling mug of fresh water, the only anomaly since I'd hidden away inside the shower. When I peered into the main room and sought a silhouette in the dark, Elowen was still as a corpse, indistinguishable from a mop of blankets on the mattress. My gaze magnetized to the back of their neck, nipped clean by the razor. In a world where dead mothers taught their lonely, biting children sympathy for strays, I was dwarfed by a gratitude so strong that it vibrated through my fingertips as I returned to the bathroom.

The dye and the trim helped very little with my unfriendly, bastard's face. Black defined my roughest pieces—enunciating the grey-blue shadows around my eyes, prying apart the little bumps and the puffy ledges around my jaw and cheek. Nauseated by the new nothing between my shoulders and my curls, I sat on the frigid tile, stalling and naked, flicking crumbs of butter crackers from my knapsack towards the toilet where two furry paws snapped outwards and knocked them away. I drained half the sleeve and made quite the mess before Tubs finally craned around the toilet to stare at me, lanky and fat the way tomcats get when they turn as old as he seemed, one opal eye sloped distrustingly towards space.

Once he realized I wasn't leaving, he gave a displeased little mewl and began to drink, checking me periodically as he went until he drained the cup and soaked his sagging face. A minuscule success but one I'd unknowingly needed; when Tubs scurried back behind the toilet with less vitriol than before, I wandered off to bed with a lightness in my step that I hadn't had since I was a girl.

I dressed enough to survive the sleep and crouched on the carpet to study Elowen's sleeping face. They left little more than a crescent of cheekbone and buried the rest in their pillow, hands splayed in front of their eyes like they'd been searching for scabbards of blood beneath their cuticles. Their lax, closed lips and their dark brows feigned anger even in sleep, an expression I'd only once seen gracing their waking face.

After some time, I laid with them in the brutal dark. Brief, passing lights glanced inside and plated the radiator with forbidden colour, leaving us with the swallowing darkness again. With my wet head on the pillow and a chill rolling down my back, I was suddenly crushed by what

V. IVAN

we were doing, what we were in pursuit of. It was a long time coming; the extraction of a blackened tooth, one which would powder at the mere touch of sunlight. Whatever was at the end of the tunnel we were barreling down was not regret but something absolved of it, something cruel and warm and bitter. Something inconceivable.

Change, regardless of regret. Change, of everything we were.

I pressed my forehead into the flat pillow aside Elowen's unmoving arm. What remained beyond my exhaustion wanted to touch them, begged my frigid wrists to reach out and soften their back, to wrangle the truth from their coiled innards. Whatever honesty looked like buried inside them, I could find solace in it, in time.

The air was different in Oregon. For the first time in quite a while, my sleep was an ice-filled bath, a crushing nothingness like a kitchen tap spewing cold air. Not once that night did I see Marian.

A Village at the Edge of the World

By the time we encroached on the outskirts of Lakeview, it was snowing hard enough to bury us.

I'd awoken that dim afternoon in a slick sweat, hosting a tumescent guilt in the nerves bundled at my sides. By then Elowen was long awake, a crafty sailor charting our route at the foot of the bed with a red pen. We scattered from the inn like half-conscious roaches, hurling our knapsacks into the truck, nabbing mini shampoos from under the spiderweb-cloaked sink.

I couldn't be rid of the guilt until I'd gotten everything I needed, and Elowen wasn't a complainer; they left inarguably to smoke under the steel awning, forcing coins into an old penny-flattening machine at the flank of the repair shop. On the cusp of their third cigarette I finally waddled outdoors. It'd begun to snow in fat, gluey globs which spackled the faded pink kennel I'd found jammed beneath the kitchenette, duct tape-labeled with the name *Bluebell*.

Tubs was so furious he didn't make a sound.

Salem was a haze of streaking yellow and low brown buildings, strangled telephone poles, long, wide streets like fungal channels dribbling into downtown. We stopped for wet cat food, two nips of Southern Comfort and a pocket-sized map book of the American West which I was both pleased and mortified to find containing a full page spread of Nevada. Tracking through with red pen, I encircled Ely like a bloody footprint, dragged the direct address in pen across the lip of the map and abandoned it in the door cubby where it remained as we fled from city to highway once again.

V. IVAN

The winter night came quickly as expected, the days eager to end and slow to begin. Trapped within the hard borders of the headlights, Elowen's eyes sank into their head from road hypnosis, their white-knuckled grip hooked on the steering wheel. I'd just worked up the courage to suggest a rest when the pitch black swell of single-lane highway gave way to a slash of neon that roused us both. Not a sign from the Gods, but a *motel*. One of the L's on their elderly signpost had burnt out, standing jagged on the split asphalt like a cross: *The Village*.

It was no bigger than three tour buses shoved together end-to-end, a dormant giant bordering a cliffside highway, cradled by wind-snapped trees and narrow gravel shoulders. Inside the truck's stale cab, Tubs and I waited with the whispers of a seventies rock station—me with my coat bound around my hips and him with his beady eyes pressed against one of the kennel's holes—until Elowen returned, a snow-powdered image of mindless resilience. Wielding a keycard which they pawned off into my hands, fatigue devoured their will to speak.

Our room reeked like the tinny mouth of an old can of spray paint left in the dirt. I freed Tubs from his crate and he slunk awkwardly into the corner, gurgling behind the nightstand until I flicked on the lamp and peeled open a can of tuna for him to eat. He fell into a mumbling, slurping trance and between Elowen's stubborn map charting at the dinette and my unspoken concern, there was little else to do but recline on the bruise-purple bedspread and listen to a blaring screening of *The Princess Bride* one room over.

Forever I was cemented to that mattress, dipping in and out of awareness, reminding myself of Nevada's sticky, dark armpit of a climate to reframe the creeping chill beneath the motel door as a blessing rather than a death sentence. At one point, hours or minutes later, Tubs sheepishly climbed onto the mattress below Elowen's pillow, gifting me his rumbling breathing in one ear, my heartbeat thundering against my bicep in the other. Somewhere along The Village's stretch of rooms, a wailing laugh rose.

"I dreamt about you," I said aloud, just to keep the room from spinning.

Elowen's scribbling withered and halted. Then the creak of the dinette chair's worn, shifting bones. "When?" came a raw voice. "Last night?"

I found the comforter's yellowed stitching, digging my nails in, uprooting it from the fabric. "A month ago. Little more, now."

The chair never made another peep, not even as Elowen cast their eyes over their shoulder and stared me down. I hadn't the courage to look at them; Westley was being revived in the other room as we spoke, and I was too busy wishing I was as lucky as a fictional farmhand. Their voice crawled lowly across the carpet.

"What's got you thinkin' about that right now?"

I waited for a lie to wash in; the shore stayed empty. "You," I said simply. "Just you, really."

"That mean you wanna talk about it?"

One of the stitches snapped free, a floss of yellow trapped between my fingertips. "No," I said honestly. "No. I just wanted you to know that I did."

A long, frigid breath passed through the motel room and their etching picked back up, unsure. Slow, repetitive, coiling circles on the edge of the map.

"I hope it was a good dream," they offered, innocently enough. "If you're still thinkin' about it."

I couldn't bring myself to see them right now. Instead, I scraped down my gelling mind for substance, forcing through my ragged imagination the image of them at the dinette, glossy around the edges, holy underneath weak lamplight and curved like a sloping ice swan, encircling routes and tracing them with crude letters. The hair I'd butchered falling above their ears and itching around their temples, their half-open eyes like wet wells of oil-drum black rimmed by exhaustive reds and purples.

Even in my mind's eye, I knew that gleam; I'd recognized it in the briefest of glances, in the smallest of their scars and the emotions that twitched in the opaline tissue. *Vulnerability,* what little that hadn't been washed out in the past. The same way they'd looked at me from the bottom of the stairwell with webs of gore in their teeth. That's how

V. IVAN

I painted them now, in the well of my skull—*fondly*, not despite all the viscera but because of it. Slathered in blood, wide-eyed and fragile. Waiting for an answer to a question they hadn't asked, a reaction to the death I'd secretly wished into existence.

I didn't have one, not then and not now. So I soured against the ambience of their persistent handwriting and melted into The Village's tacky comforter. At some point, Elowen retired to the opposite side of the mattress and Tubs begrudgingly plopped between our legs, both of them too afraid to touch me.

That was *good*. If they had, I might've given in.

F ROM OUTSIDE THE SNOW-CAKED motel came a wild, wailing scream.

There'd been screaming in the dream, too, distant and pebbling like stones on a window pane, but this was different. Not trapped within the echo chamber of my subconscious but further, and not the brutal, uncanny howl of a fox or a cat but the minced, reactionary shriek of a *man*.

Elowen slept pointed away from me, the sheets coiled around their ankles, the mountain of their side traced by slats of light poking through the half-shut blinds. Like a drunk I rose, wrangling my clothes, staggering into the television stand and bracing the teetering box so it wouldn't rattle them awake. I patted the dresser with my eyes half shut, identified the keycard and slid Elowen's boots on, creeping towards the door inside a swell of brutal dark. Mid-reaching for the doorknob, I froze—struck in the back of the head by the image of someone waiting on the other side for me, a frigid humanoid with blistered lily skin and gaping, infected slits for eyes.

In ripping it open, however, nothing was there but a brief, nibbling wind. The snow had stopped in our unconscious hours and rested now like an ironed blanket across the earth. Dome lights dangled above the motel walkway, their pale casings turning everything chalky. I crossed the parking lot and veered from the buggy hum of the roadside vacancy sign, checking both ways on that dead stretch of highway to make sure no distant headlights were roaring towards me.

Another yowl, clearer, whooping through the boughs just ahead. At the opposite shoulder where bottom heavy pines grew in troves, I hiked up the ankles of my sweatpants and maneuvered through the dead, buried overgrowth onto a low concrete ledge ribboned by old chain link, where the decline of a two-lane gravel road snaked around the tree line and into a moored baseball diamond. Easily a hundred feet below, a great roaring beast in the shape of an acid-green derby car flew through the sand like a bat out of hell, flinging caked snow and mud as it went. It spiralled across the diamond, circled by four vulnerable bodies dotting the tire-churned hail like buoys on a pale sea. Through pluming breath came their screams, hooting and hollering at the sky, jeering as the driver left a streamline of blue-grey exhaust in his wake.

I crouched at the edge of the drop off and propped myself into a sit. I must've blended into the trees like a leopard in snow, Elowen's long-borrowed jacket the only signifier of distant human life. From that angle I could rationalize each and every wicked noise, hovering in the stench of ran-smooth rubber. I rubbed one freezing wrist forcefully against my nose.

Marian would enjoy this, I thought, *if he weren't dead somewhere.*

I greeted the memory of him stiffly. If I thought too hard, he'd end up seated along the concrete wall with me, and I wasn't in the mood for company; his spilled blood would freeze in the cold, and I'd wind up leaving him and retreating to Elowen for the second time. Through the howling I was drawn back into the fray, the crunch of cold carpet under my feet, the tart scent of meat, bone and blood all melded together. Elowen's face swollen by shadows, oddly beautiful, covered in a slick of turpentine blood. There were surely others out in the world that might've thought me traumatized by the dream, but it wasn't terror that glued me to the overlook.

The feast was no longer a swirling haze of radio static but a staunch, quiet room in an unvisited hospital wing. It was terminal, my

V. IVAN

hope—that there was an answer there waiting for me, drilling straight into the first willing vein, an answer I could relax against even if it was horrifying. I didn't want beauty, or candy-coated fantasies—I just wanted to *know*.

Marian's corpse had been nibbling at my mind for weeks and yet, as I sat with the drag racers curving crop circles into the lot below, there was something even more gripping about the cloud of relief I'd been perfumed by. Even in that sleeping haze, I recognized the last coils of smoke drifting from that firing gun. It was over. For a brief while, it'd been over. The fright only came in weighing that reprieve and asking whether or not it was worth it. How terrible of a person could he be to end up another's meal? Had he *really* meant what he said, that he'd intended to hurt me? Supposing that was his intention, how long could I keep toying with death? How many times would the Devil arrive to take me and how many times could I stave off what I ultimately deserved?

Death was still ever present, creeping as it had been for years, simmering closely by. The dead man and his cursed gift of relief wouldn't last me, not long enough to live any sort of life. *That* journey was a fruitless one, and there was no turning back for the cowards that changed their minds.

I RETREATED TO THE Village's parking lot in Elowen's untied sneakers and paid for two sugary cans of soda from the vending machine outside the lobby.

Back down the stretch of doors, passing a muffled argument in 1C, I dipped into Elowen and I's shared room which was stale and dank. Assured they were still sleeping, I switched shoes and retrieved two cigarettes from the smallest pocket of my knapsack, creeping back outdoors and around the edge of the motel and shimmying through a gash of unlocked fencing. The flat backyard of smooth concrete beyond was hugged by sloping mountainside and buried unevenly beneath patches of white powder, and since my only neighbours around the lip of the emptied swimming pool were icicle-laminated deck chairs, I had little to be embarrassed of when I crept into its basin for a smoke break.

The deep end was its own universe, sliced from the reality I knew which was restlessly windy and irately cool. That separate universe housed plump groves of seagrass, bulbous strands of kelp, blade-like fish and aquatic snowfall, debris from a world I didn't belong to. I bellied each drag and pretended I was eight feet deep in muted green muck with a stomach full of rocks, pinned against the tile and looking skyward.

There were others in that pool with me. Piranhas like snapping dogs executing the blade fish, splitting chunks from my hair. Fat, blind leeches wiggling in the mud, finding shelter within the golden trinkets sprinkled amongst the gravel-slick tile and reprieve from hunger in the crooks of my fingers. Through the muck swayed a melted figure tucked in the corner, slumping over a ribless abdomen. Dark, wet matts of ringlet hair. Numbed by brine, candied by salt.

Someone eclipsed the shoreline, footsteps snapping in the half-frozen snow. I lifted my head and nothing but bubbles rose from my bloated lips.

Standing at the pool's edge, trapped in a thick sweater and a pair of twisted red pyjama pants, Elowen craned over me, their sleep-swollen face a gleaming pebble on the shoreline.

"Did I catch you just before you froze?"

"Just."

No need to wave them down—Elowen stooped carefully, taking gingerly steps down the tile slope until they reached the bottom, jamming themselves into a flank of snow opposite me like a broom-startled spider tucking itself into a bedroom corner, folding its limbs meticulously to make itself as small as possible. "Penguins huddle to conserve their heat," they said after sparking a half-spent cigarette. "Thought you should know."

"We're a bit south for penguins, aren't we?"

"Y'ever been sick on a long car ride? You don't wanna experience that."

"Let's just let *me* worry about it."

V. IVAN

With the cold seeping into my bones, I couldn't control my delivery. Each word arrived erect and blunt around the edges. Shaking snow from the gutter of my hood, I caught them watching me. Instead of carrying on, I leaned closer and stuffed the second can of soda into the bank to cool, piling it with tidied walls of snow and cracking mine harshly.

"Couldn't sleep?"

"Who's shocked?"

"Not a soul. What was it this time?" When I had nothing to *say*, they had little to *do* but trace their fingers through fresh powder until they found the courage to speak again, lower as if that might pacify me. *"Let me inside. You did once, and I didn't break anythin'."*

A rogue dart could've landed on any fleshy, self-disturbed thought. There was simply too much running around in the dark there—my body a grand meal of flesh, Myra and the polar ice caps melting, Dad and Kev and the sore ache in my larynx that never went away. Marian and his gutted features; he was inside me, breathing through my blood, tickling my nerves with brittle, dead nails, wearing my hands like silk gloves.

Words crept forward, wormed out by eye contact. The right time would never come. Just *a* time, one as silent as this, for the words to be well heard so neither of us misinterpreted things. Down there in the pool filled with imaginary water, I slid through the kelp, my ears waterlogged so badly that my voice came to me as a buried whisper.

"Elowen. Did Marian show up at Georgia's that night?"

They were a silhouette against the pool's grimy wall, motionless the way figures in a dream often idle, aching to burst from their poses and stagger in inhuman ways. But Elowen only broke their statuesque seal by wiping cigarette aftertaste on their sleeve, ashing into the snow. Pitted concern formed around their sunken eyes.

"Is that what woke you?" An exhausted sigh spilled from them. "Leo, it's the middle of the night. You'll freeze out here. Let's go in."

"It's a simple question."

Elowen's fingers found the perfect spot to snub out their smoke, the cherry giving a fizzling hiss as it died. Their lips parted and closed again, the dimpled unevenness of their mouth making each twitch a grimace.

They cast a look towards the shore of the pool, their voice stooping to a private mumble.

"He showed up past midnight. Wasn't too happy that I was the one answerin' the door, so he never *really* told me what he was doin' there. Guessing he wanted to know if you were home, if you'd thought about what he said. *I didn't—*"

"*El.*" White light had taken to the corners of my vision.

"I don't know why," Elowen lifted a hand to stop me and dropped it to their knee. "I don't know why, Leo, and I didn't fuckin' *care*, then *or* now. You might've wanted to forgive him but I wouldn't let him in after *that*, so he just—got in his car and fucked off."

I waited for them to continue and they waited for me to speak, to validate that I'd understood. The words thumbed the innards of my skull, indenting the tender underside of my brain. *He had come over. He'd been there the night he died.* Grotesque excitement crept to a rolling bubble, an impatient siphoning of my inner tension, and I drove it ferociously down.

"So that's it. That's everything. You spoke to him, he left, and then he died."

"This conversation can't happen tomorrow?"

"I want it to happen now." I searched their wind-bitten face. "So is that it?"

Could they see the rotten knowing inside of me, the clarity which I'd dug up through the roots of dream and reality, salvaged from the garbage dump of my consciousness? There was something pearly in their eyes, something understanding. Tucked into themselves, my little spider really did look small. How long did we sit, the weather burying us, before Elowen shook the sleet off of their hood and spoke? Their hands like two brackets, attempting to fasten their knees together.

I had little faith that it was the cold which prompted their trembling.

"*I stayed up. I had no plan to lay down after that shit.*" Elowen's eyes fluttered over the snow, seeking sanctuary from the truth. "Around two he came back, only he didn't bother knockin'. Didn't turn a single light

V. IVAN

on, didn't call out when he came in. He checked the knob and—crept inside, real quiet-like, 'cause he knew he wasn't supposed to be there. I was in the living room—I couldn't—I *wouldn't* sleep, see, 'cause I sort of felt like he wasn't finished."

A chill writhed upwards from the base of my spine, curving around each nodule.

"He didn't get to the stairs," Elowen added, words dangling from their tongue. "That didn't happen."

I gave colour to Marian in my mind, placed stoically inside the downstairs hallway like a miniature figurine with painted clothes and a painted scowl and a painted toothpick blade in his hands, curved at the tip to fit my throat. Slinking through the house, spinning Georgia's figurines around on their shelves. What might he have done while he was thinking about it? What was on his mind when he checked that knob and turned it slow, just to make sure nobody could hear it?

Air puffed in circles from my mouth, split by the dry cold.

"Did he leave?" I begged.

Something in the air splintered—it had to be a question, otherwise I would've broken apart in the sudden shift, in the zap that took to the air and shook us dry from the sleet. Elowen could feel it, too; as I sat willing an answer from their dark lips, their hands struggled to cease trembling. If I wasn't frozen by the image of Marian's murderous face in the sentient dark, I would've held them still with my own.

"I won't be angry, Elowen."

I couldn't be—I'd known, hadn't I? It was the same reason they were vibrating and I wasn't. I was at the mercy of the rollercoaster, flying down the summit, and they were still burdened by the incline, envisioning death at the other end.

"Elowen," I softened. *"Did he leave?"*

Their head lifted from its downward perch. "We're talkin' 'bout that dream you had. Ain't we?"

A scalding cold like menthol on broken skin slicked over my covered chest. "If he didn't leave," I tried, "then he didn't leave. I won't be angry with you."

"*When you dreamt about me,*" Elowen furthered, lifting a quaking finger, "*cause you said you did—what'd you see?*"

I took a sweeping look over them before the guillotine was set to fall. Compared their snow-burnt features to that of the hungry Wolf at the bottom of the stairs, their blood-drunken eyes glassy like wet pearls, their breath whistling in euphoric bursts.

"You," I said. "I saw you. Both of you."

One of those breaths came heaving from them, their body nothing but a punctured balloon.

"Yeah," they quieted. "*Yeah, I figured—'cause I saw you, too, Lee.*"

The tide took me. An overarching clarity like the sting of fresh chlorine gnawed at the hairs in my nose, burying me against the packed ice beneath my ass. My shoulder blades dug squarely into the tile as I tried desperately to keep from folding over.

Marian at the base of the stairs, cemented to the back of my eyelids, in their hands, organs pinched and crushed between molars like ripe tomatoes for feasting. Elowen and their palms wound in Band-Aids, flicking cereal across the counter. A laughing woman on the hilt of a knife I'd never seen before. My skull seemed to cave in, a whining relief and despair settling in the most unreachable crooks of my bones, my connective tissue punctured by memory. *Memory,* yes, because it hadn't been a dream at all. And I'd known that. Deep down, I'd *known* that.

Thank God, I told myself, knowing the horror of that thought's mere existence. *Thank God I'm only as delusional as I'd thought.*

Still the tide swept me out into the bloody deep, where I sucked in heavy gulps of kelp-laced water and drowned in the heat of it. Outstretched went my arms, my elbows locked for my forehead to lay securely. Only then did I recall the industrial crushing sound their hands had made, a then-odd, frightening realism to the cracking of teeth on bone. I sucked back the hard bile in my throat with a long sip from my can, propping it between my knees.

I'd read about these things on the internet before, back when I was in high school. Mountains of men who devoured young boys, who leathered their skin into wallets and lampshades of supple palm and

V. IVAN

throat skin, tangled lamp cords from their arterial veins with beaded decorations around their puckered lace edges. Morbidly, I'd always wondered how someone could bear to work with such a material. What did they taste like, boys? Were they as tart and bitter as their attitudes?

Dredging up the strength to look at Elowen, I found that there was no dreaded shift, no veil-lifting moment, no patiently waiting demonic gleam. All the same Elowen, their hardened face pocked by ancient acne and ribboned scar tissue, rapid exhales parting their whittled lips. Elowen, my friend. Elowen, the waiting shadow in the corner of the bedroom.

Elowen didn't make lampshades of men, but could I change my mind about them if they had? If it hadn't changed at the shifting tide, then would it ever budge? What did that say about me if nothing about them? What horrific delights could I make of the worst men in my life if no moral outcry turned me away? And if the information was in some limbo, not yet arrived at my heart and my soul, would it then drive me insane?

A wicked word wandered up to my ear, whispering scantily to me.
Good. Good.
Devour him.
My own voice no longer sounded familiar, just some airy girl who felt no shame. *"That sonovabitch was going to kill me,"* Not-Me whispered. *"Wasn't he?"*

Elowen jolted, startled by the simple sound of words instead of a blatant, terrified scream. Had they known I was still present, or had they assumed I'd taken off running?

"You were asleep. If I wasn't there, then—"

I envisioned it—the slip of a blade so cold it seemed wet against the ripples in my throat, the breathless, short ride of bleeding out. Death had been in my house, in my hallway. It'd never really left after its first visit. I'd slipped away then, too, like a thin shadow from beneath the windowsill, a pale nothingness into the night.

"But you went further. You went further than just putting an end to it, Elowen."

Their lips were pasted shut.

"You ate him," The words went free stubbornly, coagulated like old blood in the pits of my cheeks. By then, I was impressed that neither of us recoiled. "You *ate* him. *Raw.*"

Elowen's eyes snagged mine, edging on coyness. "How else should I've done it?"

I wished I had an answer. A booklet of tips, a Post-it rife with tricks. I couldn't guide them through this like dishes or laundry, couldn't help them separate the delicates from the rest. "You've gone further before?"

"D'you *want* the answer to that, Leo?"

"This is just part of us getting to know each other." Lord, I tried to sound less spiteful, but I'd exhausted myself of the circling. "That's what you *wanted*, right?"

"You'd be better off not knowing me."

My mouth opened before I could think, and what toppled out was brutal, like the truth always was.

"If I didn't, I'd be dead."

In the silence that followed, I thought about Ylenia Barbaneagra in her pearl necklace crying on the restaurant television. I debated repenting, and the sound of the word as it hissed from Marian's throat. He'd come to kill me that night, or something worse. I shelved every rationalization until nothing was left but the act, the suckling of ribs, the raw feast. The sour slash of fatty tissue wetting their lips, their widened eyes like oil drum bottoms. Idle fingers slid over my chest and I found something all the more terrifying lying there, deep under my own dissectible abdomen.

My pulse rattled along, wobbling and lilting as if I was watching cirque performers tumble from the sky attached to nothing but hairs of silken thread. I'd been in the lion's mouth and had pulled back out once more; the jackhammering of my heart now stood as proof. Relief washed horrifically over me until I was nothing but a leaf, mid-tremor.

It was adrenaline that cradled my hand; my fear paced about in someone else's body, out of sight and out of mind. My hands shook all

V. IVAN

the way as I retrieved that unopened soda from its snow-packed hole and leaned towards the Wolf in offering.

"It's happened before," Elowen confessed after a long, cleansing drink. "It'll happen again. But it's not some—fucked-up hobby. Regardless of what you *think* you know."

"Fuck-all," was an understatement.

"You're not in danger. Not now, not from *me*. I'm not gonna ask you to believe me, 'cause if tomorrow you look back at this and you finally change your mind, I'll understand."

They leveraged their eyes on my face and nodded, more to themselves than to me. A painful twang struck me like an arrow.

"I ain't holdin' you to your word, Leo, 'cause things *change*. If I wake up, and you an' all your things are gone, I'll find a way to understand it. Or if you're still here, and you figure the world can't go on with me in it, I'd just have to let you have me." The slowing snowfall kissed the back of their neck. Even then, I was immeasurably jealous. "Never really knew what to do with myself. You might finally be the one that puts my sorry ass in the ground. And if you are—once you realize what this is, and who I am—I'll understand, an' I'll never blame you for the end of it. Not once?"

I envisioned their teeth framed around my gnawed-on wrist, against a mound of pink, pretty tissue, blistering with nodules and pockets of white fat—a sensation I'd supposedly never feel. Snaking jealousy seized my throat and warped my breath.

I had no clue who I'd be by morning, but it was impossible to imagine a version of myself that would rather live peacefully without Elowen than on the tip of a blade with them. If in the morning I was a different Leo, the kind that could leave her dearest and only friend in the snow and the rain and take off back to Washington, then I'd reconsider. But for the time being, I was the Leo that sat in the snow until it covered her up, the Leo who knew all those petulant truths and still remained, heart twinkling like busted Christmas lights, knowing she'd die if Elowen left her, too. The kind of Leo who would rather be eaten right down to the bone.

IN THE END, YOU KILL US BOTH

"*I'll kill you in the morning,*" I whispered around my drink. "Right now, we need rest."

Slugging back the final potent shot of soda at the bottom of my can, the taste of hot, phantom blood painted my aching throat.

BOISE

I CREPT DOWN THE highway, balancing on the crumbling asphalt where the broken yellow lines were worn to nothingness. The road before The Village was a septic infection coiling through the patchy trees and dew-heavy cliffside. A flash of rain had struck sometime after we'd left the pool and returned to bed, killing off a sizeable amount of snow and leaving a distant mist netted across the morning sky. I was well around the bend before I realized I'd forgotten my goddamn cellphone on the TV stand.

Nothing moved but the power lines. No birds, no animals, the mountain itself as stagnant as pond water. No distant music like in those old Christmas movies, wrenching me towards a fairytale town. What little faith I had dragged behind me as an iron ball in the shape of a knapsack. I figured I could make it a mile or two before I died of frostbite, so I went forward past The Village, hoping for another inhabited building down the way where I could halt and reconsider—then subsequently figure out if I had the cowardice to backtrack.

Elowen was still asleep when I left—curled up facing the bathroom door, their face stuffed into the linen bunched inside their fists. When they slept, they looked like they were playing a coy game of hide and seek, suddenly a child again, left to struggle through dream after dream. I'd stood there watching them for so long and did so without an ounce of shame. If they'd woken up and caught me, I would've bailed at the very bat of their lashes. Instead, their chest rose and fell in light, hiccuping breaths.

I couldn't bear it. I found Tubs sleeping in the bathroom and had granted him a tender scratch across his neck and back, one he was too tired to bat away. Then, wondering if I could brave the sea of old carpet to touch them, I left without trying.

Just as the Village ducked out of sight, it soaked into me—this unbearable sting, a disproportionate piece of my heart demanding an answer. It was *right* to walk away—staying meant something else altogether—but I'd been suspicious in Olympia and I'd come anyway. I fought my own yearning like a resilient weed. Inside me stretched a wide, unforgiving plane where my remorse once lived; the chance to excavate that overgrown part of me, the vengeful, howling hurt and the stony soil of my sadness, still sat just beyond reach. It'd take the rest of my life to manicure those hedges, and then what? Was that all life was? Uprooting one ache and sowing another in its stead?

I rounded the slope, tracing the cliffside that rose to my right and stretched towards a blinding summit. Struggling waterfalls shelled in ice draped over the rock walls at my flank as I went on, wheezing. A hundred feet more and my cheeks were searing with cold, my eyelids puffy and stiff like pencil shavings. I itched at the jacketed skin above my heart and thought of Elowen, wondering which demons they were ducking from now.

The highway guardrail stretched alongside me until the steel fell away completely at a low, snaking stretch of the road, bludgeoned by a great force, its rusting edges left dangling like shredded meat. I didn't check both ways before I crossed and placed my hands against its remaining sister posts, where asphalt bled into the pebbled gravel overhang and then dropped off into nothingness. I was as tall as the treetops of those ancient conifers, looking beyond their pinecone-socked tips and towards the carpet of needles below.

My stomach pumped like an iron lung.

Fifty feet down, a passenger van laid rusted to the earth, speared by the balding stalk of one of those giants. Glassless windows rimmed with thick, orange-rind rust gaped at me, each one a stained, toothy mouth. Time had melted its colours away and one greying passenger door laid

V. IVAN

ensnared in the surrounding grass, caved in by the tumble, punched with an indent like a shadowed crucifix below its handle. Shredded branches from above hung like splayed hands, shielding the sky-facing windshield.

When I came to, I'd already torn a good chunk from my thumbnail, suckling the blood as I raked my eyes over the wreck. The moss-darkened cab tricked my eyes; shadows sculpted a pair of dice in that darkness, black with yellow velveteen spots. Thick leather upholstery, hand-worked, the sort of craft that took years to perfect. A photo dangling from the rearview window—none of it there, all of it a mirage.

I crouched and held the railing, dunking my thudding finger into the snow bank, hardly breathing.

How quick had it happened? Had they died on impact or, when escaping, had shattered bone pierced their vitals? Did lichen take to their spilled blood like a death-drinking parasite? What were they thinking—had they known what was taking place or had the car suddenly felt so *light*, so warm and refreshing and free from the asphalt carrying it that they assumed they were in heaven before the tree even gored them?

My own death lay down there, muddied in the snow, beaten by the elements. I'd asked myself these questions before at another time. There weren't any answers here nor there, but I could be okay with not knowing. I had to be. I'd walk for miles more before I ever caught a glimpse of town, and I didn't have the miles in me. Somewhere down that cold stretch of broken highway someone would find me, Elowen before anyone else, frozen against the gypsum rifts in the cliffside with my shrunken eyeballs hiding inside their sockets, my extremities stained black by frost.

Some part of me, the most *pathetic* part, ached to walk into that endless night and lay myself down with a good view to decay. But my hypothermic ass knew, right then and there, that cutting the cord to save myself from what I needed to do was a crock of shit.

I looked upon the old wagon, buttering my nerves with the now fading similarities to the cars I'd seen before, the cars I knew as a child. That death beyond the highway's bend, that devouring, punishing death—it wasn't *enough*. A more suitable death lived on in Ely, waiting patiently for my arrival. I wanted to go to it. I wanted to find the Devil and cut him limb from limb, and I wanted to be with Elowen before I went. What little life I had was better spent with them, regardless of our atrocities. Regardless of what they'd done. What we would do.

More time.

Elowen slept still against the mattress when I returned, painted by invasive morning light. Flicking the blinds closed, I stripped to the bare minimum, threw on a second pair of socks and climbed into the bed as delicately as I could, pinning myself to their sweating back, seeking heat like a missile. Quiet, languid breaths told me they were alive, so I rutted my nose against the exposed nape of their neck, studying the unclean silver seashell that'd spun in their sleep to face me. They took shape before me as the same Elowen I knew, not as a static image from the night Marian died but as another part of me, unchanged by the lifting of the veil between us. I pressed my cheek to their spine where there laid a sickening sweetness I'd never categorized, hidden beneath a skim of unwashed skin and peppery body spray, sketching out the cloying perfume of a shattered bird on the side of the road or a deer half-sunken in the ground.

Could death cling that way? Without permission? I draped an arm across their shoulder and found their mouth with my fingertips, desperate but paranoid to peel back their cracked lips and find the canines they trusted so faithfully. I craved for an understanding of their body that only they could ever wield, desperate to identify which teeth punctured first, which ripped and tore, which slid the meat from its lifeless bone.

My fingertips dusted their lips, hot breath misting my nails—if they entered the darkness between Elowen's jaws, would they come back again?

The mountains shifted and a hair-thin hand rose from the bedsheets to coil around my wrist. I was little more than a fly in their fragile grip.

"You're still here," tickled the skin of my palm.

I rested my chin against their shoulder as they roused beneath the licks of sunlight from the window. Fluttering lashes, shifting shoulders

V. IVAN

like tectonic plates, the crescent hangnail of their pale face cast my way. Oily tears left streaks against their nose and jaw.

"*And you're cold, so you're real.*" Their voice was burdened by all their smoking, on the verge of complete and utter loss. "*Is it raining?*"

"*Not much,*" I whispered. Not enough to hurry. "*It's holding off. There's time.*"

There was a dense, rolling silence in which so much could have been said and yet nothing came from them at all. Not a hushed sigh, not a shudder. The radiator buzzed and kicked to life. In the corner of the room, Tubs' blurred silhouette flexed in sleep.

"*Sure,*" Elowen finally caved, slackening against the mattress. Our fingers netted together, their palms clammy from another exhaustive slew of nightmares. "*There's time. An' y'know what Pop always told me about time?*"

I was shaking. "*No. Please tell me.*"

Their restless smile splayed my fingers.

"*Our rations won't get any bigger. We just figure out how t'stretch 'em to hell.*"

They drew my arms around them like a shawl and I *knew* it—that I'd never met their father and never would, but all he'd done and all he'd said in life had led Elowen to *this*, to *me*, and I couldn't exist as I was without him. I'd made quite the habit of only appreciating men once they were dead; I wasn't stopping anytime soon.

In an ideal world, we wouldn't ration. We'd stay in The Village, not moving towards home or away, floating in limbo like soulless thieves seeking sanctuary in a place where no one could ever track us down. What they'd done would never matter to me as much as it should. That was the problem with how I felt about Elowen; I'd *cared* about them, the fatal flaw, the last split stitch in my undoing. All things that came after would have to swelter beneath it. Disgust, fear, horror—of which I had none—would all be smothered out like a desperate coal by that care. By the singular moment I'd taken them into me.

The Devil himself couldn't crack through that. I fed that delusion deep in my pill-white marrow, in the last living threads of my soul—that for even those few bloody days on the border between one state and then next, we were alone. Together. Safe from what we'd done and what we were about to do.

Despite where and what we were heading towards, everything was so briefly beautiful.

T HE VILLAGE WAS EONS smaller in the rearview, no longer a moonlight beacon or a scattered graveyard but a simple cash motel on the edge of a lonely highway, shrinking in the nubile daylight. I watched it pass, sent jittering by half a blunt and a lukewarm can of Crush; it was all I had to save myself from jumping out of that moving truck.

We followed that winding highway hugged by leaning trees and little else for another ten miles before we reached any sign of civilization. Eight more until it dissolved into a fifty zone and a sweeping valley greeted us, bordered by tumescent mountains speckled in the last brass tacks of their fall foliage. Once we departed the mountain, the town of Burns slid down our throats in one gulp, our only stop made for cigarettes and a few cheap tabloids which I read aloud in the passenger seat all the way across town and out the other side, the clouds deepening as the day went on like fat turkey tails above the state's hilly borders.

I'd long forgotten my death on the highway when the rain struck again. Huge, eager droplets like wet grubs on the windshield, obscuring the skinned trees, unrelenting until Jordan Valley. We parked along the shoulder of a dusty back road lipped by humanoid shadows of tent rocks and sagebrush, playing a wordless, back-aching game of Twister as we flattened the backseats and folded The Village's stolen sheets down around the cushions, dressing our backpacks in wrinkled clothing and huddling for warmth under the desert's shrinking heat.

All fell silent but the wind and the sound of Tubs devouring a drained can of tuna. Elowen's body traced mine, half-dangling from the edge of the seat until I dragged them closer, ridded by an infectious

V. IVAN

anxiety. That familiar, dredging humidity made me wild and I urgently coaxed them to find me through it—flush against their sweetness, pressing an ear to the staccato pulse at the nape of their neck. Cars dribbled by once or twice in the night and never stopped. Sometime inside the still-dark morning my mouth found their throat, hungering for blood and skin, hoping to trap them between my jaws. A hand, crooked and rough, found shelter inside the lip of my jeans. One of my legs lolled and across the window above my craning face, a gush of hot breath spilled from me.

I didn't dream that night. Not of anything.

When I awoke again, we were flying between curtains of winter greenery where state lines dissolved and bowed to the ungracious volatility of unkempt highway, and each blurred yard appeared the same as the last before it. I was stretched across our makeshift bed, balancing a throbbing neck against my knapsack, patting blindly for my cell phone until I noticed Tubs reaching through his crate and batting at it, face-up on the floor mat. Dead, likely for hours, but the shrinking daylight told me it was evening. I dredged the gunk from the corner of my eyes.

"Jesus Christ, you bounce back fast. How long have we been driving?"

Elowen caught me in the rearview mirror and held me. Sometime after I passed out, they'd thrown on a second layer of knitted ivy green. "Less than an hour. We both slept in like hell—you ain't missin' much." Their hooded eyes flattened on the road ahead again, but they were *clearly* fighting a goofy smile. "Got restless. S'not a reflection of your skills."

"Ha-ha. You didn't get lost while I was out?"

"Not once."

I lifted my head, pressing my cheek to the window. The cool glass fish-hooked me and stripped me of my drowsiness. Ely never saw snow like the trees spinning by the window—a dense icing like that of a rich cupcake, the kind that caramelizes until spring.

"Can't remember the last time I saw a white Christmas in Nevada."

"*Little detour,*" said Elowen, after a swell of quiet. Wringing their palms along the steering wheel, they cast an eye out the window and I followed them—cutting lines through the Douglas fir, searching for something in the heavy thicket. "Won't take us long, I promise. We're still on course."

I stared into a wiry bolt of scar tissue at the tip of their ear, willing them to elaborate. Instead of reaching out to give them a tug, or *hell,* instead of just asking for more, I bumped a foot against the back of the driver's seat and sank into a melted recline.

"Thank God your Pop taught you how to stretch shit out."

Two tarry pupils flew to the rearview, pinched by an eager grin. "Thank God, *indeed.*"

"Pull over. Road hypnosis is eating your brain."

Our detour, as it turned out, rode the thin lines between Oregon and Nevada and skidded into the paper-white sleet of a state I didn't recognize. The moment we passed the guidance signs into Boise, the air in Elowen's truck calcified into something that was difficult to think around. The highway zigzagged into the bowl of Treasure Valley, a frigid soup of low-hanging cottonwoods and blue spruce that stood tall and stripped, cinched at their roots by carpets of cold-shrunken yarrow and shortgrass all the way into the browning chess pieces that made up that huddled city.

A mere ten-minute cruise through the city's wide streets made the memory of Olympia small and unassuming; a compact little burg in comparison to Boise's robust frame and noxious grey sky. Elowen wheeled the truck gently down a clustered bar strip, neon bulbs doubling in my sleep-latticed vision. Purples, yellows and reds in grotesque patches, signs as tall as me hoisted high above painted doorways where people filtered in and out like bees from a dispersed hive, admiring the telephone poles and their blinking Christmas wreaths, dangling candy canes and wicked grinning Santas. As the windows began to fog, I cranked the heater up all the way, pressing myself eagerly into the cushions like I might disappear into the upholstery.

"And why're we stopping?"

V. IVAN

The truck slid to a careful halt along the curb and Elowen turned to me, the powdery hairs of their cheek catching light. "It's almost Christmas," they said, fondling their seat belt buckle. "Let's take a breather. Refuel. Stretch."

"We couldn't have stopped in some bumfuck town closer to Nevada?"

Swiftly came the familiar urge to bash my face in with my fists for even speaking, enunciated by Elowen's stunned, absorbent stare. I wished I could crawl out of my body and let someone kinder fill it back up, retreat into the woods somewhere to live sheltered and solitary as the imitation of a person I'd always been.

But it was there; a twitching, withheld explanation on Elowen's face, forming around a bleak, grimacing smile.

"Cause I know this place better. You need to ease up. Me, too. Hop to it."

I idled on the sidewalk, cat carrier and knapsack in tow, as the brick wall in the adjacent alley was relaid. Elowen stole an emergency sweater from the backseat, hung it stubbornly over their bent elbow and took leading steps ahead of us, weaving through ankle-high snow around trickles of the general public. Their purposeful, zig-zagging stride was enough to quench my mind. They knew the city in a way that only lonesome people can perfect; well-versed in the splotchy desire paths threaded through fenced-in courtyards and icy passageways, the one-man offices tucked deep in the bowels of the few but leering skyscrapers and the amateur graffiti bouncing light from seemingly unreachable heights. A tango step through the dingy alleyway flanking a fish and chips joint swept us onto a well-lit and arborous sidewalk and as we pierced through a crowd I would've U-turned to avoid in Olympia, I latched onto a belt loop on their jeans and trailed helplessly and ecstatically along, handing myself over to the swish of warm, tarry air and the sheer concentration of their speed walking.

Eventually we ducked beneath a striped awning and into a moody billiards lounge where the air was warm and thick as cream, heaters cranked so high that the alcohol and persistent rotation of inebriated bodies baked the bar in a heady humidity. There, I longed to forget the memory of the first and last bar I'd ever been in. Thawing sluggishly, I waddled after Elowen towards the far bar top where our company was none but an old, singing Billy Bass and a few greyscale photos of potato farmers from Hailey cast in a film of dust. I sat Tubs down as gently as I could, his bulk tucked against the old wooden trim. Inside the kennel he stirred loosely, murmuring about the stink of wood polish and spilled liquor.

"You been here before, or did you pick the first one that looked interesting?"

"I picked one that doesn't card." The explanation sat speared upon their teeth, a comfort I envied. "Most folk bitch about the service, but that's 'cause they want a barkeep who'll talk to 'em. *Two whiskies on the rocks,*" Elowen asked the bustling man behind the counter. He returned with two ice-stuffed glasses filled with sunset amber and they slid the nearest one towards me. Bubbles clawed their way to the surface—I gave the glass a jostle, following their ascent.

"I didn't think you were inner-city," I admitted. "I thought you lived in the woods and ate bugs and shit."

Elowen took a brief, startled sip of their drink.

"That's—I dunno how accurate that is," they said, humoured by the thought, "but I ended up here when I got older, just for a little while. Long enough to know a few places, pick up a few things."

I followed their inimitable calmness as I sucked back a swig. A kind, welcoming tickle seared the pathway into my chest, rounding out holes in my gut. In the dark, when Marian began to wander back in through those very gaps, I said, "Show me a bar trick."

Elowen snorted. "I can't turn whiskey to water or anythin', if that's what you mean."

"Just show me what you've got."

When the bartender was back within earshot, Elowen ordered two shots. They arrived briskly, one clear and the other a thick, muted yellow, and Elowen fell upon them like a calculated scientist, meticulous in the burning light, oranges and reds emblazoned on their rough face as they worked. A thick plastic card scoured from the fourth-tried pocket of their jeans, seated neatly on the mouth of one shot glass. Cold, colourless fingertips flipped the covered shot face down on top of the other without spilling a drop.

The card went sideways a hair, allowing the glasses to coyly kiss. Clear began to bleed, a cool, steady trickle that diluted the yellow, spewing fluted trickles into one another until they'd successfully swapped places. I hadn't even realized I was smiling until the terrifying gesture was returned back to me.

"It's a pretty common trick. Used it to get drinks off strangers when I was a kid. I've got better methods for that now than a little shot trick."

I stared brutally into the glasses, willing them to switch back. "How come you never showed me that in Washington?"

Elowen's gaze slid over me, cogs halting. "Did we ever go out for drinks in Washington?"

"Go *out?* No, but we could've."

"Sure. But we didn't."

"Well, I've had people buy drinks for me before and I never had to use any of that stuff."

Though I was the only one thinking of *him* then, a knowing dimness clouded Elowen's wayward glance. "Well," they parroted, flattening a bill and three quarters on the counter, "that's all fine an' good, but us ugly fucks have to improvise. *You* wouldn't know."

Incredibly, I laughed.

Hard, like the sound of buckshot leaving a shotgun. Elowen tried not to panic, but their eyes flickered between my face and the resin-coated butcher block, antsy in the fallout of a sound we hadn't heard in quite some time. Before either of us could pinpoint which despairing pit inside of me it crawled from, Elowen tapped their quarters thrice and leaned, their head lolling to study the bodiless buck erected on the placard above us.

"It's *simple.*" They spoke lowly, just for me. "Ask 'em what they're drinkin'. Ask who introduced 'em to that drink. Sneak in somethin' sly, somethin' charming that'll make 'em feel young. Might even let you try it, if you're charming enough. You never *had* fancy drinks like that where you're from, there weren't any classy ladies around to be orderin' the fancy stuff. Make 'em interested. Hook and sinker. And then you just—milk it. As long as you can."

"That's assuming that every single woman you talk to has the exact same reaction. Which is—so incredibly wrong."

Elowen wagged a finger. "It's not about women or men. It's about *you*. It's a little mask you throw on, somethin' laidback to get 'em talkin' about themselves. Everybody likes talkin' about themselves. Makes 'em feel good."

I cast them a look.

"Yeah," they said around a withheld grin. "Not you, obviously."

"Not you either, right?"

"Course not. I barely fit inside those categories." Peeling themselves from the barstool, Elowen slid behind me, patting their ghostly hands on my shoulders once they knew I'd seen them coming. *"Watch, Leo,"* they whispered. *"Watch the professional."*

"I don't want anything fruity. Pick a strong drinker."

"You'll take what you get." When they caught my eye, I found wicked delight blooming in their swollen pupils. "Then you'll try it yourself. Hammer some of that stress out. We ain't all the way to Hell yet; might as well enjoy the last bits of Heaven on the itinerary."

They found their targets easily—a gaggle of mature women in leather and jean jackets, tan and coal cattleman hats and well-worn ropers, each contoured by budding drunkenness in the flushes of their cheeks, worked well into the angular wrinkles they'd spent years sculpting. Elowen was outright conversational for the first time since I'd met them; smooth and slow like a serpent. They slid past the table and halted at the sight of one precariously perched glass on the knee of a woman at the booth's edge, backtracking to ask her some muffled version of the first step as the group turned to them. I swear I saw the curtains close and the roses fly.

I tried uselessly not to stare, but there was captivation in the eyes of those women, a gleeful audience to the impossible trickster I'd brought with me. Elowen's worn fingers curled around the edge of the table as they crouched to drown out the music. One woman leaned close to speak, the sunken apples of Elowen's cheeks rose with laughter and something inside of me was gored by a cattle prod. As if I was on camera, Elowen turned in my direction and the group followed, taut by invisible strings hooked to the hems of their collar. Red-faced, I spun and studied the hanging wine glasses behind the bar. I sat for ages just gazing blearily at the backsplash and strip lights until the stool next to me cranked out from under the counter and Elowen's thin, branch-like frame was back in my sight.

"*Did I botch it?*" After a few seconds of debilitating nothing, my hands began to tingle. "I botched it," I said again, sure this time, as the passing barkeep settled two ruby-coloured cocktails before us.

I stared dumbfounded at their pink-salted rims, the arch of lime wedged upon their lips. Elowen peeled one from its paper napkin with no more than a smug glance that spoke deafening volumes. They crushed their lime with their teeth, suckling at its loose pulp. I was nauseatingly envious of the garnish, the warmth of whiskey kiting my mind elsewhere. Last night. *Last night.*

"*You're cute,*" Elowen purred after a long sip.

Every ounce of blood in my body flooded my face. I pressed a cooled hand to my closed eyelids. "What is *wrong* with you?"

Their eyes cut across the bar, admiring my burning face. "They think you're some precious, sittin' here all by yourself. They wanna shove a table together. How's that sit with you?"

I debated our options. When I came up with nothing and the blood returned to my extremities, I shouldered my paranoia and slid my cocktail across the counter until it clinked against theirs.

"I've got nowhere *better* to be."

One last confident swig of whiskey to take it all down, its uniform bitterness a cutting reminder that the evening was not an eye-of-the-storm dream. I had to allow it to be genuine in order to feel it. I had to lay down the fractal images of the dead that plagued me and step back from the stairwell to see Elowen properly. I had to know they

were there, in the flesh, and that of the few good moments I had access to, this could be one of them.
Only then would I feel it. So help me God, I wanted to feel it.

As the night grew long in Boise, I ran laps around the table, sopping up compliments and stories like a soggy paper towel.

Maryellen was an accountant, a round-faced widow of seven years who only recently got back into fly fishing to meet singles. There was her sister Denice, an orthopaedic surgeon with an eighties slasher fixation, and Marta, a dog-sledding hobbyist whose summers meant trading stocks and spending time with her children on black sand beaches. Over the table she flashed a polaroid of herself in a floral bathing suit on the coast of Tahiti, golden-brown and grinning like a jack-o-lantern.

"I have more," she said, "but they're not as appropriate." When I flushed the group of them coddled me, as if expecting I'd never seen my own chest in the mirror let alone anyone else's.

But my eyes were on Elowen all night. Melted into the booth across from me, mirrored by women twice our age, gabbing in multiple directions with an energy I'd never seen. Flashing razor teeth, the bloodied glow above our booth blurring every fleck and scar against their cheeks. The pits of my eyes ached like I was hunting for the wispy lines of the Northern lights through a foggy sky.

That was The Terrace—Maryellen, Marta, Denice—then there was The Whistling Dog, which sounded fucking *hilarious* after a few rounds of negroni and whiskey. At The Otter there were others—Julia, Nathan, Haylie—a veterinarian, a pro-bono lawyer and I couldn't remember the last one, God forbid, I was a little wasted. By the time we left The Otter, where I abandoned each name like old gum on the table, we were nearing the last hours of the evening and the hot chocolate-toting grandparents and their grandkids had long cleared out.

I was knee-deep in a snowbank, ogling at the lamppost Christmas garlands when Elowen finally coaxed me onto the sidewalk with Tubs

V. IVAN

swaying at my side. I was still punch-drunk off all that conversation, daydreaming about vacations in Polynesia and the process of castrating a domestic python. It was time to return to the truck, to feed the cat, to crawl into Elowen's clothes and warm myself up. The memory of their venous, slanted hips clenching beneath my hands at the Sixth Street apartments swung upon me like a bat to the head, and my landing foot skidded on the sidewalk.

"Careful. It's only quarter to eleven," Elowen countered when I started whining, stomping out a seat in the snow for me at the mouth of an alley and dropping that unused sweater in the fresh cavity. "Sit," they demanded softly, and I did without question. "Just catch your breath. We'll grab a bite, an' then we'll head back. Alright?"

"I thought this *was* me catching my breath," I tried to say, but I hiccupped and embarrassment claimed me.

Elowen leaned patiently into the cement wall, its crumbling ankles latticed by a fishing net of dead, ice-flattened grass. "You must be hungry."

Inside, my guts wrung responsively like a wet towel—but at least I'd given a convenience store fruit cup a chance the night before. As the brick at the back of my neck cooled me, I hiked my hood up for protection. "Christ, don't worry about *my* hunger. I'm still waiting for you to feed *yours*."

The world fell sharply quiet, eavesdropping on our little corner of the pavement. I caught Elowen's eye and something prodding peered back at me, searching my face for reason. With my wide, fat tongue laying dead in my mouth, I ducked my head.

"I didn't mean it like *that*."

A group of tourists clamoured by, stupefied by the Christmas glow of downtown Boise.

"*Uh-huh,*" Elowen murmured once they were out of earshot. "But you're thinkin' about it."

I laughed again, humourless the second time. Even Tubs startled in his crate.

Elowen turned to the street, gnawing at their fingernails with their teeth, their body carved by that insatiable hunger so long ago that they'd made an art of appearing comfortable despite starving. "You would've been better off not knowin' at all," they whispered as sirens fled past. "But I didn't have a choice in tellin' you, for the record."

A disagreeing noise shot from me. "No. No, no, no. You *had* an out. All that legal noise on the TV? You could've let me believe that instead."

"Even if I could've, it wouldn't make a difference."

"No?"

Elowen sought fresh words from the filthy snow at their ankles. Their lips split from the cold, a lashing of blood at the corner where I'd kissed them before. "You're smarter than some lazy ol' dream—you already knew. Nothin' I could've said would've changed your mind, but you'll think of me differently from now on—*forever.*" The toe of their sneaker disappeared into the slush. "I'm still tryin' to figure out which would've been worse."

"What were my choices?"

"You thinkin' of me as a monster, or you thinkin' you can't trust me."

The cogs worked tirelessly behind Elowen's darting eyes; they had been since day one. Which would've been worse: living in blind faith that Elowen was some puritan saint, or knowing that all that blood had been real then *and* before, *somewhere* else with *someone* else at some *other* point in time? That it was frequent. That it was perpetual, them wading in death.

"What's the point in knowing you if all I know is a lie?" I asked us both.

They squinted in the gleam of passing headlights. "Even if I'm a monster to you?"

When my speechlessness waned and my words finally returned, I was frostbitten with annoyance and much too drunk. It came out slurred but honest, as brutal as it needed to be. "You're not a *monster*, Elowen."

"I didn't lie to *you,* Leo. *Please,* don't—"

V. IVAN

"Oh, God, *please?*" I bubbled over, startling both of us. "Spare me. Spare me from that. You don't *do* that—that *pity* thing. Don't start now, here, with me."

For the first time in a long time, Elowen looked truly embarrassed.

"You're a *killer*," I said aloud, my voice wobbling just above a whisper as I hammered out the syllables, sobered by a single word. *"That* you are. Beyond that, you're a confusing, antisocial *prick* and a spiteful *bastard* at times, but so am I. And if that's the worst of you, that you're a bastard and a prick and a *killer,* and you don't know how to be hungry in *any* other way, then I've *still* loved worse people before you. Really, really shitty people that never gave a damn about right and wrong, or the world, or me and my wellbeing. You can talk about monsters all you *want,* but neither of us are *stupid;* you're a special degree of fucked up and I should be disgusted by you and what you've done, I know that, *I know that,* but I *won't be.* I can't get past you. I *can't.* I know evil and I'm *sorry,* but you're not it. I don't even think you're *bad.* And if I'm sitting here rationalizing it—because Marian *was* a bad person, bad enough to come to Georgia's home where her *kids* sleep just so he could hurt me—by your standards, what does that make me?"

Button eyes burrowed deep into the snowbank between us, flattened with layered footsteps from the alley out onto the street. Breath puffed from Elowen's mouth in rapid, visible bursts. I hadn't realized I'd kicked on the waterworks, not until I faced the streetlights and found they'd become wobbling, splotchy thumbprints.

"You are *fucked up,"* came their whisper after an eon of silence.

I knew that. If I didn't by then, I was *screwed.*

Elowen slowed, each word delivered in courses. "You are fucked up, but there's *nothin'* past you," they said, as if they'd studied that map through our entire trip and knew very well that the roads dropped off at the small of my back. "It's been so long since I've loved anythin' that I'd hardly recognize it if you showed it to me. Sometimes I think it's all I've got to keep my fear company, but I can't remember where I buried it. Lee—whatever's left, whatever you've managed to dig up—it's yours."

They raised their baying head, cutting right through me. "You *know* it's yours. I mean—by now, you've *gotta* know that."

A melody of feeling puddled at my feet, encouraged by liquor. At first, my reflection rippled with confusion—anger followed suit, because I just didn't *get* it. A bruising, painful heat that swam through the nodules in my throat, shrinking my tongue against the back of my jaw. Denial arrived like a brief and bloody sunset, because what could they possibly want from me that would require such an elaborate ruse? An emphatic wave like a pair of hands dug into my skull and sectioned it like citrus. Each wedge a florid emotion—guilt, confusion, terror, euphoria.

There were tears in my eyes. Big, fat, wet ones. I didn't move until they'd been sucked back, until I could put away my tools of frustration and allow the words to just float, without any frightened refusal. I forced my eyes onto the crate, between the matts in Tubs' ginger fur.

"*I'll take whatever you've got.*"

We hung there, battered by the love, exalted by it. I waited for it to dissipate only to realize it wouldn't once Elowen's fingernails had been bitten down to the tips of their frost-white fingers. With a numb ass I rose, removing my eyes from the kennel. Blobs of wiggling light danced at the corners of my eyes.

"*Y'know what we need?*" I asked earnestly, patting flecks of dirt from my pants. "Another whiskey sour."

Elowen's silhouette twitched, their chipped thumbnail wedged between canine teeth. "There's one we haven't hit," they said, tapping a cigarette from their crumpled pack. "Round the block, to the right. The Elixir Room."

"Fine. Let's hit it." When they didn't budge, I nudged their shoe with my own. "I'm getting really, really thirsty. I might die."

Instead of being roused by my pitiful attempt at lightening the mood, Elowen gestured to the sidewalk and back over their shoulder, sparking a shy flame.

"Round the block an' to the right, past the deli, past the lights at the intersection. There's a big purple sign out front, last I checked. Y'can't miss it."

V. IVAN

"Why aren't you getting up?"

They finally looked at me. Long and slow, sober but lost in something heavier than drink. "I'll follow. Jus' need a minute to finish this. That's all."

"I'll wait for you."

"Go ahead. They won't card you." Elowen wiped their palm of spilt ash. "I've been before, many times; they can't do without the cash. Go on an' get us a drink, 'kay? But *pay* for it. These ones'll take you home if you let 'em." After handing me a twenty which I took with numb fingers, they flattened themselves against the brick, drinking in my splotchy face. "I won't lose you. Believe me. Just need to wash somethin' off."

I dragged myself down the block with that bill crammed stiffly in my pocket, hooking right past a dim sandwich shop and scuffing my feet until I found The Elixir Room, as easily as Elowen had claimed. It waxed the street in shades of orchid purple, omniscient and gothic against Boise's cloak of holiday cheer.

The fluttering guts of The Elixir Room were trophy-laden, dozens of horse racing chalices on shelves with punchy, incandescent lights underneath, illuminating the gold and silver like dying stars against supernova splatters of colour. Remnants of cigarette smoke plumed like spores from the wooden floor, the motion in the room a constant, communal jitter of nicotine cravings. The bar stretched horizontally towards the furthest wall and at its end I found the first face I could make out in the tart-purple light; a thin, waning spirit with oaky hollows beneath his inch-thick eyeglasses, erected like a coat hanger beneath a turkey-grey uniform. I took a seat away from him, near a collection of pool tables overflowing with quietly chatting men and women in long, thick coats.

I looked at the door more times than I'd like to admit. Really, I did all but burn holes into it. The confidence inside me waned but I clung to it with my nails, hoarding it deep inside my skull where it retreated into the tender flesh of my brain. I'd meant each syllable, regardless of the timing, regardless of the circumstances. I'd never been confident, not once, and it was spurting out of me then but so was the alcohol, so were the bitters. *Fuck*, I had to piss. And I *just* sat down.

Regardless of his protests, I hauled Tubs along with me. Even the bathrooms were surreal—long peels of waxen orange paint along the ceiling, casting a rich, warning glow over the checkered floor. In my pursuit for relief I nearly slammed into a spindly, expensive-looking woman at the sinks, touching up the concealer beneath the corners of her narrow eyes.

"You're alright," she said in the presence of my mortified face. A thick pair of silver-rimmed glasses rested against the crest of her greying head, her sparse lashes caked with liner. Her wide, curious gaze followed me to the sink's edge where I stood idly for a moment, suddenly too shy to pee in front of a beautiful woman I didn't know. A pang of embarrassment cut me open.

Setting Tubs aside the exposed plumbing, I pumped thick, fluid soap into my hands and cranked the tap. On the edge of the neighbouring sink, an array of thick golden rings lined the porcelain. One for each finger—sparkling, bulbous faces with thin backs, horseshoes encrusted with glaring diamonds, a snarling doberman with garnet eyes. The head of a stallion, its bridle polished by emeralds.

"Someone's got wanderin' eyes."

My gaze flew upwards, lipped by trails of light. Despite my drunken dizziness, she was *gorgeous*, and not just in orange. Any light would've suited her I bet, with her dark lipstick and her tanned face like an old cat, firm and round at the hard edges of her cheekbones, her slate-grey hair a half-braided curtain that nearly reached the countertop.

"You have beautiful jewelry," I confessed.

Her lips twitched towards a vague smile, and she slotted her glasses back upon the bridge of her nose, softening the powder around her eye with her pinky. "That I do."

I'd never seen gems like those before, not even in the movies. "You must like horses."

One after the other, each ring slid down a dried finger, the doberman guarding her index knuckle. "I don't like 'em, I raise 'em. Auction 'em off to heavy rollers in Montana. Pays for the stones."

"Are horses that valuable?"

V. IVAN

"They can be." She caught her own reflection in the mirror, then mine. Something simmered there. "Depends on how good you are at takin' care of 'em. If you're shit, then they're shit. Lots of things work that way."

"You must be pretty good at it, then."

"I manage." Turning from the mirror, the woman adjusted the buttons on her collar and splayed her hands out before me. "Which one caught your eye?"

My mind ran blank, numbed by the neon buzz overhead. Only with a waggle of her fingers could I tell that her brittle nails were painted nude.

"My rings," she tried slowly. "You were starin' at 'em."

Helplessly, my eyes looped around her thick knuckles sectioned by gold, the small rivulets of scar tissue from years of being an equestrian. But the garnet caught me, still.

"Your dog."

That pleased her. She raised her knuckles, eyelashes inches from its snapping teeth. "Evil little thing, isn't it?"

"You got one?"

The woman paused. Glancing towards Tubs' carrier beneath the sink's edge, she flinched. *"A pet?* No. I keep this one around, though," she said, working the gold between her fingers. "Feels like a ward of sorts, though I suppose I haven't needed it lately. I've got other dogs that hang around. The bipedal kind." Just as easily as she slid it on, the woman peeled the doberman from her finger and tilted it, hanging from the tip of her index, towards me. "Here."

I stood frozen there, wiping my hands on my three-day-old jeans. "I don't understand."

"Take it, girl. Your hands not workin' all of a sudden?"

No, actually, they weren't. They'd gone just about as heavy as two cast iron skillets dangling from my aching wrists, and more than that, my bladder was mere moments from busting like an overstuffed balloon. Desperate to relieve myself and reddening by the second, an involuntary shudder rolled the words from me.

"I've really gotta pee."

IN THE END, YOU KILL US BOTH

The woman abruptly straightened. A long blink of her cloudy eyes sliced the air between us in two, and her hand, dangling the doberman, swept the room with little concern.

"By all means. Don't let me stop you."

Her stare cut shapes across my back as I scurried into the stall, crudely slamming the door in pursuit of not pissing myself. I barely made it—my foot crushed to the side of Tubs' kennel with my pants ridiculously askew—and thinking of that odd, ringed woman standing at the counter listening to me emptying out just complicated things. But it wasn't long before the Elixir's swinging bathroom door whimpered in her departure, and in avoiding my own reflection in the gold-rimmed vanity mirror afterwards, I made eye contact with the doberman ring sitting precariously atop a slice of paper towel, its unholy eyes glinting upwards in abandonment. It seemed cursed just sitting there and still I lifted it to the light, marvelling at its silversmith scarring in purposeful patches. I slid it halfway past the middle knuckle on my ring finger, as far as it would go. Whatever curse the doberman held, it couldn't possibly complicate things any further.

Back in the bar, the silver-haired woman stood out now like a swollen thumb alongside men that were twice her size yet shrunken by her presence, tucked politely into a corner booth within the smoking section where cheap nuts in filmy amber bowls dotted the tabletop. As I orchestrated my drunken steps back to the table I waggled the doberman at her; behind the smog from her cigarette, I could've sworn a smile passed over her face.

A deep, wading loneliness swept me out to sea. Clouding my skull was the image of Elowen down the street somewhere, hands as cold as the truck's rims, burning out the end of their smoke with no jacket. Waving my hand like a child in class, I drew the bartender, who came sluggishly to my rescue while iron-gripping a tray of dirty glasses, and ordered a half-serving of sauceless wings and water with no ice, to his *clear* lack of appreciation. I brought Tubs onto the seat next to me, his crate sandwiched between me and the wall, his coin slot eyes glaring needles into me as I tore the meat from its bones. Nostrils pinched by

V. IVAN

an oily musk, I fed the angry old man through the bars of his kennel until we both calmed down. The dim dark crept closer, enunciated by that petrifying loneliness. Marian was just threading his ghostly fingers through my hair when a known sweetness tugged me back.

Elowen slid across the booth from me. It was all I could do not to dive into them, instead tracing the coiling lines of cold pilling off their clothes like gun smoke, their snow-swollen hands pressed to the sides of their neck in desperation. I draped my own across the table, wiped free from the stench of peanut oil, and Elowen buried their icy fingertips in my palms without question. The sweater rolled off their arm and onto the seat, entirely unused.

"No drinks. You pocket that bill or what?"

The doberman sang to me, hidden beneath our hands. "I'm working my magic," I quieted, relishing in their presence. "Hook line and sinker. Just wait."

"All the buyers are off to parties now," said Elowen, rustling their fingertips like worms in dirt to stir the heat. "We can just order somethin'."

"Not all of them. Just give it a minute."

They sat back, removed their hands, dusted the chill off their shoulders. After an aching minute of no changes, they jutted an open palm towards me. "Pass me the bill. I'll pick somethin' out."

A slinking hand passed over theirs and two candy green drinks landed on the table with a deliberate *clink*.

"On the house," came the bartender's crypt-dry voice, stiff and sour like he'd rather not give us the time of day. He shuffled back to the bar, gripping the edge of his tray as he went. Inside the rippling candy green the Elixir's lights danced, and pride rolled over me like an avalanche.

"I *told* you," I gloated, sliding a glass closer for inspection, melted sugar swirling lowly like glitter. "I found one more. It was sort of an accident, actually. I almost crushed her with the bathroom door."

Elowen toyed with their glass, nursing a hesitant sip. Their lips twitched at the sweetness, casting out a plush, darting tongue so they wouldn't miss a lick of sugar, their gaze floating lazily around the room.

"Crushed with a door. *God*, you're a charmer."

"That's, like, three times tonight," I pressed, searching Elowen's unamused face. "Maybe four. I lost count. Point is, I think old women *love* me. I've found a new passion to replace—the lack of a passion I had before, I guess."

Elowen's expression was stuck, a mesh of illegible emotions netted over their rosy cheeks. I sat my glass down, envious of the sugar at the sharp corner of their lip. They lifted a stiff hand and gestured, if you could call it that, with a twitching finger across the room.

"That one. In the corner, there."

When I spun, the silver lady was watching us sternly, only she wasn't looking at our table, our drinks *or* me—her pale, feline eyes were on Elowen, firm and half-hidden behind the fur-clad throat of her newly donned coat, unwavering. I faced forward and threw back another swish.

"You mean the cougar with the glasses?"

"Yup." They were still staring.

"Bingo. Nice guess."

Something strung out lingered in Elowen's voice—an odd gleam I'd seen only once or twice, hand-painted across their tight cheeks like the glossy face of a porcelain doll. I rapped my knuckles on the table, flashing the ring as Elowen's eyes, widened and black, fell expectantly onto the doberman and solidified there.

"She gave me this," I clamoured on, desperate for their distant attention. "Just 'cause I said I liked it."

I turned to snag her attention but in the fragile seconds it took for me to look away and back, the woman was up and gone and the Elixir's double front doors swayed in her absence. I licked absinthe from my lips, bathing in a lime-green drunk as a gust of clueless gratitude swept under my jacket and stood me on my feet.

"I'm going to say thank you. To be nice."

Elowen's head jerked so hard, their neck popped. "You don't need to."

V. IVAN

"Nah, but I'm going to," I crooned. "You left me, so I'll leave you. Just for a minute."

"*Leo—*"

I was away from the booth before they could fully protest. The cold beyond the bar's entrance bit eagerly at my face, which was hot and ready from the absinthe, and I milked that languid heat as I wobbled down the steps, spotting the woman alongside an ivory Lincoln town car parked twenty meters down the sidewalk. Beside her idled a large, Slavic-looking man with a cross, hawkish concentration on his face, his wiry blonde hair greased into a ponytail that must've taken years to grow—a true dedication to looking as awkward as he did.

Upon my approach the Slav straightened, horribly threatened by the sight of a short, chubby drunk girl in a jean jacket and hoodie. The bejewelled woman reached out and shooed him towards the driver's door, adjusting her glasses to get a better look at me as he fit himself awkwardly out of the way.

"*I didn't get to thank you,*" I heaved.

She waved a limp hand. "You don't need to," she hummed, suspending me with a playful stare. "Spreading cheer on Christmas. All that."

"Expensive cheer," I countered. Awkward in the cold, I glanced between the man and her, gushing hot breath. "It was really nice of you. I'd pay you, if I could."

"That's alright. Happy to share."

"I hope you make lots of money off your horses next year."

The woman looked as if she were going to agree, or perhaps she was going to tell me she really didn't need luck, but her eyes cut bluntly past me as if drawn by the brilliant force of a distant explosion. Following her, I discovered Elowen's ghostly form atop the steps, beholding me like I was petting a drooling tiger through a live-wired fence. The handle of Tubs' kennel was cemented to their palm.

"This a friend of yours?"

Even after all this time, I was still asking myself that question, despite knowing the answer the same way I knew breathing and blinking and digesting. Just hearing it aloud drew a phantom laugh from my sore throat.

"*Sometimes.*"

The woman stepped from the side of the Lincoln and settled alongside me, the both of us studying them like a jagged mountain ridge, balancing the sun on the tip of its head. Extracted seemingly from nowhere, the woman shot her words like a gun, firing over the lessening crowd of passersby.

"*Hey, stranger.* You got any thanks for me, too?"

A sinking, thickening feeling cropped up in my gut like bad bacteria. It was dread, looming over. A tall, sinking dread, like hearing your name called through leafless woods. Like knowing something is sitting just beyond the blackened panes of your bedroom window but being too terrified to part the curtains.

"*Elowen,*" the woman beckoned, a curse drawn from my own head. "*Should never leave your friends out in the cold.*"

My blood coagulated and froze.

They weren't *surprised*—that was what frightened me the most. They stood there, posed like a department store mannequin, their wide, lightless eyes rolling back and forth between us, and not for a single *second* did the cogs in their skull grind or stutter. As the spell broke, Elowen crept down the steps in bruised silence, refusing my stare. I couldn't see anything else—only the subtle twitch of their scarred mouth, pin-straight and unhappy. Dread, milking my bones of their marrow. Dread, replacing the sugar on my tongue with something slick and bitter.

As they grew closer but not near as close as I, the woman's hands came out, reaching, grabbing.

"C'mere," she said. "Lemme look at ya."

Elowen lingered long enough to make things aggressively awkward before lifting their limp, dead hands. The woman took them, pressing her thumbs into their palms, leaving indents that I felt on my own skin—deep, repulsive rivulets in the flesh.

V. IVAN

"God," she lamented. "Been a good bit since I've seen that face. Nobody told me you were here." A slanted laugh spilled from her, and I could've sworn the ground shook. "Well, who would? Not *you*. Christ, no."

Only the woman turned to look at me—I'd lost Elowen in the fog of it all, unreachable as they glowered at the sidewalk.

"Don't be nervous," she purred, staggering me with the sudden brightness in her tone. "I've known this one since they were a sprig of grass. When you compare the two images, it's really quite something." Her hands, removed from Elowen, slid forth to cup mine, the absinthe working my body like a hamster in a mech. "Ronnie," she declared expectantly.

In the silence, I'd forgotten my own name and how to tear free. I parted my lips, but they shrank shut again.

"Summers," Ronnie tacked on like that might clear things up, her pearly eyes lowering. *"Veronica."*

"We're just passin' through," Elowen cut. Then, as if just remembering that I was present, "Leo? Time to tuck tail?"

Seemingly burned by my inability to recognize her, the fog lifted from Ronnie's stare and her head cocked to the side. *"Don't tell me you're drinking and driving."*

"I've slept it off in a truck bed before," said Elowen. Their hands went buried inside their coat pockets, writhing like unearthed snakes to shed some invisible grime. "We have blankets. We'll do fine."

"It's *freezing*," Ronnie fought. "We're heading up to the cabin right *now*. There's plenty of room for you to rest a night. You know that." Elowen's head began to shake, but Ronnie held up a ringed finger and I beheld the whole thing like a painting on the wall, banging my bloody hands on the canvas, wishing to be set free. "Your friend needs a bed. How long have you been driving? You must be exhausted. You get sick *so* easily. Better ward it off before it gets here."

"A bed would be nice."

I hadn't intended to speak, but in the moments after I did, I fought regret back down into my belly with all my strength. Was it betrayal that slicked Elowen's face? Some Frankenstein expression I'd spend the rest of the night scraping from the backs of my eyelids, grime collected alongside the fear and the dread? It burrowed deep inside of me, knotted up like a set of guts mirroring mine. It could've been anger, or panic, or fear for all I knew. I'd never *seen* them panic. If that's what this meant, then I wanted to take them away from it—once I understood.

Whatever this was, it meant *something* to them. So little I'd been given from Elowen regarding their life, their wants, their *cares*, that even though I'd rejected the urge to know them at one point in time, the cloak slid free and I bore it openly now—had always needed it despite envisioning some way around it, like a mosquito charting an escape from blood and reproduction. At that moment, the desire was parasitic. It was all I knew.

Elowen didn't argue. They fell silent to Ronnie's appeasement, moving to the Lincoln with Tubs at hand like a red carpet spectacle, the door opened for them by the Slav who had arrived cartoonishly fast at Ronnie's side when he was beckoned. I climbed inside the cab eagerly, coaxed by pluming heat the same way a child is coaxed by sweets.

The Elixir Room disappeared in the dark, Boise's Christmas decorations muted by window tint. Against the rich leather seating that gushed of fresh coconut air freshener and deep, woody herbs I rested uneasily, drawn in by the murmur of Highwayman on the radio, the Slav's low hum whittling away at my nerves as the weather began to stir and gurgle, churning dense, blinding flakes in a matter of minutes. All the way outside of town and upwards through the wind-shredded mountains, Elowen's eyes remained out the window and on the snow-spattered trees as if they'd lost something in the sleet and were searching tirelessly for a glimpse of it. A wagging flashlight beam, a hand gloved by vibrant blood—a haunted memory, of which I now knew they had plenty. Not even a hand could break them from the sights beyond the glass. Not even a whisper, not a nudge. For once, they were awash in their own worries instead of mine.

Something, somewhere waited for them out there. I prayed, if I was even capable, that it wasn't me that summoned it.

THE LONGER-LASTING ASSHOLE

I ONLY KNEW ONE car before the Lincoln that was equally as personable—a '64 Ford Falcon, my father's. I sat in the back of the Lincoln the same way I had in the Falcon; like I might bust a seam by exhaling too fast.

The Slav wound us up the mountainside through hurtling snowfall, Boise's boundary hills slanted like the lines of a weathered cross. Roadside pines rose like sky-wanting fingers and the Slav powered through with nerves of hammered steel as the tires stuttered and wobbled through densifying snow. By the time we found our traction, I'd stamped nail marks deep into my seat.

Elowen still wouldn't look at me. They huddled like a pinched nerve on the opposite seat, unmoving as the road's bumps thudded their temple softly against the frost-lined glass. In days past they'd subsided almost entirely off mitigated sleep, soda and cigarettes and the light bouncing off the Lincoln's red leather made them look mean. When I draped my hand across the seat, disgusted by my own reflection in their window, they found my fingertips and pressed them into the upholstery. It was all I could do not to weep.

Cabin lights broke through the onslaught, the crucified body of a street sign buried in a filling ditch. The ground was briefly visible again, panic retreating from my dying mind, and carved from the darkness came the outline of a cabin painted in streetlight blues. The distorted glow of an opening garage door sliced through the dark and across the windshield. Parking, the Slav climbed out of the Lincoln with well-buried reluctance, striding into the wind and sleet to shovel snow from the entry as the three of us waited in misused silence—idling around unspoken feelings like restless ghosts crowding a mausoleum.

The cabin, blanketed by the night, oozed of dryer sheet sweetness, of old wood and vinegar from canning vegetables. The front hallway poured into a wide-berthed great room with a wall of intimidating picture windows, tanned leather furniture bobbing on a sea of ancient wood, brass decorations and an elephant skull half the size of the Lincoln swarming the corner of the room that was dedicated to a television and a brick fireplace that far surpassed the stretch of my arms. Hand-woven rugs ran dogpiled across the floor, overlapping gracelessly towards the brutal, tooth-white hell outdoors, sliced by an unlit pine tree with a red and green tree skirt.

When the Slav offered to take my coat I clung to it like a lifebuoy, not for need but inability to do anything but *absorb*. I swayed for quite some time before I even realized the floor was *actively* warming up.

"Dimitri won't steal your jacket," Ronnie swore. She'd peeled off her furs in exchange for an asymmetrical woollen shawl, her working hands buried deep into the mouth of the fireplace. She went poking around nearby for kindling and settled on the mottled face of an old magazine cover. "Or your cat, for that matter. Neither is his style."

The Slav—Dimitri—stepped into the entryway, inches from me. When I moved so did Elowen, pasted to my side like a skim of old dust. Only the shuffle of their feet and the nudge of my arm reminded me of their presence.

"Ms. Summers," Dimitri beckoned. "I think I should stay, on your behalf. The storm won't let up for a while, and it'd be in your best interest not to be left without transportation."

"Oh, that's alright," Ronnie waived, glibly ignorant of the souring weather. "I've got company, and more coming. Head home. I'll call you."

Reluctantly, Dimitri retreated through the garage entry, the cold snapping at our ankles as he went. Ronnie turned from the fire, which had begun to pucker around magazine shreds and rough-cut firewood, and rested against the sofa arm. When stationary, she was little more than a gold-emblazoned puzzle piece that held the main room together, ogling

V. IVAN

at us with her glasses fitted tightly against the bridge of her nose. A cock of her head, the lace of hair around her cheeks silhouetted by firelight and somewhere in the lines of those shadows, a grimy smile bloomed like a dahlia, pointed right past me.

"*Have you been eating good in Washington?*"

I was affixed to the subject of her questions, a subject that tensed but held still beneath my cradling hands. Elowen's discomfort collected in their ever-snarling lip, in the nothingness saddling the slope of their nose where two drained pools pointed glaringly at Ronnie.

"You're taller, somehow." She squinted shamelessly. "And there's real colour in your face; not just a hiker's tan anymore." Rising from the couch, she was the first to cut eye contact, only then realizing I was present. "You're both welcome to the pantry—food, water, spirits—a shower. El can show you where it's at. Nothin' fancy 'bout it but the size. Take your choice of the guest beds; unless we cross paths, I'll hardly know you're here. Hell, I hardly do now."

The fire spat and only I startled. What transpired between Elowen and Ronnie was kept behind a door I hadn't the key to. All that crept through the cracks was a knowing sort of glare that moored Ronnie's words in my mind, in the way I felt they'd been meant: *Find a corner and stay there.*

I was dragged up a winding redwood staircase, the floor swaying and flowing beneath me. By the time I'd stashed my bag and released a shack happy Tubs to explore one of the white-walled guest rooms, it was due time for me to reevaluate how important free drinks had been. The best place for that was on my knees against the bathroom's rustic tile floor, sandwiched between an automatic toilet and a stone bathtub bigger than my bed at Georgia's. When I returned with a stomach-acid mouth, Elowen was clinging to the hallway wall like a petrified beetle, their paranoid eyes cast over the second story railing.

"I'm fine," they promised without question. Loosening, they gestured at me in the half light. "You're givin' me a look. I don't need any hail Mary's."

I peered unsurely across the banister like a thief in a mansion of window-to-window gold. "I thought you'd prefer it over another motel. But if you're scared—"

"It's *all* fine," Elowen cut into my words, shuffling towards the bathroom. "I just need a shower. I smell like shit."

"Both of us smell like shit. But I won't ask you to share."

"Leo?"

They hovered in the bathroom doorway with one ghostly hand on the trim, watching the words drip from my lips to the floor, their wide stare set behind a glossy, illegible film.

"Don't stray too far," they asked finally, trapping the bewilderment on my face and turning it over in their fussing hands. "Case I need ya."

I couldn't argue with the gutting feeling of being needed. I was too drunk. "I might have to puke," I wagered, for their sake, too. "So I'll never be far."

With the bathroom door shut, I parked myself along the railing, breathing in time with their clothing bouncing off the floor and the hesitant cranking of the faucet. Ronnie's shadow pouring from the kitchen entry was fine enough to study, puttering about to the tiring thrum of seventies rock ballads and the subtle clinking of dishes. After a few lonely minutes I slunk downstairs, my ears trained for the familiar breeze of Elowen's voice, for any worried cry that might come from the washroom.

Amongst a well of black and bronze cabinetry I found Ronnie stationed at the sink, halfway through a bloody glass of wine when I arrived as silently as a sleeper agent. On the butcher block behind her lay a board of cubed gourmet cheeses, seed-encrusted crackers and various meats in ribboned petals. My mouth welled with a thick, jaw-aching drool.

"They'll be alright," Ronnie said suddenly, to the open room. Over her shoulder she found me, her long-lobed ears and blue-jewelled earrings exposed now that she'd pinned the loose hair back from her face. "You haven't had alone time in a while, I bet. Let them enjoy theirs." She nudged an emptied crystalline drinking glass, set aside the cheeses. "Eat, please. There's more absinthe. I buy it to be drank."

V. IVAN

I hardly remembered nodding, only knowing I had as Ronnie set and doused a precariously placed sugar cube with lime bliss. In the time it took the sugar to melt I thought of Georgia and her fruity beer, the ladybug figurines, her goddamn chicken braise and her lovely perfume. With a topped-off glass in my hands I sank into a stool at the butcher block, my eyes fitted on Ronnie's shoulder blades as she snuck more wine into her glass, wishing I could bury myself once again in the coat closet at Allenview and huff the life I'd excavated there.

The scrape of a stool on old wood drew me back. Ronnie was parked across from me, her face catching the furthest glances of firelight.

"Do you find this place frightening?"

I washed away Allenview with a steep sip of liquorice gold. "It's—like a maze. Sort of."

Ronnie's smile twitched. "It can be. Not exactly what I meant, though." She waited for banter, for some sort of chipper comment, but I hadn't the energy. Without any warning, a snicker spilled from her. "It's like talkin' to a mirror. That must drive them crazy."

That arrow stung to dig out. I hunted for similarities, but they were tough and age-worn if even there. Another long sip just to burn away my nerves, instead sending them sparking and tingling like fireworks on a lightless sky.

"They told me their mom was dead."

Ronnie's face morphed suddenly, her smile skirting away. "Well—*sure*." She sifted her wine with a playful swish. "They'd know better than anyone. Besides—I hope they've come to terms with it by now. If they haven't, then I doubt they ever will." The stool croaked beneath her and when I sought her eyes, they were already on me. "You thought I was their mama?"

In the silence I stole a cracker, nibbling to fill the seconds in which I wasn't guzzling absinthe. Swallowing a mouthful of half-chewed seed, I said, "Someone's. I guess."

Wetting her lips with a dosage of wine, Ronnie's attention drifted distantly away. "It's that serious of a fuckin' stink, isn't it? Motherhood—rotting away." Her gaze zapped back to me. "Haven't been a mother for some time, and I was never theirs. No—no, I was part of their rehab team here in the city. There's an official title for what I did, but it doesn't mean much to me now. They needed a whole *team*. Even circus tigers get *one* trainer. Now what does that tell you?"

Once I'd numbed the urge to be curt, I whispered, *"I didn't know them then."*

"But you do *now*." Ronnie saw my emptied glass and rose to the occasion, pooling within it another dosage of sweetened absinthe. I had half a mind to wonder if it was poisoned. "What do you think of their new paint? The lot of us worked hard to get them in tip-top shape, but they just wouldn't *bend*. Biting and screaming and hitting all of us whenever we betrayed them by setting a godforsaken *standard* to their care. Biting, in particular, they've always had issues with."

Only when a lick of blood glazed my tongue did I realize *I'd* been biting—hard enough to break skin. *"I'm aware."*

"And you're still here. All the way in Boise, so close to their old huntin' grounds."

"They go wherever they please," I corrected, toying with the doberman around my finger. "Both of us do."

A strange, uneven grin rose to Ronnie's face, and cold fear drooled down my back. It was almost inhuman, completely *disingenuous,* save for the little scraping of her index nail against the table, thinking hard of something and wanting to scratch it all away. An invisible gun held to the back of her neck, denting her armour.

"I always thought that... by the time Kitty started to crave their little game again, *this* mouse would be long gone. Fort Collins. Maybe Jackson Hole, somewhere the air's a little wetter. Somewhere the spirits are a little bit pricier. But I'll tell you something, though—I'm spending borrowed time. I know I'm doing it, too, 'cause I should've been gone a long time ago if God's really calling the shots. I don't know if that's what this means—you two being here—but I figure if God's driving my stolen car, the least I can do is sit back and trust him. I'll pray for you from herein out, kid, if things work out." A snicker left Ronnie's lips, a woman unafraid. "You don't have a killer's face."

V. IVAN

The face I did have was wearing thin. "I don't need *prayers.*"

Ronnie sat forth. "What do you need, then? Is it money? That ring there—no, keep it," she said as I went to pry it off. "It's a nice chip in your corner. So *not* money. What, then? What's stopping you from going?"

"Going?"

"Don't be juvenile," Ronnie bit. "You know very well what I mean."

My mind rolled back twenty-four hours to the ice-molded mountains along the Village's ghost highway. To the Elowen I'd abandoned in that motel bed, curled up like a dead fox, fighting off their nicest dreams. To the tangle of my limbs against theirs, greedily devouring their little warmth.

"You think I haven't thought about it?"

"Thinking ain't enough. It's never *enough*. Why?"

I crawled further back to the breakfast from Xianne and the pocked-white of Elowen's bare back. To their sleeping body on Georgia's couch, to their wheezing breath and the liquor-sweet smell of their sweating skin. To Andy's blocks in their hands, to the seashell necklace threaded around their neck. To the smoker's corner in Georgia's bathroom and the earwig, and the way they'd seen what I'd done and never asked why, had only known even as strangers that I needed it to happen.

"I don't want to," I said, returning to the kitchen.

Ronnie took a stiff sip. In the other room, the fire dimmed and caught again, casting us in orange.

"The thing about Elowen," said Ronnie, "is that at one point or another, they went headlong into something they didn't understand, something way beyond their capabilities, and they got *cracked*. No matter how hard they try to fix it—Lord, I hate saying it, but I don't think they've ever tried very hard—they won't be able to live the way you want 'em to. Some little apartment outside the city block, sharing a cheap beater to get you two around. Grocery trips, Saturday bar hopping. Wild animals get hungry. That one'll tear you to pieces when they get too bored."

An intoxicating cold swept under me, raising gooseflesh on my covered arms. Elowen, bored and under-stimulated, could easily devour me in their excess of spare time. And yet, having seen the swollen boredom in their eyes, having observed them in the bleakest, most uneventful nights and in the middle of *feasting,* they had taken me in their arms and put me to bed.

Ronnie's fingers slid into the wells beneath her eyes. "You're stubborn. I get that. Just take one thing from this, 'cause I've got the experience." Her wide, dove-grey stare fixed on me. "When somebody *breaks* like that, it doesn't matter what you try to do to fix them. Anger doesn't matter. Love doesn't matter. None of it goddamn matters except the crack, the size of it and the time it'll take to heal, if it ever *will.* They can't care about anything that exists beyond their own *hurt.* No exceptions. Not even you."

I waited for the sting, for the barbs of Ronnie's words to tear away at my ignorance and make me see light. Nothing came. Not a breeze of clarity that hadn't already curtained me at the bottom of that swimming pool. How long had it been since they'd last stepped foot in Idaho? How had Elowen been—*who* had they been—to make someone think the very existence of love inside their wounded body was utterly impossible? That wasn't the person I carted across the states with me, the person bled in purples and reds under winter fireworks. It wasn't even the person at the bottom of the stairs, bathed in all the mess a body can give, staring with dark, blown eyes at my waking frame above. There was love in that, too. Amidst their hunger, some of the most brutal sentiments left pooled in the excess were love. Love enough to destroy. Love enough to *devour.*

I'd thought myself too broken to love. That thought came eagerly to me one day, just shortly after the last sparks of Ely drifted from my mind and I was left with the tar-black memory of what I'd done. I'd broken so terribly that I'd lost pieces indefinitely. I couldn't look my own mother in the eye. I took showers with the curtains open for months, panicking to the brink of fainting at the thought of rinsing my shampooed hair. I wept from rage well into each evening, all my contents spilt into the wind. Ruined, I guessed. I'd been *ruined.*

V. IVAN

Elowen had been ruined, too. Broken beyond comprehension in ways I'd never have the courage to ask about, in ways that changed them from a child I might've known when I was a girl. If we'd been bent in the same arc over different circumstances, just enough to synchronize for as little or as long as we were present in each other's lives, I did love them. I loved, and could be loved back. If it was all I had, then I had it still. I reached for them in the dark, mind or body, and sought them like serous fluid seeks an open wound. I sat there, broken as I seemed, and waited for the sound of their voice, needing me from the top of the stairs. It didn't fucking *matter* what Ronnie said, because she had no *clue*.

There was something other than death that could do the impossible job of making me happy. There *was*.

Down a corridor of varying, patterned tile I moved like an absinthe-powered machine.

Past doors, shut and open, bedrooms and glass-entry closets with shoe racks and old riding clothes, clear plastic bins that held vintage Halloween decorations, newspaper-wrapped china. I hooked left and the hallway thinned further, funhouse-like, before I started to worry I was walking myself into the bowels of a house that never stopped snaking into new and more obscure pathways.

But the next right greeted me with a dead-end and one exit; a doorless bedroom. Down two carpeted steps lived the dugout, only a flowery-quilted bed visible in the snowy gloom cast by two curtainless windows. When I flipped on the light, I was boxed in by walls of staggering, adolescent purple.

At the sight of the bathroom around the corner from the steps, my heart skyrocketed. It was tiny but surgically clean with thin streets of pink caulking between the wall and floor tiles and no toothbrush in the plastic cup aside the brassy sink. My desperation to give Elowen the last of their shower in complete solitude wasn't fruitless after all. I didn't even shut the door before my bare ass hit the seat. Awash with relief, I collapsed helplessly against the tank, thrilled to have made it there alive, let alone dry.

By the time I'd finished up, the purple didn't seem so bad. It was the storm and I alone in that room, and I was enamoured by the palm-sized stuffed animals against the headboard, old coins in a cut-off soda can rinsed clean and placed deliberately on the nightstand. Beneath the window overlooking the backyard was a long, thin dresser with a scratched top and little sticky pads on its ornate legs. It was hard to imagine two people waddling down the hallway to strategically place it there, of all places, for someone who'd really needed it. I nudged a fallen plastic ashtray wedged beneath the dresser and the wall, but knew if I moved anything, I would've destroyed what was ultimately a portrait. My own had never been so clean; always caked in soapy blood and button-black soot, cinched by yellow caution tape and fenced off from the world. It looked and smelled nothing like *this*—a purple bedroom with an empty hamper, a small television framed by a few lesbian pulp novels I'd never heard of, a cigarette package in the garbage, its gold strip of plastic like a live worm catching the light.

In retreating from the tomb I nearly took myself out on the bed's metal ankles, shattering the fragile memory of whoever had lived there with a nudge of the mattress. Beyond the scattered throbbing in my toe, the silence was sliced in two by the flat *thump* of something heavy toppling onto the carpet.

Call it morbid curiosity, or call it a lacking of fear that an amputated, gangrenous limb was waiting in the dark under there for me; I didn't think before I ducked my head to look under the bed.

A shy slab of manilla yellow winked at me from its fallen slouch against the wall. Someone's child had spent time in that bed, had riddled the walls with posters, large-scale faces of old celebrities and baseball players, had surely smoked through the cracked window overlooking the backyard, had been placed in the furthest reaches of the mountainside cabin to be left to their own devices. Whoever that child was, they'd hidden a folder under the edge of their dusty pillows, praying nobody would find it—or praying the very opposite.

V. IVAN

Oh, hell. I'd already shattered it; whatever case I sought to crack from under the edge of that mattress, it'd already started to unspool. So I parked myself at the foot of the bed after fishing it out and peeled the mouth of that folder apart with little shame.

Polaroids like a hefty stack of bills fell into my hands. Mellow around the corners with age, oily in the folds where fingertips once laid. There were men with fishing rods and sunburnt scalps and oversized denim overalls, wet up to the armpits, hoisting trout and pike and glinting walleye to the sky. Smiling women with ruby-red sunburns ripping weeds out of makeshift flowerbeds, obscured by water streaks that made their grinning faces oblique and unending. 1989—two muddied men talking over beers in dark lawn chairs parked inside a grove. 1990—a man in nutmeg overalls, his sweating brows painting the upper half of his face in slick, carpets of dark hair across his exposed forearms. 1988—children chalking on the inside of a half-built shack, patterns of sunlight tracing their thin-scalped heads.

There were hundreds. A group intermingling, exchanging gifts of food and talk. The construction of a greenhouse, recycled windows with snarling curls of paint rocketing off their edges. A little girl on the shoulders of a brick wall of a man, a bearded fellow with the stir-crazy face of a naturalist. A papermaker working over handmade wooden sieves, children rimming the outer walls of a sunlit cabin, the up-close face of a fiery-haired woman consumed with glee over two corn snakes, hoisted to the camera, threading her fingers. Backwards facing Polaroids, etched as the others with dates and numbers in near-illegible handwriting.

I flipped them over, and my tongue curled up at the very back of my throat.

The blood outweighed the rest. None splashed on the actual material before me, all contained within the simple squares of those polaroids—slabs of clothing sprayed in blue-black, piles of bones stashed inside a weed-encrusted wooden barrel. I could still smell it, wobbling through those last images, tracing the penned-in gashes of neutered text. *Penhurt, femur and l. foot. Gardner, M—clavicle. Clorissa, F—left tibia.*

IN THE END, YOU KILL US BOTH

Skull of unknown woman. Harnish, H—ribcage. Daughtery, T—r. arm and r. leg.

Next to the bloody potatoes and shredded hanging baskets, a living child sank against the backdrop of a mauled porch step, the same child that'd looked so free and windswept just a few images past. Her hair was glued in thick patches to her throat and forehead by dark plaster. Liquid death sat heavy in her eyes, knitted clothes with picks and frays spiralling around her gashed body, one minuscule hand clutching loosely at the torn shorts which did nothing to shield her bug-ravaged legs from the elements. Her mouth was an exit wound, two fragile, thin lips sprayed with zippered gashes still-bleeding—like she'd screamed, which she *must've,* and the sound had come out bladed. No name penned in blue ink—like she didn't deserve one.

Oh, I thought. *Oh, God, God, God. Oh, God.* And despite how quickly I dropped them onto the carpet, despite how frantically I went hands-and-knees towards the bathroom, it was the garbage can with that wiggling golden worm that received the last of my stomach's contents.

It was a collapsed mine in which I'd struck gold; I was reeling so hard that I had to lay down on the carpet just to catch a breath. I'd seen that little one before, the slope of their odd, pointy face rife with fat-trimmed gashes, more brutal than the kind you get from teetering into gravel face first. They looked so peculiar with long hair. Feminine, fragile and unprovoked, eyes glued wide with far away thoughts they couldn't yet make sense of.

The rumbling of a tired, old man was the only thing to rouse me. He spiralled around my legs, mewling incessantly, bashing his soft skull into my spine like he'd escaped just to come looking for me. Once Tubs realized I wasn't moving, he stood on two feet atop my splayed knees and waited for me to come to, which I did after moments of heaving and a terrible chill that reminded me of the week I'd spent weaning in October. Somehow among the carpet I found my footing, long enough to carefully slot the photos back into their folder so as not to crease and free any of the ghosts from their immortal frames. Then I scooped up

V. IVAN

Tubs' snarling body and moved backwards through the labyrinth, hardly feeling the nipping bites he gave as we made our way upstairs.

In my absence, the kitchen's cheese tray had made its way onto the comforter of the open guest bed, a bitter reminder of Ronnie's warning. The shower had long stopped and I carried myself to the edge of the bannister, desperate to soothe my acidic throat with nibbles on a crumbly piece of cheddar until Elowen returned, their movements silent on the hardwood floor.

I sensed them behind me—towel-wrapped, their ankles bare, crooked toes and fragile bones. The thought of them connected the fraying wires in my mind and zapped me, their bare shoulders teasing the light, scars latticed over their back and biceps and throat—the thin skim of spider silk flesh at the juncture between their collarbone and jawline grinning at me. I couldn't meet their eyes, no matter how hard I tried.

They left as quickly as they came and returned dressed. By then, the dogs Ronnie spoke of had begun to arrive through the large oaken door from which we'd entered, big, burly men like the ones she preoccupied herself with at The Elixir Room. Rough-faced and loud, hooking their dense winter coats wherever they could hang—one, then two, then a third with an American flag gaiter tugged up past his nose, hovering around a dining table cloaked in a display of thick stacked poker chips, score pads with lined paper and chunky pens and a gleaming bowl at its centre for bills and coins. Only upon offers of ice-chilled beer did the gaitered man peel off his slip, exposing a scooped-out cheek of peeling skin and exposed yellow teeth.

Elowen's socked toe grazed my hip.

"*Let's move,*" they whispered, their tone holding a phantom urgency. "*We don't need to watch this.*"

Without question I wobbled off to the bedroom where I'd first unleashed Tubs. My world leaned horribly off kilter. Now sensing a purpose in this detour which had originally been *so* purposeless, I was left gritting my teeth at the edge of the mattress, the room spinning and pulsing around me as I waded through their marshy secret and prayed that nothing would bite me. There was so much I hadn't said either and so my pain was almost *pointless,* yet it was only furthered by the gutting display of Elowen's discomfort; the turned-knob shutting of the bedroom door, draping their used towel against the crack beneath so they could smoke their cigarette without worry. There was a piece of them trapped here, a piece I yearned to recognize, fragments of their soul hidden in the cabin's floorboards or swept out into the mountains of the neighbouring cliffs.

The cold hard facts settled heavy in my belly until I began to devolve, to slip back and away into the things that I'd never told them. The things I could've admitted would've killed their version of my current self and so I'd never said anything, but weren't they the very same? How well did they know me at all? Well enough to kiss me. Well enough to love me, despite not knowing.

With all the strength I had left, I climbed across the mattress, turned on my side and faced Elowen, tracing the wet lines of their anxiously-trimmed head cut clean by moonlight, the flex of their arms as they cracked the window, expelling the stuffy heat. How cold did one have to get before they stopped noticing the winter wind?

"I think I'm ready to repent," I whispered beneath the howling.

Elowen sat themselves on the wicker chest beneath the window and sparked up. "I don't know any churches 'round here. I never went."

"That's fine. I just want to talk out loud, in case anyone's listening up there. You don't have to pay attention. But I'd like it if you could." I waited as they sucked drag after drag. My courage didn't come and so I went in afraid, as I always knew I would. "After your first time, did you feel like repenting?"

Elowen said, "Fuckin'?"

"Killing," I flushed. *"Eating."*

Elowen swayed on that chest, moved by an invisible breeze. "Lotta things told me I should've," they admitted, their fingernails like paper wasps against the chest's wooden finish. "I knew *other* people would've. I knew I was *supposed* to. But after a while, I guess I realized that other people weren't *in* my situation. And y'know—nature doesn't get to feel bad about rightin' itself. There just ain't time for all that grief over people who don't deserve it." There came a sharp, humourless snort, the kind that made me faint. "No. Repenting means you've gotta feel bad. And I just—*didn't*. I didn't have an option."

My mouth was rusted shut.

"An' I don't feel like joinin' you," they assured me. "I do feel bad about—*lots* of things. But not that. So if you're tryin' to hold communion—"

"I'm trying to find out where you align."

"With what? Proximity to bein' absolved?"

"With me." The comforter sucked me in. "How *we* align."

"There's nothin' to compare. Not in that way."

And though it sounded silly coming from my mouth, I suddenly said: "I think I killed someone, too."

Elowen stared hard, working disbelievingly over the details of my face. There was a long stretch between my words, inside which I debated if it was worth it at all—saying aloud what happened and what now sat rotting because of it, casting a hopeful line into Elowen's cool darkness—what, if anything, it would change for Elowen who had always asked for more and now sat mutely in the face of it.

Words—slowly, *slowly*—pilled at my lips.

"When my parents finally called everything quits, I thought they were gonna give me away. I know how stupid that sounds. I know how stupid *I* sound, but I cried so hard over it that I gave myself these shitty, chronic migraines for weeks and I had to spend a few nights on an IV just to get rehydrated. I wasn't really wrong, 'cause I had no fucking clue where I was going to end up. Myra couldn't care less what the distribution of me was, but Dad—he was a roofer working out near Baker, an hour and some change from home if the roads were quiet and you sped. Long shifts, twelve and fourteen hours, but on his time off he'd take me on these day-drives towards the California coast in his car—a classic car, deep green with these huge, fuzzy dice on the rearview mirror. I just liked being in it, I never—cared if we made it to the water, which is *great* because we never actually did. We talked about it, though. Going all the way someday. He was a *good* father. Birthdays, school talent shows, doctor's visits, he was all over it like flies to shit. He used to tell me he didn't need to work as much as he did, 'cause I made him rich just by being his. But Mom—"

Myra, I corrected myself. I painted her face in my mind, but younger—not her current state, something crueler. A distant projection of old love.

"Myra's got a convincing way of spinning things. Telling stories the *right* way so I'd know what she was getting at and what she wanted me to do, and I ate it up every single time because I wanted her to *want* to keep me. Mothers and daughters, y'know— they've got something unspoken built in, some connection that fathers never get to experience, not even from the outskirts, but she just talked to talk. Said what she said to make him look worse, not to make it easier for me. To make him look like a criminal. Or a bad person. She didn't *really* want me, but she fought him hard enough to force it into court and when the judge asked me about my preferences, I told her my mom got weeks off in the summer, with her stupid laryngologist job in the valley before she went North, and that my dad worked so late sometimes that I wouldn't see him for days."

My eyes floated across the knockdown ceiling.

"He got a weekend once every few months, if Myra permitted. And he *tried*—with phone calls and text messages, and letters, and these painful monthly dinners where he wouldn't do anything but question and reminisce and *apologize*. I tried, too, but the guilt ate away at me. I hid his letters so well that I've never been able to find them again. I froze whenever his calls came up. All I could see was how miserable I'd made both of them just by *being there*. Eventually I couldn't handle it anymore, so I went radio silent. I was young, barely twelve, and I still saw him a few weekends a year, so it wasn't like he was *gone*.

"He was supposed to pick me up from school this one Friday afternoon. Myra called them *conjugal* visits, the weekends that I *did* see him, but he never showed. After an hour or so of waiting, the office staff hauled me indoors and sat me in this dingy little first-aid room with an old landline phone and told me to call my mom. Myra picked up on the

V. IVAN

fourth call, first ring. I guess at that point, she was still trying to pawn off the responsibility of telling me onto someone else."

The ceiling blurred, wobbling in the dark as I excavated all that I'd done well to bury.

"He was drunk. Really, really drunk, flying down the highway at stunting speeds. That's—pretty fast, isn't it? I never had the guts to look it up. He hit a cement divider and flipped the Falcon six times going the opposite direction from my school. That car was old as fuck, but he'd spent every Sunday tuning it up for as long as I could remember; it meant everything to him. That's how I knew he was dead. She didn't need to say it. He cared about *me*, too, and I took that away from him."

The room was so silent; I had to place Elowen in my peripheral to make sure they were still there.

"I swear I could always feel it—my repentance, just waiting below the surface, biding time. I used to have really nasty dreams over it, but once I hit the Echo, y'know—they stopped for the most part. Got replaced by other things. I was convinced that the Devil would come for me in my sleep and drag me through the floor into a fiery pit, where I'd burn and burn forever. I was just little, so that seemed—real.

"Within a year of Dad, Myra started seeing this —empty-headed fuck—and she moved us into his place without thinking too much about it. I was almost out of the Devil thing, but me and him, we *despised* each other. I wasn't quiet about it. I yelled back more often than not. I used to throw things at him and he'd always come back harder. I thought maybe that was my repenting—having someone worse to make me understand what I'd given up. I stopped dreaming about the Devil, 'cause I didn't need to anymore. He was just there, living in the same house as us. Eating all our fucking cereal. Taking what he wanted."

I envisioned the dealing of cards in the dining room, followed the reddened back of the deck as it shrank.

"Two years ago, we got into a real nasty one like we always did. Something was different that day—sometimes when I'm feeling extra brave, I think hard about it and try to remember all the details, try to figure out what I did to get him going, but deep down I think those situations just sort of evolve on their own, even if you think you've got a handle on them. He tried to drown me in a sink of hot dishwater. Came—out of the blue—cracked some of the thinner bones in my throat when I hit the counter. He wanted me dead, and he wanted to do it. I almost let him, 'cause I felt I deserved it. I *did*. For letting the only man who was ever good to me die alone and unloved."

I turned to find Elowen's face, unreadable in the dim light, blurred by hot, furious tears.

"The only one, Elowen. The Devil came to kill me and when he couldn't, I tried to burn everything down with me. The house, the—the lawn, my bedroom—I—I don't know why I dreamt of Hell. It was already there. I was always there."

I didn't feel any more seen for saying it. Just stuck in the phantom memories of the rug burning day and the earwigs, the weekend trips to the coast and the ice creams afterwards, the sugar cones that left me jittery all night.

"I'm no better than that fucker for doing this," I said finally. From nowhere it seemed, some deep, gaping hole from which all my sins had bled, where a heart could still grow if only I'd let it. "And if I feel bad—which is unlikely but not impossible—I'll just end up with something else to repent for. And I'm not even fine with what I have now."

Elowen was still for a while after that, a bodiless shadow that long ago finished their cigarette. The air was soupy with it, gratefully replacing the oxygen inside of me with smog. In the aftermath of my own depressing expulsion, I was so red and so tearful that my arms and legs were nothing but pinprick tingles.

I waited for the apologies, for the sorries, for the embarrassed consoling that everyone loved to give when exposed to the things that made me. I neglected to remember that Elowen *wasn't* everyone else. They were made of wounds salted by sorries, an eternally bleeding thing in their own right. Their voice rose through the dark as a rich, infuriated whisper:

"*Why d'you have to be any better?*"

V. IVAN

I'd thought at worrisome lows that I was incapable of it—that when I saw him again, I'd crush his neck against the sink's edge with a brutal, twiggish snap. I fantasized about it—the wet soap in his hair, the suctioning of his throat—my intimate knowledge of the eye-blinding detergent sting that cauterizes the tender insides of a mouth. I was tantalized by the thought of him knowing intimately what memories he'd sown in me. How they felt. How they stack inside of me, decomposing in my temperamental stomach.

"Isn't that one of the first steps?" I turned my face towards the door, waiting out the last of the tears. "Learning how to be a bigger person?"

"The bigger person wouldn't pity their anger," said Elowen. The chest creaked beneath them as they rose, and I did my best not to flinch as they parked themselves in bed next to me. "The bigger person respects it more than that."

"If I fed my anger every time I felt it, I wouldn't be the person that I am," I assured them. It sounded positive, just for a moment—the person I might be if I let the hatred consume me entirely instead of intermittently drowning in it. "I'd lose all of this and become someone I wouldn't like. Someone *you* wouldn't like. I'd just be the longer-lasting asshole."

A great huff erupted from Elowen's nose. "Then be the longer-lasting asshole," they said. Their face was voided in shadow, but the vitriol came out frightfully clear. "Those bastards don't change, Leo. They only ever wanna convince you they changed so they aren't burdened by their own guilt. *No.*" They reclined stiffly on the mattress. "No, you *owe* it to yourself. We all do."

"What?"

"To feed it. And be angry without regrettin' it." Moonlight clipped the corner of their eye, exposing bone-white sclera. "As much as you might not believe me, I'm tellin' you now—it's alright to be a monster to other monsters in exchange for bein' good to yourself. And if you change because of it—then fuckin' *change.*"

We almost made it to the finish without the worst bits, but Elowen leaned close.

"The things that happened to you ain't layers of fuckin' *divine punishment,* Leo. They're just shitty things that shouldn't have happened, but did *anyway.* You can't outlive anger. You shouldn't try."

My eyes flooded and crammed shut. "Don't tell me how sorry you are," I wheezed. "I really—*really* don't want to hear that come out of your mouth."

"Oh, I'm not sorry. I'm *angry.*"

"And you intend to feed that?"

In Elowen's stunned quiet, the wires clipped together inside of my mind once more. One by one, flitting to life, pulsing energy into my fingertips.

"Did you not realize that?" they asked, much kinder than they could've. They caved, twisting to face me, their exhausted limbs sagging with relief. "You knew that. You must've known he was next."

"I meant to ask if you were really doing all of this just for me."

Staggered, Elowen hunted for answers in my expression. I tried to stop the words from spilling but they swelled without warning.

"You had other reasons than giving me a breather," I wagered, waiting for them to object, continuing as they refused. "We're past that white lie, I think."

The manila envelope slid into view against the backs of my eyelids. The radiation of the printed article left folded away in my knapsack weighed the room down on one side in my mind, scattering decor, smashing Elowen and I between the bed and the wall in the unavoidable tilt. Deep breaths did nothing to calm me. I said what I did with terrible haste.

"Does the owner of your knife know what you've done with it?"

For a while, I wondered if Elowen had died. If their soul had slid free from the confines of their body, drifting to the ceiling and leaving a hollowed-out carcass in bed. The remaining air in the bedroom thinned from the uttering of what very well could've been a brutal curse. I couldn't know the power of what I'd said when the words had demanded release. I only knew I had to say it, or risk tearing us both apart at the seams by locking it away.

V. IVAN

"*T.D,*" I whispered, and reached into the shadows beneath their chin, a place I boastfully knew only *I* could reach and return from with my fingers intact, trapping the silver seashell hooked around their throat between two pinching fingers. "*It belonged to a cop, right? Officer Daugherty?*"

A wisp of air slid from Elowen's lips. They weren't dead. Near to it, but not quite. As their turning head caught the light, a peculiar, touching smile fish-hooked their lips.

"*You're whip smart. Where the hell'd you find that name?*"

"The library is free," I began, once my throat allowed oxygen to pass through. "Came across an old article about shit going down in the Panhandle. I didn't go looking for it."

"Oh. It *came* to you."

"I'm not asking for a story," I promised, treading the rough waters of their memories blind. "You don't owe me anything. All I want is for you to admit you know what I'm talking about."

The brows above Elowen's searching eyes fused together. "I do," they said without question, without cover. "Yeah. Sure, I do."

"Was it you? In those photographs?"

I knew. Of course, I knew. And still, the ghostly recognition on Elowen's face, the building gloss over their gaze—it broke me.

"Could've been," they guessed, like a stranger to their own stories. "At one point in time. But I don't feel bad about that, Leo."

"I know," I said. "You were a kid. What could you have to feel bad about?"

Their head twitched towards me, latent emotion working around old scar tissue. "Livin'," they said plainly. "I could feel mighty bad about that."

A deep weight slid from my shoulders to the mattress. It was effortless and altogether painful—studying the domino collapse of their face as it melted from one trembling expression to the next, widening eyes rolling over incorporeal bodies, an aged map of a protected forest splayed out in their mind. I could beg them to stop, could apologize, could throw myself hard into them and knock them back into the room with me—but it all seemed useless. I was as efficient as a clipboard-wielding scientist behind shatterproof glass, watching a rage-filled wolf claw its own eyes out.

In the midst of all that blood, I found their hand and took it still.

"T.D," I dared. "You knew him?"

"I stole it," came a voice so far from their own that I was, for a moment, petrified. It was flattened down, removed of the familiar, languid comfort I knew. "But sure—I knew him." A pinch in their expression, disagreeing. "Thought I did. Then I didn't. So really, I guess I never did."

"But you lost him."

"An' found him." Elowen's face lolled away from me. I wanted to bring them in closer, to mash our foreheads together and wipe clear the debris, the old cabins, the bloody vegetables and the bones of the dead littered about like pinecones. Before I could build the courage to do so, they volunteered: "He was the first."

Tiny explosions of light rounded my vision.

"You don't have to believe me," said Elowen ignorantly, as they knew full well the position I held, "but he deserved it. For everythin' he *did*, everyone he *betrayed*, the—*months* of lies, an' stories, an' he—*he*—as hard as God strikes a fist down on his weakest soldiers, he fuckin' *deserved* it, Leo, *Christ*—I'd do it again if he was here. Even if I still couldn't *fix* it."

One hand lifted and came swinging down like a hammer, a meek, clenched-fist thud against their ribcage. When that fist dispersed into a flattened palm, so did their confidence, and they deflated on the mattress across from me, giving my swollen eyes a weak silhouette to climb. The tense muscles in their throat called to my fingertips. I wanted to take them by that tautness, to relieve their worn body from the exhausting consumption of him and all the others. Theirs was the face of a person that had never found comfort in the smooth side of a knife. An entire existence founded on blade-clutching had made even the peaceful haze in their eye seem violently opportunistic, had made even the brave child inside of them bleak and stone-faced.

V. IVAN

Despairingly, I cradled the thought of their cold little fingers, leaves glued to their raw knees. Brutal infection, the nauseating cold of early spring on the joints of a child too young to comprehend it. The absence of life, the inability to kill. I gripped Elowen's hand until my knuckles bled of their colour.

"*I've never been that hungry in my life.*"

Elowen laid deathly silent, chewing soundlessly at the corner of their mouth, staring blindly beyond the exposed support beams on the cabin's ceiling and into the wintery air outdoors, rationalizing with thoughts I wished to pluck from their mind and hide away. Without warning, they untangled my hand from theirs, dressing their frigid mouth with my fingertips. I didn't protest for a second.

"I'll tell you about it," they said. "One day, I will. When it's not so real."

I inched my head across the gap between the pillows, pressing my slick forehead against theirs. "I won't hold you to that."

A nasty, painful knowing crept into the back of my mind. I'd come to understand it, holed up there next to Elowen, imprisoned by its strangling grasp. It all boiled down so simply into something I could've said aloud, but feared what would be done if the words had left me.

I'd lost too much fucking time from that goddamn broken larynx.

I knew their face. Had always known their face, much like the way a child recognizes their mother before their first shared glance, but more plainly I'd known them in the week-long overlap at the Echo. I hadn't recognized them in Georgia's bathroom, not at first, but eventually the memory came crawling back. The butchered segments of long, oily hair in the shade of fresh, undiluted blood, a courtesy set of airplane-quality headphones sutured to their ears, their glue-white face a latticework puzzle I'd happily spend a lifetime solving.

That week, years ago, I'd spent what little energy I had on hiding—wrapping myself inside a sweater much too large, zipped up to my picked-at chin in a last ditch attempt to hide the foamy navy brace I'd been saddled with. I couldn't speak let alone think around the spherical pain buried deep inside my throat. I toted around an intravenous ball and

IN THE END, YOU KILL US BOTH

chain everywhere I went, sipping my meals from a plastic straw, sweating and itching and clawing and not wishing to be better but to simply be dead. It was torture to know how close I'd been to something genuine, to recall from my pill-softened memory the days in which I could've done something but was too afraid to speak. To think of the chances we could have had, to mesh it with Ronnie's checklist of Elowen's incapability—an apartment, in Idaho or anywhere. A different cat—*another cat*—and a shitty old pickup with a miniature plastic skeleton dangling where the dome light should be. A life outside of the cement bubble we'd grown into. All the impossibilities.

There'd be no absinthe or cheese boards or log-scented double sheeted beds for the both of us in that simple life, but were we so far from Heaven? I couldn't have been peeled from that bed if the world was on fire. I would've burned before lifting a finger. I would've cracked and broken and turned to powdered scabs of coal before taking my hand from their lips.

In that bed, I prayed for the capability to save us. I took the knife from that muddied child, cradled it to my chest, pulled them from the killing fields and placed them protectively at my back. I'd be the longer-lasting asshole, I *knew* I could, because I would've struck down any flimsy God just to hold onto them for a while longer, to eat cheese and dance under the redwood support beams and play cards at midnight, to fuck and kiss and never go anywhere without each other. I would've struck every motherfucking one down to the same earth I laid my bare feet on for a fraction of it. For them.

I found Elowen in the dark, ladling exhaustive kisses to the tips of my fingers. My eyes slid shut, studying the darkness at the back of my lids where no lingering images laid, no burnt-up atrocities awaiting me. How long that might last, I had no clue. I opened them again to the biting child, the wounded survivor. My Elowen, a shattering eclipse to the life I had before them, if you could call it a life at all.

"*I see you,*" I whispered, their face wobbling in a tear-stricken wave. "*I see you.*"

V. IVAN

I wetted their mouth with kisses, pulling my fingers from their nipping teeth. It was all I could do to apologize, whether they could sense it or not. It was all I could do to pray to the God cruel enough to grant me them, so that he might instill in me the strength to set it all aside and tear us apart.

WILD DOGS

THE CABIN WHISPERED TO me: ***get up, get up***. So I did, in the dead hours of the morning once the city lights rose again and the storm began to pass.

When I awoke, Elowen's empty bedside was all I could make out, impossibly cold to the touch like they'd never been there at all. I dressed rapidly in the pure dark to stave off the gut-wrenching déjà vu, wobbling on frozen hardwood as I fumbled for my pants, their sweater, my knapsack. All the while my brain was a coiling cloud of pissed off wasps, fresh guilt gnawing at the last of me and refusing any extraneous thoughts passage through my mind, which was fantastic because I didn't need anyone or anything trying to change my mind. I was hot on the Devil's scent again, a hound driven by a pulsating desire I hadn't felt in years, his wheezing breath casting thin, leaping chills down my spine. For the sacrifices I could no longer avoid, I'd strangle him with my bare hands.

In my haste I stumbled over Tubs, apologizing profusely as he scuttled beneath the bed, departing from the room without so much as a goodbye snarl from him. The hallway was lightless aside from a skiff of gold beneath the master bedroom doorway, a brief glance of light dribbling into the rest of the blackened upstairs foyer. The muffled echo of a local news station whispered down the hall and dropped off at my feet, the remaining silence as fragile as an unset bone and humid with my own paranoia. The wind cackled along the edges of the house, ruffling the shutters and rousing me from my drowsiness.

Elowen was everywhere and nowhere in the dusky guts of the cabin. I sought them out like a child awoken by a paralyzing dream, skirting

V. IVAN

by the hollow bathroom, its pale tile slicked by incandescent moonlight. Phantom blood crawled up my nose and so I breathed open-mouthed, forcing myself to the banister, a blooming dread unfolding inside my belly as my unadjusted eyes scoured the shadows.

Despite the milky dark, only carpets laid spread across the floor below. I crept downstairs into the den, a vast stadium in the wicked dark, and swore at the whimpering boards I would've memorized if the cabin had been home. I was urgent to remember that it wasn't—that this wasn't a comfort, that I'd have to traverse the mountainside if I wanted to get anywhere at all. As I approached the wall of windows I greeted that which threatened me—the wind lapping at the panes, the last remnants of that wicked, white death. My only opponent on the mountainside that wasn't born from my own tumescent desire to *stay*.

I couldn't be sure what decided it. Last night's love, or the sleep, or the sudden, staggering jolt I'd experienced in the middle of the night, staring half-awake at the ceiling with the ashen bedroom in Ely on my mind. But the plan was sure and concise—spelled out like a scattering of snow angels on a freshly powdered field. I could sense its faulty points in the cold radiating off of the ornate glass, beyond which I traced the lights of downtown through the shoulders of the mountain, beckoning me, whispering sweet, syrupy promises of gold-encrusted dinnerware, of a life spent reading books and smoking pot in Elowen's boxers on the back patio. Takeout every second Tuesday. Another cat. A smarter one. No more cloying stenches from my mind playing tricks. No more dreams.

But Christ, the smell wouldn't wash away; I wasn't even *thinking* about it anymore, not since I was on my back in the guest room, and still it swole above me like the plumes of a plug-in air freshener, frying my lungs.

The floorboards behind me wept, and all the air in the room hurtled into my lungs in one fell swoop.

Before the labyrinthian hallways alongside the kitchen entry, I carved them out of the dark, sloped and sunken into the wooden walls as nothing but a framed painting. Their dizzying stare slid over me, the detached gaze of a dead-hour bathroom trip. In the night they'd stripped off into a skim of boxers and a dark red undershirt, comforted by the cold that pocked their bare arms. The viperous chill slid across my own shoulders like a razor.

"You weren't in bed."

Confusion, or curiosity, cocked Elowen's head. Their entire silhouette wobbled like a fat tail of smoke that I could swipe away with my hands. I followed their exhaustive stumble around the couch, nestling a sharp hip on the armrest, only the lace-white of their cheek making it through the seamless shadows.

"And you're dressed," they purred.

"Why weren't you in bed?"

The house sat blindingly quiet—I feared who, or what, might hear us. Nothing could be worse right now than God, and I was sure he'd changed the channel to someone more interesting long ago. I felt his absence more than I'd ever felt his presence. And that *smell*.

Jesus. The stench of *blood.*

"Did I scare you?"

Pleading with my still beating heart, I caved. *"No. Never."*

"It's cold." Elowen angled their words towards the stairs, never losing my eyes, their arms tangled behind their back in waiting. *"Come back to bed. We got hours before the sun hits that valley."*

The floor in the foyer stretched us further and further apart. Whatever horror flick I'd clocked into, I yearned to shield my eyes, to save us from the bloodbath, but it was impossible. I *was* the brutality, the knife-wielding terror, the monster just waiting around the bend. I sucked in, waiting for the hitching violin music to cut through the tension. It never came.

"I can't."

The dark allowed me so little of them, and still I knew their expression just by the stark sound of their voice.

"You *can't.*"

With my back to the windows, the cold tongued my joints, nudging me forward. Though I loved them, there was a lancing of fear in my words when I begged, faint and hushed, *"Don't be angry."*

V. IVAN

Elowen slid around the couch, spectre-like in their lightness as they cut around it to get closer to me. *"Angry? Leo,"* they hummed, and my heart pinched with the horrid urge to hand-deliver them my steaming organs. "It's the middle of the night. You're here. *Right?* What've I got t'be angry about?"

"I know what needs to happen."

"Course you do." They paused near the coffee table, bewildered. "We talked about this. We ran over it a few times. Didn't we?"

"Yes," I said. *"Yeah. We went over it."*

"We'll head off first thing. I'll pay for breakfast n' everything. Hash browns, toast, whatever th'hell you want. But if we don't sleep, I'll have t'make you drive."

I could get no colder. Staring blankly at their hands, my rationale departed in one fell swoop. I wasn't afraid of the person I loved. I was afraid of the way *I* could hurt *them*. And the house—it was so *quiet*. Where had all the life gone?

"I can't sleep," I squeezed out. *"I can't wait."*

"Then we'll go now," they compromised, unflinching. *"But it's dark, plus the bears an' shit around here—"*

They twisted towards the stairs to find the words, pulling their slick arms from shadow, the bright clean back of their shirt bouncing sparse moonlight. Only then could I see where the white cotton ended and the red began.

The black-drying border ran along the cusp of their ribs, the front of them flooded in wine. It drooled down their thin neck and slashed across their shoulders, giving a strange tan to their skin, worn on their slack hands like surgeons gloves that went all the way to the elbow. The sight of it made the scent even stronger, promising *no, this is not a dream, has never once been a dream, and would you even prefer that it was?*

I wore the chill around my heart like a necklace, cinching my veins closed.

A blooming headache, a dawning realization creeping in like the coming sun, and all my fear fell behind me where I could at least protect it if I never intended on feeling any of it. I'd only ever seen them like this half-awake, drifting through sleep, and now the adrenaline blew my pupils and hardened their silhouette for me. This wasn't Marian at the bottom of the staircase, nor the comfort of Allenview; this was Veronica, spread across their lips, hands and clothes in a lively spray. The steadiness of their waiting body told me it was long over.

Now that there was nothing else for them to tear apart in my absence, I hesitated to leave them. I didn't want to be afraid—but nothing scared me more.

"You left her television on," I whispered.

That froze them. Fragile like a glass house, eyes seeking the stones surely clenched in my fist and awaiting an absent punchline. When none came, Elowen's chest rose and fell in one fluid motion before they ceased breathing. Their voice rose above a whisper, like the hum of an earthquake drawing near.

"D'you feel bad for her?" I heard them swallow, the struggle to get their own spit down. *"I can tell you—all about why you shouldn't. But then you'll definitely be drivin'."*

My own breath came in quiet gulps, my lungs clenching to keep my heart from becoming shrapnel. Ronnie filled the air—and as horrible as I felt for thinking it, I really did like her perfume much better.

"No," I caved. "No, she—she *knew* this was coming. She seemed—*ready*. And sure, maybe she had the intuition to know that seeing you last night meant the end was finally here. But I *know* you. I know where this leads us, what this is going to do to you—"

"Don't," crawled strangely from Elowen's throat.

"That's why I'm going. And now, *right* now, you're staying here with this. *That's* what I need from you."

The cogs *tik-tik-tiked* inside of Elowen's head, dry steel-on-steel smoking like a damp fire. When their darkening eyes drifted off and stuck unwaveringly to the floor, I knew they'd gone flying down the same old mineshaft I'd been trying to steer them from—into confusion, towards abandonment. Alone in the dead woods they'd never left.

Before they could even try, I said, "It's not because of *that.*"

V. IVAN

Elowen dripped with exhaustion, their twitchy hands fluttering about like two frantic doves. "God, Leo, don't you be the one to do this to me. *What,* you read one ancient article of sensationalized horseshit and now y'think all this needs to change 'cause of—again, *what?* Some folk I buried a damn *lifetime* ago? I don't think about 'em anymore." An open, *lying* hand swept the room. "I'm not even thinkin' about 'em *now.*"

I begged; for the horror music to kick in, for the pull of a backdrop, for a waving neon sign spelling *cut* in peony fluorescent curls. Elowen didn't raise their voice for a second—instead, they whispered through the pain of something thorny stuck in their side.

"I'm not a *fucked up little kid* anymore, Leo. I offered to do this 'cause I *can* handle it. I can handle *more,* too. However bad you think this is—I've seen *worse.*"

My stomach pinched so tightly I thought I might puke. "I know you have. I know you *can.* But you shouldn't."

"But I *am.* So why don't you just get some sleep, and tomorrow you can let me *do this* for you. I'll *do* it. And I'll live through it. You'll see. I won't even *blink.*"

I took a long look at Elowen, glowing in the haze of a death that even God couldn't stop, glorious in their love for me. Because it was love—misplaced, destructive, but love all the same. I didn't want to lie, but it was *in* me—the image of the tangle-haired child, broken-faced, sleeted by mud; I wanted to protect them the way Elowen couldn't. I wanted to shield them from the onslaught that desensitized them, that buried them deep under the cabins in the Panhandle, pinned beneath the swollen dead. What would I do if Ely shattered them? Could I continue living and loving them, knowing I'd allowed it to happen? I'd have rather died. *Wasn't that clear enough?*

I splayed my hands over my hammering heart to no avail.

"I'm going to go back to Nevada tonight," I said, "and I want you to be good to me, just like you have been, by *staying here.*"

Elowen's eyes went wide and puss-white. "Like fuckin' hell I'm doing that."

"*El.* How much do I ask of you?"

"Right now? Too much."

"It's the only thing I need from you," I bled through weaning patience. "I want everything. Elowen, I want *all* of it. But whatever I bring home, he always *takes*. And having you there won't make this any quicker. It'll just make me *sloppy*."

"Goin' alone is what's *sloppy*. How d'you think you're gonna do it all by yourself, Lee? The act of it, an' the aftermath—if you've never—"

Before they could begin rattling, they were struck so hard by an unspoken realization that their words ground to a halt. Something caught flame in their expression, some horrific, detesting gleam that made me tremble. Their features twisted alongside their sudden comprehension until they were broken in front of me, their returning voice hymnless yet holy in its weight, like they'd finally cracked open my mind and realized nothing existed inside beyond the indelible rot.

"*Oh,*" they said resolutely. "You *don't*."

At first, I didn't understand. Then the Devil, the impatience, my dead body on the side of the sidewinding highway near the motel caked in frost, my dead body abandoned in the smoked-out Ely house, my dead body at Georgia's, stabbed or beaten or even worse—it all came to me in a sudden clearing of smog.

"Of course I do," I winced, my heart rising into my throat. Lying, as I'd always been good for. "*I do.*"

"*You don't,*" came Elowen's voice again, damp with agony. I'd broken something—it was already too late to patch them up around the brooding infection. "That's why you're going. You think if you go all alone, it'll be over soon enough." They crept closed enough to touch me. "It won't be painless. It *won't* be."

"That's a dirty little trick. And it's not even working."

"It *won't* be painless, Leo. From what you've told me about the worthless bastard, I ain't gotta make assumptions—he's got no *soul*. There won't be mercy."

V. IVAN

Choking on my own pulse, spinning off the axis of my own self-control, I shook my head. "It doesn't matter. I asked you to stay, so that's what you'll do."

"*And let him kill you?*"

"Yes! Yes, yes, Jesus fucking Christ, yes!"

I slunk around the side of the couch, padding towards the entryway, uselessly cowering from the damage I'd done. In facing them once more at the edge of the room, it was clear that I hadn't kicked them hard enough; they'd turned their back on the light just to face me, their silhouette a putrid void where the pain they felt shrivelled and died.

I asked, with little will: "Or will you kill me before I can get my shoes on?"

The words didn't come from curiosity, *definitely* not belief, but from the desire to shove them away. To bar them from me, to stave off the love. I wanted to hold them yet couldn't stomach it. I wanted to keep them from harm and so I was thrusting them towards it. *That* was divine punishment.

Elowen's baying head told me everything I needed; that it'd been dutifully sharpened, my blade, and I'd plunged it into the darkness with an accuracy I'd spend the rest of my life regretting.

"*Got any more of that in you? 'Cause a little bit of cruelty's never finished me off before.*"

"I don't want to hurt you, but I will. I'll find a way."

"*Oh, don't I know it,*" was what they said first. They sawed through the shadow to get to me, softening—*weakening*—and fighting tooth and nail all the way down. "No, see—'cause you've got a thousand ways to go about hurtin' me, and I wish you'd use 'em more often. If it meant I'd believe you could do this all alone, I'd let you test 'em on me all day an' night. I'd let you grind me into dust if it made me certain you'd come right back from that hellhole. You *can* hurt me, Lee, you *have*, and I'd take it *all* again, but first you've gotta know that you're wrong, 'cause you *won't*. Not on purpose like this." Desperation cored them like an apple. "*The love's not enough? Y'want both sides, s'that it? My pain, too?*

'Cause y'don't need to walk out that door to have it. I'll give it up easy. It ain't so rare I can't grow more."

"All of it's enough. But it needs to still be here when everything's over. You know I'm right, so quit fighting me."

"You were always going to leave."

All that kept chattering was the radiator across the room. That open bullet struck me just beneath my ribs, and I just managed to pat down its gushing entry wound when I felt the tears coming.

"I—never planned to."

"No," Elowen agreed dejectedly, "but I knew eventually it'd happen. I was just holdin' out that I'd end up wrong like I've been time an' time again. It's no one's fault; things just *turn*. I knew I'd give you all the leftover bits of me, horrifying, disgusting things you never needed to know, shit I couldn't *lie* about anymore, an' eventually you'd get scared an' I'd watch you leave an' I'd never, *never* hate you for it, Leo, *never*. But why—why does it have to be *now? Why d'you gotta choose this?*"

There was no right way to break them, so I was childish as I always had been. I slid the strap of my backpack tighter to my throat, the fetal heart inside of me dying, glazed in purple splotches from my own strangling hands. The Devil would have nothing left of my soul by the time I arrived in Hell.

"It's not your turn yet," is what I settled on. "It's not yours."

I spun away before I could well up again, a sight they'd surely grown accustomed to, and moved to the front door. There were no pursuing footsteps behind me as I went. By the time I slipped on my shoes and had begun to zip myself into our jacket, Elowen was absent from the great room; somewhere amongst Ronnie's collections of night-matted brass they were waiting in the dark for a goodbye I'd never know how to give. I worried myself to bits until finally I sensed them scuffing beyond the kitchen wall, tailed by Tubs and his ragged mewling. Then there was nothing—waiting, listening. Perhaps wondering if my silence meant I loved them enough to go, or hated them enough to stay.

As I organized my knapsack by the door, they appeared in the kitchen entry, corralled by the cat circling their ankles. "You don't have

V. IVAN

to leave," they repeated, testing the waters they'd already bled in. "We can get up tomorrow and keep going, like we said. It doesn't have to be this way. I know—*I know you said it wasn't right for you, but Leo, you don't—*"

I shook my head. They sought something from my face and physically sagged when they couldn't find it, leaving to pace once more. My heart ribboned with agony; I wanted to chain them to one spot and keep them still, pin them like a butterfly in my shoddy mind. Once I returned and everything was resolved, I'd compare with fresh new eyes and kiss them with a fresh, new mouth. Then, if we wanted to disappear, I'd gladly say yes.

Elowen cycled back to the door and met me with a rattling breath that I swore shook the house. I reached for them and they folded under my fingertips, stepped in closest to me, their forehead drooping against my shoulder in final defeat, the stuffed, nasally whistle of their nose blocked by runny snot. I'd never seen them cry; I was as grateful as I'd ever been for the night that cradled us. My palms rolled over their arms, thumbs pressing into the grooves of their shoulders. A heavy sigh swelled against my neck, and Elowen trembled like a bloodletting animal.

I was foolish for them. Without reason. Without sense. And I caught a temper with them. For that, I deserved to burn. I did.

Lifting my head to rest a cheek against theirs, I whispered a listless apology.

Elowen jolted, zapped by disgust, and their fingers gripped my forearm like I'd plunged a blade of corporeal silver between their ribs. They pushed my useless bicep into the wall, forcing a cruel amount of space between us. A ruined breath hitched in their throat, buried beneath the neck of the borrowed jacket I'd thrown on, painting my skin. Offended. *In denial.*

Nothing I could say would ease their trembling. Pitiful, hurting tears welled in my eyes. *"El,"* I repeated, softer. "I really *am* sorry."

Despite feeling like prey all my life, I'd won no intuition from it; really, I had no clue at all that they were about to bite me.

No wolf had ever been so tender. Their lips sank against my skin, caving into what I thought was a kiss. Then came a slick, drooling tongue on my shoulder, usurped by a needle-imbedding, muscle-cramping pain that spasmed and took flame across my throat and chest. It rocked free the last of my tears and ceased my crying, transforming my apologies into stone. Bladed, uneven teeth sank through layers of skin that gave like softened butter, latching onto the dense muscle spooled around my clavicle. An intoxicating sting bloomed inside my ribcage like some twisted game of telephone played across nerve endings until the agony wore into my heart.

My back was jammed against the wall, the unmistakable sound of their mouth wedged against my skin sending me spiralling further and further into their jaws where pain and relief laid crosshairs I couldn't distinguish. I kneaded into Elowen's arms to assure them that it was alright, that they were good, *so* good. They didn't tear or rip or seal off that bite into a sizeable chunk of flesh to hold captive until I returned. They didn't release their hold to saw through another piece of me. Instead, they stood cradled in my palms, alligator jaws wired closed, pain pulsing and welling as something wet—saliva or blood or *both*—rolled beneath the hem of my shirt.

Release. Taking back that which filled an abscess I hadn't even realized, their teeth uprooting from my flesh. In delirium I savoured it, the grazing of their tongue on my collar, the bubbling flash of blood that cooled and wept onto the neck of our jacket as they withdrew. Their mouth suctioned around the wound, tonguing it clean with a primal tediousness. Something molten warm and confusing stirred deep inside of me.

With a blood-drunk heave, Elowen staggered and swept at their tarry lips, myself painted over the valleys of their throat, the venous backs of their hands my own vivid red. Their blown out eyes were glossy and timeless; I'd never seen them look so fragile, so handsome. Some pitiful part of me felt like I'd never see it again.

The gore hooked Elowen's mouth open, awoken by the taste of me.

V. IVAN

"I knew I wouldn't survive you," they whistled, flecks of blood lacing their relieved words. *"I knew. But Leo—I promise—if I was capable of hatin' you, you'd be nothin' but bones in my hands."*

A roaring drumbeat rose in the flesh of my macerated shoulder as I watched them retreat towards the kitchen, polishing the sandstone paint with bloodied fingertips. They surveyed me again, drunk off one meagre taste, swaying on an unseen tide.

"Go," they demanded. *"Go if you're goin'. When you get there, tell that fucker I'll see him soon."*

In me, rage brewed. A rage baited by love and still no stronger than it. Powerful enough to make my hands tremble—powerful enough to nip back like an injured animal. I could host violence, too. I could be enough—to go to Nevada and return with a bodiless head in my hands. To plunge the knife into old scar tissue and come out alive.

I leeched what fury I had in my bones and said, dishonestly, "You better fucking stay here. Or I'll kill you, too."

And somehow, that made them laugh, as unpredictable as any of Elowen's other well-dispersed occurrences of joy. With a desperate nod and a sinking smile, they knew I'd tried to mean it. I really tried.

"Too late," they promised. "Too late."

Elowen retreated and I stared fearlessly into the craters of light in their wake, the only reminder of their presence the distant scuffling of their sock feet on the staircase. My shoulder throbbed brutally, demanding tears of which I'd run dry. I stood quite still—not debating, there was no time for that, but relishing in that deliberate, welcome ache. It was bitter outside, as cold as the bones in a December corpse, yet I wasn't worried. I couldn't die from a cold I'd spent years accruing inside; I hoarded that gifted pain deep inside, bellying it to keep me warm as I opened up the door.

Still, the chill was a brass-knuckled hit to the teeth and the wind slipped an eager hand down the neck of Elowen's coat. Snow tumbled in fat, sluggish flakes as the storm lost its balance and wound down. Treasuring my wounded shoulder, I palmed for the door handle, blinded by winter's heft.

IN THE END, YOU KILL US BOTH

I couldn't help it. A long, searching look fell upon the ajar entry to that little sliver of Heaven. There was nothing for me, no whispering light, no Tubs with his patchy quilt of fur, no glimpse of salvation. They were nowhere, as I'd asked them to be. Only whipping licks of snow swept across the floor and into the hollow dark.

I snapped the door closed and stepped into the night, moving lightly around my slow-clotting wound. Down the winding slope I staggered, which was near-whiteout upon arrival and laid brutally outlined by graphite shadows in the aftermath, the cityscape below rimmed with snow-salted pines and leafless carcasses, a chessboard of homes and trees and businesses all huddled together. With snow halfway up my calves and the snot cooling to a shiny finish on my upper lip, I held myself as much as I could stand and pushed through, guided jaggedly by the sharp, turning gale and the faded divots of old tire tracks.

It was an arduous fifteen minutes before I found reprieve in the form of a mountainside convenience shack with a hand-painted poster for a sign—*Miller John's Stop,* outside which I smacked aggressively at the snow buildup on a taxi stop sign until the fleet's number peeked through. By then, all feeling in the tips of my fingers and nose had completely fallen away. When the drumming in my shoulder numbed to a halt I found leftover tears to spare, and they remained caked on my lower lashes, arrested permanently on the line of my jaw.

Miller John's Stop was closed, the little light indoors granted by two dim coolers and a neon poster board promotion for fancy lures above the counter. The building was angular—enough of an awning, enough wood piled inside a nailed-together crate out front that I could stop and think, huddling against the cover of pillbug-rotten logs. I tucked my cell phone inside the chest of Elowen's coat and huddled in the darkness it housed, gushing plumes of breath as I clumsily dialed and redialed the cab number. When another human being picked up on the fourth ring, I nearly shattered.

The taxi that rescued me ten frost-capped minutes later was stuffy with an 'everyone' smell, the yeasty aroma of varying perfumes and detergents and every cigarette-smoking wack job that's ever sat where I

V. IVAN

sat, and came rumbling up the sidewinder pathway like Death, hot as a homing missile on my heels. The sudden blast of heat upon opening the door sedated me immediately. Dangling from the back of the passenger seat were laminated licenses and certificates for forty-seven-year-old Marta-Jean Locke, whittled by time and aggressive, drunken prodding. Thick-skinned Marta-Jean eyed me from the cloudy rearview, little else but an unclean ashtray jammed between us in the middle cup holder. For a long moment, the vehicle didn't move.

"Do I pay you first?" I managed after I'd begun defrosting.

Marta-Jean stared hard at me through a pair of thin glasses, waxy yellow curls pulled tight behind her ears. "You're bleedin' pretty good, kid. Mind sittin' forward?"

Such a minute price to pay, I dropped my head against the back of the passenger seat, digging numbly through my knapsack for cigarettes. "Is that ashtray for me?"

"I don't mind." The gearshift cranked and the cab began to crawl. "That's really nasty lookin'. Somebody hurt you?"

It was my last—the final lonely joe in the pack, a threat of sorts. I took my time finagling it from the pack, lighting it with my head tucked away. "Animal got me."

"*What sorta animal?*"

The kind that I'd felt the need to kick. So painfully close to being tamed, forced to acclimate to a world that didn't want them. I kept my tongue trapped between my teeth, the bumps in the road rousing me.

"Wild dog," I guessed. "I think it was hurt."

Marta-Jean scrolled down her window and spat. The brief gasp of cold into the cab made me gag. "Nearest hospital's half an hour out. Gonna be forty bucks or so. You good with that?"

'I never said I was going to a hospital' is what I wanted to say. "Sure," is what came out instead. "Yup. *Wherever.*"

The cab carried us from the storm-weathered mountain, creeping past the edges of downtown Boise where Elowen's truck was still parked at that bar strip, cloaked by snowfall. The city was alive with the mumble of early-morning business folks and people with nowhere else to go—much like Olympia, I thought, before the cab rolled onto a brief stretch of freeway and I stripped away the memory before it could make me bleed.

After dipping in and out of consciousness for a century, the cab rolled beneath an overpass and slid off the freeway, flooding into a dozen-lane parking lot where a glass-walled million dollar bill sat like a spotlight on the city's edge. Marta-Jean pulled to a stop aside the emergency doors, right next to the no-parking signage. Five cents below forty—how many others had nearly died on that mountain to attain that accuracy?

"Keep the change," I told Marta-Jean, pawning off fifty in tens as I climbed out of the cab, my shoulder warmed and aching from the numerous, pathetic attempts I'd needed to buckle my seatbelt. Without the mountain's agonizing chill, Boise was almost peaceful—I followed the cab's dull tail lights as they disappeared from the lot, praying Marta-Jean had a safe departure as I paced before the double-doored entry, past a bike rack and a planter full of frost-smothered bergenias.

Like IV-drip, regret began to trickle in.

Snowfall kicked up once more, carried by a south wind, and I bled like a stuck pig, gazing into the waiting room which was just as full as a corner bar. I relit the tail end of my cigarette and smoked until the snow put it out, the last physical remnants of Olympia left crushed into the asphalt. Then I crossed the parking lot through rows of cars and out along the edge of the freeway where the Christmas lights and the warm drinks downtown were nothing more than a cruel, hurtful dream.

I stood on the cusp of the freeway under a gargantuan guide sign for what felt like hours before someone veered onto the gravel shoulder to pick me up. In the time that passed I'd turned red and desperate and the sky had blossomed into an infantile blue, reeling the world out of the night's endless black. At the driver's window I was met by a boy in a stained Pixies shirt with an infected nose piercing, cranking down the radio and leaning out the window, waving to quiet the group of heavy-lidded, rough-faced teenagers behind him.

"Where y'going, lady?"

V. IVAN

I looked up and down the freeway, thinking *lady, lady, lady*. Looking for her. "Where are you heading?"

He gave me an odd sort of look, which collapsed into a small, unsure smile. "Salt Lake City. We're late as fuck already. Not sure we can make any big detours."

"Sure," I said. "Salt Lake City." It was closer—much closer. My knees nearly gave at the implication of rest.

I climbed into the last available backseat next to a big girl my size with splattered freckles across her flush face. The stereo volume scrolled back up as I dropped my knapsack on my lap, my bones giving way to bouts of full-body shivers as my skin thawed once more. It was my third chance at warmth that night, and I intended to cling to it. The first I'd squandered, the second a fleeting saviour to whisk me away from sudden, whirling death. This third would carry me closer to it.

I dove into sleep so seamlessly that I might as well have been flying.

DARK WAS THE NIGHT

We were well into Glenns Ferry before the bleeding truly stopped.

From then on it was a whispering thump all the way into Twin Falls, a whole town of stooped buildings with hundreds of windowed eyes wobbling beneath an icy wind. The concert-goers stopped on the edge of town for Gatorade and piss breaks in which I abandoned them with a twenty stuffed into an empty cigarette pack. I'd been grateful for the on-off sleep in their pot-scented backseat and Salt Lake City would treat them well, but I needed to be *gone*.

I'd lived through this in Washington, this *displacement*, but that reassurance couldn't stop me from trembling; nothing could. I bumbled through that half-awake town with only word-of-mouth directions until I found the bus terminal they'd sloppily described. Ducking through the early-morning crowd and into a broom closet convenience store inside the terminal, I forked over another twenty for an overpriced pack of Elowen's Camel Crush and generic cotton balls in a half-opened box. In the station's sour bathroom I parked on a closed toilet lid, bathing my shoulder in warm water from the taps, fighting desperately not to bite my tongue off as I worked cotton over the grooves where Elowen's teeth had been.

Tonguing the marks with soapy water undid me again. I knew it would. All the ride there I'd been dangling by a hair, only tearing it out once no one could see me. I sat on the toilet lid crying through suctioned heaves and snotting on the arm of their jacket until the eye of the storm opened wide and I could breathe again, even only in small, teasing gulps.

V. IVAN

Once the comedown left me swollen and angry I tidied, dried off then devoured a stale sleeve of crackers in a hate-filled stupor and purchased a transit ticket into the next state. I couldn't get out of the mountains soon enough.

Utah crept in like a mist, my shoulder humming along with my heartbeat sending me into an unnatural, broken nap at the back of the Greyhound, startled awake by the tense voice of the bus driver shovelling me off on his last stop in SLC. Half a day had passed since I'd left and the city sky was drenched in milky, uncommitted blues, but by then I couldn't differentiate night from morning if asked. I was too focused on getting as far away as I could before I changed my mind, footing it further and further when the buses fell off schedule, checking street signs as if they meant anything at all.

There was reprieve in Salt Lake City, despite Hell pressing greedily upon its borders. Nevada hung in spitting distance, its weak winter heat levelling the heartless cold. The clouds passed in bulbous swells of mixed blue and grey; soon enough the city was slicked in darkness. I sucked back a cigarette and hoped that Elowen had fed Tubs by then, something fishy with extra juices, and had forced him leashed into the cold to relieve himself. I hoped, too, that they'd slept some. That they'd savoured my blood long into last night, and used it to calm their impatience.

What would happen if I never went forward or back again? If I dropped off the steps of that bus and planted roots wherever I'd fallen, budding in the summertimes and fading in the winters like a proper citizen. I walked alongside the evening traffic and ducked under a hotel awning to watch for a while, whittling away at all I was until I felt like no one at all. A woman with a baby tucked inside her puffer jacket passed by—*I could be that*, I thought, but even whittled down to nothing, what was left didn't deserve a child. I could've been the nearby concierge, wide-eyed and juvenile with meaty arms swinging open car doors. A passing face that nobody paid any mind to, somebody with a plasticine smile carved by hefty tips. I could buy absinthe or whiskey with my money, or all the cigarettes I wanted, and I could smoke inside the bedroom of a small city apartment where I'd live alone, all alone, and nobody would ever come looking for me.

I lingered under the awning until the concierge noticed me from inside of the hotel's polished glass doors. Down the strip I took off until I found a large enough bar to park myself outside of. The first cab there took me as far as they were willing, rolling along the cusp of Utah's freckled shoulder and into the rich, red-soiled expanse of Nevada, ending our trip at a cab stop just outside the distant, winking lights of West Wendover.

"I've got kids at home," the cabbie said, sticking his head out the window with a pitying smile formed by folded wrinkles. "Otherwise I'd take you further." He gave me the number for a Nevadan cab company and I made like I was punching it into my cell phone. "Good money around Christmas, but nothing beats time spent, and I was supposed to be done an hour ago. College kids dragged me out, then *you*. Hey, you celebrate Christmas?"

"Of course," I said. I hadn't *celebrated* Christmas in years.

He left me with a handful of pre-packaged candy canes and I ate every last one in the rich dark, awaiting a potential ride from wherever it might come. I'd charged my cellphone on the bus with an armrest port and at the ledge of the quiet desert, its digital clock claimed it was quarter to one in the morning.

I stood and willed myself to be unafraid, idling in nonexistence on the outskirts of the desert sea. Well above the distant lights of town, stars scattered like gravel dust across the sky's gritty windshield, obscured by jagged rock formations, the subtle sweat of a midnight cold creeping up the back of my neck. Briefly and for the first and only time, I remembered what I wanted to be when I'd still been young enough to want honest, sweet, unachievable things; a rip-roaring cowboy in an old Western, once a gunslinging bastard and now a man reformed though much too late, laying bank-side and nudging tumbleweeds from his spurs, succumbing to diamondback venom. I wanted to dress in hand-tanned leather with a turkey feather in the brim of my hat, my hands raw and red from braided rope. An old forgotten caricature, I swayed in the timid breeze,

V. IVAN

wondering how long it took the cabbie to make it home to his children, wondering if it was Christmas, wondering what day it was at all.

I'd never be a cowboy. But for a brief, gorgeous moment I was nothing, and that was a more familiar dream anyhow.

Hiking up my imaginary chaps, I dusted the daydream from my lap and moved towards West Wendover with fresh blood wetting our sweater, coaxed out by a humidity I'd been acclimated to when Nevada was still home. I carried on down sand-blasted streets, passing good ol' Wendover Will, until I found a 24-hour laundry. When my ass hit their glossy yellow chairs, I was out before I could consider dreaming.

Elowen, my last tangible thought.

My FINAL RIDE, A navy minivan toting an elderly woman and a dashboard of varying plastic and plush Garfields, worked its way through Nevada in the early hours of the morning like a tour bus on the blood-caked cobblestones in Hell. I kept my head down, the town nothing but a series of gore-filled collisions to me, training my exhausted eyes on the floor as the mid-morning heat cranked slowly upwards.

"I can turn the AC up, but it ain't gonna do much," the driver suggested, peering through the rearview and onto the jacket I'd zipped up to my neck. "Lots of folk aren't used to this weather. Someone say you were gonna need that coat?"

All the ride I'd prayed she couldn't smell the blood. I pressed a slick hand to my face and rubbed beads of sweat from my brow. "Bad suggestion?"

She laughed, sore and soft. Nobody who'd caught on to the blood would've done so. "Did they know you were heading to the Silver State? We don't play winter like Eastern folk."

I'd been buttered up by the cold along the journey and the fresh heat sank into my bones like tar. Ely crept upon me like a vampire—I sensed it before I'd seen it, the change in the air, the ache in my gut. Along Main Street I began sneaking peeks, micro-dosing the town in short bursts of anxiety-fed adrenaline. We rolled by a spattering of convenience and grocery stores, a gift shop on Great Basin Boulevard that I'd never been to, a drugstore that didn't open until noon. Powdery residue on my memory dusted away, the sudden realness of Ely made me tremble. The cracked, tan ground cut into my eyes and I laced my palms over my face, retreating for a while into the guttural rumbling of the tires beneath us.

Once the sunlight flares faded from the backs of my eyelids, I stuck another look out the window—seeking the glare of a burnt yellow Ford, whether consciously or not.

"What address did you say it was?" asked the driver. "It's no big detour to drop you right at home. Rather than let a little thing like you walk in this heat."

We rounded the corner past the golf club, snaking by off-white and tawny houses, garbled discussions of lunch spots on the van's sputtering radio set to a local station. The Jetson place on the edge of Grenadine Court whizzed by, Max Jetson's two exhausted Rottweilers basking on the patchy lawn behind deformed chainlink. Tilting guide signs to the railway museum, semis without their trailers parked like bodiless heads along the 93. Closer, closer and then *there, there,* like a bullet puncturing through bone—metallic black fencing pinheaded at the top, erected across the street from the charcoal remains of Passageways Church like a gross omen. My blood-soaked heart turned to stone.

"Here." I sounded like I'd been stabbed. *"Here. Right along here."*

The driver brightened at the last of my money, which was the only feasible tip I could give. I stood on the corner beneath a wide, familiar Pinyon pine and soaked in the liberating shade, gazing deliriously down the edge of an overgrown lawn. Dogs howled and bayed from some distant housing block, cars on adjacent streets whirred by, the incessant buzz of heat laying low over my head like cicada screams. The sky was a carpeted blue that day, and beading sweat hung like a pearl necklace around my throat.

Ely was home in the same way that your house is home in the middle of the night; all of the lights cut off, a blanket of glib, unseeing darkness, every scratch in the paint and every loose board a living, breathing

V. IVAN

wound. I'd been here before and had walked the streets at all hours, had run from Myra in grocery stores just down the way, had punched the face of an old classmate at the elementary school twenty minutes from that very corner. I used to watch soccer games at Steptoe Park, high as a bird, mouth Slurpee-blue.

But suddenly it was so hard to round the fence. So hard to move past the opaque, pearl and black sign that was erected from the ground. I'd never been *here*. I hadn't known—hadn't been told where to go, regardless of the wailing and screaming and hitting. Not until I was too angry to ask anymore—and at that point it'd become a mid-commute conversation, a passing fraction of Myra's time in which she'd given out the information she'd so carefully held under lock and key. As if she knew I'd spend more time with the dead than the living, given the choice.

But who knows the condition of it now, she'd said that blistering morning on my way to class, milking a red light for all its worth as she frantically paged her then-assistant, my teenage body nothing but a wavering ember of hatred in the passenger's seat. *You might not even know which one's his.*

With a throbbing chest I entered the cemetery, my eyes cutting over gravestone teeth set jagged across sunburnt grass, stepping around well-laid burial plots, ruddy pink flowers wrapped in plastic bands, teddy bears bleached by sunlight. *I'll always know which one's his,* I told myself now, criss-crossing through the grass, soaking my sneakers with dew. *Even if I couldn't see, I'd use my guilt like a compass. I'll always know.*

He was the mossiest of them all—kept in the corner, waiting like a straggler in the lobby of a fancy marble hotel. When I found him, I stayed just out of his reach—the same way I'd been when he was alive.

Myra told me Dad's body went to heaven with his soul because the earth couldn't keep him. Yet there he laid, now hidden beneath an ironically-lively blanket of lichen and sandstone. His name was engraved in silver and splotchy moss: *Noah Kavanagh, Father and Son.* Hadn't he been a husband, too? *Safely home,* it so claimed, but he hadn't gone safely home. He'd gone in a three-ton mechanical beast, wrapped in warped steel, inarguably crushed. Burnt alive, destroyed, pulverized. What about that was safe?

What about that was *fine?*

It was silly. *I* was silly. There were worse words, but my brain had long gone mushy. My father wasn't God in the face of what lived in his absence. He wasn't even a saint; the bread and wine of his being was made of tarmac, malt ice cream and adolescent DUIs. There was no opposite to the evil that I knew after he was gone—there was no man in my life, or perhaps in all of existence, worth being hailed as God. Not one of them. God was a woman, if she *was* at all, with all her spite and borderline-ecstatic indifference. God could've been Myra, with her luggage always packed and her judgment always raised like a rusty knife, hiding my dead father like a golden artifact collecting dust.

I crouched close enough that I could trace the ripples in the stone's edges and the mildewed lines of his birthday. From that half-empty pack of Camels I wiggled free a corner smoke, screwing its untouched filter into the soil just for him.

"I wish you'd left the car," I said. Then, raw behind the joke I was attempting to hash out, "I've got nothing from you now."

As if on cue, the street went quiet; no cars flooding by, no children wailing or laughing, no cackling dogs. When the silence and its clarity started to suffocate me, as it always seemed to, I stood and fixed my pants, dropping the zipper of our jacket to my collarbone. Blood awoke in the air, sour and fresh.

"I'll be back," I said, though I had little hope that I'd be buried anywhere close enough to reach him. I pictured him clawing at the earth six feet below, wailing at the soundproof soil. *Ha,* I thought. *Ha ha. Take a sip of your own medicine. Take a big, fat sip of you-flavoured goodbye, you fuck. You son of a bitch. Appear for me, you shit. Pop out of the ground like a zombie or something. I don't care if you're rotten, just come back for a moment. I'll be afraid, but it'll be of you.*

Soon enough, I'd end up right there along with the rest of them. Then all the dead with their skinless, toothy grins and their dirt-stained skulls would laugh at me for trying so hard to end something that would

V. IVAN

eventually finish up in its own way. I left the cemetery and walked until I reached Steptoe Park, until I reached the homestretch and threw my hood up and over my head and face, sweating and counting down the house numbers.

WITH NO YELLOWED TRUCK in the weed-sunken slope of the driveway, an oddly-bent American flag plugged into the porch ledge was the only flicker of movement up Carpenter Street. They'd painted the outside a meaty, opaque brown but along the back edge of the trailer the shingles were still too brand new, too polished to cloak the sutured areas where the flames had burst through and coated the still-dead grass in shattered coals.

I ripped my eyes from the pocket of Death on the corner. The other trailers in the neighbourhood had always looked *nicer*. That was totally biased, because our entire street was ten years behind the rest of this already outdated town, but it'd always been true. In the two years I'd been gone, at least someone had *tried* to catch up—there sat two new flower beds out front of the Peterson's mobile home, and the crosswalk at the neck of the neighbourhood had been recently painted. I no longer stood about in a rusted nightmare like I'd remembered it—it was only *half* rusted now. Times were changing; I couldn't help but feel responsible for the urgency.

Up the street on stiff ankles I went, slow and calculated like a fishing bear, watching for lights, for movement, for eyes. The mobiles, they all had large, wide living room windows with firmly shut curtains—*eager to watch but never to be seen doing it*. I tried calming myself by pretending I was on a post-class walk home, but that made it no better—my arms shook, my teeth gritting so hard my jaw popped in-step, moving around the inside of the driveway where the gravel dusted the street, where the tire tracks had burrowed into the dirt, patterned and unchanging.

Even the rocks beneath my feet seemed *fake*. *Fake* to the touch, *fake* to the eyes. I placed a petrified ear to the shingles and a zap of

IN THE END, YOU KILL US BOTH

static coursed through my cheek. No wandering footsteps, no lugging or scraping or deliberate chatter. No television. No raging fire, zapping the insulation into fibrous threads like cotton candy to water. Nothing.

If I gave myself time to breathe, I'd never move. One last glance at the street and I was up and around the backyard with its sun-spotted grass and lopsided lumber fencing that blocked Hell off from the rest of the world. I staggered along the overgrown gravel pathway where I used to rake out the garden hose to wash my sneakers, where I sipped warm, cheap vodka from plastic water bottles and let the sun bake me on the worst, most formidable days. There sat pails—*fuck,* my hands were vibrating— pails of bolts and tools, one half-full of mosquito larvae where the hose had long ago drowned.

Walking or floating, I crept up the peeling patio steps, ducking beneath the miniature bathroom window as I went. I'd never been so sober in my life. I wished for Elowen's knife and then for Elowen themself. Wished I hadn't mismeasured my own bravery. Despite a lack of it, I still had *balls*—I slid the patio door open an inch and pressed my ear to the partition. When only the petrifying twinkle of the ceiling fan's wobbling chain met my ears, I stepped into the damp darkness and the lived-in musk that absolved me from the direct sun.

Hell was just a boiling house in the middle of a Nevadan desert. It was made of the little things that, spread apart, seemed like they couldn't *possibly* hurt me. The tangy scent of dust-stuffed air conditioning and hot wood filled my bones. Citrus and baking soda carpet cleaner, tin and copper and red soil. The braided carpet beneath my feet, the off-kilter whisper of an ever-spinning fan, a lost pen laying on the grated floor register. Slippers in Myra's shade of purple, gathering dust beside the clay pot of a lifeless schefflera.

I was elsewhere, staring blearily at the dim space through the convex lens of an old spyglass, warped by time just like the many dreams I'd hosted there. The dining table with its infinite scratches on the old varnish, rubbed away by walnut segments, its dining chairs poorly pushed in, a plate of sauce-caked lemon china hand-stamped with ropes of bordering ivy left to spark an eventual mold. Through the archway my eyes dove

V. IVAN

into the den, across the tired, twin denim couches, a new rug juxtaposed beneath the coffee table, spattered with magazines and pocket change. The walls still the same, rosebud and eggshell, vignetted with nicotine decay.

The worst of it loomed as a steady black balloon in my peripheral vision—I sensed it like a still-warm corpse hovering over my right shoulder, my gaze rolling over the entry and dipping a toe inside where sheer, filmy curtains cast sour shades of orange and deep green over the cabinets. The kitchen—harmless in reality, and still a boulder crushing me. I took one long, sweeping look through its semicircle doorway, across the faint grey walls, over the gas stovetop, avoiding eye contact with the monstrous swell of unwashed dishes. Ungluing myself from the doorway I crept past, my eyes hooked on the floor as I went.

Not a sound reflected off the walls; the heat absorbed every whimper. The bedroom where he and Myra slept was the first door on the right, ajar an inch I chose not to exacerbate. The bathroom, with its stinking teal shower curtain and its murky tile, stood at its shoulder. The best I could do was pop my head in; three toothbrushes still perched in a cup alongside the cluttered sink, my dust-laden reflection bouncing back at me from the mirror. I made silent, distant peace with the last two rooms in the hallway, one of which was the old office Myra had worked out of before finally committing to the Yukon, now a carcass in which all memories of me had been left to breed fungus. Those memories were residue, a spillage from the last room on the right which reeked of a black, pestilent nastiness even a closed door couldn't trap. The bold, woody stench of ashes spun around my lungs and cinched.

Horribly, I expected the doorknob to be hot when I touched it. Only cold steel grazed my fingertips. I turned it clumsily and opened the kiln in which my uninspired corpse had been fired.

Those picture-perfect shingles I'd spied from the road were simply a cast. Indoors, the maroon paint I'd picked years ago dribbled in curling, waxen patches around the doorway, singed down to bare drywall at the far corners. A stapled sheet of milky plastic filled the space where a window had been, now sucking in and out like a lung, rimmed by an eyeliner of webbed curtain pasted to the wall. My burst box television slumped in the corner, my skimpy DVD collection a spray of plastic like peacock feathers at its back. Drywall and insulation and my daisy bedspread all mingled and burnt to a crisp on the floor, scabbed like a tangle of broken limbs.

I'd been sitting by the closet when it started—couldn't remember how it'd ended, or anything at all until the following days when my memories bled back in on a diluted drip. From the doorway, I traced the gaps where the slats in the closet doors had once been, its innards painted black as sin by the clothing I'd scorched.

It wasn't so hard to place the corpse of a young girl among the mess. A sudsy green zip-up, wet around the wrists and neck, spattered with dish soap. Her dark, springy hair pasted to her drenched skull. She was as real as the soot, climbing the wall like fingers. As real as I'd ever felt. Sitting right there. *Right* there.

What happened to you?

Dead Lenore turned, kneeling before flame-eaten remains of an old poster. Her puckered mouth burst from the seams of her waxen skin with an appalling crack, teeth of freshly popped golden kernels leaving ripe red gums where they'd once fitted to their sockets. Her voice rolled like a marble across the floor, nothing but a dead hum at the forefront of my skull:

You tried to kill me. Don't remember?

No. I didn't. That was somebody else.

You tried to finish his hack job. How're you gonna end it if you can't even end *it?* Her eyes widened through that splintered mask, glazed yellow with rage. *Is the Devil really chasing you, or are you chasing the Devil?*

A high, petulant whine crawled down the hallway like a funhouse wail in the middle of an empty, darkened room.

The door went whistling shut behind me as I left. I spun, facing Myra's old office door, awoken by a clarified fear oiling my innards. All I knew right then and there was that I'd broken in; the fact that I'd come all the way and ended up there, trembling in the hallway at the slightest

V. IVAN

sound, crashed over my head in a debilitating wave of nausea, my pulse a bludgeoning creature desperate to escape my ribcage.

Feverishly clinging to reality, my mind crept back to The Whistling Dog and the dried gum memory of everyone's names smashed together, then to Elowen fumbling with too many cards in their hands, their whittled mouth around their cigarettes, the weight of their bony arm around my waist. For a single, measurable moment I wanted that back more than I wanted death, and still I couldn't force myself to flee.

Instead, I crossed the carpet and cracked open the chamber of old memories, what would *still* be an office if Hell hadn't seeped through.

A warm, pudding sweetness spilled through the crack in the door. A far glimmer of light like a distant, oncoming train beamed through a filter of jade curtains, bouncing off the edges of a few moving boxes and navy storage bins; the darkness absorbed the rest. I pushed further, waiting for a howling, painted face to swing from behind the door, for a hand or a *claw* to ensnare me. My foot bounced off something on the way in, a soft and cushy thing that crinkled when kicked; incentivized, I rapidly found the light switch, flooding the room with a yellowed glow.

Dark, hand-carved wooden posts, four foot-high walls on a basis of well-balanced legs, dangling stars and moons and planets with gummy faces. Shelves tucked beneath the windowsill, sprinkled with supplements and half-folded clothing. The walls were finished in a robin's egg glaze that hadn't been there when I was still living across the hallway. Whatever storage once filled the room framed it instead, shoved and stacked hard into the right wall, boxes parting like the Red Sea towards the far corner of the room where that *wailing* had surely come from.

Nudging the unused diapers out of my path, I stepped cold-hearted into the nursery.

In truth, I expected some melting thing to be draped across the bottom of the cradle when I approached; a baseball-sized atrocity with a sickly-blue face, something so obviously inhuman that even my probing brain couldn't find some way to link it back to me. It was so much worse. All semblance of thought left my brain and departed indefinitely, cementing me at its edge as I peered in, waiting for the bomb to flay me.

IN THE END, YOU KILL US BOTH

The little thing had *curls*.

Thick, black ringlets tucked around its pink, quarter-sized ears. It wasn't moving; at first I was so horrified I thought I might faint until I realized that it was only sleeping—grumbling and moaning as it tossed and turned and settled once more, wrapped in a turpentine-orange jumper.

I didn't get it.

I didn't get it at all.

Suddenly, the torrential rain broke loose, the Red Sea swelling together once more, arcing over my frozen body. I was drowning in it, sucking in mouthful after mouthful of an ancient, glowing rage that possessed my entire body. Placing a hand on the crib to stabilize myself only made it worse; it only made it *real*.

"Don't."

Spit suctioned from my mouth into my lungs as I lurched, narrowly missing the cradle's pointy edge. I was thrust back inside the funhouse, staring into a bleeding, scabbed face I'd seen only in the sharp piques of stucco on the ceiling at Allenview. A slasher mask glaring from the top shelf of a closet—somehow alive.

All the makings of a perfect corpse stood upright before me. Somehow *fucking* alive.

Kevin was a spectre in cranberry flannel, a mere memory of the Devil I knew hidden beneath a wisp of old clothes that now wore *him*. His eyes, white-blue and shadowed beneath a slope of molten eyelids, lowered upon me like two flat coins. His wrists concave in new, terrible ways, the bones in his frail frame wrapped in a sheer layer of skin, the residue of blue collar muscle present in memory alone.

All six feet of him stood eyeing me like a mangy, ankle-biting dog, marvelling at the grime I'd built in the days past. Those odd, irregular pennies, one lagging behind the other only by a fraction, jutted towards the cradle where the little creature still slept. She hadn't any idea *what* was standing in the doorway; I *hoped* she hadn't. Terror and rage mixed at my fingertips, condensing in the furthest reaches of my body and solidifying, weighing my extremities. If I wanted to reach out and hurt him—and I did, oh, *Christ*, I always had—then I could.

V. IVAN

If I could just *move.*

Kevin lifted a bony hand to itch his chin. I didn't flinch; I would've turned golden from pride if I wasn't cowering at the very sight of his palms, his scarred knuckles, the puckered edge of his jaw where I'd clumsily slashed him open once before with an unwashed knife. It wriggled into the corner of his mouth where a scummy tongue jutted out to wet it. The ghost of him swayed into the hallway, the worn scalenes of his throat supporting the fading, displeased smile on his crooked mouth.

"Leave 'er be, and c'mon out," he wheezed, his voice as languid and dead as Marian on Georgia's runner carpet, as if I'd come home late from a gathering with friends that I'd never made. *"Keep me company out here 'til your mom gets home."*

As quickly as he came, that venomous snake slid around the door and down the hallway, leaving both us children with a rage that sank me through the floor, into the earth. It took him nine steps to reach the dining room; always had. If I could bring myself to move, it'd be the last time I'd ever have to fucking count.

GUTS

The scar I left in my absence wriggled along Kevin's lip as he stooped to aid in feeding himself.

Sacrificing his posture was all he could do to fix his vibrating hands; drained by the mid-day warmth, pumped full of goopy chemicals—he'd hiked his sleeves up as far as they could go, the untanned crook of his elbows tabbed with medical tape, buttered by old blood. Before him, a bowl of lukewarm minestrone soup was his greatest enemy. Discoloured fingertips coiled around his spoon, dredging at the bottom of the bowl and scooping, spilling, scooping, wetting the finished wood with a staining red.

The sickness preceded the day I'd met him—a deep, cauliflower illness in the beds of his caramel-coloured lungs that no doctor had ever been able to fully cut out. Cancer or something worse, if that even existed. The nameless rot zapped him of life—beneath the bounce of sunlight from the table's plum-red cloth, Kevin was less vivacious than a dust-caked candle, only a bowl of soup, a soot-caked ashtray and a large silver spoon laid out as the Devil's place setting.

"Sit, Judge," rose his hollow voice, a memory severed from my brain with a dull knife. *"Rest of the panel's got the day off. It's just you and me."*

What'd only been a pushy nightmare before was moving, breathing, trembling before me. If I wanted to reach out and grab his styrofoam cup on the coffee table, I could. The television remote would change channels if I probed its buttons. Kevin could *see* me standing there, starved and feral—if *he* wanted to touch me, he had every opportunity.

V. IVAN

That was the one thing that separated us from all the dreams I'd had—he could *reach* me now and he *knew* it. But he wasn't *trying*.

Like a dummy his head lolled dangerously close to the bowl, jerking at the yank of an invisible chain. Wide, wild eyes raked over my face.

"Or don't. Fuck if I care," he dribbled. "Should reign it in a bit, though. Someone's gonna think you're *enjoyin'* this."

I spoke, shattering the last dribbles of surreality I'd been clinging to. "Why wouldn't I be?"

Kev struggled with his spoon, slackening drunkenly against the bowl's lip before gesturing to the vase-weighted table runner where he'd piggishly left a series of varying orange bottles. "If you insist on standin' there, be useful and shove those my way."

His words didn't echo like they had in my longest running dreams. They were blunt and real and stole the air inside of me. I pinched at the skin on my palm with one hand to keep from tossing over the chair I'd bleakly refused.

"So no making amends?" I asked instead, softening the fine muscle of my palm with the hardest points of my knuckles. "That was just your typical horseshit?"

A wet, callous wheeze broke the static air. In his death-softened ears, I bet it sounded like laughter instead of the hanging bells on Hell's black iron gates.

"Oh, Christ." He muscled out a crude sigh and outstretched an arm, picking away at the medical tape to flash his needle-prodded skin. The house creaked under the sun's pressure, bouncing *pops* scattering through the kitchen like childish footfalls. His sudden, repulsive grin was only because he'd seen me jump. "Jesus Christ. Well, there's a lotta sitting around when they're pumpin' you full of fuckin' trial chemicals. Rots your brain, all that shit. Ain't got a clue what's gonna happen to ya, or what funny shit's gonna roll outta your mouth." He slurped a spoonful from the bowl's edge and debris rolled down his chin like gritty blood, ending up on the neck of his shirt. "Chalk it up to that and—fuck off. Talk to *God* about it."

The fury before had been so burdensome. Only now was it free to flex its limbs—to hoist a rage-drunk smile to my lips and shrug in the face of his weakness. What would Elowen think of this macabre rendition of him, swaying like an unmanned topsail? They would've put him down like an old dog, and they would've done it immediately. But I couldn't bear such mercy.

"No point. God won't forgive you. I don't plan on it, either."

Kevin's mannequin head lifted, his patchy skull a poorly sewn rug. "Well, I didn't fuckin' apologize. Did I?" He rolled forward, lifting a quaking arm to grab for his medication. Like a spiteful bitch, I lunged forward and swiped them from reach, distracted from our proximity by the delightful anger that flooded his eyes. "Fuckin' *cunt*."

With my fingers on the top of his medication, I spun the childproof cap back and forth in my palm, the sea of vitriol pooling around my ankles, dribbling into the dining room from all the way down the hall. The thumping headache; I submitted to it, allowing it to take me.

"*Whose idea was it?*"

Kevin gazed stupidly at me, the whites of his hateful eyes dampened by yellowed exhaustion.

"Not yours," I figured. "There's no way. No, you fucking *hate* kids."

Wryly, Kevin picked at the edge of the ashtray with dirty nails. "She thought it would be nice company. And y'know, I'll admit, at first it wasn't all that bad. Hardly cried, hardly kicked a fuss. Gave it a real sweet name—*Mindy*. Then a few months passed and it lost the charm. It started *needing* things. Surprised the shit outta *her*. Like this is her first fuckin' rodeo."

"Should've gotten a goldfish. When it dies from neglect, you won't have to feel so bad."

Kevin's eyes cut knowingly across my sweating face. He was a bloodsucker—vaguely aware of the idea of emotional pain, but never personally knowing such disadvantages. The sunlight traced him with an ironic halo.

"Feel bad?" Thick, unkempt brows hung over his glare, one quivering finger jutted towards me. "Feel *bad*. Okay—okay, *sure*, a—a *baby*

V. IVAN

that I didn't want—for that I'd still feel *something*. But you're not talkin' about that fuckin' *baby*. You're goddamn pussyfootin' like you always did." Kevin sought a chipped cigarette case from his flannel pocket, tracing the lines of his sentence through smoke as thick as oil. "I was waitin' to hear that you'd gotten your hands on a soda can tab and slit your wrists in that joint. Impressed you made it here—just a shame it ain't in a box." He flicked a clinging ember into the ashtray. "She didn't want a goldfish. She wants another shot, since the first one broke."

The sudden, unavoidable image of that dead girl drowning in a flood of murky dishwater removed me from the room. Briefly I stood before a sea of old blood, faded browns and infected reds rising to my chin, suffocating me with a frozen hatred as great as that of God. There was no confusion as to why Myra hadn't left; they prowled in the same fields, crept into the same roosts to feed, stoked the same fires. Only he was *conscious* of it.

It could've been so simple. They wanted a child that was good? A child that wasn't broken? All they had to do was *nothing*. All they had to do was *leave me be*.

I *was* good. I *was*.

"Sit," said Kevin, "and eat."

"I'm not touching that *shit*."

The edge of his fist hammered down on the table, spraying soup across its finished surface, tossing pill bottles onto their side, popping free a screw from the nearest leg. I flinched, driven deeper towards the rolling bubble at the base of my anger. Those slanted coins beneath his sparse lashes narrowed upon me.

"Finish up," he demanded. His knuckles were plastic white around the spoon's handle, the tendons of his wrist stretched taut like clothesline wires. "I'm sick of looking at your sad fucking face. I know what you want, but you can't goddamn *have* it. I can't feel a damn thing. Oh, you can sure try—maybe that'll do you, but it ain't gonna be much. I can appreciate the *effort*." He tipped the spoon's glinting head at me. "Cause I really did a number on you. Didn't I?"

Kevin took in a tense breath; it *sounded* cancerous. If I'd given all of this a few more months, I could've danced on his grave and gone back to the small but mighty life I'd built instead of fighting with the idea that killing him might be a mercy.

"*When will she be home?*"

His face drooped, offset by the pain of lacking his medication. "Soon," he suspected, sucking down a long, fat dredge of smoke. Rays of humid light caught its artful swirls and he craned closer, laying his elbows crudely on the table. "Soon. So do it. Pick a knife you won't butterfinger this time." He snubbed his smoke on the lip of his ashtray. "Or pass me my goddamn meds. I'll do it myself. Go ahead," Kevin demanded when I didn't move. "Go. Don't pussy out now."

It was all off-kilter. A pig that sought the slaughter tools was all too aware of death's mercy to be slaughtered with pride. I eyed the distance between the kitchen entry and his unmoving silhouette at the end of the table, waiting to jump me. I didn't risk it—couldn't bring myself to—collecting my body and mind before moving swiftly to the opposite entry, staggering to a halt under the archway like a horse at the lip of a cliff, too afraid to look anywhere but down.

Before me sat the void from which all the dreams started and ended.

It was identical to memory, only at present there was no blood on the edge of the sink, no sopping, overlapped towels on the floor where filthy water had sloshed and spilled from the overflowing basin. No matted chunks of my own hair glued to the countertop, squirming like tubifex worms in gunk and refuse. There were only dishes, piled towards the detachable tap with a skim of low, scummy water caulking the cracks between them.

The space didn't remember me or the wounds it inflicted. Graciously and horrifically all at once, the sink was just a sink. The tap, just a tap. Placing my feet at the very edge of that which had given me no grip when I'd truly needed it, grief's broken body crawled to me. The slick tile was gone, hidden beneath a gripped mat the colour of old wicker.

The sink was just a device for nothing but dishes, now that I'd been washed clean.

V. IVAN

I shook the probingly sweet decay from my nostrils, backing into the fridge with a dull shuffle of its heft. Nothing in the kitchen moved but me—nothing creaked, nothing whispered, not a devil laughed. *Knives*, I reminded myself, spinning towards the countertop and hunting for the right drawers, that word swirling like a cloud behind my dry eyes. *Knives*.

On the front of the fridge, something red hooked my attention.

There were glimpses of her everywhere; the woman I recognized but no longer knew. Fragments of soul in the religiously polished dinnerware she kept on the cabinet tops, in the stacked tabloids she used to read shoeless and tanned on the back porch of the old house. They were still around, just as her magnetic calendar stuck to the fridge door, peppered with tiny notes, appointments, marker X's for days when she'd be far up north with the polar bears and her snow-crazy patients.

I thumbed away a streak of old, scarlet dry erase, painting my fingertip a cartoony shade.

Readying myself for the knives, my eyes fumbled over the dates. I'd given up on keeping track the moment we left Washington, but there was plenty of red there to be had. She'd arrived—I rolled my eyes across it—in Olympia on the 10th of December, and had only been around for three days before she'd pissed off. Yet the X's, they stretched eagerly into the end of December—perhaps ever further, though the space ran out.

From down the hallway came a distant gurgling from the baby, as blissfully unaware as I was.

When the blunt force of a palm thudded into the back of my head and smashed my nose into the fridge door, my world became nothing more than the snapping of my own teeth against steel, followed by a swallowing, all-consuming pain that erupted like a shotgun blast across my face and throat.

I didn't have time to clutch for the pieces; my head hit the door again, shards of black and white splashing my vision, irreverent pain like lightning splitting my jaw in two. Chunks of teeth, sharp corners that would embed a foot like Lego if stepped upon, skittered across the floor like broken dominoes as my knees struck tile. I hadn't even known I was headed for the ground until I bounced off it. A great gush of blood flooded my mouth and slid invasively into my lungs.

He hovered over me, silhouetted by my drifting vision and the lame sunlight. A machine gun pulse rang in my gums, drilling pain into the shattered bone, but there was no scream within me to override it. A hand rounded the collar of my sweater and hiked me onto strengthless feet, hoisting me through the beams of sunlight that bled through the kitchen curtains.

Briefly, I thought I'd gone to Heaven.

The hair on the sink was so far away; I was light years from there, my conscious mind vying for escape the way I'd so gracelessly gone before. Only this time I was a colicky child, trying to wriggle free from leaving. I'd die if I slid away, if I silently handed my body over to whatever was next; my arms dangling as deflated balloons, pieces of me fading in and out. I willed myself to remain, but with every influx of pain my head flopped back, disjointed from it all.

My eardrums snapped with a horrific *crunch* as my body went hurtling into the backyard, scraping across the steel tracks of the patio door. Brute daylight painted my blood an orange, iridescent colour. I gagged on the light.

Kevin's voice echoed above. *C'mon*, it boomed. *Get outside. I don't want your blood in here.*

Grass licked my bare ankles. I'd lost a shoe in the process and when I collapsed upon the dry earth, I sucked back a mouthful of blood and began violently hacking, each cough a thrum of black around my useless eyes.

You've got a lot of guts coming back here, Kevin was saying, states away. *Y'know, hitchhikers—lots of 'em die on their way to wherever they're going. And most of 'em, they don't even know where that is, but they're just dying to get there.*

I laid wheezing as if I'd swallowed the burning cherry of a cigarette, the world a hemorrhaging pink lung, pulsing around each breath. I dug my hands into the soil like it was the very source of my fear, tearing through it in a pitiful attempt to amputate it.

V. IVAN

Who knows you're here?

In trying to speak, the exposed nerves of my front teeth sang with anguish. What came out was nothing but a bloody groan, a bubbling noise in the back of my throat like gargling soapy water. Elowen's face shrouded my thoughts and a wet mist of tears blinded me further.

I'd never asked how they wanted me to speak of them, if they wanted me to say anything at all. I might never get to. The tectonic plates shifted.

I tried rolling over and was kicked forcefully onto whatever rib had popped out of place against the door runner. A filthy work boot came down against my throat and my body and soul flew head-on into each other, clawing frantically at the rubber that threatened to crush my windpipe. Snapping nails against his ankles, driving my hands up and under his denim pant legs to dig their shattered ends into his calves. His heel drifted from my throat, though it felt like he'd gone nowhere. My uncoordinated arms, looping around his leg, hauling with what staggered strength I had. The boot came once more, the very tip sledge-hammering into my cheek with a cold, splintering stab in the depths of my ear.

I shrank—a salted leech in the soil, seeing only stars and light.

Stay here, he cut, scraping my blood off his heel and into the grass. *Or I'll open you up and let you drain on the fuckin' lawn.*

His footsteps dribbled, hushed by an unrelenting ringing. I fought for the hair-fine brackets of air that criss-crossed inside of my lungs; they didn't feel good going down but they went down anyway, vomit threatening to stifle them. The Nevadan sun pinned me to the lawn, casting blindness over my swollen eyes in which I painted myself at the kitchen table at Georgia's, at The Village with my head on a cool, dusty pillowcase, in Elowen's bedroom on Sixth with their arms weaved around me.

The only thing gluing my consciousness to my fractured body was *rage*.

I wouldn't die in the midday like a deer sidelined on the highway. I gathered every shred of strength I could find and rolled, sucking back the bile dripping from my blood-leaking lips, managing narrowly not to wail

IN THE END, YOU KILL US BOTH

as I kicked off my remaining sneaker. Even my feet were bleeding—if I could've laughed, I would've. The toenail I'd busted at Allenview was ripped clean off and nowhere to be found; blood alone quieted my bumbling, half-alive footsteps into the house.

I hated that fucking shell more than I'd ever hated myself. When I came upwards and grappled onto the edge of the sliding door, it didn't even shift under my weight. A hot tongue of nausea slicked me all over. Oh, I *hated* it, but I knew where every creaking board was. I knew every cupboard and each noise it made, the drawers, how slowly to open them. Even the half-dead corpse of myself, clumsy as I was, could fumble through without leaving but a heaving breath and a trail of blood.

He didn't come for me from the shadows like I'd expected, waiting to ambush me; he must've felt quite cocky about killing me today. Instead of waiting, I drug myself to the kitchen counter and peeled open drawer after drawer until I saw her—wide, *sharp* and clean. I groped for a handle and latched onto cheap plastic, warping my bleeding fingers around a set of grooved handles. Braced against the counter, I froze like a mouse waiting for heavy paws on linoleum. His presence dribbled from down the hallway, pacing, digging, the thudding of a door being opened.

The thread-thin tendons in my hands were screaming. I knew what four seconds away sounded like; I built a life on measuring time. When his foot thudded on that squeaking board like it always did, just past the bathroom door and before the hall closet, I padded across the kitchen like a witch out of hell, each step pulsating around my doubled vision in waves of dying light.

The corner of Kevin's face lapsed the kitchen entry's white trim. Without a hitch in my breath, I hoisted the dullard pair of scissors and plunged them into his fucking shoulder.

He howled like a ravenous demon, jerking wildly from me and ripping the scissors from my slick hands, hammering them deeper between shelves of bone, bludgeoning and puncturing through his dense flannel as he staggered into the half-wall behind him. For a fractioned second I swayed, watching him claw at his back until his fingernails caught the handle and yanked. Blood lashed across the flooring and the wall beside

V. IVAN

him as he whipped the scissors onto the carpet, where they bounced beneath the coffee table. I'd given him a wide, pearl-white mouth across his drooling collarbone; the only gift he ever deserved.

When I swung on him, he crushed my wrist into the wall and drug me down, a mess of my hair in his locked fist, the pain rendering my legs useless. Across the kitchen we went, back into the sunlight with a force I hadn't felt in ages. When my back hit the ground, I wrangled all my strength and kicked as hard as I could. I struck his thigh with the brunt of my heel and it caved in with the sickening give of rubber in a place where rubber couldn't exist.

He grabbed for me, his presence just a smattering of colour streaking by like jets through the sky. A searing, ripping ache like all my teeth springing free at once, my scalp screaming from a peeling sensation I knew was impossible, the side of my swelling cheekbone jammed into the tough dirt, pinning my mouth and nostrils shut. Drowning in something less moveable than water, less avoidable. I couldn't reach him. *I couldn't breathe.* A rock grazed my teeth, and lightning took my sight.

I left.

I fought it. I did. Harder than the first time when I hadn't anticipated it. I could've pinpointed all of the signs if I really thought back to it, but none of it seemed to matter anymore. Instead, I left the same way I'd returned: through a resolved exhale, failing to cling to my body. I deserved so little, yet I deserved more than suffocating in the dirt like something subhuman. I deserved more than this. Hadn't I deserved more than this?

Before I shut the door behind me, I peeled back the film coating my memory and found Elowen at the long dining table in the middle of the mountain cabin, seated before a plate of cold eggs and untouched bacon, not knowing where I was. Listening to me like I wanted them to and not knowing, never knowing. Tubs at their feet, begging for cold breakfast, circling their ankles. Would they talk to him? Would they take care of him? Would they kiss him and love him without me? I asked them to stay there for their own protection, but in reality I'd knowingly left them both alone.

As I was flipped over, the blue sky shot a blank into my forehead.

I spat out a gritty mouthful of bloodied dirt as air funnelled into my mouth and nose, crushed free from my windpipe. Panic swelled once again in a brutal wave. There was little fight left in me, and what remained was swollen and bruised and bleeding, and what *wasn't* sore was *about* to be, and the sudden crushing of hands on my throat sent a drilling headache to the front of my skull. He was above me, half-muddied himself, bleeding profusely from the shoulder where I'd stabbed him right through. That made me smile, but whatever came out was gnarled and spit-laden like a rabies-infected beast. He pressed harder and the blue sky above us grew ripe and green, then white, then piss yellow. He mouthed something distant, something spiteful and cruel and resilient, but I couldn't hear him.

The clouds flooded with red stars.

Kevin's head jerked backwards, his attention divided, and his hands slackened with a wet, abrupt *thunk*.

Scalding air stabbed into my crushed chest like morphine. His fingers, long and scarred, loosened around my throat and the sudden influx of air enraged me. Whatever resolve I'd had was left in the dirt nearby and whatever sadistic reprieve had paused him, I wanted nothing of it. I wanted an end. The front tooth I'd shattered was the least of the pain, and though it rang when I shrieked, I shrieked anyway.

"Hurry th'fugup! Hurry up an' kill me, y'fuggin' asshole!"

Sun cut through my eyes and snagged on something brilliant and glowing at the very centre of Kev's neck. Lifting a lolling hand, I rubbed dirt from my caked lashes, slashing through my ruined vision to observe the glinting star wedged between his throat's finest muscles.

Without warning, the twinkling thing curved beneath the skin like a nervous worm, scraping along bone, and Kevin's whole body slackened into mine. His face swole to an airless pink, a sudden gush of blood flooding from his punctured throat and across my chest like pungent diesel. One hundred pounds of withering muscle came down on me. Wailing, I hoisted my own weight and Kev toppled into the grass, that coy little star punched through his throat as a blackened blade, his hands

V. IVAN

groping pitifully for the earth as my knees drove into his ribs, my heart thrumming so hard in my ears that I knew I'd go mad if it didn't cease.

The blade didn't exist to me. What came down on him was the unflinching, shredded peaks of my knuckles, pummelling into his chest with heave after heave. Adrenaline surrounded me. A rib popped, the whites of his eyes as pink as school erasers, forced so far upwards they were devoid of their pupils. I sucked back a scream and came down harder, a closed fist to his face. He bobbled like a dashboard accessory, a weakened fizzle of air spilling from his swollen, split lips.

The Devil had come for me. *At last, at last. Take me*, I thought, drinking from the air like a fish in water, not realizing he was dying. *I'll go down with you, but I'm taking your fucking head with me.*

Freckled arms like fresh milk, powdered with my own blood, hauled me into the grass with violent urgency. I swung a fist, missed, then drove my elbow backwards into a set of ribs, earning a scattered breath from the demon at my back. My assailing arm was pinned back from the earth, held against the abdomen I'd surely bruised.

"*Leo,*" they wheezed, wrangling my flying limb against their chest. "Stop. Stop. *Stop.*"

The smell of them—sweet as a rotten peach—rose above the stink of iron.

The grass was just grass. The blood was just blood. The kitchen sink merely a kitchen sink. The hard sun glanced across the bleached ground, mud skewing my vision, their thin, angular arms loosening from the dangerous blow I'd delivered. My wounded body caught up with me, pulsating from every brutal swing. I clung to the familiar scratchiness of their wrists, hoisting them closer, the soft, irregular cut of their hair drifting along the sides of my swollen cheeks. They were frigid. I imagined it was because they were still in Idaho, still in a dream, not really there at all.

I turned my neck, wound tight by old and new wounds, and caught the corner of their sharp, scar-kissed face.

"*I had it,*" I wheezed through a skim of spit and blood. "*I had it.*"

I slackened upon them without asking. The sight, even warped by pain, brought forth a relief so brilliant that I fell into sobs. Elowen lifted a hand, slowly but calmly, and reached for my mouth, candied by blood and dirt and spit. At the relaxing of my shoulders, I allowed them the smallest grace—they placed a finger between my bruised lips and parted them, exposing the raw edge of my shattered tooth to the humid air.

Light dribbled from their eyes as their touch darted away.

"Fugyou," I whimpered. *"Fugyou. I had it."*

Kevin took a wet, rattling inhale.

Beneath Elowen's arms, I gazed into the low angle of his seizing chest. He was fading away at my feet like he was supposed to, yet it was all too kind to watch it happen without dragging it out to the end of the world and back, without prolonging his suffering until he could remember nothing but. A cauldron of jealousy melted inside of my throat and clawed unrelenting towards my tongue, which sat heavy and exhausted on my slacked jaw.

I climbed forward, balancing on my feet within a few feeble attempts. It was much easier to see the last of him from above. His eyes lolled, face unrecognizable from my knuckle-snapping blows. His hands uselessly scrubbed at the siphoning of his blood, hands that had hurt me, that had beaten me, that had ripped out pieces of my hair; they could barely hold onto his throat where that pillar of blackened steel was erected. The fury—I was molded of it now, not built *around* it—eased off of my heart, but a burning, aching scream still sat waiting. Hovering just beyond deliverance.

Kev's eyes rolled upwards to me, rimmed in disgust. They darted towards Elowen, the very same way he'd looked at me.

And he grimaced.

I crossed the dirt and the grass and the blood and hoisted my leg high. The rubber band of my mind split and snapped, and when I stamped my bleeding heel into his face, it caved through into a gushing, shapeless nothingness like a spoiled pumpkin.

For the first time since he'd entered my life, Kevin was silent.

V. IVAN

Only then did I haul myself towards the house, painting myself on its shingles. My adrenaline cooled into a fine glass, my joints rotting with an ache I'd never, ever felt. Instead of demanding to be held, I gazed across the lawn through doubled lenses—Elowen hovered over his slackened body, peering down into the last dribbles that I couldn't bear to watch. They stooped to steal his last gulps of air, their face angled in intimidating proximity to Kevin's agape mouth. I was eager to watch, having baked in mere memories for terrible, unending days—the familiar slowness of their calculated movements, the smattering of my blood on their borrowed t-shirt a gift following the endless, seamless torment.

Elowen fingers slotted into Kevin's hair, hoisting his head forward like a bowling ball, retrieving their knife from the back of his throat. It popped free, a suctioned sound like a wet hand sliding free from a glove, dripping eagerly in the soupy humidity. They held him the way I imagined they'd held plenty of pigs in the Panhandle—carefully, kindly, for even the creatures who do not know anything but violence need careful cutting.

There was no need to ask for what they wanted—yet still, they waited. As faithful as ever.

"Please," I bid them, sinking into the shingling. *"Please."*

They went wordlessly to the knife like an old friend, gripping it between their palms and driving a knee against the bone which they subsequently lined up and plunged their steel into. There came a lively jerk from the airless body beneath them, a jerk which made even me flinch, and then nothing but a faint hiss of hot air escaping around the blade.

Something froze them in their tracks. For a moment I thought they might speak, try to explain that they couldn't have listened if they tried, that they followed me all the way there without giving a damn about my demands. They did none of that. They didn't even ask if I was alright, but I felt no pain over it; we both knew I wasn't. Instead the knife, which had been wedged into his chest and left there, was taken up once more by their unflinching hands, yanked down with the zippered *rrrp* of drawing a time-stiffened lever, ripping down the core of his chest and splintering his ribcage. I laid wheezing as they sectioned him, their hands diving into that indescribable heat without warning. What couldn't be cut or wedged free by the knife was torn out by their sharp fingernails. Only once they'd dug deep enough did they finally look up, incapable of meeting my eyes.

As clear as day, they were humiliated. To be seen like that, arms tar-and-feathered in viscera and dirt, congealed around the creases in their skin. There was a hunger buried there that didn't ask for my permission but wondered if I might give it anyways.

If I'd had a thank you buried somewhere deep inside of me, there was no way it was coming out.

"Eat," I managed, instead. "Eat. He's yours."

The Wolf burrowed inside that cavity, nipping membranes as they went, dashing away webs of fat and muscle like wheat with a scythe. Not long after, their hands emerged, cradling a fair piece of him. They'd been in similar depths many times, but as I watched them cradle the bulbous organ they'd freed with their blade, I was shocked they'd managed to find one inside him.

Their thumbs worked over the slick valleys, the lopped-off tails of flesh, the well of blood in its translucent belly. They held him close like none other had, not even in life, tilting him against their cheek as if to find some ghost of an old heartbeat. Almost as careful as they'd been with me on my way out of Boise.

A wet, hideous *give*. What once laid in the cradles of their palms then gushed like an overfilled chalice.

Blood rolled like warmed molasses down their forearms as they devoured the heart they'd worked so hard to excavate. Tearing away flat bites of curved aorta like chicken fat, ripped free by their eager teeth, suckling back mouthfuls of drool. Blue-black blood cloaked their fingers in a rich, lively bleed, creeping down to their elbows in gluey streaks, spattering onto the jean blue of their muddied pants.

They worked down to the last torn pieces of that useless organ and suddenly, without much balance, they rose to their feet and wobbled in the low grass. Drenched in him, they met me at the edge of the

V. IVAN

house where I could finally see them best—their widened eyes which once seemed so dark now held an indescribable ecstasy, a molten umber eclipsed by ecstatic pupils, breath hitching in their throat, trembling but overjoyed. It pooled off them, so dense that it caressed my skin as it passed by and brought me back from the verge of death. *Brown.* Their eyes were awake and distant, but *brown.*

Towards me came one outstretched hand, palm to the sky.

Feasted upon scraps laid against their skin, a bite-sized chunk of him deliberately placed there. The human heart—it was not pink but purple and white-capped blue, as faded as a photo bleached by sunlight with no body to command the blood through its vestibules. The indents of their teeth so well preserved in its rich flesh made me shudder.

Their hand didn't waver.

I listened for the child crying inside, but no sound came from the furthest reaches of that cursed hallway. My own functioning heart throbbed inside of me as I remembered my splintered teeth shattered on the kitchen floor, the blood on the fridge, the smug fucking look he'd had when he thought he'd had me. He thought he'd had me.

Though its lingering heat nearly made me drop it, there was no delay between my mouth and my hands, and what my tongue found at the expense of their meal was something *incomparable.*

The heart inside was the only tender piece of him; if he hadn't knocked my teeth into splinters, I wouldn't have winced as it slid down my throat. Deeply sour on my tongue at first, burning past a ripe, bitter metallic and melting towards a strange, tingling sweetness. My canines sank through its giving, buttery flesh without a hitch. A new wave of agony was the only thing that made me gag. Irony like a river pebble and then not so, something dense and foreign in the curved well of my tongue. My breath caught, wheezing and gasping lessening from the faded but crushing memory of those hands on my neck. Elowen observed me from beginning to end, the twitch of my mouth as I'd sucked the blood from its silken meat, all the way through as it slid down the fractured tunnel of my throat. As *he* traced the lines of my esophagus and dove into my hollow stomach.

IN THE END, YOU KILL US BOTH

Wordlessly, Elowen leaned forward and pasted me to the siding with a wet, frightened kiss to the forehead. Then they turned from me as if I'd proven a point, and retreated to be with the dead.

I compared the brave little survivor to the daylight feast before me. They were almost identical, ravaged by death yet set aflame by its essence. Something I was not. Something I couldn't be. *You don't want this life,* said Elowen's working hands as they returned to their harvest. *If you can escape it, then you should.*

I didn't *want* to be the Wolf. I knew that. I wobbled to my feet, using the shingles as leverage. I'd never be a Wolf, not so skillfully, but I could be something akin to it, enough for us to den together, to eat in the same house, to love and sleep in the same bed. It was Elowen that the sun couldn't touch, craned over and snapping pieces from the defenceless parts of their meal. It was the Wolf that had little faith in coexisting outside of its pack. But their pack was stone-cold dead in the mountains, themselves pushing desperately towards a communion that could never happen, and I wanted to go to them. I wanted to hawk down another piece of him, just for them to see that I'd done it, that it could be done.

It wouldn't mean a thing. Kevin was dead. Whatever was left, I wanted no servings saved.

My gut, which now housed that rotten, ruined heart, was alive with a lucidity that could've lasted forever. I left Elowen there, hauling myself through the sliding glass door, praying they'd stay put. Staggering past the dining room where blood streaked nastily across the floor in dark swipes, through the kitchen to the sink where there was no matted hair but a groping handprint of chestnut-red, I flushed myself from the countertop with cold water, spatters of earthen blood painting the emptied half of the sink in a grotesque black-brown. I dipped my head and it jerked on its lazy neck, muscles worn to exhaustion, trembling inconsolably as I bent to wet my scalding face with white-cold tap water.

Weakly patting everything down with a dense ball of paper towel, I caught my reflection in the window and withheld a scream—the only thing that could've given me away in that dead, silent house.

V. IVAN

There was so *much*, bruised and smeared and pasted, that even after a good dousing of water I hardly recognized myself. The blood, the grime, flecks of torn-up grass—they were but a lingering shadow in the creases of my face, but I still didn't know the person that looked back at me. Pudgy, bruised and dissolved by violence, a red-eyed wonder with a detached nothingness that at first made me cower. I took that paper towel, folded the dirty half inward and used the dry bits to pat blood from my gums. When I checked that Elowen was still in the yard, I was pleased to find them there—hunched over, occupied. Just as I'd left them.

I drifted down the hallway, but not into the ashen graveyard where I'd left the Lenore I recognized. I wandered through the stench of her decaying memory—the powdery residue of old report cards and manila folders full of drawings, of a longboard half-charred, of my television which had puckered and exploded like a flame-kissed tire. Before traversing the tidy carpet across the hall I took my socks off, rubbed my sore feet against my jeans and stepped inwards.

Mindy was awake. Making gummy noises, turning over in her crib. I hovered over her like an intruder, which was half right, and in noticing her staring I half expected her to start crying. Instead she simply squirmed, her eyes two huge, sunny marbles gazing in infantile amazement at me.

"*Hi,*" I whispered. "*Hi, sweet baby.*"

Mindy's miniature hands groped for me.

"*You're so little.*" Whatever words came to me were short and blunt; my mouth half numb, the syllables blended in a sloshing mess. *Small. Bright. Beautiful.* I swayed, tilting my head back and forth at her in equal amazement, neglecting the spasming muscles in my neck.

Though I'd never felt the urge before in my life, I reached into the crib and offered out my fingers. Instantly, she was magnetized to me.

Lenore was dead, of course, but I felt her still at the nape of my neck, the last shred of myself observing from the open doorway. The more I thought about her, the more the absence of her ached inside me. Myra wasn't going anywhere: not then, not never. She left Mindy with him the way she'd left me, not with trust or no other option but with no care to consider something better. How long Mindy must've been here with him in those Yukon months, yet she was bright eyed and curious, and she didn't flinch when I reached for her, which was numbingly surreal.

Oh, it wasn't *bad*. It meant there was *time*, that there was something to be prevented rather than healed. The bomb hadn't yet gone off; six seconds on the clock and I'd stopped it. I gazed at Mindy and found none of Kev within her round face or her wide features. A deep, foreboding grief swept through the room.

The poor, dead Lenore I'd left behind gave a great, shivering sigh from the hall and disappeared.

If I had any control, of which I seemed suddenly in excess, I wouldn't let her be alone. I couldn't abandon her. I couldn't leave her on a nearby porch and become my mother, shirking the responsibility onto someone who'd heard that dead girl screaming and shouting and drowning and had let her die. I picked Mindy up carefully, the way Georgia had taught me to pick up Andy when he was ready for bed; cradling the back of her head and tilting her against my chest, which was still heaving, one arm swept beneath her to bear what little she weighed. I reached upwards and grazed the tip of her puny nose, the same bulbous thing that I had, then hooked my wrist around a purple takeaway sack of her things and rose, taking a sweeping look around at what remained.

"You're so little," I told her again, and she didn't get angry at me or whine or do anything but fuss with the strings on my sweater as the tears came again, for the millionth time.

The two of us retreated through the house and into the backyard. With her eyes shielded against my chest, nestled away from the viscera in the grass, I sank onto the door tracks and let Mindy's weight slope against me, her petite hands tugging on bits of my hair where the scalp had grown fiery and sensitive. She didn't yank hard—somehow, I felt she knew not to—and I allowed her the entertainment as I struggled to get my sneakers back on, assessing Elowen's still form—no longer eating.

I was tying the second knots when their voice bounced across the grass, sour and stiff.

V. IVAN

"Go away."

"I'm putting my shoes on." I spoke carefully around exposed nerves. "Go 'head. Continue."

Elowen knelt amongst the dead, stalling in the midst of their feeding. They were covered in it—opaque streaks of blood cloaking their chin, swiped and sprayed up to their ears, their lashes. Their knife was nowhere to be seen.

"The truck. It's a block over. Up the hill, away from the main road."

"Of course." I removed my raw fingers from my laces. I had little energy to —surely they could see that. "When you're done."

"I'll finish it. Just go the fuck away."

Staggered, I sat upright. Elowen found me beyond their mess of slow-drying blood and held me there. When I didn't budge, they reached into the pocket of their jeans and fired their truck keys into the soil before my feet, wiping their mouth against the back of their hand and facing the clouds.

"Y'know, I want all of it, too," they said, sucking on the words like they fought against coming out. "But right now, all I need is for you to leave me."

I'd seen these sort of mournful statues before in magazines and photographs, like the images of the Farnese Atlas in art history textbooks. The weight of a marble boulder set between their shoulders—their love inescapable, devouring them whole.

"Elowen?"

Their head twisted, fists limp in their filthied lap. I leaned on throbbing knees and plucked their keys from the grass, waiting for their eyes to meet mine—to know that even in the blood-drunk haze where they remained, I was still with them. I draped a hand against the door's edge to help us up.

"Burn it," I said. "All of it. I'll see you in Boise on the way out."

Elowen didn't nod, or grin, or gesture. They only stared with a plague-like grief I'd come to understand in the following days. Even then, I couldn't shovel it off—it went with me through the untidy walkway around the house as the sun dipped lower and lower, deepening the blue of the late afternoon sky.

I left through the path from which I'd come, my shattered teeth in my pocket and my shoes back on, held down only by the bundle gargling sleepily in my arms. Halfway up the street and around the corner I finally spotted the truck, a swollen orange sun on the glib horizon. It was then, coming upon its recognizable shape in the mirage of heat, that something deep inside of me cracked in two like a piece of wet cartilage. I heard it with my own two ears and still I kept on walking; whatever weakened thing inside me that thought it could kill me was no better than the one I'd just swallowed for company.

Baked in the hurtful scent of the truck cab, I nestled Mindy into the passenger's seat, cushioned by one of Elowen's stripped-off sweaters, and drove without setting an eye on the rearview. The truck puttered along and I craned for its pedals which I refused to adjust, doing my best with mirrors I didn't dare fix. I worked the truck along the edge of town until the asphalt wore down to dirt and gravel. Once the trees around us rose high on their stalks and Elowen's worn headlights did little more than glint on the road's midline, I pulled us onto the gravel shoulder and kept the cab warm, stepping onto the uneven road, walking until the headlights couldn't touch me.

The last of my fury poured forth like a punctured oil drum, a throat-shredding roar that superseded me. I wailed into the night knowing that anyone nearby would think me murdered, would expect a dead body flung across the road's yellow dividers in the morning's commute. I screamed until my throat was raked clean, until there was no air left to expel. As the oxygen cleared my lungs I begged for my rage to cradle my emptiness, only to find I'd left every ounce of my anger back at Carpenter, and as the pain dribbled from my swollen throat I sounded so small, and so afraid.

Still, nobody came.

LITTLE HEAVEN

THE JOURNEY TO MILLER John's Stop in Elowen's old faithful stretched on through twilight and into the early morning, shaped by a lonely highway that felt increasingly endless. By the time we hit the sidewinder and the lily-white of that *open* sign cut shapes across the hood, this night had become the longest of our lives. There'd never be another like it again.

With a functional passenger, it could've been shorter; someone to feed the little girl who was lulled for half the trip by the truck's vibration, someone to check the map so that I didn't have to haul over every fifteen minutes to make sure I hadn't fucked us. Instead I arrived sore and restless, subsiding completely on the handful of bills that Elowen left keenly stacked inside the glovebox, fuel and cigarettes, baby formula, snack foods from vending machines inside middle-of-nowhere gas stations, too afraid to show my face.

Instead of hauling off and grabbing a motel room for only a few hours, we slept inexpertly in the truck—my aching back stretched across the cushions, Mindy tucked securely beneath my arm, grabbing puny fistfuls of my shirt as she dreamt of whatever babies dream of. I hoped, as I laid painfully still, that it was something good. That wherever she was when she wasn't conscious, it was not reminiscent of Ely. In a few weeks time, she could forget Nevada altogether.

It was envy that kept me awake.

Along the shoulder of the now-motionless mountain, I parked the truck and lifted the sleeve of Elowen's jacket like a child seeking salamanders beneath a wet stone. Mindy was well asleep, her lips flooded pink from the attack she'd made on a bottle of carrot and apple puree not long before. I cradled her against the bloodless sweater I'd unearthed from the trunk, my oily hair pinned languidly at the nape of my neck by a clip I'd stolen from Georgia months before, and entered Miller John's with two twenties in my jacket pocket, flinching at the familiar cold as the door zipped shut behind me. There, a middle-aged clerk with a round, unshaven face and white-capped fingers sold me canned tuna, dried fruit in a Ziploc bag and a hot pink charger cable, gazing at me the entire time I counted my change. I could only cover so much; my face remained swollen and stained around a set of broken teeth and the pressure of that vice grip around my throat had made the whites of my eyes pink and irate—as purple-tinged and red-rimmed as the inner flesh of a grape, hidden poorly behind a two-dollar pair of sunglasses.

"My sister has a newbie like yours," the man claimed, waiving the cable's price. "It ain't easy; costly in more ways than one. You don't look much older than my girl. I've got a number you can call," he lowered his tone, though no one else was around. *"Somewhere to go. I can give it to you."*

On a clearer day I might've burst into tears. Instead, I bagged my pickings into my knapsack and sidestepped around his words. "Is there any way up to the cabins on this road besides driving? I'm not confident about the truck. Would it be alright sitting out front for a couple days?"

The man gave me a pitiful look, and hesitated to drop the subject. "Cabbing," he suggested, skimming over the truck as if he couldn't care less. "But even they'd have trouble. Walking—that's a good hike uphill. I can lift you up there if you need. Save you the fare. The plow *has* been through—not *efficiently*, mind *you*—"

"It's alright. My boyfriend's waiting for me. You got a phone? Or an outlet?"

"Really, I don't mind the trip," he explained. "Might be messy, but I've handled worse. Lived on these roads myself, 'til I got tired of that mountain pass."

V. IVAN

I studied him, cradling Mindy's head against the crook in my arm like I'd imagined Georgia doing for Bela a million times. She huffed, readjusted then settled once more, appeased by my efforts.

"Phone?" I forced around a worn smile. "I'll make it quick."

Hesitantly, the man guided us towards the back of the store past mint green palettes of canned vegetables and a cooler jammed with pollock and deer steaks the size of Mindy. Beyond a box-hut of old pasta sauce jars, he pointed me to a payphone and pawned a few quarters from his own pocket into the machine.

"Least I can do," he said. "I'd do it for my girl. You're somebody's girl, ain't you?"

I thought about it. *Really* thought.

"Sure I am," I agreed quietly. *Somebody's.*

Using Mindy's breathing as a ticking weight to keep me anchored, I spun a few numbers into the rotary dial and pressed the receiver to my ear, hoping to God for the best. After a few puncturing seconds their voicemail whistled through, old and painful in its familiarity; I pressed my forehead to the wall just to keep from hitting the ground. It warmed my aching limbs, threading stale sanity through me with each lilt, each pause, each breath. I inhaled in unison, pretending I was taking in their excess.

When the beep passed, I collected what few tangible thoughts I could form. The baby girl in my arms slept without understanding, and I told myself that if I had any wit left about me after all I'd done, she'd never have to.

"It's warm on the mountain today," I explained softly, Mindy's whispering breath glazing my arms. My forehead ached against the drywall. "You don't have to answer; I didn't expect you to. But I hope we're on the same page. Listen to me, Elowen. Please, this time. I swear I'll never ask again."

I hung up and crept out the door furthest from the cash, past the pyramid of sauce jars and freshly-killed cuts, back into the waning cold. When I peered through the frosted windows, standing in the weak cold with my arms taut around the little girl I'd kept, the man was no longer standing at the counter. He must've slunk away—put off by the memory of his daughter. I hoped he thought of her fondly. If she was anything like me, then someone ought to.

Collecting the last dribbles of our things from Elowen's truck, I began the trek up the road into the mountain, listening to the snow melt as we went, traveling underneath the bright, warming sun.

THE CARCASS OF OUR little Heaven laid silent in the snow, frosted over without the whisper of card games and a well-fed flame in the brick fireplace. Someone had plowed out the winding road in the days previous yet it was still glossy with a skim of new snow, no tire tracks or lights indoors to trigger the sirens in my head; that was *good*. Nobody knew Ronnie was dead yet.

I was climbing the walkway in my slippery sneakers when Mindy began to sniffle and toss. Her nose was light pink and snuffly and she gripped for the warmth of our shared jacket, suckling from my body heat like a parasite. I scoured the edge of the building all the way around the kited glass windows by the mountain overlook until I found a metal sliding box beneath the edge of a gutter pipe.

It was of little necessity; in trying the front door I found it unlocked, shoved tightly closed but disbarred. An explosive blast cracked open the back of my skull as I stomped the snow from my shoes on the outdoor mat; Elowen always had a feeble relationship with security. I'd hardly convinced them to start closing the dangling lock on their locker at the Anchor in the months before. As I carried Mindy inside, the bones of the cabin tensed from the gush of cool air that swept behind us. The rooms inside were frigid, the floor no longer heated to perfection, and I was hardly in the foyer with the door closed before the darkness yowled in defence, claws padding across the floor with delirious urgency.

Out of the shadows in the archways, from the snow-brightened windows stretching up the side of the cabin, a yellow-orange spectre darted between my legs.

V. IVAN

"*Hey, Old Man,*" I whispered to Tubs, my shoulder screaming and my fingertips near purple from the knapsack's tourniquet gripe. Carving him from shadow, my stomach sank. He was roughly as stocky as before, but there was a gritty unhappiness in his pudgy face. I'd seen him briskly inside a daydream since we'd left Ely, frozen mid-meow like an ice swan in the Idaho snow. I silently prayed that in Elowen's travels back to me, they'd think to squander change for cat chow.

Ronnie was nowhere. Not scraped across the floor, not blotted on the furniture. Not even the scent of her lingered, powdery and mature, suffixed by wine. I crept about the house just to make sure—through the upstairs bedrooms, into the bathrooms, into the master where I'd last known her presence as a farce of buttery light from beneath her door. It was as tidy as a hotel room, no stray clothing, no jewelry, no cups on the nightstand. Surgically clean, the scent of blunt detergent smacking my nose like a square punch. I didn't hang around.

Little Heaven was without company but the three of us, a starving band of thieves, glued to the kitchen counter as the rising wind kissed the tightly-sealed windows around us. Tubs wasn't picky; he settled for leftover diced steak tips from the fridge, reheated and glossy with grease. The power still worked and as the floor began to heat I stood against the counter and watched him suck it down, gagging on and off as I pleaded for him to chew. My meal consisted primarily of a sleeve of dry saltines from the cupboard, using them to shovel the remainder of an opened can of tuna into my mouth. In seeking more sustenance, I lost my appetite at the sight of the cheese platter stuffed into the bottom of the half-naked fridge.

I crept into the great room and shied from the balcony, nestling Mindy against the carpet and stooping next to the fireplace. Tubs circled us as I formulated a makeshift pillow crib out of blankets and throws, mewling about some heartbroken grudge as I futzed with the fire, hurling coffee table magazine scraps into its belly, igniting it with a busted lighter that hardly started. A splash of candy red flame snagged and caught before my eyes like windswept ribbon.

IN THE END, YOU KILL US BOTH

As the heat took, I retreated to the bathroom with Tubs in tow, screaming all the way. By the time we returned to the living room with wet tissues and cloth and towels, Mindy was struggling against the cushy pillows I'd sandwiched at her sides.

"I know," I told Tubs, "I know, I'm an amateur. But you don't even have the opposable thumbs to do it, so quit the bitching."

Tubs made a hacking noise and sneezed on the carpet, circling before the fireplace, seeking phantom heat as the flames rose.

"Don't," I scolded as he parked his butt on the edge of the stone pan before the flame guard. "You stay right there. I need your company for a little longer."

He looked back at me, disgruntled as I tendered the baby, wiping her clean and ignoring his incessant complaints.

"I know," I told him, feeling the glance of heat against my frost-numbed arms. "You and I both. But when they get back, it won't matter. I'll forgive if you can."

The temperature rose sluggishly. Mindy tried her hardest to watch me but her body crept eagerly towards sleep, her peachy-brown eyes fluttering over the fire. In the relieving silence I bundled her back up, looking her over as she fell calmly unconscious before the heat. With my sweater still zipped to my throat and my hair heavy and unkempt, I stole away the nearest throw and sank onto the carpet next to them, pressing my ear to the floor, absorbing the sound of the cabin crackling in the winter cold as the eager warmth climbed the back of my neck and delved into my scalp.

W HEN I AWOKE, RICH, fat clouds powdered the sky and a deep, setting indigo painted the outdoors, casting bleak light into the foyer and over the sleeping bodies of the two adopted babies resting on the rug.

I knelt over Mindy, sweating and red-faced, the feeling in the tips of my fingers and toes a welcome return. In the fluttering dance of fireplace

V. IVAN

gold, her plump cheeks had ripened and the dark curls of hair on her head had dried into a fluffy skiff. I had no idea how often babies needed to be fed. I had no idea how any facet of her dependent life operated. All I could do for a while was look down into her sleeping face and wonder, lost, why she looked so much like the dead man I resembled.

During sleep it'd begun to snow again, light and airy, the feeblest kind. Rising, I tested the switches through the kitchen, unable to trust even the most logical kindnesses from the universe, and loosened up as they flipped on one after the next, settling for the dim stove light and hunting down a pack of powdered baby formula I'd purchased at an overnight grocery in Elko. My swollen eyes glided over the curves of written instructions but I absorbed nothing, instead preoccupied by the low, burning sensation deep within my stomach, oddly cognizant of guilt. I was hyper all the same, the adrenaline from days past beading from me like sweat, slow and sticky. I'd had no access to a television; if conversations had begun about a burning house in Ely, about a dead body found in the wreckage, I was unaware. I could only hope that if something had been aired, it hadn't anything yet to do with me.

I paced about the tile and forced my focus, my bloodied socks the only thing saving me from the frosty floor. *Measure water and add to clean bottle, attach nipple and shake well,* but the words were getting all muddled and confusing. The lines crossed in my exhausted vision. *Measure the blood and add to clean bottle. Attach teeth. Shake until braindead. Heat until scalding. You killed that awful sonovabitch. You let him die. You should give yourself a pat on the back. This is what you wanted.*

Feed the baby.

When I returned to the den, Mindy was just beginning to stir. I sacrificed another log to the fireplace before scooping her into my arms, placating her hunger and walking the both of us to the wall of windows to look over downtown, a million stars glinting on its flat, foam-white sea. She balked once and settled on the bottle without another sound and I thanked her; I wasn't in the mood for small talk, either.

I was tempted to hate her, and felt like I was *supposed* to, but I couldn't even pretend. My eyes, sore at their roots, traced over her rounded, spaced out features and the dark crop of hair. I *recognized* her. There should've been a part of me that felt sorry or worried for the things that would happen, the fates I'd altered by taking her with me, and yet I stood there in peaceful silence and watched, her only drive in that moment to eat and be fed, and that alone was enough reason. She was awash in safety, silent and warm and away from it all, bordering on another lolling, peaceful sleep. The part of me that should've housed guilt for keeping her was the same unit within which I'd stored all memory of my mother. Inside, together, I felt them uniting.

I appreciated the importance of security. *That* door locked from the outside.

If I couldn't take care of myself, at least I could take care of her. I was inexperienced, occasionally stupid and I wouldn't make it far, but if I was the only capable of doing it, then I would do it damn well. I carried us both upstairs and tucked Mindy into the bed Elowen and I shared, leaving their side pointedly untouched as I propped a pillow behind her fragile back to keep her sideways, folding cotton swaths of blanket to pack the heat. She murmured and drooled and didn't even thank me, but I could look past that. She was out once more before I could properly shut everything down, and fear crept eagerly into the room with us.

She hadn't cried more than twice in the time it took to get back to Idaho. Both times she'd been satiated and off to a hefty nap once again without complaint. The uncertainty blooming in my chest made my hands tingle, made me *fearful*, and that made not a lick of sense. She wasn't even mine. I grimaced and wiped my hands on my shirt, awkwardly showing myself out with a dusting of worry that felt wrong to withhold. I kept an ear out for her the entire way through.

Though the cabin had been mysterious and golden during our first stay, it was dull and airless and cool that night, the heat from the fireplace ascending the stairs in timid steps. I felt like a surgical doctor wandering the bones of some otherworldly behemoth, alone in a halfway cabin for cowboys and outlaws, walls dusted with brass-framed horse racing photos and gold medals.

V. IVAN

I was free to rummage; through the two guest bedrooms on the second floor which housed little else but bibles in their dressers and hand lotions in the nightstands, through the kitchen for more crackers and a tin of peanuts, which I brought back upstairs and into the master bedroom with me, still paranoid of its medical cleanliness. The entire room was licked down in baby blues with white and gold trim and rattan furniture, a hefty crescent bed frame with a neat, polished jewelry holder in the shape of a clawed hand reaching out from the nightstand. The bed was hospitably made, the lead-off bathroom encompassed in darkness. I approached the television strung upon the wall and futzed around its edges until something depressed beneath my fingertips and the screen zapped on. Unearthing the remote from the lip of the duvet, the only proof that someone had lived there at all, I scrolled through hundreds of channels until I landed on a spotty national news broadcast.

A backsplash of abstract swirls in varying hues glanced over the screen, and distant voice echoed from the TV's quieted speakers; a newscaster with purple jewel earrings and thin, wiry hair faded into frame behind a C-shaped desk, gliding through a brief lifestyle segment and into evening features, skimming over a drive-by shooting in Chandler and a meth lab bust on the outskirts of the Vegas like they were nothing but cotton filler. When I heard nothing about missing men, nothing about bodies or houses charred in the soil, I carried myself to the bathroom, cradling the remote and pinching the gummy rubber buttons to distract myself.

Toying with the switches, the room exploded with blinding blue-white light and I blinked away the stars around the corners of my vision, cranking a number-dotted nodule alongside the light switch, listening, waiting. When the tile beneath my feet began to warm, I let out a pathetic grunt of relief and peeled off my clothes like old paint, first the layers thieved from the backseat and then the stiff, bloodied slabs beneath. Bare and trembling, my flesh a map of splotchy red-brown continents, I dove for the shower and halted at the wink of a dangling, metallic omen encircling the shower head.

IN THE END, YOU KILL US BOTH

I thought of it as a gift; if I read it as an accident, I'd never make it out of that room. A dredging heaviness overcame me as I unhooked it, turning it over in the plush of my palm. The petite seashell sparkled, polished and frozen in my hands.

Was it hope or fear that sent me to the floor? I'd never be sure. Still I went, a shrinking violet propped against the bathtub. Though the television was on and the house itself listened with me, nothing moved. I rested the charm against my knee and turned it over and over again, ogling at the silver clasp, wondering how many times they'd worked it, how many other hands had held the same clasps before them.

If they were still in Nevada, they'd be sweltering in the heat. I wondered about the body, the blood, if there was any of it left. Had they burnt it down as I'd asked or had they left it an infectious tomb, themselves chronically terrible at listening? I'd started to shake a little bit, angry enough to tug the chain between my fingertips.

What hadn't I already seen that prevented me from waiting for them? In what world had running been easier than sparking the flames myself? I'd done it before and I'd been ready to do it again. If they'd listened to me, we could've been washing each other clean right now. There'd be no blind waiting, seeking a pulse of some kind from any source I could find. If they'd listened to me, all would be well and good. All would be perfect. All would be fresh orange juice in the fridge and the baby sleeping between us, midnight at The Whistling Dog, absinthe for breakfast, each other for dinner.

It felt good to lie to myself, even just to momentarily avoid the cruel, obvious truth. If they'd listened, I would've been the dead body in the grass. If they'd listened, I would've been vacuum sealed in a plastic bag, hidden in the basement, dropped in a lake, something other than alive and in Boise. My limbs would've been taken from me, and my mouth, my voice, my air. Would that have been better?

I strung the seashell around my neck, revering the worn silver against my larynx. It hovered above the sunken pocket at the forefront of my throat and I left it there even as I started up the shower, even as I climbed inside and framed myself within its walls, the water running bitter cold

V. IVAN

and then strikingly hot until I could manage it where I wanted. Silt and blood pooled from me, curling in the puddles around my sore feet, spiralling down the drain. My busted hands worked into every crack and dip, massaging free the grime ingrained by the folds of my clothes, in the deep coils of my hair. I thrust my head under the stream, the heat soothing my taut scalp, loosening the frost from my throbbing joints.

For the first time since I turned seventeen, my eyes fell closed without a hitch. It wasn't completely gone, the fear—it permeated deep within my heart, lessened by his absence but ever-present. It was never simply that he was around and alive—it was that something had happened at one point, something strong enough to echo inside of me long after he was gone. Only *now*, it was easier. There was no creeping thing behind me wearing his face, waiting to bust my neck on the sink's edge, to fill my lungs with filthy dishwater. I could close my eyes and the fear would still be there, an angered ghost of him, but no more than that.

In the darkness behind my eyelids, there was nothing spectacular. No radiating, green-for-go sign congratulating me, marking me safe. There was only blackness—the sound of water flooding my face, pounding alongside my eardrums like rainfall. Little peace in his death—but loneliness, yes. Plenty.

I don't know. I could've done with eyes-open showers for the rest of my life, if Elowen was the most frightening thing waiting beyond the curtain.

W HEN I RETURNED TO the master bedroom wrapped in a thick, floor-warmed towel, it was splattered across the television, warping the darkness of Ronnie's bedroom with a blazing spray of furious, blood-red abstraction.

... took control of the blaze before it could reach neighbouring homes, but the damage ...

I'd left the room dark—what baked me then was a smattering of death's colour as I stepped before the television, scooping the remote

IN THE END, YOU KILL US BOTH

from the bathroom sink and cranking the volume higher. My eyes wide like marbles, sucking in the visual.

... have considered any sign of foul play, but believe that rising temperatures in the region have led to ...

Phantom warmth crept through the television, ringlets of flame lapping at the gashes where windowpanes had once sat, busted through by an unquenchable heat. The roof toppled inwards as the camera panned—swaths of jettisoned water cutting through the smog, clusters of onlookers mingling about on the sidewalk, separated from the blaze like cattle by firefighters. *Cut*—as viewers, we followed one fluorescent suit as they stepped through the aftermath of the blaze, past the fragments of the patio door now hanging like a beaded curtain.

... and no survivors. The casualties, believed to be forty-nine-year-old Kevin Joshua Welch and his nine-month-old ...

He was there. Blurred by news censors, but there. His flannel slashed away by eager flames, torn from his body like a shredded kite, positioned perfectly on a destroyed couch. A single pixel of melted ashtray in hand, the residue of his existence boiled down to a large, smouldering coal tampered around his bones, a dozen half-baked pixels and nothing more.

... say that the tenant fell asleep while smoking, and fire safety officials would like to take this time to urge ...

I crushed the power button on the remote and the bedroom fell into mute, viscous nothingness, leaving me alone in the abscess. I ached with it—every washed clean crevice, every heartbeat, each point where my pulse pounded inside of me. Delight and fear arrived intertwined, inseparable in the dark where I could not see their limited differences.

Once the relief had bled from it all and I was miserable, I whisked myself down the hall and into bed, into the slip of the mattress where Elowen had slept aside me for one last, warm evening. I pressed my nose deep into the pillow and willed them back, painted myself the bleary image of their butchered haircut through the window above the kitchen sink, until sleep took the Devil's place and claimed me for its own.

V. IVAN

I DREAMT OF THE Ford Falcon that night.

Driving a steady two-hundred miles an hour down a prairie road I couldn't place, clay-red pavement splayed out ahead and behind as far as I could see. At first I had no clue where I was, and had to remind myself through a haze of dreamy rationale that I wasn't *anywhere*. Stalks of wheat sprouted in horizon-cinching waves along the gravel shoulders and webs of wild onion and purple-tinged weeds poked through the exposed earth, mown down by the Falcon, whizzing by at such a speed that the passing scenery held less substance than the dripping mirage of heat beyond the dashboard.

The car was beautiful; always had been, as long as Dad had been its caretaker. Ivy green and twinkling beneath the frozen sunrise, as glossy and clean as the day it was built. I'd never taken an appreciative look at it when I was younger, but I could see all its details perfectly now; handworked tan upholstery and crochet dice bouncing with each lilt in the road, an eight-ball gear shift gleaming like an eyeball in the pearlescent daylight, a keychain photo of me on the only fishing trip I'd ever gone on dangling from the keys, wielding a rainbow trout with a hideous Chiclet grin.

I was still wearing the clothing I'd nearly drowned in, only my hair was dark and short and my hands fell right through my face when I patted for yesterday's bruises. That's how *brittle* this was. The whole dream was a quilt of bliss and terror tethered by a single layer of crepe paper, like the subtlest movement back in the Real World might shock me out of it; Mindy rolling over or whimpering, one of my hands slipping off the bed, a hard gust against the roofing. The surreality of it dangled in my helpless hands, dripping from my fingers like webbing. I could've crashed the car if I wanted, if I'd had the courage to reach over and pry the wheel from his hands.

Dad from '81 was there, and he drove like he'd been born to do nothing but. He was just as he'd looked in the sparse old photos I'd seen with his thick carbon curls and a year-old beard, reeking of dense shaving cream and car grease and menthol, a few straggler ringlets wafting into his eyes, the same watchful almond shape as mine but cadet-blue and lively. His gaze was fixed on the road, calloused hands wringing the thin wrap around the wheel, watching through a pair of citrine aviators for cars that would never come.

I ached to say something but my voice fell mute each time I opened my lips, the wretched strain of my throat the sole signifier that I was trying. Only when I managed to squeak out a meagre whimper of his name did Dad finally turn and look through me, like I was nothing but a veil of thinning clouds and pink skyline catching his loving eye.

Beyond both of our control, though Dad sure seemed like he'd expected it, the car rose and angled skyward, taking off like a jet fighter that weighed nothing at all.

Dad kept on staring through me and I kept on trying to speak. I needed to ask him more than I'd ever get the time to; where he'd ended up, why he hadn't taken me with him all that time ago, if he knew that I still loved him and that I hadn't left him, that I loved him still like a dying bird on the road, like a playground injury years after the scar tissue formed. But he only smiled— the bemused sort of smile that adults give when their kid's doing something that's a mix of wildly embarrassing and devastatingly sweet. He didn't say a damn thing until we were miles from the ground, my eyes darting outside the window, bulging, terrified. Knuckles birch-white against the door handle, I screamed bloody murder but nothing came out.

Dad's lips parted peacefully and as clear as day, in a voice I hadn't heard in nearly nine years, he whispered:

You can't keep waiting on ghosts, Lee.

Like falling from a skyscraper into the pavement, the atmosphere solidified and the Falcon collided with the air, slamming head first against a titanium wall of clouds, our bodies flung through the windshield and painted against the constellations as a crimson ink stain. Glass scattered in snowy fractals before my dying eyes, free of the gravity that separated waking life from dreams and earth from space.

My jellied body drifted outwards. A slick, morphine chill fled with my soul, escaping my body like air in a punctured balloon. My skin was shredded by starlight, blinding agony surging through my fingertips,

V. IVAN

my scalp, the sensitive flesh of my armpits aflame and blistering, the drone of the prairies, wind whistling through like a morbid show tune, my mother's voice humming in the early morning, my father reaching out to me as I laid broken in half, calloused palms and the smell of burning wood and lavender soap, shouting at me or *for* me, something in between, but I was dying.

I was dying.

After I settled my waking hyperventilation, I laid clutching the pieces of that dream which had drilled themselves into the very deepest crooks of me. When Elowen came home I would tell them about my findings and I wouldn't cry the way I was in bed that evening, drilling those humiliating noises into a pillow I'd cradled tightly against my bruised rib cage.

I didn't want to be dead anymore. The appeal of it burned away, no longer a resolute escape as much as an endless car crash, not unlike staring into the back of my eyes for the rest of eternity. I didn't want to die, not as much as I had before. There was so much more beyond death by now, wasn't there? And so much less at the same time.

They'd be so proud of me. Something better would come from this. It had to.

DAYS LATER, MYRA PHONED me.

At some point in the morning, before I'd roused myself from a thick, sweating sleep and gone to feed and dress Mindy for the outdoors. Her number appeared there on the screen, a thumbprint of an old life that I scrubbed with a tongued patch of my shirt like it might disappear. There came a voicemail, too—a waving red dot dancing around the screen's corner, waiting to be heard. I'd stood in the kitchen at the cabin for a long while, half-buttoned into Elowen's jacket which I'd failed to wash the day before, debating whether or not to call her back.

The voicemail sat still in its box as I went down the mountain to get cat food, which at Miller John's meant dried fish and broth and small cans of nearly-expired pumpkin purée because somehow, somewhere, I'd heard that cats liked it. I kept Mindy tucked into a makeshift swaddle against my chest, a homing missile for whom I promised to mind my footfalls so as not to slip and rattle her from her careful rest. Most of me was hidden beneath a thick, white scarf that I found and stole from Ronnie's closet and I carried the truck keys with me like rosary beads, the mountainside thawed enough that Elowen's poor old beater could surely clear the last dredges of slush on the road. My face had paled to a swallow-colored spattering of deep yellows and light blues, and the bruises on my throat had begun to disperse into light purple slashes.

The front windows of Miller John's were vignetted by branches of frost and an *Open But Away* note scrawled on highlighter pink paper hung like a bullseye in the door, which seemed eerily irresponsible. The lights were dimmed and a break sign slouched on the counter, pointed towards three. I dumped my last twenty onto the counter and went to work stacking my knapsack full of canned dried minnows, canned tuna, pumpkin and powdered formula packets that I found hidden in the depressing, dust-filled cosmetics corner of the store. Mindy and Tubs had been down for a shared nap on the plush guest bed before we left, and though the store was only a brisk walk downhill she'd grown restless and annoyed at the zapped heat on the inside of my jacket. As I was rounding out the total with a few ten-cent sticks of cinnamon gum she began to cry, soft little mewls until she was fretting and grunting and squirming to get out of my jacket.

I abandoned the counter and moved to the back of the store where the rickety shuffle of the metal roof couldn't disturb her, stooping against the wall beneath two racks of dry-cured meats and the payphone, nestled like a raccoon in someone's attic hiding from the elements. Mindy got it out of her system and I coached her through it, suddenly so frightfully aware of everything all at once that my own breath began to snag.

It would've been funny if not for how fucking depressing it was—two great big babies, sensitive girls with frightening tears pilling in our eyes, relearning the basics of breathing. I held her to my chest, hoping it might make her feel better to know that she wasn't the only one miserable in the cold. I said, *"It's okay, it's alright,"* and *"I know it's cold, but I'll keep us warm,"* and *"When we get home, we'll play with the kitty and have something to eat, okay?"* and in doing so I made myself horribly sad. Without fix, I left our money pinned beneath a Red Rose owl figurine at the register and carried our sustenance to the truck, popping open the driver door and climbing inside to give the ignition a forceful turn. The beast chug-chugged and then started grouchily, complaining as I cranked the heat against the frozen windshields.

After an aching minute of squirming and babbling, Mindy fell still and rested her warming forehead against my neck, falling begrudgingly asleep. Praying that the tires weren't cemented to the earth, I slid my phone free from my jacket pocket and with cold-drunk fingers I dialed their number by heart, pressing the cool metal to my ear. It managed a single, measly ring before cutting into brute silence.

A voice broke through. One of those mechanical bastards, the sort that aren't real people but sound suspiciously so. I brought the screen up to my eyes, harsh dial up following the monotonous inhuman cadence of the automatic operator. I'd dialed right. Of *course* I had. So I waited, in the chance that it was an error, for Elowen's voicemail to cut through. For their whisper, slow and careful and patient, to glide through the receiver and take my heart.

The operator repeated itself for the third time. I hung up the phone, my entire face aflame.

We sat until the clock neared three. Then I rose like foam on a wave, white-capped and bitter, and bundled my sister carefully into the passenger's seat, tucking her fragile head into a well of the fleecy, iron-scented jacket I'd given up just for her. I'd wash it well once I found the courage to strip them off it. When I thought I heard the sound of footsteps shuffling around the back entrance of Miller John's, I drove away and up the mountain as gently as I could before we were offered more help.

IN THE END, YOU KILL US BOTH

CHRISTMAS ROLLED OVER ON a long, bitter Saturday morning. I'd turned on the tree lights as if it truly mattered, a rickety bleed of reds, whites and blues. We'd spent a well over a week in Idaho—nearly two. Eventually it'd be time to reconsider Washington, and whether that was even an option anymore. My brain wouldn't yet allow it; I clung to hope like a bad stink I couldn't wash out.

And I'd tried.

Buried deep in the early morning bloom of orange sunlight across Boise's metallic cityscape, the three of us had fallen into a post-dinner coma the night before following a feast fit for a kingdom. Christmas Eve marked my first solo attempt at braised chicken, which I'd thawed from Ronnie's freezer and stuffed just the way Georgia had taught me, ballparking a temperature on the high-tech oven and burning the Christ right out of its bones. Mindy had suckled on a saved packet of pureed apricots and banana, the last of Myra's influence now sitting in the bottom of her grape-sized stomach, while Tubs and I devoured the skinless remains of charred bird, the three of us seated on the warm hearth rug like ousted kings.

Myra called me more than once in the midst of that afternoon's nap on the couch, buried beneath a sea of found quilts and pillows with Mindy in my arms and Tubs at my feet, the chicken working inside of him like a sedative. I was awoken—unaware that I'd even dozed off—by my phone blaring and the jingle of the television rattling on unwatched before me. When I flipped open my cell without thinking and pressed it to my ear, nothing came at first. In a single, earth-shattering second I realized what I'd done by not screening the number; at any moment her voice would crawl from the dull, crackly speaker of my cellphone, calling out my name, knowing what I'd done and cursing me for it.

But my mother never spoke. Instead, a choir of voices split the silence like the shattering of a polar cap, enunciated by two childish, gleeful squeals:

Merry Christmas! Merry Christmas!

V. IVAN

The living room split apart, the dull thrum of a Hallmark movie dancing about in my exposed ear. When had the news finished up? How long had we been out?

"Oh my *God*," came Georgia, whistling with disbelief, the kids now deliberately absent. "Hello? *Happy Holidays?* Come on."

In came the sudden, bold sketch of Georgia's living room and the Christmas tree lit up with glittering bulbs, the three of them crowded around the couch with the cell phone perched on Georgia's manicured fingers, awaiting me. I couldn't keep a breath.

"I'm sorry. *Very* Merry Christmas."

"I know you've been hibernating," Georgia speculated, her voice thinning from its former blissful chant, "but I don't care how bad Elowen is at sharing. Your mom's plenty fucked off by now, so quit hiding. I'll come over there and haul you outside myself if you won't spend a *chunk* of your Christmas here. Don't fuckin' *test* me."

Her voice lilted at the end, the way it always did when she punctured the severity of her genuine worries with an easy joke. My heart throbbed to be there with her. Every cell inside of me wailed—*take the shortest way back to Olympia. Georgia would do anything for you. Anything at all.*

"I was thinking about taking a walk downtown before everything gets stripped," she spilled on, refusing my silence. "No—big pressure. Just you, me, the kids and the lights. And the *big ass crowd,* but if that's a concern, we could always head out before dark."

I sat there for a wide moment, forgetting that Georgia couldn't see me—I wondered what she'd say if she could. She'd cry, I bet. I couldn't go back and make her cry.

"I might make that," I tried, rounding out my words so that they sounded calmer, relaxed. "Elowen and their roommates are doing some Christmas festivities. I offered to help out."

From the other end of the call came a surprised hum. "There's folks inside the Echo that would eat up your attempt at being completely regular."

"Sure," I whispered, turning my mouth from Mindy's sleeping frame. "I'm involved."

"You're acclimating. Better than the rest of us. Just tell me you're at *least* coming around for dinner. Bring your kidnapper, if you must."

"Possibly."

"I won't save any for you!" Georgia swore, flattened by sarcasm. "So if you're coming, it's first come first serve. Don't be late."

All this talk would go nowhere—I knew as we spoke that I was making plans that would fall into redundancy once the evening passed and the holiday lights came down. I wouldn't be there to watch Georgia's kids open their presents. I wouldn't see our home at its most lighthearted, at its most careful, kind and warm. I wouldn't see Christmas breakfast, new pyjamas, candy cane coffee creamer. I didn't have enough money to get them a single thing. I'd spent everything I had just to get to Ely, and the glovebox's excess was bleeding away. Eventually I'd have no choice. I'd have to go back. What we had would be irreparable by then, wouldn't it?

I was worth only so much in Boise, where nobody knew who I was or what I'd done. I painted Georgia in my mind, standing in the foyer with a sweater bundled all the way up around her neck, some kiddy Christmas hoodie with tacky pinstripes, a half-filled cup of hot chocolate in her soft, freckled hands. Waiting for the both of us, safely held across town in her mind.

"*Merry Christmas,*" I gave once more.

Just to hear the lilt in their voices as Georgia collected them both, presenting the cell phone's speaker as a funnel straight into my heart, their choral voices clumsy and misaligned, a glitching holiday wish through the static. I closed the cellphone and pressed the opening joint against my dry lips.

When it rang once more half an hour later, the digital green number of a contact I'd never bothered to save, I rose from the couch and spilled my heat, draping Mindy's sleeping body in the oven where I'd been laying and padding across the cabin. I crept through the entryway and drove my still-sore feet into my sneakers, slipping out the doorway against Tubs' frantic complaints and moving coatless down the driveway.

V. IVAN

At its end, with as much strength as I could collect, I whipped my cellphone across the pine tops. It soared for a few graceful seconds before it dove, crashing with a dry snap and toppling down the mountain's slope into the nearby woods, out of my view. Once the hills devoured that sound and things fell silent again, I retreated indoors to the couch and the heat and my infant sister, who murmured eagerly as I crept back beneath the blankets and took her into my arms where I knew I couldn't hurt her.

Through the slats in the heavy-lidded blinds above the kitchen sink, the sun inched her way across the mountain peaks. I flipped to the end of the channel guide where dated holiday movies and new, soapy romances bounced in and out of control. *Our Vines Have Tender Grapes* was due to screen in fifteen minutes. I'd never seen it. Neither had Mindy, surely. I wasn't sure how much it would entertain her.

It didn't matter. Nestled between the arm of the couch and me, she was already halfway to sleep. I nudged her closer, tilting her forward into the crook of my armpit where she slackened comfortably. My mouth pooled with spit and I sat as motionless as I could beneath the blanket I stretched over the both of us, her breathing deepening as she finally slipped away, hunger quenched, lulled by the warmth of my body.

I was sturdy enough for her. If that was all I was good for, then that was enough. Oh, the world seemed so small then, trapped within the confines of the cabin's den, an unmissable draft slicing through my body. So small because at that moment, it was made up of Mindy alone.

Somewhere out there, a crucial vein stretched out and away until the horizon swallowed it whole and I could no longer track it. I tried to picture it as I'd tried for the past week but each time I let myself slide into it, I disappeared completely. My hands stopped looking like my hands. I forgot to eat for hours. All I could think about was where that vein stopped and started, whether I would feel the smooth pulse of blood flowing through it again.

Were they cold out there? Were they in Idaho or had they hidden away in Nevada? Were they somewhere else than that? I wouldn't know if they were walking up the drive unless I sat at the entrance and waited for them like some forlorn house pet. There was a baby against me and I had *her* to care for, but if I was alone I would've done just that; cemented myself against the front door's neighbouring windows, frozen by the chilly castoff from outside. I would've waited there for them until I began to decay. Beyond that, even.

Once more. Only once more, I let myself slip.

The rolling credits made it easier to dribble away like a bead of blood along that distant vein. The last time I'd seen them was through that patio door, out on the shrub-trimmed yard where Kevin's body painted the grass in warm, pungent blood. Hovering over him, frozen for what felt like forever before it began. The digging, the raking, all-consuming. Too familiar with the scent of tainted meat, moving aside what would eventually be burnt and destroyed. I could see them perfectly if I tried hard enough.

That's what I did; I let my eyes fog over.

There they were—through a casement window where the light bounced off the walls in sacred rays, through the glass into a house with shitty air conditioning and lots of cupboard space and room for the both of us, together. Not the Ely house but some dreamlike version of it, devoid of the bloodied flooring, of the bedroom which had become a furnace to my flammable memory, of the sink with its gunk and the medication that did little to keep Kevin alive. In that daydream we were perpetually separated by the glass, looking at each other through the window of a home that could've been ours if things had gone differently.

In an ideal world, the privacy fencing would be shredded and torn away, replaced by flower-dense bushels and leafy trees, a bench beneath their arcing boughs. There would be no work boots at the door, no ruddy, built-up nicotine yellow on every surface. I'd display photos of Mindy and Georgia, Andy and Kennedy, and *Elowen*—for no reason other than my own desire to see them in every room they weren't immediately occupying. I'd beg them not to dye their hair so the red could shine through. I'd serve them raw, bleeding things on fine china if they wanted. I'd kill those things with my bare hands if that was what they needed, or they could spend all day outside in the woods doing just that, coming home through an old wooden fence gate that held so much character, their clothes marbled by deer and fox and man blood, kissing me on the mouth until I told them that they could stop, which wouldn't come fast at all.

    A curling smile touched my lips. A sharp splitting of the dried skin there threatened to reel me in, but I was already adrift.

    We slept in the same bed in that world. The sheets we'd picked out budded with roses and little bees and miniature stars, scattered about like flung crumbs, and I washed them every week so they'd never suffer a rough sleep again. Tragedy was equipped to our lives in every universe, even the ones I found myself fabricating, but I could tame it into submission. Could control it in a way it could no longer control us.

    That was the Little Heaven. That, there, with them. The cabin would remain a loveless carcass until they arrived in my dreams, the only place it seemed I might see them again. When they came through those slatted wooden gates, I would tell them I loved them. I would tell them I was ready. I would tell them that I was brand new and it might not be true, but it would eventually. I'd tell them everything. *Everything.*

    I'll keep an ear out for them until then.

Milton Keynes UK
Ingram Content Group UK Ltd.
UKHW041845121024
449535UK00004B/350